Water's Dance

Fire & Water

Gracey Hall

Freedom is not a gift bestowed, but a right reclaimed.

1

—— · ₒ° ☆: *.) .* :☆° . ——

The streets of Oasia, Varidia's capital are a chaotic mix of vendors hawking their wares, beggars pleading for water or food, and people rushing to and fro on urgent business. The buildings that line the streets are a mix of opulent palaces and crumbling tenements, reflecting the vast disparities of wealth and power that exist in this society.

Survival here is a battle against the relentless thirst, one that requires not just strength, but ingenuity and a dash of magic. At the apex of society are an aristocratic class of water-controlling mages. They are revered not just for their magical prowess but for their crucial role in the survival of the realm. It's them who summon the rain and create fresh water. These mages often wear adornments made from Lyrium, a rare and valuable metal known to amplify their abilities.

Beneath the mages are the Nulls, ordinary humans with no magical ability. Their life is one of hardship, toiling under the relentless sun, relying on the mages for their water, and performing menial tasks that keep the society functioning. They view the mages with a mix of reverence, envy, and resentment, aware that their lives are wholly dependent on the whims and benevolence of these water manipulators. The lowest stratum of society is formed by the Vashka, a subjugated race of demons. Powerful, resilient, but bound by magical constraints, the Vashka are forced to work in the perilous Lyrium mines. Their innate resistance to the heat and physical endurance make them ideal miners, but their lives are a ceaseless torment, devoid of freedom and dignity.

Under the relentless onslaught of the sun, the Varidians tackle their daily activities, their visages lined with stress and weariness. Dust and perspiration permeate the air, mingling with the cacophonous clamor of animal cries and human voices.

Breaking through this tumult, a magnificent golden carriage, pulled by a string of well-groomed black horses, seamlessly traverses the street. The carriage's surface is embellished with complex carvings and expensive gems, symbolizing the affluence and might of its inhabitants. Guards, well-versed in combat, lead the procession, their blades reflecting the sunlight in a rhythmical dance. The golden carriage's passing compels the Varidians to halt, awestruck by its grandeur. Many lower their heads or kneel, recognizing the emblem adorning the carriage as that of the royal water mage family. Some simply stare wide-eyed, unable to comprehend the extreme luxury of the carriage and its entourage.

Temporarily, the carriage's passage eclipses Varidia's chaos and poverty, serving as a tangible reminder of the dominance and privileges that the water mages exert over this realm. The discipline of marching feet and rhythmic sound of the carriage wheels are shattered by a distant uproar, a discordant chorus of harsh yells that intensify with proximity. The carriage comes to a standstill, the disturbance linked to a ragged group of Vhaska demons, their bodies slick with sweat and grime, their chains jingling ominously as they are driven by a handful of Null guards. From within the confines of the carriage, a figure of ethereal allure emerges, starkly contrasting the severe Varidian surroundings. She is a captivating sight, dressed in an azure silk gown reflecting her blazing blue eyes - eyes that, despite their captivating hue, are keen and discerning, suggesting an impending maelstrom of magic. Her ebony hair, entwined with strands of Lyrium, tumbles down her back, fluttering in the soft desert wind.

Her skin is an alabaster hue, an unusual trait among the sun-kissed populace of Varidia, making her stand out even more. But it is not just her physical allure that captures the onlookers; it is her unmistakable air of authority, her raw magical energy that fills the air, making the atmosphere around her thrum with anticipation. She steps down, her silken skirts rustling softly against the hot sand, her jeweled sandals whispering tales of the wealth and power she wields. Her expression is one of curiosity and barely veiled annoyance at the disruption. The crowd parts for her like the sea at the command of a storm, their murmurs hushed, their gazes both fearful and awestruck.

She strides confidently towards the commotion, her guards trailing a few steps behind. The Vashka demons fall silent at her approach, their scarlet eyes wide and watchful, their collective breaths held in dread and anticipation. The Null guards stiffen under her gaze, their armor clinking as they stand to attention.

"What is the meaning of this disturbance?"

Her voice slices through the tension like a knife, clear and commanding. One of the guards, a burly man with sun-baked skin and a tightly braided beard, steps forward to address her.

"These slaves were causing a disturbance, your highness," he responds, his voice a low rumble, eyes trained on a spot over her shoulder rather than meeting her gaze directly.

"We were simply trying to keep them in line."

"Is that so?" her response is icily calm, her piercing blue eyes narrowing as she shifts her gaze to the group of demons.

Among the huddled, weary figures, one scene draws her attention immediately: on the ground, writhing in pain, is an old and feeble demon. His skin is wrinkled and weathered, his muscles atrophied from years of back-breaking labor in the mines. He gasps for air, his breaths shallow and ragged. Standing protectively in front of him is a much younger demon, his colossal size and muscular frame hinting at a daunting strength. His crimson eyes burn fiercely, his sharp horns gleaming under the sunlight. His chest heaves with restrained rage, the thick chains around his wrists rattling ominously. The defiance in his posture is clear and unapologetic, a challenge to the guards and perhaps, to the system itself.

For a brief moment, the young demons gaze settles on her, studying her in a way that seemed almost mesmerized. His brow furrowed ever so slightly, as if he was trying to make sense of something. Against the chorus of worried whispers and her guard's protest, she continues her stride toward the demon, a small smile playing on her lips. She stops a few feet away from the young demon who has dropped to his knees, his defiance replaced by an act of submission. His head is bowed low, but his immense form still looms large

From up close, she takes in the details of the young demon who, despite his kneeling position, exudes an intimidating aura. The features of his kind, the Vashka, are usually obscured by their hard labor and weather-beaten appearances. But up close, she finds herself intrigued by the individuality etched into his unique form.

His hair, dark as a moonless night, cascades past his broad shoulders in a wild disarray, hiding part of his sharp, horned profile. Yet when the strands catch the sun-rays they seem to ignite, taking on a hue reminiscent of blood at its darkest. The red of a setting sun meeting the ruthless black of the night, combining to create a fire that dances in his hair and mirrors the flames that flicker in his gaze. It was his eyes that caught her attention next, the color seemingly to change with his emotions. One moment an unusual golden hue, akin to a topaz glinting under the desert sun and the next moment igniting into a fierce, glowing red.

In a voice laced with desperation, he pleads.

"The old one is sick. He struggles to keep the pace. I ask your permission to carry him."

"What good is a weak slave? If he can't keep up the pace now, he won't be able to mine any Lyrium once he reaches the mines," she responds, her voice steady and emotionless.

The young demon's face twists in anger, his teeth grinding together as he speaks through clenched jaws.

"He is weak now, but if he is given a chance to rest, he will regain his strength."

He glances back at the old demon, a flicker of protective concern passing over his features before returning his attention to her.

"In the meantime, I will do his work as well as mine. The Lyrium will still be mined, and the old one gets to live. You lose nothing, my lady."

The young woman can't help the small, amused smirk that tugs at the corner of her lips.

"Ah, yes! And then I might have two sick demons who aren't working at full capacity," she replies, her tone layered with sarcasm.

"Forcing yourself to do his work will eventually weaken you as well."

She kneels down to his level, the lavish fabric of her dress pooling around her in a wave of silken colors. With a gentle hand, she reaches out, her slender fingers lifting his chin, forcing him to meet her gaze. He does not resist, allowing her touch without protest, his fiery gaze burning into hers. His sharp, defined features hold a wild, rugged beauty, the beauty of a creature shaped and molded by the relentless desert and the cruelness of life.

"Tell me, what is your name?" she asks. Her voice is soft, devoid of the earlier harshness, yet still commanding.

"I am called Ash, my lady," he replies, his voice echoing with a strange, entrancing resonance, as raw and powerful as the desert winds.

A chuckle escapes her lips at his answer.

"And do you know who I am, Ash?" she asks, her voice carrying a playful lilt. The question is unnecessary, more a rhetorical taunt than a genuine inquiry. Her status and identity are known to all of importance in the kingdom.

"No"

"But you are someone of importance, I assume," his eyes flick to the guards that surround them, their postures rigid and their faces unreadable.

"Is that so?" she muses, her smirk widening.

"And what makes you think that?"

"Your clothes," Ash answers without missing a beat, his gaze falling to her fine dress.

"The guards. Their fear of you." He gestures with his chained hands, the metallic clink of his shackles filling the silence between them.

"And what if I told you I am a Princess?" Raena questions, her tone low, almost a whisper.

Ash held her gaze, the fires of his eyes revealing no surprise, only a smoldering intensity. He broke the silence with a grave nod, acknowledging her revelation without a trace of reverence.

"Then it would explain the entitlement," he remarked, the corner of his mouth tugging upward in a half-smile.

She laughed at his response, a sound that rang out sharp and clear against the murmur of the guards and the now quiet hum of the city.

"Quite the sharp tongue for a slave," she remarked.

"I hope you comprehend the gravity of your words, Ash," she said, the teasing note in her voice replaced with an icy edge.

"Your actions here, your disobedience... they could have consequences. Severe ones."

The slave's half-smile didn't waver, but his eyes took on a hardened edge. His shackled hands clenched into fists at his sides. "I am no stranger to consequences, Princess," he said "But a chance for him," he glanced back at the older demon, "is worth any consequences."

"And what if the consequences were not yours to bear alone?" she countered, the wind playing with loose strands of her hair.

A smirk still lingered on her lips as she stood, dusting off her silken dress. She looked at the demon for a long moment, her eyes glinting with a sort of grim amusement.

"Few would dare speak so boldly in my presence", she said, her tone as smooth as velvet.

"My name is Raena by the way."

"Your friend is too old to work in the mines any longer," she declared. A gasp rippled through the surrounding guards, but she paid them no mind, her focus solely on the two demons in front of her.

"So, he will now serve in the palace as one of my personal servants."
Ash blinked in surprise, his stubborn resolve faltering for a moment.
He had been prepared to fight, to argue, to take whatever punishment
this arrogant princess would dole out. But this... this was unexpected.
"My lady! No demon has ever served in the palace, no matter their
age," one of the guards suddenly burst out, disbelief etched onto his
face.
"Good," Raena responded coolly, her attention never leaving Ash as
she answered.
"There is a first time for everything, and this will be it."

A murmur of shock ran through the guards, their eyes wide
and their mouths agape. They looked amongst each other, confusion
clouding their faces, before eventually bowing their heads in
submission to their princess's command. Two guards moved towards
the elderly demon, helping him to his feet with surprising gentleness.
"This one," Raena commanded, her gaze falling upon Ash once
more, her finger pointed in his direction, "will not be punished for
his words. Is that clear?"

There was a chorus of hesitant nods and murmurs of
agreement from the guards, their faces a mixture of surprise,
curiosity, and a slight sense of fear. It was not often their princess's
commands deviated so much from the norm, and it was clear they
didn't know what to make of it.
Leaning in, Raena's voice was low as she whispered into the demons
ear.
"Until we meet again."
As she moved to turn away, Ash's voice rang out in the sudden quiet.
"Thank you for your kindness, Princess."
She paused, turning back to him with a grin.
"Oh, it wasn't kindness. I simply didn't want to waste a good servant."

With those final words, she turned on her heel, the silk dress
swishing around her as she made her way back to her carriage, her
guards quickly falling in line behind her. Ash watched her go, a
strange mix of relief and uncertainty stirring within him. The

marketplace, once filled with hushed whispers and muffled exchanges, fell into stunned silence. They all watched as the princess's carriage rode away, their princess showing a mercy none of them had anticipated.

—— · ˳° ☆: *.☽ .* :☆° . ——

2

In the solace of my private bath chamber, the world outside ceased to exist. The steam from the bath embraced me like a shroud, veiling the opulence of my surroundings in a misty haze. I submerged myself further into the warmth of the water, letting it wash away the weariness of the day. The water cradled me, lapped at my skin, and the faint scent of jasmine hung in the air, soothing my senses. My mind floats away, drifting in the ether. Amid the foggy veil, I could see a faint outline, a lone figure standing against a vivid crimson backdrop, the desert I knew so well. I recognized the rugged form of a man, his silhouette illuminated by the fiery orb of the setting sun. But there was something different, something... unnerving about his figure.

His eyes burned brighter than the sun, blinding in their intensity, and in his hand, he held a chain. But it wasn't a chain of servitude; it was the chain of a king, the links shaped like roaring lions, their eyes as aflame as his. He extended the chain towards me, a silent offering, his eyes never wavering from mine. As I reach out to touch it, I hear a distant echo, like a whisper carried by the wind. The whisper grows into a chorus of voices, thousands upon thousands of them, each a thread in the grand tapestry of life. They speak of histories long forgotten, futures yet unseen, of battles lost and love won. It is a symphony of existence, all lives intertwined.

The vision abruptly shatters as a polite knock echoes through the room.

"Your Highness," a soft voice calls from beyond the door.

"May I enter?"

Startled from my dream-like state, I sit up, feeling the sudden chill of reality. I clear my throat, trying to shake off the vivid images of my dream.

"Yes, Binda, come in."

The door creaks open, and in steps Binda, my most trusted and loyal maid. Binda is a tall, elegant figure, moving with the grace of a lifelong servant who had perfected the art of being almost invisible, yet always present when needed. Her dark hair, streaked with strands of silver, is always meticulously coiffed into a neat bun at the nape of her neck. Her brown eyes, hold a world of wisdom and untold stories. Her attire is modest but impeccably clean and well-fitted. Her face, lined with age and experience, is like an open book, each wrinkle a chapter from her life. But there's a stern, stoic demeanor that veils her, like a fortress guarding the secrets of a lifetime spent in the royal household.

Her relationship with me, though primarily one of servitude, has the complexity of an older sister, a guardian, and a confidante. Her stern exterior often gives way to a tender affection, a fondness that has grown over the years.

"Your highness," Binda says, curtseying.

"I hope I'm not interrupting anything important."

I shake my head, giving her a smile.

"Not at all. I was just enjoying a moment of peace and quiet."

Binda nods, taking a step closer.

"I wanted to speak with you about the old demon you brought with you today, he has arrived at the palace. He's been seen to by the healers as you commanded." Her voice is steady, yet I can see a flicker of concern in her eyes. A memory of my mystic dream washes over me, but I quickly shake it off. This is reality, not the echo of my imagination. "Good," I reply, nodding. "See to it that he is comfortable."

"As you wish, your Highness," she says.

Binda hesitates before continuing, her eyes betraying a hint of concern.

"Still…, it's not safe to bring a Vashka demon into the palace. They are not to be trusted."

I roll my eyes, feeling the old familiar feeling of rebellion stirring in my chest.

"Oh please, Binda. You sound like my mother. I'm sure he's harmless. And besides, he has done nothing wrong. He deserves a chance to prove himself."

Binda nods, a small smile playing at her lips.

"I know, your highness. You've always been one to see the best in people. It's one of the things I admire most about you."

"Still I fear that he may not be safe here," she says, wringing her hands nervously.

"The other servants, they don't take kindly to his kind. They might try to harm him."

"Don't worry, Binda. I won't let anything happen to him. He deserves a chance to live a better life than the one he had before."

Binda nods, her eyes softening.

"I worry, your highness. You know how the other nobles view demons. It wouldn't do for any trouble to arise because of him."

I wave a dismissive hand.

"Binda, you know me better than that. I'm not afraid of a little trouble. The other mages don't dare question my families rule, their very life depends on it."

Binda smiles, shaking her head.

"Oh, you always were a headstrong one. But please, be careful."

I nod, giving her a playful wink.

"Always am."

As Binda helps me dry off my hair and brushes it, I can't help but feel a sense of gratitude for her. Even though she's just a servant, she's like a second mother to me, always looking out for my best interests.

"Thank you, Binda," I say softly, feeling a wave of affection wash over me.

She smiles, setting the brush down.

"Anything for you, your highness. You know that."

I nod, a mischievous grin spreading across my face.

"Well in that case, how about you sneak me some of those sweets you've been hiding in the kitchen? I'm in the mood for a little indulgence."

Binda chuckles, shaking her head.

"You and your sweet tooth. Very well, your highness. I'll see what I can do."

Once Binda disappears, I finally allow myself the space to think, really think, about what happened earlier. I cross the room and sink into a plush armchair, the soft velvet cushioning me as I lean back.

"Ash," I murmur, his name foreign on my lips.

"The audacity," I muse aloud, he dared to challenge me, in public no less, with an audacity I'd seldom seen. It was refreshing, to say the least. His fierce independence and rebellious streak were so different from the people I was used to being around. It was refreshing, in a way. My mind can't help but linger on his handsome features and his fiery spirit. I let out a frustrated sigh.

"Come on, Raena," I say to myself, rolling my eyes.

"You're not seriously crushing on a demon, are you?"

I laugh out loud at the absurdity of the thought. Me, a royal princess, finding a demon attractive? It's too ridiculous to even contemplate.

"Why do I find him intriguing?" I wonder.

"He is but a common demon, a slave."

Yet, the image of his fiery eyes refuses to fade. Those eyes held defiance, as if he dared to challenge the world. It was almost as if I could feel the heat radiating from them, even from a distance.

"*But he's more than that,*" I thought.

"*He stood up for an older demon, risked his life. There's a bravery in him that is rare, especially among his kind.*"

I lean back as I recall the way he spoke, his voice carrying a raw intensity.

"A warrior at heart, no doubt. But there's something else, something I can't quite place..."

"*He's dangerous,*" a small voice in my head whispers.

"*He could hurt you or the people you care about.*"

I scoff at the thought.

"*Please, I've faced much greater dangers than him. He's just a demon, nothing I can't handle.*"

My musings are interrupted by a loud, resonating gong. The evening bell. It's time for the royal feast. With the echo of the bell still resonating, I rise from the armchair, discarding the towel in exchange for the elegant robe that is laid out for me on the chaise lounge.

"I suppose I'll have to play the dutiful princess tonight," I mutter, "Charms and pleasantries for all the boring nobles."

As I'm lost in my thoughts, a knock resounds on the door before it creaks open, revealing a small fleet of maids waiting with an array of dresses, jewelry, and cosmetics.

***

With the evening sun setting over the capitol city of Oasia, Princess Raena prepares to join her royal family for a formal dinner. The atmosphere is one of elegance and opulence, with the grand dining hall adorned with glittering chandeliers and ornate decorations.

Raena, as always, is impeccably dressed in a gown of shimmering gold, her hair styled in intricate braids that cascade down her back. She exudes an air of confidence and arrogance, a result of growing up with all the privileges that come with being a royal. Taking her seat at the long, polished dining table, surrounded by her family and the most powerful mages of the noble families, Raena can't help but feel a sense of ennui. She's had these formal dinners countless times before, and the rigid customs and traditions of royal society have always grated on her mischievous nature. Nevertheless, Raena maintains her composure, as befits her station.

The first course was a colorful salad of crisp, crunchy leaves of the Venethian cactus plant, sprinkled with delicate flakes of Fornian snow pepper, and drizzled with a dressing made from the juice of the rare Emirian starfruit.

The mages discuss politics and the state of the city, Raena listens with a polite but disinterested air. She found herself sitting next to Lord Eran, a water mage and a member of one of the most powerful noble families in the city. Meanwhile, at the other end of the table, the king and queen were engaged in a heated discussion with Lord Aric, another nobleman, about the treatment of the Nulls in the slums. The king argued that they should be given more support and resources, while Lord Aric insisted that they were a drain on the city's economy and should be left to fend for themselves.

As the main course was served, a slow-roasted blackened venison, tender and juicy, basted with a tangy sauce made from the rare spice of the Maramian fire peppers. The side dish were crispy Hassurian yams, which had been glazed with a sweet syrup extracted from the Boralian moonflower. Alongside the venison was a fragrant dish of roasted Okori roots, which had been slow-cooked with a mixture of herbs and spices that included the fiery Deldorin chili, the delicate Anghari cinnamon, and the aromatic leaves of the Kaltorian breeze flower.

Raena couldn't help but notice the stark contrast between the lavishness of the royal feast and the poverty and squalor she had witnessed in the streets earlier that day. She wondered if the nobles were aware of the suffering of the common people, or if they were too caught up in their own power struggles to care.

One of the mages, Lord Cadmus, spoke up.

"Without us, the Nulls would be nothing. They rely on us for everything, from providing clean water to protecting them from demons."

Raena, feeling a bit mischievous, decided to challenge him.

"But why should they have to rely on you? Why can't they have their own power?"

Lord Cadmus raised an eyebrow at Raena's challenge.

"My dear princess, it is not a matter of deserving power. It is a matter of having the gift and the responsibility that comes with it. We have been blessed with the ability to control water, and with great power comes great responsibility."

Lady Lysandra nodded in agreement.

"The Nulls are simply not equipped to handle such power. They lack the sophistication and finesse required to control the ebb and flow of water. It is our duty to guide them, to protect them, and to provide for them."

"But at what cost, Lady Lysandra?" Raena countered.

"The Nulls live in squalor while the water mages bask in luxury. It is not right to profit from their suffering."

Lord Cadmus scoffed.

"You do not understand the natural order of things, Princess. The strong rule over the weak. It is not a matter of right or wrong, but of power and control."

Raena narrowed her eyes, her frustration mounting as she remembered Ashes words .

"But what about the Vashka? They are sentient beings, just like us. They deserve respect and freedom, not enslavement and forced labor."

The other noble at the table sneered.

"The Vashka are demons, my dear. They are not like us. They do not deserve the same treatment."

Raena's eyes flashed with anger.

"The Vashka are a species with their own rights and dignity. It is not our place to enslave them and use their powers for our own gain. We should treat them with the same respect as we do each other."

Lord Cadmus leaned forward, his voice low and menacing.

"You speak of things you do not understand, Princess. The Vashka are dangerous creatures. They are a threat to our way of life, and must be controlled."

King Lucius, who had been listening intently to the conversation, finally spoke up.

"Enough!"

His voice boomed throughout the dining hall, silencing the bickering nobles.

"This discussion is not one to be had over dinner. We are here to celebrate the unity and prosperity of our great city, not to argue about the class disparities that exist within it."

Queen Isadora, sensing the tension in the room, spoke up in a more soothing tone.

"Indeed, my love. Let us enjoy the rest of this delicious meal and continue our conversations in a more appropriate setting. After all, we must remember that we are all part of the same community, and it is only by working together that we can continue to thrive."

The tension dissipated somewhat as the servants cleared the table and began to bring out dessert. Raena couldn't help but feel a sense of frustration and anger towards the nobles at the table. The guests were served a selection of sweets, including a light and airy mousse made from the pulpy flesh of the nan starfruit, a sticky and sweet syrup extracted from the sap of the Rostavian honey tree, and a plate of delicate pastry shells filled with a creamy mixture of ground hazelnuts and the rare Tarsian vanilla bean.

As they enjoyed these treats, Lord Eran whispered to Raena off his sympathy for the Vashkas plight and his desire to see them treated more fairly. Raena smiled gratefully at Lord Eran's words.

"Thank you, Lord Eran. It's comforting to know that there are still those among us who value justice and fairness above their own self-interest."

Lord Eran nodded solemnly.

"I believe it is our duty as nobles to use our power and privilege for the greater good, not just our own personal gain."

─── · ｡˚ ☆: *.☽ .* :☆˚. ───

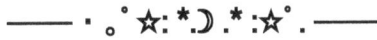

3

The sand sears my bare feet, a constant punishment in this hell I was born into - a reminder that my kind is on the lowest rung of this twisted society. My wrists ache, chafed raw by the chains that bind us all, while the relentless sun overhead bakes us in our own sweat. The growl that claws its way out of my throat sounds more like a death rattle, a bitter echo against the surrounding dunes. Around me, the guards snarl, their disdain and contempt for us matching the cruel chill in their eyes. Water Mages, the noble bastards who lord over us with their uncanny power over water. Their power is the cruelest of ironies in this parched desert landscape. Below them are the Nulls, pitiful humans stripped of magic, but even they sit a step above us - demons, born only to serve. Our purpose? To extract lyrium, the precious metal these mages covet for their magic. As our footfalls march us closer to the mines, my gut coils in dread. Each of us shares the same fate, the same dread etched into our faces. It's a destiny steeped in the promise of backbreaking work, grinding us down day after day.

The distant rumble of the mines is like the growl of a starving beast, reaching out with claws of dread and anticipation. Each step quickens my pulse, my heart pounding an angry beat against my chest. The weight of the day's events presses heavily against me, making every breath an act of defiance. The memory of Elras, stumbling, gasping, and frail, sends a surge of anger coursing through my veins. I had moved to shield him from the whip, to shoulder his punishment. It was all for naught until she intervened.

Her - the woman whose name I didn't know at the time. I'd only recognized the authority in her stance, the way the guards had faltered. She was a princess, a damn Water Mage who surprisingly saved Elras from the mines, elevating him to a palace servant. When

I thanked her, her cold reply hit me like a bucket of ice. She hadn't done it out of kindness, but practicality. Her words did nothing to quench the tiny spark of hope, of gratitude that flickered within me. Someone had finally noticed us, noticed our plight.

But I can't afford to dwell on it. I can't afford hope, I am a demon born in chains, but I'll be damned if these chains will break me.

The colossal doors of the mine loom before us, a monstrosity carved into the mountainside, its insatiable maw ready to swallow us whole. A bulky guard, the stench of his sweat mixed with the dust of the desert, steps forward from the entrance, an expectant grin etched onto his weathered face. He stops before the leader of our escort, a superior sneer plastered on his face. The two of them exchange a few words, their voices carried away by the merciless wind.

Handing over a scroll, our escort reports.

"Twenty-nine of these horned bastards. Supposed to be thirty, but one of 'em was...reassigned."

The bulky guard chuckles, a cold, cruel sound that sends a chill running down my spine despite the burning heat.

"Unfortunate for him. Harder fate awaits those who escape the mines," the guard says, scanning the lot of us with a disdainful gaze.

"Actually," the escort commander corrects him, "the lucky fucker got sent to the palace."

My chest tightens at the mention, my mind instantly drawn to Elras. Despite the cruel mockery, the guard's words spark a small fire within me. Maybe the palace wouldn't be an escape for Elras, but at least it was not this hellhole, not this mine where we are nothing but bodies to be used and discarded.

He then points at me, his eyes narrowed in thinly veiled contempt. "Keep a close watch on this one," he growls, spitting out a vile curse. "He's got a knack for stirring up trouble."

The mine guard turns his gaze towards me, a malicious grin pulling at the corners of his mouth. His eyes gleam in anticipation, like a cat that's just spotted a wounded mouse.

"Troublemakers, eh? They're always my favorite kind," he says, laughter oozing out of him like venom from a serpent's fang.

His words crawl under my skin, stirring a rage that I've long grown familiar with. I meet his gaze unflinchingly, my jaw set. The fact that my defiance amuses him only fuels the flames of my fury. I won't be broken. Not by the likes of him. As he takes a step towards me, I meet his gaze squarely, refusing to let fear show in my eyes. A sense of rebellion pulses through my veins, a bitter reminder of the hate that has been carved into the very marrow of my being. I am not just a demon, a slave, a tool for these mages and their despised magic. "Defiant. I like it," he says, taking a step back.

"It makes the breaking all the more enjoyable."

It's a challenge. A warning. But I am no stranger to threats, no stranger to the looming shadow of pain. The harsh reality of my life has been nothing but a bitter cycle of endurance.

"Get moving," he orders, his humor vanishing as quickly as it had surfaced. The grin is replaced by a grim line, his eyes turning to steel. He pushes me forward, sending me stumbling into the open jaws of the mine.

We're herded into the beast's maw like cattle to the slaughter, the only sounds our shackles scraping against the hard ground, and the harsh laughter of the guards echoing off the stone walls.

The first level of the mine is teeming with life. Slaves, demons like me and some nulls, the unlucky ones who got caught in the wrong place at the wrong time, are toiling away. The pickaxes hit the lyrium-laced rocks, the sound an irregular, jarring rhythm. The air is heavy with dust, the precious mineral glittering in the meager light of the mage-lit lanterns. Bare-chested, their bodies gleam with sweat, muscles straining with each swing of their tools. It's a sight that's simultaneously inspiring and horrifying - the raw strength of my people turned into a commodity for these Water Mages.

The newbies, the ones not yet familiar with the mine's unforgiving nature, stumble around me, their breath hitching at the sight before them. I don't blame them. Even after years in the pits, the harsh reality still claws at my guts.

A figure steps forward from the gloom, a foreman by the looks of him. His eyes flit across us, his expression void of any sympathy. "You're property of the mine now," he begins, his voice echoing in the cavernous space.

"You work until you can't. If you drop, you'll be replaced."

The guards disperse us among the toiling slaves. I'm assigned to a crew working a vein of lyrium on the second level. As I step into line with them, a few familiar faces nod at me, their eyes hollow yet fiery with unspoken resolve.

We are handed pickaxes, the cold weight familiar in my hands. The guard who brought me in grins at me again, a malicious twinkle in his eyes.

"Have fun, troublemaker," he says, before turning on his heel and leaving me to my fate.

The work is grueling, each swing of the pickaxe a test of endurance. My muscles scream in protest, but I push on. The supervisor watch from above, his faces a mask of indifference as he oversee this kingdom of slaves. But I am not one to wallow in despair. As I drive the pickaxe into the rock, I let my anger fuel me. Each swing is a promise. Each spark that flies from the rock is a symbol of my resolve.

I will endure. I will resist. Because I am the unyielding fire in a world of water. And I will not be extinguished.

4

Dawn has broken over the capital city, painting the sky in a gentle palette of pinks and purples. However, inside the palace, I'm oblivious to the beauty unfolding outside. Instead, I am nestled comfortably beneath my heavy silk sheets, still in the thrall of dreams. The first rays of sunlight pierce through the diaphanous curtains, splaying golden streaks across the floor of my spacious chamber. Still, I linger in the warm cocoon of my bed, buried beneath an avalanche of rich, silken pillows. I roll over in the soft bedding, a small groan escaping my lips. Mornings have never been my favorite, and I relish these last few moments of peace before the palace springs to life.

The sound of light footsteps interrupts my blissful morning lull. Without opening my eyes, I know who it is.

"Five more minutes, Binda," I murmur, pulling a pillow over my head.

However, the voice that replies is not Binda's, it's deeper, more amused.

"Your wish is my command, princess," Zarek says with a chuckle.

I groan, burrowing deeper into the pillows, but a soft laugh breaks through my barriers, drawing a smile from me.

"Zarek, what are you doing here so early?" I grumble, pulling the pillow away to peek at him.

Zarek, my fiancé, stands by the foot of my bed, a mischievous smile dancing on his lips. He's tall and well-built, his shoulders broad and his frame athletic, as well as it should be considering the countless hours he spends training in the palace grounds. His hair is light, and his eyes are an entrancing blend of emerald green and gold, like an oasis in our desert kingdom. He's clad in a tailored outfit that hugs his physique, making him look every bit the charismatic lord he is. We had been promised to each other since we were children, a political match, but one I had grown to appreciate over time.

"Early? Raena, it's almost noon," he teases, raising a brow at me.

I groan, letting the pillow fall back onto my face.

"That's still early for me," I mumble, my voice muffled.

Zarek's laughter fills the room, a pleasant sound that sparks a small flame of contentment within me.

"Come on, lazybones," he says, pulling the covers off me.

With a yawn, I sit up, rubbing the sleep from my eyes.

"I could have you executed for that," I grumble, throwing him a mock glare.

His smile broadens.

"But then who would you have to tease and torment? You'd be bored within a week."

I can't help but laugh, shaking my head at his antics. It was true; our relationship had always been filled with banter and playful jibes, something most unusual from the strict decorum of court life.

"Can't deny that," I quip back, throwing my legs over the side of the bed.

I glance around my chamber, spacious and airy, is filled with a variety of luxurious furnishings, each piece thoughtfully curated. My bed, a grand four-poster draped with gossamer silk curtains, sits in the center, an island amidst a sea of sumptuous rugs and polished marble floors. Large, tall doors open onto a wide balcony. They're free from ornate carvings or decorations, their smooth wood grain instead adding an element of natural warmth to the room.

To the left of the balcony, sits my vanity, a large, beautifully crafted piece made of rich, dark wood. The mirror is large and ornately framed, reflecting the lavish room in its polished surface. Around the vanity there are shelves and drawers, filled with cosmetics, jewelry, and other trinkets, some of which are from lands far beyond our kingdom.

On the opposite side of the room, a seating area is arranged, featuring plush armchairs and a low table. A few scrolls and books are strewn haphazardly across the table, curtesy of my fondness for late-night reading sessions. Zarek takes my hand gently, pulling me from my moment of reminiscence.

"Care to join me for tea, princess?" he asked.

I eyed him, suspicious.

"It's not poisoned, is it?" I retorted playfully, knowing full well that he understood my banter. His laughter echoed in the room, a sound that I had grown to find endearing.

"Of course not," he said with a playful smirk on his lips.

"I would be a terrible assassin, considering I'm the one who'll drink it with you."

With a chuckle, I take his hand, standing from my perch at the edge of the bed. Together, we move towards the open balcony doors. Stepping out onto the cool stone floor of the balcony, a gentle breeze tugs at my loose hair, bringing with it the fresh, verdant scent of the palace gardens. The view is breathtaking. The palace gardens stretch out before us, an oasis in the midst of a desert. Tall palm trees sway gently, casting long, wavering shadows over beds of brilliantly colored flowers. Canals of water, drawn from our underground reservoirs and manipulated by the palace's water mages, wind their way through the garden like veins, nourishing the vibrant greenery.

Birds chirp melodiously in the trees, their songs mingling with the faint, soothing sound of trickling water. Butterflies and bees flit from flower to flower, a busy tableau of life against the vibrant backdrop. Amidst the harsh desert, the garden is a display to our powers and the prosperity of our kingdom. The balcony itself is spacious, with comfortable, cushioned seating and a low table made of the same dark wood as my vanity. It is an extension of my room - simple yet elegant, mirroring the oasis that is the garden with its sense of tranquility.

"It's so beutiful, isn't it?" I say, leaning on the balcony railing.

Zarek smiles, watching the gardens with me.

"That it is my love," he admits.

Before I can respond, I hear soft footsteps approaching. Turning around, I see a couple of palace maids, their arms laden with trays. I recognize the familiar gleam of a silver teapot, the delicate china cups, the assortments of pastries and fruits. With practiced ease, the maids set the table, their movements so synchronized they might as well have been dancing. Within minutes, they're gone, leaving behind the tantalizing aroma of freshly brewed tea. Zarek, as a gentleman, pulls out a chair for me. As I sit down, he pours us each a cup of tea, the steam curling into the crisp morning air and mixing with the fragrance of the garden.

"This is one of the few advantages of rising early," he says, a playful twinkle in his eyes.

I smirk, accepting the cup he offers.

"Or in your case, Zarek, staying up till dawn."

His laugh is soft, a mere exhale of amusement as he takes a sip of his own tea.

"Guilty as charged."

I lift my cup to my lips, the scent of the brew filling my senses. It's a unique blend, floral with a touch of sweetness, a signature of our kingdom.

"Jasmine and honeydew," I note, closing my eyes to appreciate the aroma better.

Zarek nods.

"One of your favorite. I thought it might make an early morning more palatable for you."

The warm liquid slides down my throat, a perfect balance of flavors. The sweetness of the honeydew mellows out the floral notes of the jasmine, creating a harmony that lingers on my tongue.

"This is...perfect," I admit, a smile pulling at my lips.

"Perfect enough to make you a morning person?" he asks, a teasing lilt in his voice.

I pretend to consider it, placing my cup down onto the table.

"Let's not get ahead of ourselves."

"You missed the royal feast last night," I mention, my voice soft. Zarek's expression falters, guilt clouding his vibrant eyes.

"I'm sorry, Raena, I was occupied, I'm afraid. There's been a dispute at the western border, nothing to worry about but it required my attention."

He's been working late often, taking care of matters of the kingdom. Despite our age, both of us have had responsibilities thrust upon us, the price of being born into nobility. I reach across the table, placing my hand on top of his. He looks up, his eyes meeting mine.

"You can't fix everything, Zarek. You need to rest too," I say, the sincerity in my voice silencing his protest. He smiles, a small, tired one, but it reaches his eyes.

"I know, Raena. But I can't ignore my duties either. Not when I'm capable," he responds, wrapping his fingers around my hand. The chill from his skin, a side effect of our water magic, sends a pleasant tingle up my arm.

I let out a soft sigh, brushing my thumb over his hand.

"I know, Zarek, I know," I reply. "I just don't want you to burn out." His gaze lingers on mine a moment longer before he diverts it, looking down at our entwined hands. His voice is a low rumble when he finally speaks.

"I won't, not if I have you."

"Speaking of duties," he says, lifting our joined hands and placing a soft kiss on my knuckles.

"I heard from father you had a...rather interesting suggestion for him last night."

I blink, the comment throwing me off guard. I tilt my head at him, my eyebrows furrowing in confusion.

"Interesting suggestion?" I ask, trying to recall what I had said. "Oh...are you talking about the caste system?"

Zarek nods, his eyes sparkling with amusement.

"Yes, my love, the very same. Father seemed rather taken aback by your proposal to...how did he put it? Oh yes, 'dismantle the very foundation of our society'."

I snort, rolling my eyes.

"Well, when you put it like that, it sounds so dramatic. It wasn't a proposal, really, just a passing comment," I clarify, taking another sip of my tea.

"I didn't think anyone would take it seriously."

His chuckle fills the quiet morning, soft and warm.

"Only you would consider abolishing the caste system a passing comment, Raena," he says, shaking his head in disbelief.

"I think Lord Cadmus nearly choked on his wine," I add, giggling at the memory of his father's aghast expression.

Zarek's laughter joins mine, filling the balcony with lightness and joy.

"I wish I had been there to see that," he says, wiping a tear from his eye.

"Anything that ruffles my father's feathers is worth witnessing."

As our laughter subsides, I reach for a small pastry on the tray - a tiny work of art with intricate sugar glaze atop a flaky crust. I offer it to Zarek, who accepts it with a grateful nod.

"You're spoiling me, Ren," he says, before taking a small bite of the pastry. He hums appreciatively.

"Delicious. Almost makes up for missing the feast."

I smile at his playful comment, picking a pastry for myself.

"Well, the feast was quite something. Roast pheasant, seared fish, platters of fresh fruits... you missed quite a spread."

His gaze grows distant at my description, likely imagining the scene. I feel a pang of guilt. Zarek works so hard for the kingdom, and often at the cost of his own comforts.

"Next time, you must join us," I insist.

"You work too hard, Zarek. You deserve to enjoy the fruits of your labor."

He chuckles, shaking his head.

"And who would protect the kingdom if I were to indulge as you suggest?" His tone is light, but I detect a trace of regret.

I frown slightly, pausing to choose my words.

"Zarek, protecting the kingdom doesn't rest solely on your shoulders. You're surrounded by capable people who can share the burden."

He looks at me for a moment before sighing, his expression softening.

"It's not so much that I don't trust them. It's just...well, the system, it's flawed."

I tilt my head curiously, the half-eaten pastry still in my hand.

"What do you mean?"

He sighs, his hands reaching for his tea, a crumb from the pastry still stuck to the corner of his lips.

"You mentioned the caste system," he begins, pausing as if he's carefully weighing his words.

"I believe... I believe there are some merits to your 'passing comment'."

I blink, surprised.

"You...agree?"

He nods, setting his cup on the table and looking at me seriously.

"I see it every day, Raena. Prestigious families with heirs who have neither the aptitude nor the desire for leadership, being handed crucial positions of power due to their birthright. That's a birthright lottery. It's an unproductive system, fostering incompetence and resentment."

A frown pulls at his brows as he continues.

"We need capable hands, not just prestigious ones. And I believe those hands could just as easily be found among the nulls. I've seen their potential during our combat trainings. Some of them are better strategists and warriors than half of our high-ranking mages."

His words catch me off guard. It's a radical idea, especially coming from Zarek, who's usually so dedicated to preserving tradition.

"I... I think that's a wonderful idea and a risky one. Not many would agree with it," I finally say, knowing how deep-seated the caste system is in our society. To challenge it would be to challenge the foundation of our culture, our traditions.

"To reward skill and dedication, rather than lineage... it would change everything."

Zarek sighs, a somber note to the otherwise light-hearted morning. "I am aware. It would upset many, especially the families who benefit from the current system. They might see it as a threat to their status, their influence."

He pauses, his gaze wandering over the lush, green garden below us. "But as a military leader, it's my duty to place the kingdom's well-being over personal comfort. If a change in the system can contribute to that, then I believe it's a risk worth taking."

"I'm proud of you, Zarek," I tell him, my hand finding its way to his over the table.

He looks at me, his smile softer now.

"Thank you, Raena. Your support means more than you can imagine."

Suddenly, Zarek chuckles.

"Father would have a fit if he were to hear about this."

I laugh, the sound ringing clear and bright in the early morning air. "Oh, to be a fly on the wall when you tell him. He'd probably choke on his own words."

Zarek joins my laughter, his eyes meet mine, twinkling with mischief. "Perhaps we could stage it during another extravagant feast. That way, at least he'll have something good to eat while swallowing the bitter pill of change."

"Deal. It'll be a feast to remember."

"Poor Lord Cadmus," I say, feigning a pout.

"Imagine, a rebellious future daughter-in-law and a son who's ready to topple the social order. He's got his work cut out for him, hasn't he?"

Zarek grins, his eyes crinkling at the corners.

"He did always say he enjoyed a good challenge."

"But did he ever mention he wanted his family to be the challenge?" I retort, teasing.

Zarek throws his head back and laughs, his delight infectious. I join in, our laughter filling the morning air. It feels good to be so carefree, even if just for a moment.

"Maybe he should have been more specific," Zarek finally manages, wiping a tear of mirth from his eye. We lapse into a comfortable silence, savoring our pastries and tea as we watch the sun continue its ascent in the sky. The gardens below us are alive with activity, the water mages at work, maintaining the lush greenery in the heart of the desert.

Zarek breaks the silence, his tone more serious.

"When we're king and queen and if we decide to walk that path I do hope father will come to understand, in time. He has always been so... resolute in his beliefs. Stubborn, even."

I reach out, giving his hand a comforting squeeze.

"Change isn't easy, Zarek. But with enough patience and understanding, even the most stubborn of minds can be swayed."

He turns his hand under mine, fingers lacing together in a warm hold.

"I know. I just hope it doesn't drive a wedge between us. Father and I... we've always had our differences, but this... this could be a breaking point."

"Perhaps," I say, thinking it over.

"But, Zarek, remember this - you are proposing change for the betterment of the kingdom, for the future of our people. It's a noble cause. And in the end, isn't that what being a leader is all about? Making the tough decisions, for the good of the many?"

He nods, a small smile tugging at his lips.

"You always have a way of making things seem simpler, Raena."

I shrug, my smile matching his.

"Well, someone has to balance out your knack for complexity."

He chuckles at my comment, his eyes gleaming with amusement. As the laughter fades, Zarek leans back in his chair, eyeing me with a thoughtful look.

"Speaking of complexity, I've heard a curious rumor." His voice is casual, but there's a spark of curiosity in his eyes.

"They say you've done something rather... unusual."

"Oh?" I reply, feigning innocence.

"And what might that be?"

He grins, leaning in closer.

"It appears that the Princess has welcomed a Vashka demon into the palace. As a servant, no less. Now, I find that quite intriguing. Especially since you've never shown much interest in demons before."

I can't help but laugh. He has a way of making even the most outrageous things sound completely normal.

"My, my, news certainly travels fast in this palace, doesn't it? Especially when one stays up all night."

Zarek raises his hands in mock defense.

"I can't help it if my men enjoy their palace gossip."

"But you're right," I admit, picking up my tea cup.

"I did bring a Vashka demon into the palace. His name is Elras. I think he'll make a good servant."

Zarek's eyes widen slightly. He's clearly surprised by my candid response.

"Really? A Vashka demon... here? In the palace?"

I nod, my eyes meeting his.

"But why, Raena?" He asks, his voice carrying a note of genuine curiosity.

"Why bring a demon here? You've never given them much thought before."

"Yes, it's true," I admit, brushing a stray curl off my forehead.

"I never did. I suppose I simply accepted our society's attitude towards them without question. But a recent event has...made me reconsider. I saw how these so-called 'dangerous' creatures were being treated, and it didn't sit well with me."

Zarek raises an eyebrow, leaning back into his chair, looking at me with curiosity.

"Oh? And what might this event be?"

I gather my thoughts, trying to decide how best to describe the scene that changed my perspective.

"The other day, on the way to the market, a group of Vhaska demons were being marched down the street, chained and exhausted. One of them, an old demon, was too weak to keep up and collapsed. A younger demon, was trying to help him, pleading with the guards for mercy, but the guards didn't care."

Zarek frowns, the wrinkles on his forehead deepening.

"The guards aren't usually known for their compassion."

"Yes, and I realized something," I continue, setting my cup down with a soft clink.

"We've been treating these demons as if they're some kind of monstrous enemy. But they're not. They're just... beings. Beings who can feel pain and empathy, who can show kindness and compassion. Just like us."

Zarek listens quietly, absorbing my words.

"Elras couldn't go to the mines, he would have died there," I go on. "So, I brought him here instead. He'll serve in the palace, where he can live out his days in peace."

Zarek leans in closer.

"So, you brought Elras to the palace out of pity?"

I shake my head, meeting his gaze.

"No, not out of pity. Out of respect. Respect for the young demons commitment to Elras. Respect for their resilience, their strength in the face of adversity. Demons are not just our slaves. They are sentient beings, with their own culture and society, their own bonds and alliances. Their own strengths and weaknesses."

I pause, looking at my hands folded in my lap.

"And they have their own dignity, Zarek. We just choose not to see it."

Zarek is silent for a moment, processing what I've just said. The usual playful spark in his eyes has given way to a more thoughtful expression. Finally, he speaks.

"Raena, you've surprised me."

"Good," I reply, my voice tinged with light humor.

"I was getting bored of being predictable."

He chuckles, but there's a serious undertone to his response.

"I suppose this means we'll have to adjust to having a demon around the palace?"

"Indeed," I say, lifting my tea cup to my lips.

"And you, as the future king, will set the example for our court."

He gives a mock sigh, placing a hand dramatically on his chest.

"Ah, I suppose I can't say no to that, can I?"

"Well, we'll pretend you can, but actually you can't," I retort, reaching over to playfully swat his arm. His grin only widens, his eyes sparkling with humor.

"Fair enough, my lady," he concedes, lifting his tea cup in a mock toast.

"To our new palace servant, then."

—— · ｡˚☆: *.☽ .* :☆˚. ——

5

Later that day, I sit on an ornate chair in my private study, the afternoon sunlight filtering through the windows, casting an array of light and shadows across the room. Elras, the old Vhaska demon, shuffles in under the watchful eye of Binda. Despite the complexity of the situation, I feel a strong determination to make his transition as smooth as possible.

"Your Highness," Binda greets me with a curtsey, her voice perfectly measured and respectful.

"Elras, Binda," I nod in acknowledgment, trying to put the old demon at ease.

"There's no need for formality. Please, take a seat."

Elras looks apprehensive but follows my command, his body awkward on the delicate, ornate chair. Binda takes a seat next to him, her hands folded neatly in her lap.

"I've brought you here, Elras, because I wanted to welcome you personally," I begin, meeting the demon's bewildered gaze.

"From today onwards, you will be serving in this palace, not the mines."

"Binda will guide you through your duties and familiarize you with the palace," I explain, turning to my trusted maid.

"You will be assisting her with household tasks. If there are any problems or if you need anything, Binda is the person you should talk to."

Binda gives a small nod, her face impassive but her eyes understanding.

"Of course, my lady. I'll ensure Elras here becomes well acquainted with his responsibilities and the palace's routine."

I smile at the both of them, a sense of satisfaction settling within me. "I am hopeful that you will find your place here, Elras. And remember, you are no longer a slave. You are a servant of this palace, and you should be treated as such."

The old demon looks at me, his eyes reflecting a mix of gratitude and disbelief. He lowers his head in a humble bow.

"Thank ya, my lady. I'll do me best, I promise ya that."

His relief is palpable, but beneath it, I can see remnants of old pain, of hardship and years of grueling labor in the unforgiving mines. His weathered hands, thick with calluses, rest uneasily on his lap, the toughened skin a stark contrast to the finely woven fabrics of the palace.

"Elras," I begin, my tone soft yet firm.

"I would like to understand your past better, to learn about the life you led before you came here. If you are comfortable sharing, I want to know about your time in the mines."

He flinches, just slightly, and his gaze drops to his hands. The room grows quiet, save for the distant song of birds from the garden and the rustle of wind against the window. Elras takes a deep breath, his chest heaving underneath his worn-out clothes.

"Aye, my lady, if it's what ya wish," he starts slowly, his voice low and husky.

"Life in them mines... it ain't something I'd wish on anyone, not even me worst enemy."

He describes the harsh conditions, the endless days of toil, the scarce meals, and the punishing heat of the desert. His words paint a picture of hopelessness, of endless suffering in the pursuit of lyrium, precious gems and metals that his kind weren't allowed to touch. His account is raw and painful, an unfiltered look into a life of servitude. His story is interrupted by quiet sobs. I look over to find Binda discreetly wiping her eyes, her composed façade crumbling under the weight of Elras's words. It is a rare show of emotion from her.

"Thank you for sharing your story, Elras," I say once he has finished, my voice steady.

"I can't erase your past, but I can promise you that your future here will be different."

Elras lifts his gaze, meeting my eyes.

"Thank ya, my lady. That's more than I ever hoped for."

A moment passes before I speak again. The silence is filled with the echoes of Elras' account, resonating deeply within me. I take a steadying breath, my heart heavy with the painful reality that Elras, and many others like him, have endured.

"Elras," I begin, the words careful and considerate.

"There is one more thing I would like to ask you. The demon named Ash... the one who tried to help you at the market. Can you tell me more about him?"

The old demon looks at me, a hint of surprise in his eyes before he takes a moment to gather his thoughts.

"Ash....? Aye, I can tell ya about 'im."

He pauses, drawing in a deep breath, as if the mere mention of the name brings forth a wave of emotions.

"Ash, he's a good lad, strong, resilient. He's been in the mines for a couple of years now, brought in as a young one, not much older than a whelp. Tougher than any of us though, he is."

Elras looks into the distance, as though looking past the lush gardens and into the harsh, sun-scorched mines.

"Life in the mines ain't been kind to 'im, just like the rest of us. But he's a fighter, always helping others when he can, always standing up to the overseers when they push us too far."

His expression turns somber, his voice dropping to a whisper.

"It's earned him more than his fair share of beatings, it has. But he don't care. Says it's better him than any of us."

"Much like when he tried to help you in the market?" I ask, thinking back to the memory of that day. A fleeting moment that brought forth significant change.

"Aye, my lady," he nods, a hint of pride lining his voice.

"He's always been that way. Puttin' others before himself, risking his own skin to lend a hand. He didn't have to step in that day, could've kept his head low and minded his business. But he saw me struggling and stepped in, even if he knew the consequence."

"And how is Ash faring now?" I ask, I can only imagine the conditions he must be facing after that day, how his act of kindness may have drawn unwanted attention.

Elras's expression hardens slightly, a shadow passing over his face.

"I can't say for sure, my lady," he admits, his voice tinged with concern. "The mines ain't kind to those who step outta line. I reckon they'd be harder on 'im after that day. But knowing Ash, he'd endure it, bear it with that stubborn pride of his."

The tales of the mines are horrific.

"Thank you, Elras," I say softly, finally lifting my gaze to meet his. "Thank you for sharing about Ash. Your words... they've given me much to think about."

"Binda," I start, my voice firm yet gentle.

"I want you to take care of Elras. Ensure he is comfortable and well-fed. Help him learn his duties around the palace and assist him in adapting to this new life."

"Of course, your highness," Binda replies, her voice steady.

"I will do my utmost to see to Elras's well-being and smooth transition into palace life."

I then turn back to Elras, offering him a warm, reassuring smile.

"Elras, Binda is one of the most reliable people I know. She will help you navigate through your new duties and ensure you're treated with respect."

Elras looks at me, then to Binda, before dipping his head in a sign of gratitude.

"Thank ya, both of ya. I... I don't know what to say."

"Just do your best, Elras," I tell him, offering a comforting smile. "And welcome to your new home."

7

—— · ˳˚ ☆: *.☽ .* :☆˚. ——

Weeks turn into an endless blur of pickaxes and pain, the sun doesn't reach us down here in the belly of the mountain, the void illuminated only by the dim, flickering glow of torchlight. My mornings start with the dull, echoing sound of the guard's whip, a crude symphony that lulls us out of restless sleep and into another day of toil. A harsh shove to my shoulder announces the beginning of a new day, the guard grinning down at me as if my existence were a joke to him. The sight of his sneering face fills me with a familiar, burning rage, but I bite it down. It's the same routine every day; resentment won't change that.

The day drags on in a haze of dust and sweat. Our pickaxes chip away at the stone walls, the grating sound gnawing at the edges of my sanity. Each strike brings forth a shower of sparks, a fleeting moment of brilliance in the grim darkness.

Suddenly, a desperate shriek slices through the monotonous rhythm. My heart skips a beat. An accident. It's not uncommon in these mines, where safety is as scarce as our rations.

A young demon named Kiran, a lad who was barely of age when he was thrust into this torment, lies writhing in the dirt. His pickaxe slipped and skidded into his leg, blood gushing from the wound. The guards stand by, their laughter echoing through the cavern, while Kiran's screams fill the air. Rage flares in me. Kiran is a good kid, stubborn, but he didn't deserve this. None of us did.

Ignoring the guards' warnings, I drop my pickaxe and rush towards Kiran. His eyes are wide with fear, the blood draining from his face at an alarming rate. I rip a strip from my already tattered clothes, pressing it against the wound in a futile attempt to stem the bleeding. A rough hand yanks me away, and I'm met with the guard's gleeful gaze.

"What's this? Playing hero, are we?" he taunts. But I don't back down, meeting his gaze with a glare as fierce as the desert sun.

"You're gonna let him die? For what? Your amusement?" I spit, my voice echoing throughout the cavern.

The guard only chuckles.

"It's survival of the fittest down here, demon. Remember that."

There's no time for me to argue, no time to start a fight I can't win. All I can do is turn my attention back to Kiran, whispering words of reassurance as his life ebbs away. His grip on my hand tightens for a moment before going slack, his eyes glazing over. My fists clench as the last bit of life slips out of Kiran's eyes, his body going cold beneath my trembling hands. There ain't no dignity in death, not down here. It's raw and ugly, a cruel joke to the guards and a painful reminder to us. Just like that, another brother lost to the endless greed of these fuckin' mages.

"Ain't you done enough?" I growl, glaring at the guard who's still laughing, that bastard. His grin widens, the sight of it lighting a wild rage in me.

"Get the fuck away from him!"

The guard only smirks, a cruel twist of his lips.

"Such a big heart for a demon. That's cute."

Cute? I see nothing cute in our misery. Nothing cute about our reality. My heart aches for Kiran, for his pain, his fear. But what can I do? Fight? Rage? All it would earn me is a lash or a quick trip to an early grave.

Fuck them.

Work resumes as if nothing has happened, as if one of us hadn't just been erased from existence. They think we're just bodies to use and dispose of. But they're wrong. Each of us matters, each of us feels. We're not just numbers, not just tools for their precious mages.

The sharp sting of a whip cuts through the murmurings of my thoughts. I flinch, but don't cry out - giving them the satisfaction would be worse than the lash itself. With clenched teeth, I pick up my pickaxe and join the others, swinging into the unforgiving stone with renewed anger. Every chip of lyrium that we pry from these fucking walls only fuels the mages' power, strengthens the chains that bind us.

Kael's on my right, his jaw set with determination. He's not as big or strong as some of us, but what he lacks in brute force he makes up for with a sharp mind and even sharper tongue. Always thinking, always planning, always pushing us to survive. He's a tether to sanity in this mad, mad world. A reminder that we're more than what they say we are.

On my left, Gavril. The guy's built like a mountain, muscles forged in the fires of this hellhole. There's a raw, wild strength to him. If I didn't know him, I'd probably be scared shitless. But Gavril's loyalty is as sturdy as his build. He'd rather rip a guard's throat out than let one of us fall - and believe me, I've seen him come close.

With a grunt, Gavril strikes the wall with his pickaxe, sending a cascade of dust and debris down on us.

"Bastards," he grunts, sweeping a hand across his face to rid it of the dirt.

I nod, too choked up with grief and anger to say anything. Bastards. That's putting it mildly. Beside me, Kael's face hardens, his silver eyes gleaming in the dim light.

"We can't let this continue," he says quietly, his voice barely audible over the clinking of pickaxes. He's right. We can't. But what the fuck can we do?

"We need to stand together," Kael continues, his gaze steady. "Wait for the right moment. They can't kill all of us."

Gavril snorts, the sound reverberating through the cavern.

"And when's that? When we're all half-dead?"

Kael shakes his head, a grim smile tugging at his lips.

"No. When they least expect it."

The day drags on, each chime of the pickaxe a muffled tribute to Kiran. The familiar ache in my muscles feels trivial in comparison to the hollow pang in my chest. When the guard finally announces the end of the shift, there's no relief, just a numbing emptiness.

Food's a meager gruel, the taste as bitter as our lives. But hunger gnaws at my insides, so I eat, choking down each spoonful with a mixture of resignation and rage. Around me, the others do the same. We're all survivors here, each one of us held captive by the chains of survival.

As night blankets the mines, the guards return to their quarters, leaving us in a darkness that matches the one within us. We huddle together for warmth, our shared misery a twisted form of companionship. Suddenly, a soft whimper pierces the silence. A small demon, the newest addition to our unfortunate lot, cries into his thin blanket. The others ignore him, their eyes too heavy with sleep and despair. But I can't. Sliding next to him, I murmur softly.

"Hey, it's gonna be alright."

His eyes, wide with fear and confusion, latch onto me.

"Why did they let Kiran die?"

His question stabs me like a dagger, my chest tightening.

"Because they're fucking heartless," I reply, my voice bitter.

"But why don't we fight back?" he whispers, his voice trembling with a fragile hope.

I look at him, at this innocent being thrust into the cruel reality of our lives.

"Because right now, survival is our fight," I tell him, my voice barely audible.

"But remember, kid, anger is a gift. Use it. We may be in chains, but we've got a fire burning within us. They can't extinguish that."

The kid nods, his eyes glinting with a spark of resolve. As sleep finally claims us, I make a silent vow to myself. I'll turn this fucking hell upside down if I have to. For Kiran, for this kid, for all of us.

***

In the darkness of the mines, a few stolen moments of respite are more precious than the lyrium we break our backs to extract. That's where we are now, tucked away in a cranny of this hell, away from the prying eyes of the guards. Kael looks at us, his silver eyes glinting with a mixture of resolve and anticipation. He's been quiet for the past few days, his mind whirring faster than usual. Now, it seems he's ready to break the silence.

"My friends, listen" he begins, his voice barely more than a whisper against the ever-present clang of pickaxes.

Gavril grunts, his massive form folded on the ground as he catches his breath.

"What's it, Kael?"

"I've been thinking..." Kael starts, his gaze flitting nervously from Gavril to me.

"I've been observing the guards, their routines."

"What? You planning to join 'em?" Gavril snorts, but there's no heat in his words, only exhaustion.

Kael shakes his head, leaning in closer.

"I believe I found a flaw in their vigilance. At the deepest hours of the night, when the guards change shift, there's a brief moment of... weakness."

"Weakness?" I echo, my interest piqued despite myself.

"A window. A time when we might escape."

I blink at Kael, letting his words sink in. An escape? From this place? It's madness, sheer madness. We're demons, for fuck's sake. Vashka demons, easily spotted, easily hunted down. And yet, as I look into Kael's earnest eyes, I find myself considering it.

"Even if we manage to escape, Kael, where'd we go?" I ask, voicing the question that's gnawing at me.

"We can't exactly blend in, can we?"

Kael's smile is a grim line in the torchlight.

"There's a place... not far from here. A settlement where Nulls and Vashka live. Outcasts, deserters, and those disillusioned with the regime."

Gavril snorts, a bitter sound.

"And you think they'll just welcome us? We're slaves, Kael."

"Not slaves, Gavril," Kael retorts, his voice filled with a conviction I've never heard before.

"Survivors. They know the pain of oppression as much as we do."

"And where'd you get that nugget of hope?" Gavril questions, his hard eyes locked on Kael. I'm interested too. Kael's smart, but he's been a slave his whole life, same as us. Where could he have heard about a place like that?

A shadow passes over Kael's eyes, a darkness I've seen there before but never questioned.

"During my time serving the mages," he confesses, voice barely a whisper.

The mere mention of the mages stirs a bitter taste in my mouth, a revulsion I can't control. Kael had it worse than any of us, forced to satisfy the twisted desires of our captors. Just the thought makes my fists clench, the old chains around my wrists biting into the skin.

"And you believe the words of those fuckers?"

Gavril scoffs, echoing my doubts. Trusting the words of our captors seems like a fool's game. Kael just stares at him, calm as a still pond, his silver eyes holding a spark of defiance.

"I do," he states, his voice carrying an undercurrent of steely determination.

"Because it was whispered in secret, a glimmer of rebellion from a water mage tired of the oppression. It was spoken not as a command, but as a desperate plea."

He falls silent, the echo of his words lingering in the tense air between us. The hope, that small flicker of something better, it's infectious. It's reckless and dangerous and probably a goddamn death sentence, but it's also the most alive I've felt since...well, ever.

"I have carried this secret with me ever since," Kael continues, his gaze not leaving ours.

"A flickering flame of hope amidst the darkness of my life. And now, I share it with you, my brothers, so that we might find our way to the promise of a better tomorrow."

Gavril is silent, his usually quick retorts nowhere to be heard. He's considering it, I realize. The big lug's actually considering it. As for me, I can't deny the appeal. A chance at freedom, no matter how slim...it's a hell of a lot better than dying in these godforsaken mines. I look at Kael, this demon who was enslaved like us but still clings to hope like a lifeline. It's brave. It's stupid, but it's also brave. And as I meet his hopeful gaze, I find myself nodding.

"We're in," I say, and the look of relief that washes over Kael's face tells me everything I need to know. We're all desperate to escape this hell. But more than that, we're desperate to believe that there might be something better out there for us.

For the first time in my life, I dare to dream of freedom.

8

—— · ₒ˚ ☆: *.) .* :☆˚ . ——

Raena sat in her study, the flickering candles giving the room a cozy glow. It was her retreat from the constant dramas and formalities of the palace. Binda and Elras were working quietly in the room, while Raena sat lost in thought in a comfortable chair, her attention far away despite the open book in her lap. Suddenly, she asked Elras a question.

"Elras, did Ash like sweets? I'm curious about what he likes."

Elras seemed a bit taken aback, but answered her anyway.

"My lady, in the mines, something like a sweet would be a real luxury. Any of us would consider it a special treat."

Raena nodded, a thoughtful smile on her face.

"So, the small pleasures mean a lot when life is tough, then."

"How tragic," she added softly.

Elras nodded, his voice quiet.

"True, my lady. In the mines, even small joys feel like treasures. Brief moments of happiness help us forget the darkness."

Raena nodded, deep in thought, and then turned to Binda.

"Binda, ask the chef to make ten boxes of my favorite treats."

"Heavens whatever for your highness?!" asked Binda in a surprised tone.

"Just tell him that it's for a very important diplomatic mission and we need them for tomorrow", she said waving a hand dismissively.

Binda raised an eyebrow, her expression a blend of amusement and curiosity.

"A diplomatic mission, Your Highness?" she inquired, a wry smile playing at the corners of her lips.

"I think the head chef might have a heart attack when he hears we want them by tomorrow morning"

Raena's eyes lit up with a playful glint, and a cheeky grin tugged at her lips.

"Well, we can't have him getting bored now, can we?" she said, her voice a mix of confidence and good humor.

"We need to keep those cooking skills of his sharp, right?"

Binda gave a small, amused shake of her head, caught up in Raena's light-hearted mood.

"I'll make sure he gets the message, Your Highness."

Elras, watching their interaction, asked hesitantly.

"What's all this about treats, then, Your Highness?"

Raena's expression turned coy, a coquettish smile dancing on her lips.

"Let's just say, dear Elras, that I have a newfound appreciation for the power of simple pleasures."

Binda narrowed her eyes at her.

"I've known you too long to think that this is a good idea," she warned.

"Big boxes Binda, specify big boxes," said Raena with a smile on her lips.

Binda sighed, her tone a blend of exasperation and affection.

"Very well, I shall ensure the head chef understands the gravity of the situation and the... enormity of the boxes."

Still not quite sure what was going on, Elras decided to just go along with it. He nodded, a quiet understanding in his eyes.

"I may not know what's going on, Your Highness, but I trust that it's for a good reason."

Raena burst into laughter, the sound ringing through the room.

"Oh Elras, you're giving me too much credit. Sometimes, a treat is just a treat — a little bit of happiness in a world that could use more of it."

***

Binda strode into the bustling kitchen, her gaze focused and determined. The head chef, a flamboyant and passionate character by the name of Auguste, was in the midst of orchestrating a culinary symphony, his hands deftly dancing between various pots and pans as he shouted orders at his scurrying underlings.

"Auguste, I must speak with you," Binda announced, her tone firm yet respectful.

Auguste paused, his dramatic flair momentarily suspended. He turned to face her, his vibrant eyes narrowing as he assessed her purpose.

"My dear Binda, can't you see I am in the throes of culinary creation? What could possibly be so urgent as to pull me from my art?"

Binda wasted no time, her voice unwavering.

"Her Highness, Princess Raena, requests that you prepare ten large boxes of her favorite sweets for a most important diplomatic mission. She requires them by tomorrow morning.

Auguste's eyes widened, and he threw his hands into the air, a gesture of exaggerated incredulity.

"By tomorrow morning? Mon Deus, does the princess not understand the intricate nature of my confections? The delicate balance of flavors, the sublime marriage of textures? Such things cannot be rushed!"

Binda, suppressing a smile at his theatrics, replied with a gentle firmness.

"Her Highness is well aware of your unparalleled talents, Auguste. She believes that only you can accomplish this feat and elevate these sweets to the heights of perfection."

Auguste scoffed, his eyes rolling dramatically.

"The heights of perfection? I alone can reach those, but in such a short time? You ask the impossible! Even for a culinary genius like myself, there are limits!"

Just as Auguste finished his impassioned protest, a loud crash echoed through the kitchen, followed by the splatter of sauce on the floor. One of his underlings, a young chef-in-training, had accidentally dropped a pot, its contents spreading across the tiles in a messy red pool.

Auguste's eyes narrowed, his nostrils flaring with indignation.

"By the holy goddess! What imbecile dares to interrupt my culinary sorcery with such a careless blunder?"

He stormed over to the hapless young chef, his voice rising in a torrent of dramatic, colorful curses.

"You bumbling buffoon! You...you culinary catastrophe! You have the dexterity of an intoxicated walrus! The finesse of a rampaging minotaur! What possessed you to darken my kitchen with your presence?"

The young chef, trembling like a leaf, stammered an apology.

"I-I'm s-sorry, Chef Auguste. I...I didn't mean to—"

Auguste cut him off, his tone dripping with disdain.

"Silence, you gastronomic disaster! Remove yourself from my sight before you bring further ruin to my kitchen! And ponder the enormity of your failure while scrubbing every inch of this floor!"

The crestfallen chef scurried away, broom and mop in hand, as Auguste returned his attention to Binda.

"Now, where were we? Ah, yes. The impossible task."

Binda, struggling to maintain her composure after witnessing the chef's dramatic tirade, cleared her throat.

"Auguste, I understand that this is a challenging request, but Princess Raena has faith in your abilities. If anyone can accomplish this feat, it is you."

The head chef sighed, his arrogance momentarily giving way to pragmatism.

"Very well, my dear Binda. For the sake of our dear princess and the kingdom, I shall attempt this Herculean task. But remember, I make no promises! The confections may be exquisite, but their true potential may remain just out of reach."

As Auguste returned to his culinary ballet, Binda shook her head in bemusement, secretly admiring the passionate chef's unwavering dedication to his craft. She had no doubt that the treats would be nothing short of exquisite. Auguste set to work, his hands weaving intricate patterns in the air as he conjured an orchestra of tastes and textures, his energy renewed by the daunting challenge before him – and the fervent hope that no more calamities would befall his precious kitchen. Binda watched in awe as the kitchen transformed into a stage, with Auguste as the star performer, his every movement an elegant dance.

Throughout the night, the kitchen bustled with activity as Auguste guided his team through the complicated process of creating the princess's favorite sweets. His booming voice echoed through the air, directing each member of his staff with an unyielding precision. The atmosphere was tense, but a palpable excitement coursed through the room. As dawn approached, the once chaotic kitchen had transformed into a sea of calm, the air fragrant with the aroma of the freshly made confections. Ten large boxes, each adorned with the royal crest, sat proudly on a long table, the result of a night filled with hard work and dedication.

Binda returned to the kitchen early in the morning, her eyes widening in amazement at the sight of the ten beautiful boxes. Just as she marveled at the extraordinary results, the door to the kitchen swung open, revealing Princess Raena herself, eager to witness the fruits of Auguste's labor. The princess approached the table, her eyes sparkling with delight.

"Auguste, you have truly outdone yourself! These look absolutely divine."

Auguste, exhausted but proud, bowed his head in gratitude.

"Thank you, Your Highness. It was a challenging endeavor, but I am pleased with the results."

Princess Raena turned to Binda, her expression serious but excited. "Binda, please make sure a carriage is prepared to transport these boxes safely. They must arrive in perfect condition."

"Of course, Your Highness," Binda replied, shaking her head but going to make the necessary arrangements nonetheless.

—— · 。˚ ☆: *.☽ .* :☆˚. ——

9

On the desert horizon, a small black speck could be seen, gradually growing larger with each passing minute. As the wind swept across the vast expanse of sand, the speck revealed itself to be a small procession composed of two ornate carriages, one carrying the precious cargo of ten boxes filled with exquisite sweets, and the other transporting two figures. A handful of guards rode alongside on camels, their keen eyes scanning the surroundings for potential threats. The small procession moved slowly through the harsh desert landscape, the unforgiving sun beating down on them as the wind whipped up sand that threatened to invade every crevice.

Princess Raena sat in the carriage, her face shaded by a delicate silk veil as she gazed out at the endless expanse of sand, her eyes betraying a mischievous gleam. Beside her sat Elras, the former Vashka demon slave miner she had saved just a month prior. He was still adjusting to his new life in her service, his demeanor cautious yet grateful. Elras squinted at the horizon, his rough voice apprehensive. "This place be unforgiving, Your Highness. Ain't no place for a royal like you."

Raena smirked, her confident tone in stark contrast to his. "Nonsense, Elras. Royalty or not, I can handle a little sand and sun." The Vashka demon shook his head, still trying to comprehend this strange girl that has given him a new life.

"Still, I reckon there must be somethin' mighty important to drag you out here, all the way from the palace."

"Oh, indeed," Raena replied.

"You'll see soon enough, Elras. For now, just trust that I know what I'm doing."

The guards on their camels flanked the two carriages, their eyes scanning the dunes for any sign of danger. The desert was a treacherous place, and they knew all too well the threats that could lie hidden beneath its surface. The journey through the desert continued, the procession trudging along under the relentless sun. As the sun began to dip lower in the sky, the landscape started to change. The endless expanse of sand gave way to a rocky terrain, marked by the telltale signs of mining activity. The guards grew more alert, their eyes scanning the environment for any potential danger. As the procession drew closer to their destination, the entrance to a sprawling mine came into view.

Upon arriving at the mine, the carriages pulled to a stop, and Raena and Elras stepped out, their eyes adjusting to the dimmer light. The princess looked around, taking in the vast network of tunnels and scaffolding.

"Here we are, Elras. The Zulnar Mines," Raena announced.

"These mines supply our kingdom with precious metals and minerals and of course lyrium."

Elras shifted uncomfortably, his memories of his time as a slave miner still raw and painful. He looked around, observing his surrounding still unsure. For a moment a horrible thought past thru his mind that the princess might have bored with him and decided to return him to his old life.

"Lyrium...." Elras muttered, his voice heavy with apprehension. "That stuff's dangerous, Your Highness. I've seen what it can do to people."

Raena glanced at him.

"I'm well aware of its dangers, Elras. But it's also a valuable resource, and we need it to survive."

Elras clenched his fists, trying to push away his fears.

"If you say so, Your Highness. But what do you want me to do here?"

Just as Raena was about to respond, a group of stern-looking guards approached them, their weapons drawn and their expressions wary. The mine's own security detail had spotted the unfamiliar party and were now demanding answers.

"Halt!" one of the guards bellowed, his voice echoing through the canyon as he stepped forward to block their path.

"This area falls under the jurisdiction of the royal family, and unauthorized entry is strictly prohibited. Declare your intentions here without delay!"

Raena's chief guard, a seasoned warrior named Darius, took a calculated step forward. He spoke in a voice that was both harsh and commanding, like the crack of a whip.

"Do you truly dare to question the presence of Her Royal Highness, Princess Raena Seraphina Isabella Evangeline, the Radiant Jewel of the Desert, and the Rightful Heir to the Throne!?"

The mine guards hesitated, the uncertainty in their eyes betraying their sudden unease. It was evident that they hadn't recognized the princess until this very moment. Darius continued, his tone dripping with disdain and authority.

"In the presence of your future sovereign, it is only fitting that you bow."

As if struck by a powerful, invisible force, the mine guards immediately dropped to their knees, their heads bowed low in submission. They offered their apologies, their voices trembling with fear.

"Forgive us, Your Highness," one stammered.

"We failed to recognize you."

Raena regarded them with a mixture of amusement and annoyance, her hands resting on her hips, her posture exuding confidence.

"That much is painfully clear. Now, rise and pay close attention. I have come to inspect the conditions of this mine and ensure that its workers are treated with the fairness they deserve. As the princess and your future ruler, I demand nothing less than your unwavering cooperation."

The mine guards scrambled to their feet, their faces flushed with embarrassment as they nodded fervently.

"As you wish, Your Highness. We are at your service."

Raena cast a sidelong glance at the guards and then, with a decisive nod, addressed them.

"Take us to the one in charge of this mine. We have matters to discuss."

The guards exchanged nervous glances, but one of them stepped forward, his voice cracking slightly as he spoke.

"Yes, Your Highness. Our overseer is stationed in the main office just inside the mine entrance. We'll take you there right away."

The group, guided by the now subservient mine guards, made their way deeper into the mine. The air grew colder and more damp as they ventured further into the depths, the sounds of mining tools echoing off the cavern walls. Elras, still feeling uneasy about their surroundings, couldn't help but cast furtive glances at the workers toiling away. The memories of his own time as a slave miner coming back to him. As they approached the main office, a stout, middle-aged man with a grizzled beard emerged from within. He looked startled at the sight of the princess and her entourage, quickly adjusting his dirty cap as a sign of respect.

"Your Highness," he stammered.

"I-I wasn't aware of your visit. My apologies for not being prepared to receive you."

Raena waved a dismissive hand, her expression a mixture of curiosity and determination.

"No matter. I am here to ensure that the workers in this mine are treated fairly. I trust you have been upholding our kingdom's standards in this regard?"

The overseer swallowed hard, beads of sweat forming on his brow.

"Y-yes, of course, Your Highness. But umm the kingdoms standards? These are creatures." replied the overseer unsure.

Raena raised an eyebrow.

"Creatures or not, they are still under the protection of our kingdom. And as your future queen, I expect them to be treated as such. Now, let's continue with the inspection, shall we?"

The overseer's face paled.

"Yes, Your Highness," he stammered, bowing his head in submission.

With a flourish, Raena led her entourage deeper into the mine, her eyes taking in every detail, her curiosity piqued. Elras followed closely, still tense but feeling a newfound respect for the princess. As they continued their inspection, the group observed the Vashka, all laboring away to extract the precious resources buried within the earth. Raena, never one to shy away from an opportunity to assert her authority, questioned the overseer at every turn, demanding explanations for the working conditions, the workers' rights, and their safety. The overseer, visibly flustered by the princess's relentless questioning, tried his best to appease her, but it was clear that his answers weren't entirely satisfactory. Raena's expression grew more serious with each passing moment, and her tone became sharper, revealing her growing displeasure.

"Overseer," Raena finally declared, her voice icy and commanding. "I find the conditions here to be unacceptable."

The overseer paled, his eyes wide with fear.

"Your Highness, I assure you, I have always done my best to ensure that the mine is run efficiently and safely. If there are any concerns, I will address them immediately."

Raena regarded him skeptically, her piercing blue gaze unwavering. "Very well, we will certainly worked on that, but for now I want to speak to one of the Vashka here", her eyes looking around.

The overseer's surprise was evident on his face, his mouth opening and closing a few times before he managed to respond.

"Y-yes, of course, Your Highness," he stammered, his nerves clearly getting the better of him.

"I'll fetch one right away."

Raena left out a small laugh and corrected him.

"You misunderstand, I wish to speak to a particular Vashka, my servant Elras and one of my guards will go with one of your men to find him."

The overseer hesitated for a moment, clearly taken aback by Raena's request.

"As you wish, Your Highness," he replied, still visibly nervous.

"I'll have one of my men accompany your servant and guard to find the Vashka you seek."

Raena nodded, satisfied with the overseer's compliance. She turned to Elras and one of her guards, a tall, muscular man named Avric.

"Elras, you know who I wish to find, Avric, you will accompany him to locate the specific Vashka I wish to speak with. I trust you will find him without issue."

Elras and Avric exchanged a quick glance before offering a respectful bow.

"As you command, Your Highness," they said in unison.

The overseer gestured to one of his subordinates, a young man with a somewhat timid demeanor.

"Take them to find the one they want" he instructed.

With a nod, the young man led Elras and Avric further into the mine, navigating the twisting tunnels with practiced ease.

In the serpentine heart of the mine, Elras and Avric led by the young man delved into a labyrinthine abyss, an eerie chiaroscuro painting of darkness and flickering light. The walls, whispering tales of toil and sorrow, were adorned with filigrees of lyrium that gleamed like the stars of a long-lost constellation. As Elras, Avric, and the young man ventured deeper into the mine, the conditions around them became increasingly harsh. The dimly lit tunnels were narrow and claustrophobic, the air heavy with a stifling mix of dust, sweat, and the acrid scent of lyrium. The flickering light from the scattered torches cast eerie shadows on the walls, giving the impression of an ever-present darkness lurking just beyond their vision.

The air was humid and suffocating, making each breath feel labored, and the temperature rose steadily as they descended further into the bowels of the mine. The heat radiating from the lyrium veins pulsated against their skin, a constant reminder of the dangerous and volatile nature of the substance they were extracting. As they searched various tunnels, they witnessed the brutal working conditions the Vashka were subjected to. The Vashka labored tirelessly, their bodies hunched and contorted to fit the cramped spaces as they swung their picks at the unyielding rock walls. Their chains rattled and clanked with every movement, a cruel reminder of their enslavement. The safety measures were evidently lacking. The tunnels were supported by crude wooden beams, which seemed to be barely holding up the tons of rock above them.

There were no signs of any ventilation systems, leaving the Vashka to breathe the polluted air, heavy with mineral dust and the noxious fumes emitted by the lyrium. It was clear that the Vashka's health and well-being were far from a priority in these mines. As they continued their search, the group passed by several exhausted Vashka slumped against the walls, their faces gaunt and hollow from malnutrition and overexertion. Their eyes held a mix of despair and resignation, as though they had long given up hope for a better life. Everywhere they looked, Elras and Avric saw evidence of the overseer's cruelty and negligence. The Vashka's living quarters were cramped and squalid, with thin, filthy straw mats serving as their only bedding. Food and water were scarce, and many of the Vashka appeared severely undernourished.

Despite the wretchedness that enveloped them, Elras persevered in his quest for his friend. He scrutinized each Vashka they encountered, their faces ghostly apparitions cloaked in a veil of grime and sorrow. Yet the similarities in their appearance, the ragged clothes, and the soot-streaked visages rendered the task of identifying him a Herculean endeavor.

"It's a veritable purgatory," Avric muttered, his voice tinged with despair.

"How can the overseer justify subjecting these poor souls to such inhumane conditions?"

Elras, could not hide his disquiet.

"It's a cruel irony," he said, the shadows dancing across his face as he spoke.

"The Vashka are forced to mine the very substance that fuels the power of their oppressors."

As they continued their search, they entered a chamber where a group of Vashka toiled beneath the oppressive gloom. Elras's gaze was drawn to a trio in particular, their visages obscured by soot and grime yet somehow familiar. He cautiously approached, his heart pounding in his chest like a wild tempest. In the dim light, his gaze landed to a figure whose presence seemed to defy the darkness. The man's hair, cascaded in untamed waves down to his shoulders, to a face that bore the scars of tribulation yet retained its striking allure. Streaks of soot, like calligraphic brushstrokes, accentuated the proud contours of his chiseled jaw and prominent cheekbones.

Though malnutrition and overexertion had etched themselves upon his body, the man's muscular frame remained, as imposing as a granite cliff. His sinewy limbs bespoke an indomitable spirit, an unyielding defiance against the crushing weight of adversity. His countenance shaped by the merciless conditions of the mine, yet his essence undimmed, like a distant star through the blackest night. Beside him stood two others, equally battle-worn and fatigued, yet just as stubbornly defiant. In the hollow silence, a single word punctured the gloom, the name uttered with a mix of disbelief and relief.

"Ash."

Ash's lips, cracked and parched, curved into a semblance of a smile.

"Elras," he murmured, his voice a mere wraith.

"I didn't think I'd ever see you again."

Elras's eyes flickered to Kael and Gavril.

"And you two," he whispered, the shadows of sorrow and guilt weaving a tapestry in his eyes.

"I'm so sorry."

"I never thought our paths would cross again."

Kael, his voice hoarse from the dust and grime, managed a weak chuckle.

"Fate has a twisted sense of humor, doesn't it?"

Gavril, his expression a mixture of surprise and apprehension, couldn't help but ask.

"Elras, what are you doing here? How did you find us?"

Elras quickly glanced at Avric and the young guide, who remained at a respectful distance and said in a hushed tone.

"We must be cautious. I cannot help you now, but know that I will do everything in my power to find a way."

His eyes landed on Ash.

"The princess is here, she sent me to find you."

"Princess?" Gavril spits out the word like it's poison.

"You're shittin' me."

"Water mage princess?" Ash couldn't keep the disbelief from his voice. In his head, he could see a memory of her. Young, too clean for a place like this, with eyes that held a bit of the desert storm in them. Raena, he remembered her name well.

"Yes," Elras confirms, looking even more nervous at the mention of her title.

"She... She took me to the palace."

"The palace?"

Kael's voice is soft but deadly. They've all heard the stories of the mages, of the decadence and debauchery, the cruel games played by bored mages. A demon in the palace isn't a servant. It's a plaything.

"Y-yeah," Elras stammers, a red flush creeping up his neck.

"But it's not... It ain't like that. She's different."

"Different," Ash asks.

He is unable to forget her. The first mage who ever looked at him like a sentient being, not a thing. But she was still a mage. Still one of them. She was still the enemy.

"Why are you here, Elras?" Gavril's questions. The old demon shrugs, his gaze dropping to the floor.

"She... She wants to see Ash."

"Me?" he blinks, surprised.

"Why would she want to see me?"

Elras gives a helpless shrug.

"I don't rightly know, Ash," he admits, meeting his gaze with an apologetic one.

"She's a strange one, that princess, ain't like the others. In a good way, I mean."

He turns to the silent figure at the mouth of the tunnel, the one they now realize is the princess's guard.

"Avric, we found who we were lookin' for. Let's get him to the princess."

The man nods, his impassive gaze flicking between Elras and Ash. "Very well, let's return."

As they retraced their steps through the winding tunnels, Elras couldn't help but feel a mixture of joy and trepidation. Joy for the reunion with his old friends, and trepidation for the uncertainty that lay ahead. He didn't fully understand Raena's intentions, but he knew one thing for certain: he would do whatever it took to free his friends from the oppressive chains of the mine.

10

─── · ₀˚ ☆: *.☽ .* :☆˚. ───

Raena stood by the table, her royal attire a stark contrast to the grim surroundings. Her eyes, bright and inquisitive, betrayed her keen intellect and curiosity. Ash, on the other hand, seemed to merge with the shadows, his fiery gaze locked on her, his pupils dilating as if trying to drink in every detail of her visage. As the weight of recognition settled upon him, an insidious thought crept into Ash's mind. The memory of their first encounter was not a figment of his imagination, nor a fleeting dream spawned by feverish exhaustion. It was undeniably, unnervingly real. A tempest of emotions surged through him: anger, confusion, and a sense of betrayal so profound it consumed him like wildfire. His pupils turned black as coal, swallowing the molten gold that once blazed within. His heart pounded like a war drum, each beat a call to arms against the perceived deception.

"You!" he roared.

"What treachery is this? Are you not content with the suffering your kind has inflicted upon us, that you now seek to ensnare me with this vile charade?"

Fury coursed through his veins, compelling him to lunge at the unsuspecting princess with the intention of breaking her delicate neck. He wrapped his hands around her throat, determined to crush the life out of her, putting an end to this abominable betrayal. Raena, though shocked, managed to channel her powers and summon a wave of water that pushed him aside.

"Witch!" he cried out with indignation.

"What have you done to me!?

Small clouds of vapor began to rise from him as the water droplets on his skin started to sizzle and evaporate. The room's temperature rapidly increased, though he remained oblivious to this, consumed by his rage. Raena couldn't help but take a step back in fear at this unexpected turn of events. Gathering her courage, she spoke with a commanding tone that belied her anxiety.

"What are you talking about? I haven't done anything to you!"

"Dear goddess, he is mad! she said out loud.

***

There she stood, like a mirage, resplendent in her regal attire, a ray of light trespassing into the very heart of darkness. Her eyes, pierced the veil of my soul, igniting a dormant ember buried within the depths of my being. My thoughts enshrouded in a fog of confusion and disbelief, I could not help but be drawn back to that fateful day in Oasia, where our paths had first crossed, as we were being lead to this blasted hellhole, she had appeared, a vision of unparalleled beauty that had, for a moment, brought the world to a standstill.

Even then, in the throes of that ephemeral encounter, I had felt the stirrings of something inexplicable, a tremor in the very fabric of my being that I had dismissed as a fleeting fancy. But now, as I stood before her, the memory of that moment burgeoned like an insistent tide, washing over me with the force of a tempest. Yet, as the swell of emotions threatened to engulf me, the specter of doubt, relentless in its pursuit, continued to gnaw at the edges of my conviction.

Was it possible that this burgeoning connection was nothing more than a cruel illusion, a diabolical ruse orchestrated by those who sought to manipulate and control me? I fought with the conflict within, a voice, at once tender and fierce, whispered from the depths of my soul. It was the voice of my ancestors, who had carried the legacy of our kin through the annals of time. They spoke of the ancient bond of kinship, a bond that transcended the ephemeral and reached into the very essence of creation, they told me she was mine. And yet, even as their wisdom offered solace, the knowledge of the mages' sinister machinations cast a pall over the serenity of their counsel.

How could I trust in the veracity of this connection when I knew that the masters of deception had the means to conjure phantoms that mimicked the very essence of our soul?

In the midst of this maelstrom of doubt and desire, Raena's gaze remained steadfast, a beacon of light that pierced the encroaching darkness. As I looked into the depths of her cerulean eyes, I found myself teetering on the brink of surrender, torn between the call of destiny and the whispers of trepidation.

And then I gave into my rage....

The dam of restraint, battered by the torrents of fury and indignation that coursed through my veins, finally gave way. The tempest of emotions, long simmering beneath the surface, erupted with the force of a volcanic cataclysm, shattering the fragile veneer of civility that had cloaked our encounter thus far.

"You!" I roared, my voice a maelstrom of accusation and pain.

"What treachery is this? Are you not content with the suffering your kind has inflicted upon us, that you now seek to ensnare me with this vile charade?"

My heart, a cauldron of molten rage, hammered against my ribcage with each breath, the seething heat of my anger threatening to consume me from within. I yearned for retribution, an inferno of vengeance to scour away the injustice that had been heaped upon my people. All thoughts of reason and restraint vanished like smoke before the wind as I resolved to crush the life from her, to put an end to this. As my fingers closed around her delicate neck, I felt the warmth of her flesh beneath my grasp and the rapid pulsing of her heartbeat. In that instant, I was both executioner and savior, poised to snuff out the flame of her life and free myself from the torment of my conflicted heart.

But fate, it seemed, had other plans.

A torrent surged forth with the primal might of a raging sea, casting me aside like driftwood upon the shore.

As I lay there, my rage undiminished, I felt the heat within me intensify, an inferno threatening to escape.

"Witch!" I cried out with indignation.

"What have you done to me!?"

Raena, her eyes wide with fear, took a step back, recoiling from the tempest, I could sense my rage quelling giving way to a primal need to comfort her.

"What are you talking about? I haven't done anything to you!"

"Dear goddess, he is mad!" she whispered.

I growled, my instincts screamed at me to trust in the voice of my ancestors, to surrender to the call of destiny, but the seeds of doubt snuffed those voices.

"Have you used anything on yourself or brought something with you that would make me in any way attracted to you?"

I managed to growl clenching my fists in suppressed rage.

Raena stared at me, her eyes wide with shock and confusion, clearly taken aback by my question.

"I don't need magic to be attractive," she scoffed, her tone dripping with condescension.

"But if it makes you feel better, I can assure you I've done nothing to manipulate your feelings. It's not my fault you can't handle your emotions."

"Though if that's how you express your affection, goddess help any woman you set your eyes on."

Her words stung, but I couldn't deny the spark of truth that lay within them. I took a deep breath, my eyes never leaving Raena's as I grappled with the implications of their meaning. If that were true I knew without a doubt that she was my soulmate, the other half of my soul, my vesha as we demons call it. The realization sent a shiver down my spine, a mix of awe and terror. How could it be possible? A demon and a princess of Varidia, bound together by fate? It seemed too preposterous, too dangerous to even entertain the thought.

But as I searched her eyes, looking for any hint of recognition, any sign that she might share this unbreakable bond, I saw nothing but bewilderment and fear. It was clear that she had no idea of the connection between us, and I knew that I had to tread carefully if I wanted to protect both of us from the potentially disastrous consequences of our bond. Taking a deep breath, I forced my anger and confusion aside, and spoke as calmly and clearly as I could manage.

"Your Highness, I apologize for my outburst. I do not understand what came over me, but I can assure you, I meant you no harm. My people have suffered greatly at the hands of the mages, and I fear that my frustration and despair may have clouded my judgment."

Raena eyed me warily, her stance still defensive, but a hint of understanding softened her gaze.

"Very well," the edge in her voice receding ever so slightly.

"We all have our demons to battle, figuratively speaking," she said with a small smile tugging at her lips.

"But don't think that just because you've apologized, I'll be letting my guard down around you."

"Nor should you," I agreed, a bitter smile twisting my lips.

"We are both pawns in the game of fate, it seems."

Her eyes narrowed, and I could sense the wheels turning in her mind.

"Hmmm, what do you mean by that?"

I hesitated, my mind a whirlwind of conflicting emotions. Part of me yearned to reveal the truth, to lay bare the bond that connected us, while another part shuddered at the thought of the danger such a revelation might bring.

In the end, caution won out and I decided to change the subject, "Why are you here?"

She paused for a moment, seemingly contemplating whether to reveal her intentions. Then, with a flourish, she grabbed an ornate box from the table and showed it to me. It was exquisitely crafted, adorned with the royal crest.

"I brought these for you," she said, her voice softening ever so slightly, "and for the Vashka slaves working in the mines. A small token of goodwill, if you will."

I eyed the box with suspicion, my gut instinct warning me against accepting anything from mages.

"What is it?" I asked, my voice tinged with wariness.

"Sweet delicacies," Raena replied, a mischievous glint in her eyes. "Skillfully made by the royal chef himself. Umm....Elras mentioned it would be a special treat for anyone here."

I couldn't help but raise an eyebrow at her unexpected gesture feeling a flicker of gratitude. It was a small gesture, to be sure, but it was more than any of the mages had ever offered my people.

"Thank you," I said, my voice barely above a whisper.

"Your kindness is unexpected, but not unwelcome."

"Try one", she baited me, putting the opened box back on the table and taking a few steps back so I could approach while maintaining a distance between us.

'Really now, she's going to treat me like a mad hound?', I ponder internally, though who could blame her, it was a miracle she hadn't yet called her guards to have me killed.

"You don't have to be weary of me", I tell her.

"What happened before won't happen again, I would never hurt you."

"Says the one who a few minutes ago was chocking me."

I winced, her words cutting deep.

"You're right," I admitted, my gaze fixed on the floor.

"I can understand why you'd be hesitant to trust me after that. But I swear to you, it was not my intention to harm you. My anger and frustration got the better of me, and for that, I am truly sorry."

Raena studied me for a moment, her eyes searching for any hint of deception. Finally, she sighed and offered a small nod.

"Very well, I'll accept your apology. But actions speak louder than words. If you truly mean to make amends, then show me through your actions, not just your words."

Her challenge stirred something within me, a determination to prove my sincerity.

"I will," I promised, my voice firm and resolute.

Raena's lips curled into a half-smile, a glimmer of approval in her eyes.

"Good," she said, her tone softening and gesturing towards the box of delicacies.

"Now, go on. Try one. You might find them to your liking."

Despite my lingering suspicions, I approached the table, my curiosity piqued. I picked up one of the sweet treats, studying its intricate design and marveling at the craftsmanship. Tentatively I took a bite, the rich, sweet flavors exploded on my tongue, and I couldn't help but close my eyes and savor the taste.

"It's... delicious," I conceded, opening my eyes to find Raena watching me with an amused grin.

"See?" she teased.

"I told you so."

I couldn't help but chuckle at her playful tone, she really is strange like Elras said. The tension between us seemed to ebb away, replaced by a cautious curiosity. Emboldened, I asked.

"May I approach you, Your Highness?"

My voice was soft, yet unwavering, and I could see the surprise flicker in her eyes. Raena hesitated for a moment before giving a cautious nod, her eyes never leaving mine as I slowly closed the distance between us. As I stood before her, I couldn't help but be captivated by her beauty, my hand reached out tentatively, my fingers gently brushing the delicate silk veil that obscured part of her face.

"May I?" I whispered, my heart pounding in my chest.

Raena hesitated for a moment, but then gave a slight nod.

With trembling fingers, I lifted the veil, revealing her face in its entirety. Her face was even more enchanting than I remembered, her features a delicate balance of strength and grace. Raena's eyes widened at my proximity, but she didn't pull away. Instead, she held her ground, her expression a mixture of defiance and vulnerability that I found both intriguing and endearing.

"What are you doing?" she asked, her voice barely above a whisper, her eyes searching mine for an answer.

"I wanted to see you," I replied honestly, my voice equally hushed. "On the day we first met, with the rush of events I couldn't, now in this quiet room I can commit your face to memory."

Raena glanced back at me, her eyes reflecting a mixture of emotions – uncertainty, curiosity, and perhaps even a hint of admiration.

"You are an enigma, Ash," she said softly.

"I do not know what to make of you."

I smiled wryly.

"I could say the same of you, Your Highness."

As I lowered the veil back into place our conversation was interrupted by the sound of approaching footsteps, and I quickly stepped back, giving Raena her space.

——· ₒ˚ ☆: *.) .* :☆˚ . ——

There was a firm knock at the door, followed by a gruff voice.

"Your Highness, are you alright? We heard a commotion."

Raena composed herself swiftly, her regal demeanor returning in full force.

"I'm fine," she called out, her voice steady and confident.

"There's no need for concern."

"Your Highness, with all due respect, we must check on you. It is our duty," Darius insisted, his voice laced with concern.

Raena exchanged a glance with Ash before addressing the door once more.

"Very well, enter."

The door opened, revealing the mine overseer and Raena's guards, all with expressions of concern and curiosity. Their eyes immediately fell on the demon, distrust evident in their gaze. "As you can see all is well, I am done with my discussion with this Vashka. Chief overseer I now have a task for you."

The mine overseer straightened his posture, giving Raena his full attention.

"Of course, Your Highness. What do you require?"

Raena gestured towards the royal boxes of sweets that her guards had brought from the palace.

"I want you to distribute these sweet delights to every slave in the mine," she instructed, her tone firm.

The overseer's eyes widened in surprise, and he hesitated for a moment before responding.

"Your Highness, are you certain? These are precious royal treats. Surely there must be a better use for them."

Raena cut him off with a dismissive wave of her hand.

"I am well aware, but I have made my decision. I believe that everyone deserves a small moment of happiness, no matter their circumstance. Now, please see that my orders are carried out."

The mine overseer bowed his head, clearly taken aback by Raena's unexpected generosity but unable to object.

"As you wish, Your Highness."

The overseer left to carry out her orders, quietly asking one of his underlying in a puzzled tone.

"Did that slave seem cleaner to you?"

Ash murmured a barely audible "Thank you" in her direction.

Raena winked at him as a form of acknowledgement, leaving him both amused and more surprised with her personality.

***

Feeling both physically and mentally drained from the day's events, Raena returned to the palace. She made her way to the royal bathhouse, eager to soak away her worries and relax.

The bathhouse was an oasis of serenity, with intricately carved marble pillars and soothing, tinkling fountains. The walls were adorned with mosaics depicting scenes of nature, and the air was filled with the soft scent of jasmine and rose petals. As Raena slipped into the warm, fragrant water, she let out a contented sigh, feeling the tension begin to melt away. Binda, her trusted handmaiden, approached her, a silver comb in hand.

"My lady, may I?" Binda asked, her eyes glancing at Raena's wet hair. Raena nodded and leaned back against the edge of the bath, closing her eyes as Binda began to gently comb through her hair.

"So, who got Auguste's precious sweets?" Binda inquired, her voice full of curiosity.

Raena couldn't help but chuckle at the mention of Auguste, the palace's renowned pastry chef who
was known for his legendary possessiveness over his confections.

"Well, you wouldn't believe it, but I gave them to the slaves at The Zulnar Mines," she replied, her voice light and amused.

Binda's eyes widened in surprise, and she nearly dropped the comb into the bath.

"You did what?!" she exclaimed, unable to hide her disbelief.

"Oh, Auguste is going to have a fit when he finds out!"

Raena grinned, imagining the pastry chef's reaction.

"I know. But he won't, in fact please give him my praise and arrange for a gift for him, something he'd enjoy. Tell him the mission was a success and all thanks to him."

"Very well, Your Highness. I'll make sure to pass on your praise and see to it that he receives a suitable gift. Perhaps some rare spices or exotic ingredients for his kitchen?"

Raena nodded, her eyes twinkling.

"That sounds perfect. Auguste might be protective of his sweets, but I'm sure he'll be pleased to have some new ingredients to experiment with."

Binda paused in her combing for a moment, her expression turning more serious.

"Raena, if I may be so bold, what possessed you to give the royal sweets to the slaves? And what happened at the mines? I've known you since you were a child, and you've never shown much interest in the slaves before."

Raena's expression sobered, and she opened her eyes to look directly at Binda.

"You're right, Binda. I haven't really cared much for them before. But something happened that changed my perspective. "

Binda regarded Raena thoughtfully, her eyes filled with curiosity and concern.

"What happened, Raena? You seem... different. You can tell me, you know I'm always here to listen and offer advice."

Raena hesitated for a moment, reluctant to reveal too much about Ash.

"I... I met someone," she finally said.

"Someone who made me see things differently."

Binda regarded Raena thoughtfully, her eyes filled with a mixture of surprise and concern.

"This person... are they trustworthy? You know how dangerous it can be to get involved with the wrong people, especially when it comes to matters of the kingdom."

Raena looked away, her cheeks flushing slightly at the mention of trust.

"I believe so," she replied.

"He's... different, Binda. There's a fire in him that I've never seen before. He made me realize that they're not just slaves, but people who deserve a chance at a better life."

Binda raised an eyebrow.

"So it's a he that's gotten to have such an impact on you?"

Raena's cheeks flushed an even deeper shade of red.

"Yes, it's a he," she admitted, feeling both embarrassed and defensive. "But that's not the point. He's passionate about his people and their well-being, and it's... contagious."

Binda sighed and put the comb down, looking at Raena with a mix of affection and worry.

"Raena, you know I care about you and have your best interests at heart. It's wonderful that you've found a cause to be passionate about, but I must advise caution. You're the princess, and there are many who would try to take advantage of your position."

"Wait did you say his people?"

Raena hesitated, realizing she had inadvertently revealed more than she intended.

"Well, yes," she said, trying to play it off casually.

"He's one of the slaves from the mines."

Binda's eyes widened in shock, and she quickly grabbed Raena's arm, her voice filled with urgency.

"Raena, do you realize what you're saying? You're the princess! Getting involved with a slave, especially one from the mines, is incredibly dangerous, not to mention forbidden. You must end this immediately."

Raena pulled her arm back gently, a hint of frustration creeping into her voice.

"I know, Binda. I know it's dangerous and foolish, but there's just something, it's a pull, I don't know what it is."

Binda sighed and put her hand on Raena's shoulder and sighted.

"My lady you're the princess, if it's just lust…tho as much as I'm against it and I don't understand, a meeting can be arranged."

Raena looked at Binda, surprised at her sudden change of heart. "What? Binda, I thought you were against this. Now you're suggesting a meeting?"

Binda sighed again, shaking her head.

"I don't approve of it, but if it's just carnal lust, I've heard of other nobles indulging in such pleasures with the slaves."

Raena looked at Binda, stunned.

"Other nobles? You mean this is common practice?" she asked, incredulous.

Binda nodded gravely.

"Unfortunately, it is, my lady. Many of the nobles view the slaves as nothing more than objects to be used for their pleasure. It's a cruel and despicable practice, but it's one that is all too common."

Raena's expression turned to one of disgust.

"I had no idea," she said.

"I had heard rumors, of course, but I never thought it could be true. It's sickening."

Binda nodded in agreement.

"I know, my lady. It's a shameful practice, but unfortunately, it's not uncommon among some of the nobles. If this is truly just a physical attraction, I would rather you explore it safely and discreetly, rather than risking your reputation and your life."

"I understand what you're saying, Binda," she said finally," but it's not just physical. There's something... deeper there. I can't explain it, but it's like I've found a part of myself that I never knew existed. And I could never do something like that," she said after a while, her voice filled with disgust.

"I may be spoiled and arrogant, but I'm not heartless. I don't want to use him for my own pleasure and then discard him like he's nothing. I want to help him and his people, to give them a chance at a better life."

Binda looked at Raena, her concern softening into understanding.

"I apologize, my lady. I didn't mean to insinuate that you would behave like those other nobles. I was just trying to find a solution that would keep you safe."

Raena gave a small smile, appreciating Binda's intentions.

"I know, Binda, and I appreciate your concern. But I am not some simpering fool who can't handle the consequences of her own actions. I am the princess of this kingdom, after all."

Binda sighed, seeing the determination in Raena's eyes. She knew that once the princess had set her mind on something, it was nearly impossible to sway her.

"That you are, my lady. But please, be careful, I don't want to see you hurt."

Raena grinned.

"Don't worry, Binda. I know what I'm doing, and I have you to keep me in check."

As they continued their conversation, Binda carefully selected a delicate crystal bottle filled with the most exquisite and expensive aromatic oils from a nearby shelf. The scent was an intoxicating blend of jasmine, sandalwood, and exotic spices. Uncorking the bottle, she poured a generous amount of the golden liquid into her palms, rubbing them together to warm the oil. The heady fragrance filled the air as Binda approached Raena.

With great care and attention, Binda began to work the oils into Raena's hair. She separated the thick strands with her fingers, starting from the roots and gently massaging the oil into the scalp in slow, circular motions. Raena closed her eyes, enjoying the soothing sensation and the luxurious scent that enveloped her. Binda continued to apply the oil, working her way down to the ends of

Raena's hair, ensuring that every strand was coated in the nourishing elixir.

Once her hair was thoroughly saturated with the oil, Binda moved on to Raena's shoulders. She placed her hands on the princess's tense muscles and began to knead them gently, applying pressure and working out any knots she encountered. The combination of the fragrant oil and Binda's skilled touch brought Raena a sense of deep relaxation. Binda, now excited to learn more about the intriguing slave who had captivated her mistress, couldn't contain her curiosity.

"So, my lady, you've got to tell me more about this intriguing fellow. What does he look like? What's he like? And what's his name?" she asked, her tone playful and conspiratorial.

Raena rolled her eyes playfully, a grin spreading across her face.

"You sound like a giddy schoolgirl, Binda. But fine, I'll indulge you. His name is Ash. As for his appearance…." Raena paused, considering how to best describe him.

"Imagine strands of midnight, each as dark as the abyss, yet woven through with the fiery essence of a burning ember. That is the hue of his hair, a shade so unique it seems to defy nature itself, so dark that you might mistake it for black. But when the light hits it just right, it reveals its true red hues, like the embers of a dying fire. It's quite striking, really. It's as if the fire that burns within him has left its mark on his hair."

Binda's eyes widened, her interest piqued.

"Oh, that sounds positively entrancing. Do go on."

Raena continued, her voice animated as she recounted Ash's features. "His eyes are like the heart of an inferno, a smoldering blend of amber and gold that dances with an inner flame. They possess an intensity that is both alluring and unnerving, as if they hold secrets one is both drawn to and fears."

Binda leaned in closer.

"And what of his physique? Surely he must be a sight to behold."

Raena smirked, clearly enjoying Binda's fascination.

"Well, if you must know, his body is not bad on the eyes either despite the harsh conditions of the mines. He is tall with strong, well-defined muscles that show he spent most of his lifetime doing physical labor. And yet, there's a grace to his movements, like a dancer or a predator on the hunt. Also he is a demon after all so he has these curved horns that sweep back from his forehead, giving him an air of regality and power, they are solid and sharp, reminiscent of the finest obsidian blades."

Binda gasped dramatically, pressing a hand to her heart.

"Oh, my! Our little princess has quite the eye for strapping young men, it seems."

Raena laughed, swatting at Binda playfully.

"Enough of that! But yes, he's certainly easy on the eyes. Tho as I mentioned before, it's not his physical appearance, his presence made an impression, he has a deep, unwavering commitment to his people and their well-being, and it's impossible not to be drawn to that."

Binda chuckled, enjoying the conspiratorial atmosphere between them.

"Oh, my lady, it sounds like you've fallen quite hard for him."

Raena scoffed, but her smile remained.

"Please, Binda, I haven't 'fallen' for anyone. I just find him... intriguing. And as for what happened at the mines, well, it was an eye-opening experience. The conditions there are deplorable, and I can't believe we've let it go on for so long."

Binda nodded sympathetically as she continued massaging Raena's shoulders.

"It's a harsh reality, my lady that's true enough."

Raena rolled her eyes but couldn't help smiling.

"Yes, well, now that I've seen it with my own eyes, I'm determined to do something about it. While at the mines I've also used my magic to provide the slaves with fresh drinking water and warned the overseer not to sell it or misuse it."

Binda grinned.

"Well, who would've thought that our princess, who until recently barely spared a glance at the slaves, would become their champion?" Raena smirked, accepting the tease.

"I know, it's a shocking!"

Binda chuckled, giving Raena's shoulder a gentle squeeze.

"I've always known you have a good heart. And now, it seems, you've found a cause worthy of your passion."

Raena giggled.

"Oh, you should have seen the overseers face, Binda! It was priceless. The man looked like he'd swallowed a lemon, all puckered and sour. He could hardly believe that the princess herself was giving him orders and interfering in his 'domain. I could tell he was torn between trying to appease me and maintain his authority over the slaves."

Binda laughed.

"I wish I could have been there to see it! I bet he didn't know whether to bow or scowl. The poor man probably never expected a royal visit, controls on the mines have been lax for years."

Raena smirked, her eyes sparkling with mischief.

"You're not wrong. It was rather enjoyable to see him squirm. I can only imagine the stories he'll tell of the day the spoiled princess came to his mine. But in all seriousness, I made it clear that I won't tolerate the mistreatment of the slaves any longer. Changes need to be made, and I'm going to ensure they happen."

"But now, enough of that," Raena said, stifling a yawn as she stretched languidly.

"It's getting late, and even spoiled princesses need their beauty sleep."

Binda chuckled, nodding in agreement.

"Yes, my lady, it has been a long day. I'll tell the maids to come and help you dry off while I prepare your bed for you."

"Thank you, Binda," Raena replied, her voice softening as she prepared to leave the warmth of the bath.

Binda nodded and stepped out of the bathhouse, fetching the maids to assist Raena. The maids entered with warm, fluffy towels and helped the princess out of the bath, gently patting her skin dry.

Raena stretched her limbs luxuriously, enjoying the sensation of the soft fabric against her skin. As Raena stood wrapped in the towel, one of the maids fetched a nightgown of fine silk, the color of moonlight, adorned with delicate lace. Raena slipped into the gown, the smooth fabric gliding over her body like a whisper. The maids then attended to her hair, carefully combing and drying the long, lustrous locks before braiding them into a loose plait that cascaded over her shoulder. With a grateful nod, Raena dismissed the maids, her gaze turning to the open door that led to her bedroom. The flickering light of candles illuminated the opulent chamber. Large windows were draped with sheer, flowing fabrics that danced gently in the warm evening breeze, offering a breathtaking view of the moonlit landscape outside.

Binda stood by the bed, having just finished arranging the linens with her usual meticulous attention to detail. Raena couldn't help but smile at her friend's dedication to her duties.

"All set, my lady. Sleep well, and may your dreams be filled with handsome, rebellious demons" Binda teased, stepping back to allow Raena to admire the freshly made bed.

Raena smirked at Binda's teasing tone.

"Oh, do stop with the dramatics, Binda. But thank you, it looks delightful as always."

Raena suppressing another yawn as she approached the bed. She slid between the soft, inviting sheets, feeling their luxurious embrace as she settled into the plush mattress. Binda moved to the side of the bed, snuffing out the candles one by one until only the silvery moonlight filtered into the room. As the door clicked softly shut behind Binda, Raena allowed herself to fully relax, the comforting darkness of the room enveloping her.

——— · ₒ˚ ☆: *.) .* :☆˚ . ———

The air hung heavy with the oppressive scent of sweat and grime, the sighs and murmurs of the exhausted slaves resonating throughout the cavernous enclosure as they sought comfort in the temporary solace of slumber. Lying there, my body battered and bruised by the unrelenting demands of the day, I found my thoughts drifting back to the events of today, the memory of Raena's presence still lingering in the air like a haunting melody.

For the first time in as long as I could remember, we had been granted a small, fleeting taste of what life could be like beyond the stifling confines of the mines. The sweets she had given us were like manna from the heavens, their delicate sweetness a balm for our ravaged spirits. And the water, cool and clear as the tears of the gods themselves, had felt like a benediction, a promise of hope and salvation that quenched our thirst and stirred our hearts.

But even as I reveled in these simple pleasures, the specter of doubt and mistrust continued to gnaw at my soul, a serpent coiled within the depths of my being, its venomous fangs poised to strike at the fragile threads that bound us together. As I struggled to reconcile the conflicting emotions that warred within me, I felt the comforting presence of Kael and Gavril, my comrades in suffering, and the closest semblance of family I had ever known. We huddled together in the darkness, our whispered voices barely audible above the cacophony of dreams and nightmares that swirled around us.

"I still can't fathom it," Kael murmured, his voice tinged with awe and disbelief.

"A princess, in this hellhole."

Gavril snorted softly, his tone laced with cynicism.

"And what does it matter? One visit won't change anything. We're still slaves, condemned to a life of misery and suffering."

Torn between these opposing perspectives, the optimist and the cynic, I grappled with the discord that plagued my tormented soul. I sought refuge in the darkness, drawing a deep, steadying breath, and spoke with quiet conviction.

"You're both right," I conceded quietly.

"Raena's visit may not change our circumstances, but it has gifted us something we have long been deprived of: hope. And hope, my brothers, can be a powerful weapon. For the first time our people have been given a glimpse of something more, of something beyond suffering and toil. However small it might be. "

Gavril's eyes glinted in the dim light, the embers of hope and defiance flickering within their depths.

"Perhaps there is some truth to your words, Ash. We must not squander this gift, but use it to inspire our people and ignite the flames of rebellion."

"This visit doesn't change our plan," I said firmly, my voice a low growl, heavy with determination.

"We still need to escape the mines. We must find a way to rid ourselves of these chains and make our move under the cover of night."

Kael nodded, his eyes shining with determination.

"I've been observing the guards, and I think I've found a weakness in their patrols. There's a small window of time when they change shifts, leaving a gap in their surveillance. It might be our best chance."

Gavril nodded in agreement, his gaze drifting toward the cruel iron shackles that encircled our wrists, the symbols of our enslavement.

"That's a start, but we still need to find a way to remove these cursed chains."

I couldn't help but agree with Gavril, but a plan had already begun to form in my mind.

"I've been thinking about that," I admitted, my voice low and steady.

"The yearly rain summoning is approaching, and the guards will be busy and distracted gathering the precious rainwater. That might be our best opportunity to make our move."

Kael's eyes widened, realizing the potential of my suggestion.

"You're right, Ash. During that time, we could use the opportunity to slip away."

Gavril nodded, the fire of determination burning in his eyes.

"Very well, we'll use the rain summoning as our window. But we still need to find a way to remove these chains."

I glanced down at the heavy iron bands that encircled our wrists, the very symbols of our oppression and closed my eyes, focusing inward, searching for a solution within the depths of my own thoughts. I knew I had to be careful, for the enemy's eyes were everywhere. As my thoughts wandered, the memory of Raena's visit returned, her face etched in my mind with striking clarity. Her beauty, her defiance, her compassion – it all left an indelible mark on my soul. But more than that, her actions that day sparked a renewed sense of purpose within me. If a princess could risk her own safety for the sake of the enslaved, then perhaps it was time to take matters into our own hands and fight for our freedom.

"We need something to break or pick the locks," I mused aloud.

A slow grin spread across my face as the gears in my mind continued to turn.

"I have an idea," I said, my voice barely more than a whisper.

"It's a long shot, but if we can pull it off, it might just work."

Kael leaned in closer, his interest piqued.

"What is it, Ash?"

"I've noticed that the mineral deposits in the mines have unique properties. Some of the ores are highly conductive, while others seem to have a more...explosive nature," I explained, the memory of a small, accidental explosion from a few weeks prior still fresh in my mind.

Gavril raised an eyebrow, clearly intrigued.

"Go on."

"What if we could harness the power of these minerals to create a makeshift explosive or acid capable of breaking the chains?" I suggested, fully aware of the risks involved.

"We would need to be extremely careful and precise, but if we can control the reaction, it might be enough to free us from these shackles."

Kael's eyes lit up with excitement.

"That's brilliant, Ash! With my knowledge of alchemy, I can help determine which minerals would be the most effective and how to combine them safely."

Gavril nodded thoughtfully, weighing the risks and rewards of our plan.

"It's dangerous, but it's our best shot. We should start gathering the necessary materials and experimenting to see if this will work. Luckily there's still 2 weeks left before the rain summoning so we still have plenty of time to prepare. "

A spark of hope ignited in my friends' eyes as they contemplated the prospect of liberation. It was time to turn hope into action and rise up against the shackles that bound us, both literally and metaphorically.

"We must be prepared for anything," I said, my voice resolute.

"We must trust in each other, and we will make it through the darkness. When the time comes, we will emerge from these mines, not as broken slaves, but as free men, ready to reclaim our rightful place in this world and we will not stop until we will free all our brethren."

As we discussed the details of our plan, I couldn't help but feel the weight of responsibility on my shoulders. I knew that I had to share with them the truth about Raena's visit and what it meant for me. Taking a deep breath, I looked at my brothers in arms, my voice steady and resolute.

"There's something else you should know about my meeting with the princess."

Kael and Gavril exchanged puzzled glances before turning their attention back to me, curiosity etched on their faces.

"What is it, Ash?" Kael inquired, his tone gentle.

I hesitated, my emotions tangled in a complex web of conflict, unsure of how to put my turmoil into words.

"When I met Raena, something inexplicable occurred. It was as if our souls resonated, intertwining with an ethereal familiarity, and in that fleeting moment, I knew... She is my mine, she's the other part of my soul I've been missing, she's my vesha" I admitted, the words tasting bittersweet as they escaped my lips.

Gavril's eyes widened in surprise, while Kael's expression darkened, a storm brewing behind his gaze.

"That's... unexpected," Gavril murmured, struggling to process the revelation.

Kael's voice trembled with fury, the shadows of his past experiences looming like specters.

"No, Ash, it cannot be. She is deceiving you, manipulating your emotions to serve her own ends. I've experienced this treachery firsthand, and you must not fall prey to her enchantments."

I could see the flicker of rage within Kael's eyes as they seemed to recede into the depths of his tormented memories. The air around us grew heavy, charged with his dark emotions as he began to recount his harrowing ordeal in vivid and chilling detail.

"Before my imprisonment in these wretched mines, I was a plaything for the mages – a pleasure slave, as you both know" Kael snarled, his voice strained with the effort to contain his fury.

"I was passed around like a piece of meat from one hand to the next, used and discarded. They used their magic to enhance my senses, making every touch, every kiss, every act of pleasure ten times more intense than anything I had ever felt before. At first, I thought it was heaven, the ultimate dream come true. But it was a trap, a hellish cycle of pleasure and pain that never ended."

"But that's only the surface of the nightmare that consumed me."

He took a deep breath and continued, his voice low and haunted.

"Within the opulent halls of the brothels, I encountered a female mage whose wickedness knew no bounds, and she took particular interest in me. She was a master of deception, weaving a web of lies and illusions to ensnare me in her twisted game. And she broke me, in ways I cannot even begin to describe."

Kael's voice dropped to a near-whisper, the words emerging like venomous serpents from his lips.

"This sadistic sorceress concocted an elixir that altered her very essence, making me believe she was my soulmate. I was ensnared, my heart torn open and vulnerable as I willingly surrendered to the illusion of a bond that never truly existed."

Kael's voice trembled, as if the memories themselves were a physical weight on his chest.

"As a pleasure slave, my body was not my own. It belonged to her, to be used and abused as she saw fit," he continued, his tone laced with bitterness.

"I was shackled, bound by chains and magic, leaving me powerless to resist her twisted desires, not that I wanted to, with the impression she was my mate I was willing to do anything to make her happy, her smallest smile brought me infinite joy."

He paused, taking a deep, shuddering breath before delving deeper into the darkness of his past.

"She delighted in exploiting my vulnerability, her eyes alight with sadistic glee as she inflicted pain and humiliation upon me."

Kael's hands clenched into fists, knuckles white as he struggled to maintain his composure.

"Her perversions knew no bounds. She used her magic to manipulate my senses, distorting my perceptions of reality, and blurring the lines between pleasure and pain. She toyed with me, pushing me to the brink of madness, only to pull me back again, laughing as I clung to the tattered shreds of my sanity."

"She reveled in my agony, her laughter echoing through the chambers as she subjected me to unspeakable torment. With each act of cruelty, she took perverse pleasure in shattering the remnants of my spirit.

Every violation, every debasement, etched deep into my soul, leaving scars that will never fade. She wielded her magic as a weapon, searing my flesh and chilling my bones, twisting and contorting my body in unnatural ways. Each night, I was broken anew, a living testament to her boundless cruelty."

His voice cracked, the raw anguish of his ordeal seeping into his words.

"Even when the physical torment ceased, she continued to taunt me, her presence an ever-present specter that haunted my dreams and tormented my waking hours. Her insatiable appetite for suffering pushed me to the brink of madness, my mind fraying at the edges, torn between the desire for relief and the need for vengeance. And then, when she had grown bored of her sadistic games, she cast me aside like a broken toy, condemning me to a fate worse than death."

The air around us hung heavy with the weight of his pain, the gravity of his experiences leaving an indelible mark on our hearts. Kael's voice, thick with emotion, trembled as he shared the final chapter of his torment.

"In a moment of desperation, fueled by the last remnants of my sanity, I found the strength to strike back. In a frenzy of retribution, I managed to seize a shard of glass and plunged it into her throat, relishing in the sight of her lifeblood spilling from the wound."

His eyes met mine, the depths of his sorrow mirrored in their darkened hue.

"That was the day I sealed my fate. The day I was condemned to these hellish mines. I killed her, Ash. I killed the monster who had tormented me for so long, but in doing so, I became a prisoner of a different kind."

As Kael recounted his harrowing experiences, I found myself grappling with a tempest of emotions. Rage and sorrow swirled within me, threatening to consume me. My heart ached for my friend, and I felt a fierce resolve take root within me, a flame that burned with the intensity of a thousand suns. I vowed that we would break free from our chains, that we would reclaim our freedom and our dignity, and that we would never again allow ourselves to be subjected to such depravity. We would not let the mages break us. I would not allow their cruelty to define me or my people. We would rise, phoenix-like, from the ashes of our suffering, and we would reclaim our freedom, no matter the cost. Kael's voice trembled with a mixture of fury and sorrow, as if each word were ripped from the depths of his tormented soul.

"That accursed elixir... whatever vile concoction it was... has forever scarred my very essence. Even now, after all the horrors I've endured, I find myself mourning her, a sentiment that repulses me to the very core of my being. I despise the lingering, insidious influence she holds over me, even beyond the grave."

He scoffed bitterly, his voice laced with a deep-seated self-loathing. "Such a twisted paradox, isn't it? To grieve for the one who brought me to the brink of destruction, to long for the embrace of the monster that reveled in my torment."

His gaze locked onto mine, and I could feel the searing heat of his resolve.

"I will not allow that fate to befall you, Ash. I cannot stand idly by as another mage weaves a web of treachery around you. If Raena dares to manipulate your heart, I will not think twice before driving a blade through hers. The very thought of witnessing you endure the suffering that I have faced... it is a burden too heavy to bear."

The air between us grew thick with the weight of his words, a somber oath born from the depths of his anguish. As I peered into his eyes, I saw the flames of his determination, a fierce inferno that refused to be quenched. The atmosphere between us grew thick with the weight of his words, a solemn oath forged in the crucible of his anguish. As I peered into his eyes, I saw the flames of his determination, a fierce inferno that refused to be extinguished.

"Kael," I began, my voice laden with emotion, "when I first encountered Raena, I, too, believed her intentions to be malevolent. The suspicion that she sought to ensnare me in a web of deceit and manipulation clouded my judgment, and I acted with instinctive wrath."

I paused, the memory of my hands tightening around her fragile throat still vivid in my mind.

"In that moment, I sought to choke the life out of her, driven by a primal need to shield myself from her perceived treachery."

Closing my eyes, I took a deep breath, allowing the memory to envelop me like a suffocating shroud.

"But in the midst of my rage, she retaliated with a sudden blast of water, a torrent that forced me to release her. As I gazed into her eyes, I saw that she was confused and afraid, yet there was a sincerity within them that pierced through the haze of my suspicions. In that moment, I could no longer deny the truth that resonated deep within my being – our connection was real and undeniable."

As I shared my experience with Kael, I felt the turmoil within me subside, giving way to a sense of clarity and purpose.

"I understand your fears, Kael," I said softly, acknowledging the weight of his concerns.

"Your experiences have left you scarred and wary, and I do not take your words lightly. But I must trust in the truth that I feel."

My gaze hardened, and I spoke with an unwavering conviction.

"If she is indeed tricking me, if her intentions are as sinister as you fear, I will kill her myself. I will not allow a mage to play with my heart and soul."

Kael's eyes were haunted, a storm of emotion surging within them. "Ash, what if you can't bring yourself to do it? What if you're ensnared in her web before you even realize you're trapped?"

His voice trembled, a plea for me to grasp the severity of the situation.

Gavril, who had been silently observing our conversation, spoke, his voice steady and calm, a striking counterpoint to the maelstrom that threatened to engulf me.

"Kael, perhaps we must trust in Ash's judgment. We each have our own path to traverse, our own fears to conquer. It is through these trials that we learn and grow stronger."

I glanced between Gavril and Kael, their words resonating in the dark recesses of my soul. My heart ached beneath the burden of their concerns and the gravity of my own decisions. Yet, I recognized that I could not let fear dictate my actions or cloud my judgment.

"Kael, I hear your fears, and I appreciate the wisdom born from your pain," I said, my voice resolute but compassionate.

"And I vow not to let my guard down. I will not be seduced by a mirage or trust without reason."

Kael's eyes searched mine, a tempest of despair and trepidation swirling within their depths. He struggled to find solace in my words, to relinquish the grip of his past traumas and trust in my determination.

How could I trust Raena, knowing the heinous acts her kind had perpetrated against my people? How could I reconcile the bond I felt with her, with the inferno of rage ignited within me by the mages' atrocities?

"I will be ever watchful," I continued, the fire in my eyes steadfast. "And if the moment arrives when I must confront Raena and put an end to her deception, I will not waver. I will do whatever it takes to safeguard our people and secure their freedom."

Kael's eyes flickered with a mixture of resignation and understanding. "I will stand by you, Ash, no matter what path you choose. I trust in your judgment, but know this: if she betrays you, if she brings harm upon you or our people, and you cannot keep your promise, I will not hesitate to exact retribution."

I nod, understanding completely and not wishing it to be any other way. United, we stood, bound by the unrelenting resolve that had carried us through the darkest times. We would not waver in our pursuit of justice and liberation. We would fight to reclaim the destiny snatched from us—for ourselves, for our people, and for future generations. Our hearts were bound, entwined by the unbreakable bond that only those who have been forged in the crucible of shared suffering could truly comprehend.

13

—— · ｡˚☆: *.☽ .* :☆˚. ——

As we lay intertwined, our limbs tangled together like the roots of an ancient tree, I felt the warmth of Zarek's body seep into my very core. My mind was a whirlwind of emotions, a storm that threatened to engulf me, yet at its eye lay the stillness and comfort that Zarek provided. The first tendrils of dawn crept across the desert horizon, bathing my chamber in a gentle, rosy light, I tried to focus on the here and now, to bask in the love and passion we shared. Zarek's voice, low and husky, whispered against my ear.

"You're trembling, my love. What's troubling you?"

I hesitated for a moment, my heart torn between revealing my inner turmoil and protecting the sanctity of our bond.

"It's nothing," I murmured, forcing a smile to my lips.

"Just the remnants of a restless dream."

His fingers traced the curve of my hip, slowly moving upward to cup my breast, his thumb teasing my nipple.

"Let me chase away those shadows for you," he suggested, his voice sultry and seductive. As if in response to his touch, my body ached for him, the fire within me reigniting with fervor. I pressed my lips to his, our tongues dancing together in a passionate waltz, as we lost ourselves in the intoxicating rhythm of our desire.

Zarek's hands roamed my body with a skilled familiarity, his touch both tender and possessive. He explored every curve, every sensitive peak and valley, leaving a trail of shivers in his wake. My breath hitched as he dipped his head to capture my nipple between his lips, suckling gently before grazing it with his teeth. My legs parted slightly, seeking friction between them, but Zarek stopped short of entering me. Instead, he kissed his way down my neck, whispering endearments as he caressed me with his tongue, sending tingles coursing through my veins. The heat between my thighs grew hotter with each passing second, making it difficult to concentrate on anything but the pleasure he offered.

His fingers moved from my breasts to trace the contours of my abdomen, cupping my mound and parting me to expose my wet pussy to his gaze. With one hand he thrust a finger deep inside me, stretching me open, while his other hand teased my clit with feather-light touches. I cried out, arching toward him, desperate for more. He plunged two fingers inside me, eliciting another cry of pleasure from my lips, then quickly added a third. As he continued to stroke his fingers against my sensitive spot, my body became a furnace of desire, my muscles clenching in anticipation.

"Zarek..." I breathed his name, unable to contain my rising need. "Please... I need you."

"Not yet, my love." His voice was soft, his tone gentle. "We have all morning. Don't rush things."

The thought of waiting made me groan, my hips moving against his fingers. I strained to reach him, craving the feel of his body pressing against mine. With a mischievous glint in his eyes, Zarek gently disentangled himself from our embrace and climbed out of the bed. As he crossed the room, his toned, muscular body gleamed in the soft morning light, a living work of art that never failed to leave me breathless. He picked up a glass and filled it with water from a nearby pitcher. Turning back to me, he raised his free hand and whispered an incantation under his breath. A subtle shimmer of magic danced across the surface of the water, and I watched in as it transformed before my eyes. The water in the glass coalesced and took on a new shape, forming a smooth, phallic object that elicited a gasp from my lips. Zarek chuckled at my reaction, his voice rich with teasing warmth.

"I thought you might enjoy a little morning surprise," he said, raising an eyebrow playfully. He returned to our bed, the transformed water held carefully in his hand, and I couldn't help but laugh at the absurdity and delight of the situation.

The moment the transformed water touched my skin, I felt a shiver course through my body, the stark contrast between the coolness of the water and the warmth of my body creating a sensation that left me breathless. The texture was smooth and fluid, yet it held its form with a gentle firmness that was intriguing.

Zarek watched my reaction with an appreciative smirk, his eyes alight with desire and a hint of the satisfaction he derived from my pleasure. "Do you like it?" he asked, his voice husky with desire and anticipation.

"I... it's different," I managed to stutter, my mind momentarily blank as I processed the unique sensation.

The unexpected coolness of the water was a delightful contrast to the rising heat within me. Zarek's hand held the water creation expertly, a painter in command of his brush, tracing a line of anticipation down my body. As he moved it slowly, teasingly lower, I found my breath hitching.

"Zarek," I gasped, the name falling from my lips as a plea.

"Mmm?" he hummed, leaning in to kiss the curve of my neck. His lips were warm against my skin, adding to the symphony of sensations that played out across my body.

The water creation finally found its destination, pressing gently against my arousal. A gasp escaped my lips at the new sensation; the coolness of the water only seemed to stoke the fire within me further. Zarek guided the water phallus into me with a slow, deliberate care that had me arching my back and clutching at the silken sheets beneath us. The intrusion was as gentle as it was firm, the water adapting to my body in a way no solid object could. I bit my lip, a moan escaping as he began to move the creation within me, each movement sending ripples of pleasure coursing through me. "I want to see you lose yourself in pleasure, my love," Zarek murmured in my ear, his words punctuated by a thrust that made my breath hitch.

"Feel everything... let it consume you.".

He continued to stimulate the water phallus inside me, the coolness giving way to a warm, smooth sensation that sent a waves of pleasure coursing through my body. Zarek watched my reaction with a tender, lustful gaze.

"It's... incredible," I breathed, my voice trembling with desire.

"It's so smooth and gentle, yet so deeply stimulating."

With a knowing smile, Zarek continued to manipulate the water phallus, expertly adjusting its shape and movements to heighten my pleasure. It seemed to mold itself to my body, filling me in the most deliciously satisfying way. As he pushed it deeper, I couldn't help but moan, my body arching in response to the exquisite sensations.

"Raena, you're so beautiful like this," Zarek murmured, leaning in to capture my lips in a passionate kiss.

I wrapped my arms around his neck, my body pressing against his, as he continued to pleasure me with the magical creation. We moved together in a sensual dance, our bodies entwined, our breaths mingling as one. The water phallus ebbed and flowed within me, adapting to my every need, every desire, with an almost otherworldly precision. With each stroke, the pleasure mounted, building towards a crescendo that left me breathless with anticipation.

"Zarek," I whispered, my voice laden with passion and love.

"I'm so close..."

He grinned wickedly, his eyes gleaming with pure adoration.

"There are so many ways I can make you come."

I moaned out loud at his words, my body throbbing with need, craving release. The water phallus was sliding easily between my walls, while he was licking my clit and caressing my swollen breasts. His fingers stroked my skin with a gentle care, sending shocks of pleasure through my body, while he gently licked my engorged nub. The sensations were overwhelming, almost too much for me to bear.

"Are you ready to let go?"

"Yes," I gasped, my voice betraying my need.

"Then let go, my love. Surrender to the pleasure and let it wash over you."

Zarek's lips left mine, his mouth moving to my breasts. He sucked hard on my nipples, taking no mercy as he tormented me with his tongue, tugging on my hard buds with a tender bite. The water phallus moving inside me, adding to the sensation of having my insides stretched wide by the enchanted toy, Zareks tongue and hands moving feverishly from my clit to my tender breasts, it was too much, I couldn't take any more. My body went rigid, my entire being consumed in a white-hot blaze of ecstasy. I screamed out, my voice reverberating around the room. My body convulsed, my muscles tightening, my insides clenching uncontrollably around the magically enhanced phallus. For several long moments, I simply floated above the world, bathed in the afterglow of my release.

When I regained control of my senses, I glanced over at Zarek, who sat beside me, stroking my hair with a tender touch, a smile on his lips.

"That was amazing, we need to try that water trick more often" I murmured, turning toward him.

His smile widened, and he laughed.

"You liked it?"

"Very much!" I exclaimed, my face flushed.

He leaned forward and brushed his lips against mine, tasting me, savoring the taste of my arousal on his tongue.

"Did you like it when you came?"

I nodded, my cheeks heating.

"As always it was amazing," I replied shyly. Zarek's hands slid down my sides until they reached the swell of my hips, his fingers pressing against my clit. A jolt of electricity shot through me, my body arching upward.

"I can feel you are still wet," he said softly. His hand moved between my legs, fingering me gently, prolonging my pleasure.

"Do you want to come again?"

I moaned at the thought of it.

"I wouldn't mind, but this time with you inside of me."

"I'd like that, too." He smiled.

His fingers circled my clit, teasing me with a slow, steady circle preparing me for another round. I began to caress his chest while with my free hand stroke his cock. It responded immediately, hardening even more before my eyes. I decided to use the same trick as him and used my magic to make the water encircle his shaft and caress him without mercy. Zarek groaned, his head falling back. I had no idea what my powers could do to him, but it felt good. With each pass of the water, it became harder and thicker until it looked almost impossible. I continued to tease him while he writhed in pleasure.

"I want to feel you inside of me," I whispered.

He gripped my hips, pulling me closer, his cock pushing into me slowly. The feeling was indescribable. Each inch he took sent ripples throughout my body.

"Hold on," he said hoarsely, his gaze burning into mine.

"It's going to be fast."

I wrapped my arms around his neck, my breasts pressed against his bare chest, and closed my eyes. My heart raced, blood pulsing through me. And then he thrust himself deep inside of me. A sharp cry escaped my lips, my body spasming. I held onto him tightly, my nails digging into his shoulders. Slowly he withdrew and pushed into me again and again, the water moving between us, caressing our bodies, creating waves and currents that surrounded us. Each thrust was punctuated with a growl of pleasure. Our bodies moved as one, our movements perfectly synchronized.

His long fingers slid from my waist to cup my breast, his hand grabbing on to them like his life depended on it. I bit down on his shoulder, moaning loudly as he sucked in a sharp breath. Then I arched my back, biting down harder on his shoulder as another wave of pleasure tore through me. He groaned and bit down in turn, sucking hard on my neck as the tension built up within me once more.

The water made the world around us foggy, but it didn't stop me from seeing the fierce look on his face as he continued to move inside me, slamming against me repeatedly.

"You're so tight," he said roughly, and I knew he meant every word, "It feels incredible."

He moved faster now, pounding into me over and over, his hips slapping against mine. The sound echoing, filling the air with something primal and carnal, dampened only by the shield of water our magic created to enhance our pleasure.

"By the gods!" His voice was hoarse, and then he dropped his head and kissed me hard.

He gritted his teeth, his body tensing, his movements becoming erratic. My body tightened, and my stomach clenched, and I cried out as the pressure finally exploded throughout my entire being. My muscles clamped down on him, trying to squeeze everything he had inside of me. He let out a loud roar and I felt every hot drop of his seed fill me up. Spent he collapsed against me, both of us panting hard, my skin tingling and my muscles trembling as if I had just run a marathon. We lay there for a while, just enjoying the closeness and warmth of each other's bodies and I couldn't help but smile at the sight of him lying next to me, naked.

With the morning sun streaming through the window, casting its golden light upon us, I took a moment to truly appreciate the man beside me. His tousled, light hair framed his strong, chiseled features, the sunlight playing across his deep-set eyes, revealing their rich, emerald green hue. His muscular physique, sculpted by years of training, spoke of his power and grace, and his arms wrapped around me felt like the embrace of a warrior and a lover, all in one.

After a few minutes, he pulled back and looked down at me, his expression soft once again.

"What are you smiling about?" he asked softly.

"Because this is exactly what I wanted."

He nodded slowly, his eyes darkening as he stared down at me.

"I can't believe how amazing you feel. You're going to drive me crazy."

"Good."

I licked my lips.

"It's been too long since I've seen you like this."

He laughed and leaned down to brush my lips with his own.

"I have something planned for us today, my love," Zarek said, his voice playful and teasing.

"I think you'll enjoy it."

Curiosity piqued, I raised an eyebrow.

"Oh? And what might that be?"

He flashed me a mischievous grin, his eyes twinkling with delight. "That, my dear Raena, is a surprise. But rest assured, it involves pampering, relaxation, and a bit of adventure."

I couldn't help but laugh at his cryptic description, my spirits lifting as I leaned in to give him a lingering kiss.

"You know me so well, Zarek. I'm looking forward to it."

As we rose from the bed and prepared for the day ahead, I would not let my thoughts be consumed by anything else, today was about Zarek and me, and the love we shared. Not knowing what adventure Zarek planned I selected a silk tunic and pants that hugged my curves and accentuated my figure. Zarek watched me with an amused smile, no doubt appreciating the sight, I too couldn't help but steal glances at him. His light hair, tousled from our morning activities, caught the sun's rays, giving him an almost ethereal glow. His emerald green eyes, always so full of love, sparkled like jewels as he met my gaze. The tailored tunic and breeches he chose accentuated his strong, lean form, and I felt a surge of pride knowing that he was mine.

"Alright, my love," I said playfully, taking Zarek's offered arm.

"Lead the way to this mysterious adventure."

Zarek grinned, and together we made our way through the palace halls, eventually stepping out into the warm sunlight of the palace courtyard. I noticed that several servants had gathered, each carrying an assortment of baskets and bundles.

"Is this part of your surprise?" I asked curiously, raising an eyebrow. Zarek nodded, his eyes gleaming with excitement.

"Indeed, my dear. Today, we shall embark on a private hot air balloon ride, soaring high above the desert and enjoying a luxurious picnic, complete with drinks and relaxation."

My eyes widened in delight at his revelation. I had never been on a hot air balloon ride before, and the thought of experiencing it with Zarek filled me with excitement.

"You never cease to amaze me, Zarek," I admitted, squeezing his arm affectionately.

Zarek chuckled, his own excitement palpable as he helped me into the hot air balloon's spacious basket. As the servants loaded the baskets and bundles, I could see an array of my favorite foods and drinks, as well as some sumptuous cushions and blankets to ensure our comfort during the journey. Once we were settled and the balloon was ready, we began our ascent, the ground below us slowly receding as we climbed higher and higher into the sky. The sensation of floating effortlessly through the air was both exhilarating and calming, and I found myself captivated by the breathtaking view of the desert landscape stretching out as far as the eye could see.

The desert, a place so familiar to me, took on a new beauty from this vantage point. The sun cast a golden glow on the endless dunes, their shadows dancing and shifting with each gust of wind. Zarek, sensing my awe, reached over and took my hand in his, giving it a gentle squeeze.

"It's breathtaking, isn't it?" he murmured, his eyes reflecting the wonder of the world below us.

"It truly is," I agreed, my heart swelling with appreciation for the moment we were sharing. We had experienced so much together, and this adventure was another treasured memory in the making.

"Look at the way the sunlight glistens on the sand," I breathed in awe.

"It's like an ocean of gold."

Zarek smiled at my observation.

"An ocean of gold for my golden queen," he replied, his voice filled with warmth and affection.

I playfully rolled my eyes at his flattery but couldn't help the grin that spread across my face.

"You have such a silver tongue, my love. How do you expect me to resist your charms?"

He chuckled and pulled me closer, our bodies pressed together as we shared the view.

"I don't," he whispered into my ear, sending shivers down my spine. "That's the whole point."

As we continued to float through the sky, we took turns pointing out landmarks and features of the desert below. Our conversation was light and full of banter, our laughter ringing out into the vast expanse around us.

"See that oasis over there?" Zarek asked, gesturing toward a small, lush green patch in the distance.

"That's where I first learned to swim."

"Really?" I replied, feigning surprise.

"I would have thought the royal palace pool would have been more your style lord Xantheer", calling Zarek by his family name.

Zarek shook his head, grinning.

"Even those born into wealth need to escape the confines of the palace from time to time," he said, his eyes twinkling.

"Besides, swimming in a natural oasis has a certain charm that no palace pool can match. On our next adventure maybe we should go there."

I smirked at the suggestion.

"Perhaps, Lord Xantheer, but only if you promise to regale me with tales of your mischievous youth while we're there", I teased, enjoying our playful banter.

Zarek's laughter filled the air, and I found myself reveling in the sound.

"Deal, my precious jewel," he agreed, using the nicknamed derived from my title.

"But be warned, some of those tales might shock even you."

I raised an eyebrow, intrigued.

"I highly doubt that, but I look forward to finding out," I countered, challenging him with a sly grin.

The hot air balloon continued to drift effortlessly through the sky and we shared stories of our pasts, laughter and loving gazes exchanged between us. The world below seemed to disappear as we lost ourselves in each other's company. Time seemed to stand still, but eventually, the sun began to dip below the horizon, bathing the desert in a warm, golden light. The sky transformed into a canvas of brilliant oranges and purples, a sight that took my breath away.

"Have you ever seen anything so beautiful?" I asked, my voice barely above a whisper.

Zarek's eyes never left mine as he replied.

"Only when I look at you, Ren."

I blushed at his compliment, touched by his heartfelt words. Our tender moment, however, was interrupted as the temperature began to drop. The once warm desert air turned cooler as the sun dipped lower in the sky. Despite my best efforts to ignore it, I couldn't help but shiver, my body involuntarily reacting to the chill. Zarek, ever attentive to my needs, immediately noticed my discomfort.

"Raena, my love, you're shivering," he said with concern, his brow furrowing slightly.

I tried to dismiss his worry with a casual wave of my hand.

"It's nothing, just a little chill in the air," I replied, not wanting to ruin moment.

But Zarek would hear none of it.

"Wait here," he insisted, before swiftly moving to the corner, he rummaged through the various baskets and bundles, finally producing a thick, plush blanket embroidered with intricate patterns.

With a triumphant smile, he returned to my side, carefully draping the blanket around my shoulders. The warmth of the fabric was instantaneous, enveloping me in a cocoon of comfort that chased away the chill.

"There," Zarek said, satisfaction evident in his voice.

"That should keep you warm."

I couldn't help but smile at his thoughtfulness.

"Thank you, Zarek," I murmured, snuggling deeper into the blanket.

"You always know how to take care of me."

He grinned.

"It's my pleasure, I would do anything to ensure your happiness and well-being."

As the sun continued its descent, casting a warm glow over us, Zarek suddenly grew serious. His eyes, which had been filled with laughter moments before, now held a different kind of intensity, they held a seriousness I had rarely seen before.

"Raena, there's something I've been wanting to tell you for a long time," he began, a hint of nervousness creeping into his usually confident voice.

Curiosity piqued, I looked at him expectantly.

"What is it, Zarek?"

He took a deep breath and slowly lowered himself onto one knee before me. I blinked in surprise, not expecting such a gesture.

"Raena," he began, his voice earnest and full of emotion.

"I know that our engagement was arranged at birth for political reasons. But over the years, as we've grown together and shared countless memories, I've come to realize just how deeply I've fallen in love with you. Our love has grown beyond the confines of duty and obligation."

He reached for my hand, his gaze never wavering.

"You are the most intelligent, beautiful, and captivating woman I've ever known. Your strength, courage, and spirit leave me in awe every day, and I consider myself the luckiest man alive to be by your side.

I love you not because I have to, but because I can't imagine my life without you."

A warmth spread through my chest at his heartfelt words, my own emotions swelling within me.

"I want you to know," he continued, "that even if we hadn't been betrothed at birth, I would still choose you, Raena. I would choose you a thousand times over, in every lifetime, because you are the one who completes me."

A grin spread across his face.

"So, my dear, stubborn, enchanting Raena, I ask you, not as a political obligation but as a man deeply and irrevocably in love, will you marry me and make me the happiest man in Varidia? Will you allow me the honor of being your partner in life, not just in name, but in spirit as well?"

A sudden pang of guilt washed over me as Zarek's heartfelt plea reached my ears. My mind involuntarily drifted back to the demon I had encountered, the one who had stirred something unfamiliar in my heart. The pull I felt towards him was inexplicable, and it frightened me. But was it fair to compare that fleeting encounter with the deep love and connection Zarek and I had built over the years? And yet, despite my own internal rebukes, the demon's image continued to haunt me. The undeniable attraction I felt for him gnawed at my conscience, making it difficult to focus on the man kneeling before me. My heart raced as I looked into Zarek's eyes, filled with sincerity and hope. Could I really let this newfound curiosity for a stranger, a slave, overshadow the love and commitment Zarek had shown me throughout our lives? Was I willing to throw away everything we had built together for a mere infatuation?

I felt torn. How could I say yes when I harbored such thoughts and feelings? But then I reminded myself that Zarek had always been there for me, his love steadfast and unwavering, and he deserved my whole heart.

It's just a stupid infatuation, I told myself, trying to dismiss the unsettling thoughts that plagued me.

Zarek is the one I am meant to be with, the one who truly knows and loves me. I cannot let a fleeting fancy for a stranger sway my heart.

No, I couldn't let this brief fascination cloud my judgment. I had to remember what truly mattered, and that was the love and trust Zarek and I shared. He was my rock, my support, and my constant in a world that was often uncertain. Taking a deep breath, I pushed away the lingering thoughts of the demon and focused on the man before me, the man who loved me without question or hesitation. I looked into his eyes, now filled with a mix of vulnerability and anticipation, and made my decision.

"Oh, Zarek," I whispered, my voice thick with emotion.

"Of course, I will marry you. I love you more than words can express, and I can't wait to spend the rest of my life with you."

His face lit up with joy, and he rose from his kneeling position to embrace me, our arms wrapping tightly around one another. We shared a tender, passionate kiss, sealing our promise to each other as the sun dipped below the horizon, leaving the sky awash in a symphony of colors. As we held each other close, I couldn't help but feel a twinge of regret for the feelings I had been harboring for the demon. How could I be so torn between two beings? Zarek, my betrothed, my love, my rock; and the demon, a stranger, a slave, and yet...But I knew that I had made the right choice. Zarek was my future, and I would not let anything, or anyone, stand in the way of our happiness.

That night, as Zarek and I lay entwined in each other's arms, I couldn't shake the thoughts of the demon from my mind. It was as if he had etched himself into the very fabric of my soul, refusing to be forgotten or dismissed. I wrestled with the guilt and confusion that swirled within me, wondering how I could ever be completely true to Zarek when a part of me still yearned for a stranger.

"You're a fool", I scolded myself, clenching my eyes shut in a futile attempt to block out the haunting image of the demon's captivating

gaze. *"Zarek is your everything, your love, your partner, and your future. You cannot let a stranger's allure threaten everything you have built together."*

Yet, despite my internal rebukes, I couldn't help but feel that something had shifted within me. The demon had awakened a longing I had never known, a desire that refused to be quelled by reason or logic. How could I reconcile my love for Zarek with this newfound passion that burned within me? As I lay there, my thoughts a tempest of doubt and desire, I knew that I had to find a way to resolve the conflict that raged within me. I owed it to Zarek, and to myself, to confront these feelings head-on, rather than allowing them to fester and poison the love we shared. I decided that I would speak to the demon once more, to try and understand the allure he held over me. Perhaps, by facing this temptation, I could dispel its power and find my way back to Zarek, my heart whole and undivided. Only then would I be able to give him the love and devotion he deserved, free from the shadows that clouded my heart.

But for now, I would cherish the warmth and security of Zarek's embrace, his love a comforting balm that soothed my troubled soul. And as I drifted off to sleep, my mind filled with a kaleidoscope of memories and dreams.

14

— · ˳°☆: *.☽ .* :☆° . —

After the day's grueling work, I collapsed onto the hard, unforgiving ground of our shared slave quarters. My muscles screamed in protest, every inch of me coated in a thick layer of dust and grime. Sweat trickled down my brow, stinging my eyes, mingling with the ever-present dust. The meager cot beneath me offered no comfort, the coarse fabric rough against my aching body. Around me, the other demons lay in similar states of exhaustion. The stench of toil and desperation hung heavy in the air, each breath tasting of dust and defeat. In the harsh, unforgiving world of the mines, we had become more than slaves. We were brethren, forged in the crucible of shared suffering. Sleep, when it came, was a fleeting escape from the harsh reality of our existence. But tonight, sleep was elusive, driven away by the storm of thoughts that raged within my mind.

The very notion of soulmates, of two souls so perfectly intertwined that they became as one, was a concept I had always struggled to comprehend. In the brutal world in which I lived, the idea of such a sacred bond seemed a cruel joke, a whispered promise of happiness that was forever just beyond my reach. But there was no denying the yearning that took root in my chest whenever I thought of her, a sweet ache that was as puzzling as it was profound. It was as if a piece of me I never knew was missing had been returned, filling a void I never knew existed.

Yet, even with the undeniable bond pulling at my soul, I remained wary. Trust was a luxury a slave could ill afford. But as much as I tried to dismiss it, to ignore the lingering warmth that spread through my chest when I thought of her, it clung to me, a persistent reminder of the strange twist of fate. The elders used to speak of it - the sacred bond between souls, the invisible tether that linked two beings across space and time. It was woven into our songs, our stories, our very essence. A gift from the gods, a blessing bestowed upon those fortunate enough to find their other half. As I pondered this notion, the fires of doubt and anger burned within me, their flames fanned by the reality of my own situation. For it seemed that fate had played a cruel hand, leading me to find my soulmate in the most unlikely of places - within the walls of the palace that housed the very oppressors who had enslaved my people.

A fucking water mage, and my goddamn soulmate. The universe was laughing in my face, a torment only a god with a cruel sense of humor could have conceived and all I could do was grit my teeth and bear it. The embodiment of everything I detested. And yet, my damned demonic blood screamed otherwise. Vesha. The word echoed in my mind, a mantra, a curse. How could she be my vesha, my soulmate? My heart was a tempest, my soul aflame with a myriad of conflicting emotions. I yearned for the tender touch of her hand, the softness of her lips against mine, and the warmth of her embrace, yet at the same time, I was consumed by anger and resentment toward the mages who had enslaved my people.

I should've been repulsed, should've scoffed at the absurdity of it all. But instead, her presence felt like a cool, soothing rain in the arid wasteland of my heart. The water mages, her kin, were the reason my people suffered, the reason we had shackles binding our hands instead of freedom. The thought of loving her was as foreign as the idea of freedom. The irony was not lost on me. Born a slave, yet bound by the soul to a princess. She was mine. Mine in a way no one else could claim. But could I trust her? Could I let myself believe in the faint glimmer of hope she presented?

Worse than slavery was the unbearable thought of her kindness, her sympathy being nothing more than a façade. If she was like the rest of her kind... I'd rather face the whip a thousand times over. I couldn't afford to be thinking about her, not like this, not when every fiber of my being screamed danger. The mages... If they discovered this bond, they would exploit it, tear us apart, and use it to their sadistic advantage. As a slave, I was expendable, but she was a princess. To the mages, I was just another set of hands to dig for lyrium, but she... She was valuable. I couldn't let her become a pawn in their twisted games. I clenched my fists, the harsh reality gnawing at me. I couldn't tell her, couldn't allow her to be put in danger because of me. She was a beacon of light in my dismal existence, a spark of something... hope?

I had to keep her at a distance. A fucking difficult task when every pulse of my demonic blood resonated with hers. Every instinct in me screamed to claim her, to find solace in our shared bond. But it was a luxury I couldn't afford. The thought of what this connection to Raena meant left me feeling more vulnerable than I had ever felt in my life, I had to protect her, even if it meant from myself.
What a goddamn mess.

In the depths of my soul, I could feel the indomitable spirit of my ancestors urging me to fight, to never yield in the face of adversity. I would not bow to the whims of fate, nor would I surrender to the tyranny of the mages.

—— · ˳ ˚ ☆: *.☽ .* :☆˚ . ——

15

A few days had passed since my emotional conflict, and I had yet to go see Ash again. I told myself I would find the right time, but part of me was afraid of what I might discover about myself when I finally faced him. Unbeknownst to me, my brother, Prince Caspian, had returned from his diplomatic visit to the neighboring kingdom, accompanied by a friend. The throne room was alive with excitement as my parents, King Lucius and Queen Isadora, greeted our esteemed guests with warm smiles and open arms. I could hear their voices echoing through the corridors as I made my way towards them. As I entered the throne room, the sight of my brother brought a genuine smile to my face. It had been months since I had last seen him, and I had missed his warm presence and easy laughter. He looked more mature and confident, a testament to his experiences abroad.

"Raena!" Caspian exclaimed, spotting me and making his way through the crowd to embrace me.

"It's been too long, little sister!"

I hugged him back tightly, the scent of his familiar cologne bringing back fond memories of our childhood.

"Welcome home, Caspian," I replied, my voice filled with affection. "You've been sorely missed."

Caspian grinned and stepped back, gesturing to the tall, handsome man standing beside him.

"Raena, I'd like you to meet Prince Aldric. Aldric, this is my sister, Princess Raena."

Prince Aldric bowed gracefully, his dark eyes meeting mine with a respectful glint.

"It's a pleasure to meet the Jewel of the Desert herself, the stories of your beauty pale in comparison to the real thing. I've heard much about you from Caspian."

I curtsied in response, my cheeks warming slightly under his intense gaze.

"The pleasure is mine, Prince Aldric. I hope you enjoy your time in our kingdom."

He straightened up and smiled warmly.

"I have no doubt that I will, with such gracious hosts."

My parents approached us then, welcoming Aldric once more and expressing their eagerness to show him the wonders of our kingdom. As the conversation flowed around me, I couldn't help but feel a sense of normalcy returning to my life. The presence of my family and our esteemed guest seemed to ground me, reminding me of my duty to my kingdom and my upcoming marriage to Zarek. That evening, a grand dinner was held in the palace to celebrate the arrival of Prince Aldric and the upcoming rain summoning ceremony. The long, elegantly adorned table was filled with a plethora of sumptuous dishes, and the room was filled with laughter and light-hearted conversation. As I took my seat between Zarek and my brother, I couldn't help but feel a twinge of happiness at the lively atmosphere. I caught Zarek's eyes as he leaned in and whispered.

"You look absolutely stunning tonight, Raena. The room seems to glow with your presence."

I smiled at his compliment, grateful for his unwavering affection. "Thank you, Zarek. You're quite dashing yourself," I replied, appreciating his effort to keep me in high spirits. He caught my eye and winked, making me smile.

The conversation flowed easily, mainly centered on Caspian's adventures in the neighboring kingdom and the upcoming rain summoning. Caspian regaled us with amusing anecdotes from his journey, each tale more entertaining than the last.

"…and then, just as we were about to leave the feast, a goat wandered into the banquet hall!" Caspian exclaimed, chuckling at the memory.

"It caused quite the commotion, but Aldric here managed to catch it and save the day."

Aldric grinned, accepting the praise with modesty.

"I merely did what needed to be done, but I admit it was rather comical."

The laughter around the table was infectious, and even I couldn't help but join in. It was moments like these when I felt truly content, surrounded by those I loved and cherished.

As the meal progressed, the topic turned to the rain summoning ceremony. My father, King Lucius, addressed Aldric with enthusiasm.

"Prince Aldric, we are honored to have you witness this vital event for our kingdom. It's a long-held tradition, and we hope it will leave a lasting impression."

Aldric nodded thoughtfully.

"I am eager to learn more, Your Majesty. I've heard tales of the rain summoning's beauty and power, and I am grateful for the opportunity to be a part of it."

My mother, Queen Isadora, added.

"The rain summoning is performed only by the female mages of our family. Raena will be the one to perform the ritual this year, as I have done so in the past. It is a great responsibility and honor for her."

My chest swelled with a mix of pride and anxiety as all eyes turned to me. This would be my first time performing the rain summoning, and the weight of its importance pressed heavily on my shoulders.

Aldric looked at me with admiration, his dark eyes sparkling.

"I have no doubt that you will succeed, Princess Raena. The wellbeing of all Varidia depend on the rain you will summon. I am eager to witness this marvelous event."

Zarek chimed in, his voice filled with pride.

"Raena has been training diligently for this moment. She is more than ready to take on this responsibility. I have the utmost confidence in her abilities."

Tho I appreciated their support, I couldn't help but feel the pressure mounting. The importance of the rain summoning ceremony was immense, as it would bring rain to the entire of Varidia for seven full days. The people would collect and store as much water as possible during this time, ensuring their survival for the rest of the year. The ceremony would also leave me drained for days, unable to get out of bed, but it was a sacrifice I was willing to make for my people. I took a deep breath and forced a smile, trying to keep my nerves at bay.

"Thank you, Prince Aldric, and thank you, Zarek. I am indeed honored to perform the rain summoning this year, and I hope to make everyone proud."

Aldric, raising his glass, said.

"A toast to the Radiant Jewel of the Desert! May her rain summoning bring us an abundance of water and joy."

Everyone raised their glasses in unison, and I couldn't help but feel a surge of pride.

"Thank you, Prince Aldric," I said graciously, raising my own glass in return.

"To the prosperity of our kingdoms and the friendship that binds us."

As we clinked glasses, I stole a glance at Zarek, who was beaming with love and pride. His unwavering support in the face of such a monumental task was a comfort to me, and I knew I could rely on him during the challenging days to come. The dinner continued, the conversation light and filled with laughter. Caspian and Aldric exchanged amusing tales of their travels, while Zarek's father, Lord Cadmus and a few nobles discussed the upcoming trade negotiations. I listened intently, occasionally chiming in with my own opinions or stories. Zarek, ever the witty and clever companion, teased me gently.

"I'm surprised you haven't tried to convince Aldric to import some of those exotic fruits you love so much, Raena," he said with a smirk.

I rolled my eyes, a smile spreading across my face.

"There's still time, Zarek. Besides, I think everyone should have the chance to experience the delight of biting into a fresh kavara fruit." Aldric chuckled.

"I must admit, I haven't had the pleasure of trying one. But with such a passionate endorsement from you, Princess, I'm eager to taste them for myself."

The evening wore on, my worries seemed to fade into the background, replaced by the warmth and camaraderie of those around me. With the dinner drawing to a close my mother rose from her seat to address the gathering.

"We thank you all for joining us this evening. We look forward to the rain summoning ceremony and the many blessings it will bring to our kingdom and our people."

With a round of applause and murmurs of agreement, the guests began to disperse, leaving me to share a quiet moment with Zarek. He took my hand, his eyes filled with love and concern.

"You're going to do wonderfully, Raena. I know it's a tremendous responsibility, but you were born for this."

His words of encouragement warmed my heart, and I squeezed his hand in response.

"Thank you, Zarek. Your faith in me means more than you know."

We said our goodnights and retired to our separate quarters and I couldn't help but reflect on the evening. The laughter, the camaraderie, and the unwavering support of my loved ones had buoyed my spirits and given me the strength I needed to face the upcoming challenge. It was a heavy burden to bear, but one that I would carry with pride and determination.

—— · ˚ ☆: *.☽ .* :☆˚ . ——

16

The days wore on and we continued our clandestine operations, stealing what little moments we could to gather the essential materials and refine our strategy. Each of us knew the risks all too well, but the tantalizing prospect of freedom fueled our determination, driving us to defy the ever-present danger that stalked our every step. Our every movement became calculated and precise, each step a carefully choreographed performance designed to avoid detection. The mines, once a place of misery and despair, transformed into a stage upon which we played out our desperate gambit for freedom. As the days dwindled and the hour of our escape drew ever closer, an electric current of tension hummed through the cavernous depths, casting a pall of apprehension over even the most mundane of tasks. We communicated in furtive whispers and subtle glances, our words laden with unspoken meaning. The slightest misstep or careless word could have unraveled the intricate tapestry of our plan, plunging us headlong into catastrophe. Each successful transfer of materials or exchange of information felt like a small victory snatched from the jaws of defeat, fueling our hope even as it underscored the precariousness of our situation.

Our efforts nearly failed on one harrowing instance, as I covertly gathered a particularly reactive mineral from a secluded corner of the mine. I could feel the heat of the gaze of one of the guards on my back, the unspoken threat of punishment that lingered in the air like a dark cloud. Clutching the precious mineral in my trembling hand, I offered a silent prayer to whatever gods might be listening, my breath catching in my throat as I heard the guard's footsteps draw near. I concealed the reactive mineral within the folds of my ragged clothing, my palms were slick with sweat, betraying the fear that coursed through my veins. I strained to maintain a mask of calm, my eyes fixed on the dull rock face before me, even as my mind raced with visions of discovery and the brutal consequences that would surely follow.

The guard's footsteps echoed through the mine, each heavy thud bringing him closer to me. With each passing second, the tension wound tighter, the oppressive atmosphere of the mine seeming to constrict around me like a vice. I could hear the ragged rasp of my own breath, the beat of my heart like a drum in my ears, and I fought to keep my mounting panic at bay. In my peripheral vision, I could see the guard's imposing silhouette looming ever closer, his eyes narrowing as he scanned the ranks of slaves, searching for any sign of disobedience or dissent. He approached, barking out a command, his voice cold and harsh.

"Keep working, scum! No slacking!"

I knew that if he were to notice the bulge in my clothing or the tremor in my hands, it would be the end for me – and likely for my friends as well. As the guard drew closer, I summoned every last ounce of my resolve, willing my body to remain still and my face to betray no hint of my inner turmoil. The air was thick with tension, the silence heavy with unspoken menace. For a moment, I dared to believe that I had escaped detection, that my desperate gamble had paid off. But then, the guard paused, his eyes narrowing as they fixed on me. He took a step toward me, his hand reaching out to grasp my shoulder, and I could feel the icy grip of despair tighten around my heart.

"Hey, you! What are you hiding?" the guard growled, suspicion etched across his hardened face.

When his fingers brushed against the rough fabric of my clothing, a distant commotion suddenly erupted, pulling his attention away from me. Another guard was shouting angrily, his voice carrying across the cavernous expanse of the mine.

"Damn it, one of the slaves has collapsed! Get over here!"

The guard who had been about to apprehend me hesitated, torn between his suspicions and the pressing need to investigate the disturbance. With a final, lingering glare, he released his grip on my shoulder and hurried toward the source of the commotion, leaving me to exhale a shaky breath of relief.

"Thank the gods," I whispered under my breath, my heart continuing to hammer in my chest.

I knew that I had been mere moments from disaster. The close call had left me shaken to my core, a stark reminder of the risks we were taking and the stakes for which we were playing. In the aftermath of that harrowing encounter, my resolve only hardened.

I knew that the path we had chosen was fraught with danger and uncertainty, but the alternative – a life of enslavement and suffering – was a fate that I could not accept.

—— · ₒ˚ ☆: *.) .* :☆˚ . ——

The morning sun streamed through the tall, arched windows, bathing the opulent breakfast room in a warm, golden glow. The room was adorned with exquisite tapestries and paintings, each carefully selected to showcase the wealth and taste of the royal family. A long, polished table stood in the center of the room, laden with an array of mouthwatering dishes. The aroma of freshly baked pastries, sizzling bacon, and sweet, ripe fruits filled the air. Seated around the table were Princess Raena, her brother Prince Caspian, Zarek, and their esteemed guest, Prince Aldric. The king and queen were attending to other matters of state, leaving the four of them to a more informal meal. They were all dressed casually, ready for a day of exploring the city and showing Aldric the best of what the kingdom had to offer. While they began to serve themselves, Caspian clumsily knocked over a pitcher of orange juice, causing it to spill all over the table.

"Oh, not again," he groaned, trying to salvage the situation as they all burst into laughter.

Zarek teased Caspian playfully.

"Caspian, my brother, I do believe your coordination skills could use some polishing. Perhaps we need some magic spill-proof tableware just for you."

Aldric joined in, chuckling as he observed the situation.

"I must say, your enthusiasm for breakfast is truly unparalleled, dear Caspian."

Raena rolled her eyes, a smile playing on her lips.

"I suppose we should be grateful he hasn't managed to flood the entire room yet. But the day is still young, isn't it, dear brother?"

Caspian, good-natured as always, laughed along.

"One can only hope my clumsiness is limited to the dining table. But I do apologize for the mess."

Elras, Raena's demon servant, quickly appeared at Caspian's side, ready to clean up the spill. As he mopped up the juice, his expression remained neutral, giving away none of his personal feelings. As Elras mopped up the orange juice, Raena gave him a reassuring smile. She knew he was still adjusting to his new surroundings. Aldric, noticing Elras for the first time, looked at him with a mix of surprise and curiosity.

"I must admit, Princess Raena, I am quite amazed to see a demon serving as your personal attendant. It is rather unusual, isn't it?"

Zarek, sensing Aldric's curiosity, decided to explain the situation. "Yes, Prince Aldric, it is indeed unusual, Raena saved him about a month ago. She saw him on the streets when he was being transferred to the Zulmar mines, the guards were abusing him and she took pity on him and decided to bring him into her service. It is quite a unique arrangement, but so far there have been no issues."

Raena nodded in agreement, adding.

"He has been a valuable addition to our household, and I believe that everyone deserves a second chance, regardless of their origins. While he may be a demon, he has been adapting well to his new surroundings and is no less deserving of kindness and respect than any other being."

Caspian looked at his sister, his eyes wide with amazement.

"Ren, I had no idea you intervened on behalf of a demon. That's quite... unexpected."

Raena shrugged nonchalantly, enjoying the reactions her choice of servant had provoked.

"Sometimes, dear brother, even the most unconventional decisions can have the most intriguing outcomes."

Aldric, still somewhat skeptical, nodded thoughtfully.

"I suppose that's true. It will be interesting to see how your choice plays out. Tho that is a fascinating story, Princess Raena, your benevolence and compassion are truly commendable."

With the orange juice incident resolved and the conversation flowing easily, the group continued to enjoy their delicious breakfast. They discussed their plans for the day, eager to show Aldric the best their city had to offer.

"So, Prince Aldric," Caspian chimed in, "what do you hope to see most during your tour of our fair city?"

Aldric considered the question thoughtfully.

"I've heard marvelous things about your marketplace and the vibrant array of goods on offer. I'm also keen to see your renowned botanical gardens. They are said to be a sight to behold."

Zarek nodded in agreement.

"The gardens are indeed a jewel of our kingdom. Raena and I often spend hours wandering the pathways, marveling at the exotic flora."

Caspian grinned and added.

"And speaking of marvels, we mustn't forget the pièce de résistance of our city – the heavenly confections created by our head chef, Auguste. His creations are nothing short of divine, and I daresay you'll find them a hidden attraction worth experiencing."

Raena laughed, nodding in agreement.

"Caspian is quite right. Auguste's sweets are the talk of the kingdom. The man himself is as flamboyant and dramatic as the desserts he creates. You simply must indulge in his artistry while you're here."

Zarek chuckled.

"Indeed, a visit to our city wouldn't be complete without a taste of Auguste's culinary masterpieces. The man is truly gifted, and his passion for his craft is unrivaled."

Aldric's eyes sparkled with anticipation.

"Well, with such high praise, I would be remiss not to sample his creations. I eagerly await the opportunity to meet this culinary virtuoso and taste his legendary sweets."

With the breakfast conversation coming to a close, the group decided to pay a visit to chef Auguste in his domain – the royal kitchen. When the group approached the royal kitchen, they could hear the lively chatter of the staff and the clattering of pots and pans.

The grand double doors swung open, revealing a bustling scene filled with chefs darting about, their faces flushed from the heat of the stoves. No sooner had they entered the kitchen than a young sous-chef carrying a towering stack of plates nearly collided with Zarek. The young chef yelped in surprise, the plates teetering precariously in his arms. Zarek, quick on his feet, managed to catch the top few plates before they crashed to the floor, earning a round of applause from his companions.

"Ah, Princess Raena, Prince Caspian, and Lord Zarek! What an unexpected pleasure to have you grace my humble domain."

Auguste greeted them, sweeping into the room with a grandiose flourish of his hand. He wore a vibrant pink chef's hat perched jauntily atop his head, the color a perfect match for his flamboyant personality.

"And who might this fine gentleman be?"

Raena, basking in Auguste's effusive greeting, introduced their guest.

"Auguste, this is Prince Aldric of the neighboring kingdom. We thought it only fitting to treat him to the exquisite taste of your culinary creations."

Auguste bowed gracefully, his eyes twinkling with delight.

"Your Highness, it is an honor to meet you. I assure you, I will prepare a veritable feast for your senses, showcasing the very best of our kingdom's gastronomic delights."

While Auguste spoke, a pastry chef in the corner of the room attempted to add a delicate spun sugar decoration to a cake. He spun the fine strands of sugar a bit too enthusiastically, and they tangled in his hair instead of adorning the dessert. Auguste, catching sight of the mishap, sighed dramatically.

"Ah, the perils of sugar artistry," he mused, striding over to the pastry chef and expertly untangling the sugar strands.

"Remember, my dear, elegance and restraint are the keys to success in our craft."

Caspian chimed in.

"Auguste, we would be most grateful if you could create some of your legendary sweets for Aldric to sample when we return from our city tour. We have been singing your praises all morning, and we simply must share the experience with our esteemed guest."

Auguste placed a hand on his chest, his eyes sparkling with excitement.

"But of course, Prince Caspian! It would be my absolute pleasure to craft an array of my most exquisite masterpieces for Prince Aldric's enjoyment. I assure you, when you return from your delightful excursion, a veritable feast for the senses shall await you."

Zarek, said with a smile.

"Auguste, we expect nothing less than perfection, as always. I daresay our dear friend Aldric may find himself wishing to extend his stay, once he's had a taste of your remarkable talents."

Aldric chuckled, feeling both intrigued and amused by the animated chef.

"Well, with such high expectations, I cannot wait to savor your culinary wonders, Master Auguste."

With their request placed in the capable hands of the flamboyant chef, the group set off to explore the city, confident that Auguste would not disappoint.

***

For this desert world, the upcoming rain summoning was an event of unparalleled importance. The anticipation had reached fever pitch as citizens prepared for a week-long deluge that would bring life-giving water to the parched land they inhabited. Every corner of the city buzzed with energy and excitement, as the summoning would not only bless the kingdom but the entire world with seven days of continuous rain. In the heart of the marketplace, merchants and craftsmen worked tirelessly to prepare for the coming rain. Colorful awnings were erected to protect their wares from the impending deluge, while stalls overflowed with rainwater-catching devices, ranging from simple clay pots to ornately carved vessels. The people eagerly purchased these items, hoping to store as much of the precious water as possible for the dry months ahead. Laughter and lively conversations filled the air, and the marketplace thrived with a vibrancy that was rarely seen in a world where water was so scarce. The air was fragrant with the scent of exotic spices, while the tantalizing aroma of freshly baked goods and sizzling meats wafted from the food stalls. As the summoning approached, the entire kingdom, from the highest-ranking nobles to the lowliest Nulls, would be united in celebration and awe.

For seven days, the perpetual rain would fall upon the parched land, nourishing the soil and filling the wells, cisterns, and reservoirs that were the lifeblood of the kingdom. This miraculous event would bring a measure of relief and abundance to all, regardless of their social standing. In the days leading up to the summoning, the city would be alive with various events and activities designed to foster a sense of unity and shared purpose. Free meals would be provided in the plazas, allowing people from all walks of life to break bread together and share in the joy and anticipation of the rains. Performers and storytellers would regale the crowds with tales of past summonings, while musicians and dancers filled the streets with rhythm and movement.

The well-to-do water mages and affluent citizens enjoyed a life of luxury, their homes adorned with lavish decorations in anticipation of the summoning. They held extravagant feasts and threw lavish parties, reveling in their good fortune and the gifts that the rain would bring. Meanwhile, the less fortunate members of society – the Nulls and the poor – struggled to make ends meet in the shadow of the city's opulence. They lived in ramshackle dwellings on the outskirts of town, their homes devoid of the extravagant decorations that adorned the mansions of the wealthy. While they too looked forward to the rain summoning, their celebrations were marked by a quiet resilience rather than ostentatious displays of wealth. With the afternoon sun blazing overhead, casting its sweltering heat upon the city, the preparations for the rain summoning continued unabated. Workers toiled tirelessly to erect stages and pavilions where musicians and performers would entertain the crowds during the week-long celebration. Food vendors set up stalls offering a smorgasbord of exotic dishes and delicacies, their fragrant aromas wafting through the air.

In the city's public spaces, murals and sculptures depicting the miraculous power of the water mages were being created, each piece of art a testament to the vital role these gifted individuals played in their society. The rain summoning was a time to honor and celebrate the mages, but it also served as a poignant reminder of the deep divisions that existed within their world. People from all walks of life mingled together, their faces alight with excitement and anticipation for the rain that would soon bless their arid land.

"Ah, the marketplace," Caspian exclaimed, "a veritable treasure trove of delights and curiosities. It's always such a treat to explore its many offerings."

Raena nodded in agreement, her eyes scanning the vibrant stalls for anything that caught her fancy.

"Indeed, dear brother. And it's even more bustling than usual, given the upcoming summoning. I do love the energy and vitality of this place."

While they strolled through the marketplace, the stark contrast between the opulent displays and the ragged street vendors was apparent. The rich and powerful water mages, adorned in extravagant robes, browsed through luxurious wares, while the Nulls, dressed in tattered clothing, scrambled to make a living with their meager offerings. Zarek, navigated the market with ease, his head held high as he led the group through the bustling crowd while holding Raenas hand.

"Come, my friends," Zarek urged them.

"I know of a fascinating spot that specializes in magical artifacts and weaponry. I think you'll find it most intriguing, Prince Aldric."

As they approached the stall, they were greeted by a dazzling array of enchanted items, each one shimmering with its own unique aura. Swords that seemed to hum with energy hung alongside enchanted amulets, and crystal orbs glowed with the promise of untold power. Aldric's eyes widened with curiosity as he examined the array of magical artifacts.

"This is truly a remarkable collection, Zarek. I've never seen such an assortment of enchanted items in one place."

Zarek grinned, clearly pleased with Aldric's reaction.

"I thought you might appreciate it. The merchant who runs this stall has a knack for finding the most extraordinary pieces."

Caspian, accidentally knocked over a small stack of enchanted parchments, causing them to emit a shower of sparks as they fluttered to the ground.

"Oops," he chuckled sheepishly, "my apologies. It seems I'm a bit of a hazard in these close quarters."

Raena smirked, rolling her eyes playfully at her brother's clumsiness. "Caspian, you could trip over a shadow if given the chance. But we wouldn't have you any other way."

The merchant, a wily old man with a twinkle in his eye, seized the opportunity presented by Caspian's blunder.

"Ah, young sir," he said with a knowing smile," it seems that fate has conspired to introduce you to my collection of enchanted parchments. These are no ordinary scrolls, I assure you. They contain spells and incantations from far-off lands, some of which are lost to the sands of time."

Aldric, intrigued by the merchant's sales pitch, picked up one of the fallen parchments and examined it closely.

"Fascinating," he mused.

"I've never seen such an eclectic mix of spells. How did you come by them?"

The merchant leaned in conspiratorially, his voice dropping to a whisper.

"Ah, my dear sir, that is a tale best left for another time. Suffice it to say, I have traveled far and wide, and I have made some rather unusual acquaintances in my time."

Raena, her interest piqued, picked up another parchment and began to read its contents.

"The writing on these parchments is not something I'm familiar with."

Zarek, intrigued by the mysterious parchments, examined one as well.

"I must admit, I haven't seen anything quite like this either. What language is this written in?"

The merchant flashed a sly grin.

"Ah, that is part of their allure, my lord. The language is an ancient dialect, known only to a select few. It is said that some contain spells of great power, while others hold the secrets to long-lost magics. They are truly one-of-a-kind treasures."

Zarek, raised a skeptical eyebrow.

"And how do we know these spells are genuine? I imagine deciphering their true nature would be no small feat."

The merchant chuckled knowingly.

"That is the beauty of these parchments, my lord. The very mystery that surrounds them only adds to their value. Acquiring the knowledge to decipher them is a journey unto itself, and one that could lead to untold power and wisdom."

Raena, her interest piqued, decided to negotiate for the parchments.

"Very well, how much do you ask for these mysterious scrolls?"

The merchant rubbed his hands together, sensing an opportunity for profit.

"For such rare and enigmatic items, I must ask for 300 gold pieces."

Caspian let out a low whistle and Zarek, scoffed at the asking price.

"300 gold pieces? I daresay that's a rather steep price for items whose value is still uncertain."

Raena smirked.

"Indeed, while these parchments may hold great potential, it seems their value is as enigmatic as their contents. I would offer you 30 gold pieces for the lot."

The merchant feigned offense, clutching his chest in mock shock.

"My dear lady, you wound me with such a low offer. These treasures are beyond compare, and their price should reflect their rarity. I could part with them for no less than 250 gold pieces."

Zarek, countered with a sly grin.

"Good merchant, we are not disputing the potential value of these parchments. However, we must also consider the time and resources we will need to invest in deciphering their secrets. As such, I believe 50 gold pieces is a fair price."

The merchant, sighed in resignation.

" Very well. It is clear that your keen minds will not be swayed. I accept your offer of 50 gold pieces. May the knowledge contained within these scrolls serve you well on your journeys."

Aldric, pleased by the haggling prowess of his companions, handed over the agreed-upon sum.

"Thank you, good merchant. I trust that we shall find these parchments to be well worth the investment."

With their new acquisition secured, the group continued their exploration of the marketplace, their noble status evident in their attire and bearing, they were treated with deference by merchants eager to secure their patronage. Continuing their journey through the market, the group encountered a young boy, no older than twelve, attempting to sell handmade clay pots. His clothes were ragged and dirty, and his eyes held a desperation that belied his years. He was a Null, one of the many unfortunate souls born without any magical abilities.

"Please, my lords and lady," the boy pleaded, holding out a small, crude pot.

"I've made these pots myself. I need to sell them to buy food for my family."

Zarek, his appearance softened by the boy's plight, exchanged a glance with the group before nodding.

"Very well, young man. I'll take two of your finest pots. And here, take these extra coins as well. It should help you and your family."

The boy's eyes lit up with gratitude, and he thanked him profusely before scurrying off to attend to other customers.

As they moved on, Raena wrapped his arm around Zarek, whispering.

"That was a kind and generous act, my love."

Zarek smiled gently.

"Even with the great divide between us, we are all part of this kingdom. We must remember that and do what we can to uplift one another."

——— · . ˚ ☆: *.) .* :☆˚ . ———

18

The day progressed and Raena guided the group towards the Temple of Melusine, a sacred place where water mages sought the goddess's blessing before important rituals. This year, Raena will perform the sacred Rain Summoning instead of her mother, and she wished to offer her prayers to Melusine for a successful ceremony. With the city eagerly awaiting the rain summoning ceremony, the Temple of the Water Goddess Melusine took center stage in the preparations. The temple, a magnificent structure made of shimmering blue stone, stood proudly in the heart of the city as a symbol of hope and renewal. Its tall, graceful spires seemed to reach for the heavens, as if pleading for the blessing of the rain.

The temple's exterior was adorned with intricate carvings and reliefs depicting Melusine, the goddess of water, along with scenes of rain, rivers, and fertile lands. The goddess was often depicted with a serpentine lower body, symbolizing her connection to the life-giving waters. As the day of the summoning approached, the temple was draped with lush, cascading garlands of flowers, their vibrant colors and sweet fragrance enveloping the sacred space in an air of reverence and celebration. Within the temple, the atmosphere was one of quiet intensity as the priests and priestesses of Melusine readied themselves for the pivotal ceremony. Dressed in flowing, azure robes embroidered with silver thread, they moved gracefully through the hallowed halls, their voices a soft murmur of prayers and incantations dedicated to their patron goddess.

The temple's interior was a reflection of the world they sought to create through the rain summoning – a lush, fertile oasis amid the arid desert landscape. The walls were adorned with rich tapestries depicting the goddess Melusine and the abundant life that water could bring, while the floors were laid with smooth tiles that mimicked the flow of water. In the center of the temple stood a large, circular pool of crystal-clear water, its surface reflecting the flickering light of the numerous candles that illuminated the sacred space, and an enormous statue of Melusine, resplendent in her flowing robes and holding her sacred water staff, her benevolent gaze inspiring both awe and reverence in all who beheld her. The high priestess of Melusine, a wise and regal woman with deep, knowing eyes, led her fellow priests and priestesses in a series of sacred rituals. They gathered around the central pool, their voices raised in a hauntingly beautiful chant that echoed through the temple, sending shivers down the spines of those who heard it.

In the days leading up to the ceremony, the priests and priestesses spent long hours in meditation and prayer, honing their connection to the goddess Melusine and the elemental forces of water. They practiced their most potent water spells, the air around them alive with the energy of their magic, and submerged themselves in the central pool, seeking communion with the very essence of water itself. With the group approaching the Temple of Melusine, Aldric couldn't help but marvel at the breathtaking architecture and the palpable energy that seemed to radiate from the sacred structure. Raena, sensing Aldric's awe, gave him a smile.

"You've never seen anything quite like this, have you, Prince Aldric?" she teased.

"You're about to witness the very heart of our world's magic and the hope it brings to our people."

Zarek nodded in agreement, his eyes filled with pride as he looked upon the temple.

"Indeed, this is the source of our power and the key to our survival." Caspian, chimed in with a chuckle.

"Just imagine, dear sister, the fate of our world resting in your delicate hands. No pressure, of course."

Raena laughed and swatted at Caspian, feigning annoyance but secretly relishing the challenge that lay ahead.

"You always know how to make everything sound so dramatic, Caspian. But in all seriousness, I am prepared and honored to perform the ritual."

As they entered the temple, Aldric could feel the weight of the spiritual significance that permeated the sacred space. The air was charged with energy and anticipation, as if the very walls were alive with the power of the water mages and the prayers of the people.

Raena, eager to share her knowledge explained about the sacred relic they keep in the temple.

"The temple is also home to the Water Hearth. During the Rain Summoning ritual, I will channel my powers through the crystal, allowing me to summon a deluge of rain that will nourish our world for another year."

Aldric, unable to contain his curiosity, asked.

"So, what exactly is the Water Hearth? I've heard tales of its power, but I've never seen it up close."

Zarek decided to share some of the history and lore surrounding the Rain Summoning and the Water Hearth.

"The Water Hearth itself is a truly unique and enigmatic artifact. It is said to be a fragment of the heart of the goddess Melusine, imbued with her divine essence. As the legend goes, Melusine wept for our world's suffering, and her tears crystallized to form the Water Hearth. To this day, it remains the most potent source of water magic in our world."

Aldric, fascinated by the rich history and lore, asked, "And how did your people come to possess such a treasure?"

Raena, her eyes sparkling with pride, answered, "It's said that our ancestors were guided by Melusine to the heart of the desert, where they found the crystal. They built this temple around it to honor the goddess and to safeguard the crystal's power. And since that time, the water mages have been responsible for the Rain Summoning ritual, ensuring the survival of our people."

Caspian chimed in.

"But the power of the Water Hearth must be wielded with great care and responsibility. The ritual itself is very taxing on the summoner and it requires the water mage to enter a deep meditative state, where they commune with the goddess Melusine herself. It is during this communion that they receive her guidance and blessing to summon the rain."

The group continued their tour of the temple, coming across a magnificent mural depicting the history of the Rain Summoning and the royal family's connection to Melusine. Raena gestured towards it and said.

"As you can see, our family is said to be direct descendants of Melusine herself, which is why only we can harness enough power to perform the Rain Summoning. It is our birthright and our duty to ensure the survival and prosperity of our people"

Aldric studied the mural, awestruck by the intricate details and vibrant colors.

"The artistry is incredible. It must have taken years to complete."

Zarek nodded, his eyes tracing the mural's timeline.

"Indeed. The mural serves as a reminder of our people's struggle, resilience, and our sacred duty to provide for them."

Caspian, pointed to a particularly dramatic scene on the mural.

"Ah, look at that! There's our great-great-grandmother performing the ritual. I've heard she summoned the most torrential rains the kingdom had ever seen! That year, the crops were so bountiful, they had feasts for months."

Raena laughed and shook her head.

Aldric curios asked.

"What happens if the water mage fails to properly commune with Melusine? Is there a risk involved in performing the ritual?"

Raena's expression grew somber.

"There is always an element of risk, Prince Aldric. In the past, there have been instances where water mages were unable to establish a connection with Melusine, leading to a failed summoning. The consequences of such a failure can be dire, as our world relies heavily on the water summoned during the ritual."

Zarek placed a reassuring hand on Raena's shoulder.

"Worry not, my love. I have every confidence in your abilities, and I know you've trained extensively for this moment. Our people believe in you, and so do I."

Raena smiled at Zarek's unwavering support, her eyes filled with determination.

"Thank you, Zarek. I will do everything in my power to ensure a successful Rain Summoning."

As they neared the inner sanctum of the temple, Raena explained her intention to offer a silent prayer to Melusine, seeking the goddess's guidance and blessings for the upcoming ritual. The group entered the inner sanctum, and Aldric's breath caught in his throat as he beheld the stunning statue of the water goddess Melusine. The craftsmanship was exquisite, with flowing lines and intricate details that captured the essence of the goddess. It was almost as if Melusine herself was standing before them, her divine presence filling the space. Raena knelt before the statue, her hands clasped in prayer, while Zarek, Caspian, and Aldric stood a respectful distance away, giving her a moment of privacy. As Aldric studied the statue, he couldn't help but notice the uncanny resemblance between Raena and the depiction of Melusine. It was as if the goddess's features were mirrored in Raena's own, from the curve of her cheekbones to the shape of her eyes.

Aldric, intrigued, turned to Zarek and whispered.

"Do you see the resemblance between Raena and the statue of Melusine? It's quite remarkable."

Zarek, glancing at the statue and then back at Raena, chuckled softly.

"You know, I've never really noticed it before, but now that you mention it, the resemblance is indeed uncanny."

Caspian chuckled and added.

"Well, they do say our family is directly descended from Melusine. Perhaps her divine beauty has been passed down through the generations."

He then turned to Raena, who had just finished her prayer, and jokingly said.

"Raena, dear sister, have you been holding out on us? Are you secretly the goddess Melusine in disguise?"

Raena rolled her eyes and laughed, her previous solemnity replaced by a lighthearted air.

"If I were truly the goddess Melusine in disguise," Raena retorted playfully, "I wouldn't have let you get away with so many outrageous antics growing up, dear brother."

Caspian feigned shock, pressing a hand to his chest.

"Why, Ren, whatever do you mean? I was the very model of propriety."

Raena raised an eyebrow and listed off a few incidents with a smirk.

"Oh, like the time you replaced my perfume with fish oil? Or when you filled Zarek's boots with slime just before the Spring Ball? And let's not forget the infamous incident involving a barrel of frogs and the royal council meeting."

Zarek shook his head, laughing.

"Ah, yes, the great frog fiasco. That one will go down in history."

Caspian grinned, unrepentant.

"All in good fun, I assure you. I was merely keeping things lively at court."

Raena scoffed, amused.

"Well, if I were truly Melusine, I would have smote you for some of those pranks. But alas, I am but a mere mortal, destined to endure my brother's mischief."

The group shared a laugh, their spirits light and jovial as they left the temple. Aldric felt welcomed and warmed by the camaraderie between Raena, Zarek, and Caspian, and he looked forward to witnessing the Rain Summoning and supporting Raena in her sacred role.

—— · ｡˚ ☆: *.☽ .* :☆˚ . ——

19

A week before the Rain Summoning ritual, Raena began her preparations in earnest. There were numerous tasks and ceremonies she had to complete to be fully prepared for the sacred event. The royal family, the priests, and the priestesses all had their respective roles to play, ensuring that every aspect of the ritual was perfectly executed. Raena started her week by attending a purification ceremony held by the high priestess. She was led to a sacred pool within the temple, where the waters were said to have been blessed by Melusine herself. The high priestess chanted ancient prayers as she carefully washed Raena's body, symbolically cleansing her of any impurities and preparing her for the divine task ahead. Following the purification, Raena entered a period of fasting and reflection, designed to heighten her spiritual connection with Melusine. She consumed only small amounts of fruits, nuts, and water, and spent hours each day in quiet contemplation within the temple's meditation chambers. These chambers were adorned with beautiful murals depicting the many forms and aspects of Melusine, further inspiring Raena's connection to the goddess.

Throughout the week, Raena attended lessons with the temple's priests and priestesses, refining her mastery of water magic. They taught her intricate incantations, delicate hand gestures, and powerful chants, all aimed at enhancing her abilities for the Rain Summoning. The priests and priestesses also shared the rich history of the ritual, impressing upon Raena the importance of her role in the survival of their people. Zarek, Caspian, and Aldric observed Raena's preparations with admiration and awe. They offered their unwavering support, attending the ceremonies and lessons as spectators, and providing Raena with encouragement and comfort in her moments of doubt or exhaustion. The day before the ritual, Raena and the temple's clergy participated in a rehearsal. They practiced the complex choreography of the Rain Summoning, ensuring that each movement, each word, and each gesture was perfectly synchronized.

The priests and priestesses performed blessings and invocations, calling upon Melusine's favor and asking for her guidance in the ritual. Incense filled the temple with a sweet, heady aroma, and the sound of their voices melded into a haunting, beautiful melody that echoed through the hallowed halls.

The final night before the Rain Summoning, Raena was given a ceremonial robe crafted by the temple's most skilled artisans. The robe was made of the finest silks and embroidered with intricate patterns representing the water element and the goddess Melusine. The royal family gathered in the temple for a solemn vigil, praying for the success of the ritual and the continued prosperity of their people.

***

Within the shadows of the mine, Kael worked in secret, his makeshift laboratory hidden deep within a narrow crevice. His focus never wavered as he delicately measured and mixed the volatile components, his eyes narrowed in concentration, sweat beading on his brow. The smallest error could result in catastrophe, and he was all too aware of the stakes that rested upon his shoulders. The air within the crevice was heavy with the acrid scent of the chemicals, a constant reminder of the precariousness of our situation. As Kael continued his painstaking work, the rest of us carried on with our assigned tasks, our hearts heavy with apprehension and our minds filled with worry for our comrade. At times, Kael would emerge from the shadows, his face drawn and pale, but his eyes shining with determination. He would share his progress with us in hushed tones, each new discovery a glimmer of hope in the darkness that enveloped us. Despite the weight of the burden he bore, Kael never faltered, and his unyielding resolve only served to strengthen our own.

As the days passed, the tension within the mine grew palpable. Each creak of a support beam or distant rumble of machinery seemed to reverberate through our very souls, setting our nerves on edge. The guards, sensing the unrest, became more watchful and unpredictable, their eyes narrowed in suspicion as they prowled the tunnels, seeking any sign of treachery or deceit. Our clandestine meetings became fraught with danger, every whispered word and furtive glance carrying the potential to betray our secret. Each time we gathered to discuss our progress or refine our plans, we risked discovery, and the ever-present threat of retribution loomed large over our heads.

One particularly tense evening, as we huddled in the shadows, Kael shared his latest breakthrough – a potent concoction that he believed could dissolve the metal of our shackles without harming our flesh. His voice trembled with a mixture of excitement and fear, his hands shaking as he held up a vial of the viscous liquid. "We must be careful," he warned, his eyes meeting each of ours in turn.

"One false move, and this could all go up in flames."

Gavril nodded solemnly, his eyes reflecting the weight of our situation.

"We can't afford to make any mistakes. Our lives, and the lives of our people, depend on our success."

I swallowed hard, feeling the pressure mounting as the gravity of our plan settled upon me.

"What's our next move, Kael?" I asked, my voice barely audible, even within the confines of our hidden alcove.

Kael took a deep breath, steadying himself.

"First, we need to test the concoction on a small piece of metal, similar to our shackles. If it works as intended, we can proceed with confidence."

As we dispersed to resume our duties, I couldn't shake the feeling that we were being watched, that the very shadows themselves held secrets we could not fathom. The tension in the air was palpable, like a noose tightening around our necks. In the following days, we worked tirelessly, stealing moments when we could to gather the materials needed for our daring escape. Our hearts raced with every close call, our breaths caught in our throats as we narrowly evaded the watchful eyes of our captors. Late one night, as we reconvened in the darkness, Kael revealed the results of his test.

"It worked," he whispered, his voice shaking with a mixture of relief and trepidation.

"The metal dissolved, just as we hoped."

A collective sigh of relief passed through our group, and for the first time, we allowed ourselves to believe that freedom might be within our grasp.

"Remember," Gavril cautioned, his voice low and urgent, "we cannot let our guard down. The most dangerous part of our plan is yet to come. We must be prepared for anything."

20

─── · ₀° ☆: *.) .* :☆° . ───

The day of the Rain Summoning Ritual finally arrived, and the atmosphere in the city was a mixture of excitement and nervous anticipation. The streets were filled with citizens from all walks of life, each one eager to bear witness to the sacred event that would determine the fate of their kingdom. Vibrant banners and garlands of fresh flowers adorned the buildings, while the pleasant scent of incense filled the air, invoking a sense of reverence and unity among the people. The sun casted a warm golden light upon the city, as if the goddess Melusine herself was smiling down upon her subjects. The royal guards lined the procession route, their polished armor gleaming in the sunlight, while musicians played joyful tunes on their instruments, further adding to the festive atmosphere. In the heart of the city stood the grand temple of Melusine, a magnificent structure of white marble with intricate carvings depicting the goddess's many forms and the history of the Rain Summoning Ritual. The temple's entrance was flanked by two enormous statues of Melusine, her graceful figure serving as a constant reminder of the divine presence that guided and protected the kingdom.

With the time for the ritual drewing near, the citizens began to gather around the temple, their faces a mixture of hope and anxiety. The temple's courtyard was transformed into an open-air amphitheater, where the people could observe the sacred proceedings. A raised platform had been erected in the center, upon which Raena and the temple's clergy would perform the ritual, visible to all who had come to witness the event. Hours before the ritual was set to begin, Raena undergone a final series of preparations. These rites were steeped in ancient tradition, drawing on the wisdom and experiences of countless generations of water mages who had come before her. The sanctum's walls were adorned with intricate murals depicting the legends of the goddess Melusine and the past Rain Summoning rituals, each scene a reminder of the gravity and honor of the task that lay before her. In the dimly lit chamber, Raena stood before the high priestess, who held a delicate clay bowl filled with a mixture of sacred oils and crushed gemstones. Each ingredient was carefully chosen for its unique properties and connections to the goddess Melusine. The high priestess applied the fragrant, shimmering paste to Raena's forehead and she began to recite an ancient prayer, her voice steady and resonant.

"By the grace of Melusine, we anoint you with the essence of her divine spirit. May this elixir grant you the protection and favor of the goddess, as you seek to summon the life-giving rains."

The high priestess then continued to anoint Raena's wrists and ankles, all the while reciting more sacred verses that evoked the power and wisdom of Melusine. As the oils soaked into Raena's skin, she felt a profound sense of calm and confidence wash over her, as if the goddess herself was infusing her with the strength and assurance she needed to succeed. With the anointment complete, Raena gazed into the eyes of the high priestess, who offered her a reassuring smile.

"You are ready, Princess Raena. The goddess's blessing is upon you, and we all have faith in your abilities. Carry the hopes of our people with you as you perform the sacred ritual."

The sun dipped below the horizon, signaling the start of the evening's proceedings, Raena joined her family and the temple's clergy in a solemn procession through the city streets. The citizens watched in awe and reverence as the princess, resplendent in her ceremonial attire and imbued with the power of the elements, made her way towards the temple courtyard. Hushed whispers filled the air, as the onlookers marveled at Raena's regal bearing and the sense of divine purpose that radiated from her. The procession wound its way through the city, a path illuminated by flickering torchlight, the citizens lining the streets bowed their heads in reverence. They marveled not only at Raena's grace and beauty but also at the presence of Queen Isadora, who walked beside her daughter, providing a comforting presence. The queen, dressed in her own ceremonial attire, looked every bit as regal and dignified as her daughter. Her eyes held a mixture of pride and concern, knowing the tremendous responsibility and burden that Raena was about to shoulder.

Upon reaching the temple courtyard, the crowd parted, allowing Raena and her entourage to ascend the steps leading to the raised platform. The temple's grand facade was illuminated by torchlight, casting a warm, inviting glow over the sacred space. Raena and her mother, Queen Isadora took their place on the platform. The high priestess, with a solemn and reverent expression beckoned to a group of acolytes, who emerged from the temple, carrying a stunning artifact known as the Hearth of Water. This ancient artifact, said to have been crafted by the goddess Melusine herself, was a breathtaking sight to behold. Made of a crystalline material that shimmered with iridescent hues, the Hearth of Water was carved into the shape of a lotus blossom, its petals gently cradling a pool of the purest water known to mankind. The water within the Hearth was believed to be a direct conduit to Melusine's realm, and it was this sacred liquid that Raena would use to summon the much-needed rains.

The high priestess handed the queen and Raena a ceremonial dagger, its blade gleaming in the torchlight. With a nod of understanding, both mother and daughter made a small, precise cut on the palm of their hands, allowing a few drops of their royal blood to fall into the sacred waters of the Hearth. The blood swirled within the crystal-clear liquid, merging with the divine essence of Melusine. With the blood sacrifice offered, the high priestess intoned a powerful incantation, her voice resonating throughout the temple courtyard. The crowd watched in awe, holding their breath as they awaited the outcome of the ritual. Raena, her eyes closed in deep concentration, began to move her body in a graceful, flowing dance.

This was the Water Dance, a sacred and ancient performance passed down through generations of water mages. Her movements were fluid and elegant, each step and gesture carefully choreographed to channel the goddess's power and summon the life-giving rains.

Queen Isadora, standing at Raena's side, supported her daughter's efforts by providing a steady flow of her own magical energy.

With each elegant step and fluid gesture, Raena summoned forth her innate magical energies, focusing her entire being on the task at hand. This was a feat that demanded incredible strength and focus, as she sought to channel the very essence of the goddess and her dominion over the waters of the world.

As the intensity of her dance increased, Raena began to weave intricate patterns in the air with her hands, her movements precise and mesmerizing. As she did so, the sacred waters within the Hearth of Water began to respond, stirred by the power of her magic. The crystal-clear liquid began to rise, coiling around Raena like a shimmering serpent, its sparkling droplets catching the torchlight in a dazzling display of refracted light. The crowd watched in awe as Raena became enshrouded in a vortex of swirling water, her powerful magic seeming to defy the very laws of nature. The water, guided by her will and her connection to Melusine, danced around her in an elaborate, ever-shifting pattern, a testament to the strength of her abilities. The high priestess and the assembled clergy continued their haunting incantations, their voices rising and falling in time with Raena's movements, further amplifying the magical energies at play.

The crowd watched, their collective breath held, as the air above the temple began to shimmer and undulate. Slowly, almost imperceptibly at first, wisps of clouds began to form in the sky, gradually coalescing into thick, heavy storm clouds. Raena's dance reached a fevered pitch, her body moving with the fluidity and grace of water itself, her magic becoming an almost tangible force. The clouds darkened, and a hushed, anticipatory silence fell over the gathered crowd, the first drops of rain began to fall. The life-giving droplets kissed the parched earth, and a collective cheer erupted from the throng of onlookers. The Rain Summoning had been successful. However, Raena's dance did not cease. Instead, she continued to weave her intricate patterns, her connection to Melusine deepening, her power growing exponentially. The water vortex surrounding her surged and swirled, the droplets now reflecting a myriad of colors as they caught the light, creating an ethereal and otherworldly spectacle.

The rain intensified, spreading outwards, encompassing the entirety of the desert planet. The power and scope of the summoning were unparalleled, a testament to Raena's strength of her magic. The high priestess and the clergy marveled at the sheer magnitude of the rain, which continued to fall unabated. Their voices, now hushed and reverent, echoed the power and mystery of the divine as they bore witness to this miraculous event. For seven days and seven nights, the rain would continue to fall, nourishing the earth and replenishing the parched lands. Yet, as the vortex of water surrounding Raena began to dissipate, her body trembled with the strain of maintaining the summoning. Her breathing grew shallow, her movements faltering, as the energy required to perform the ritual threatened to consume her.

Queen Isadora, sensing her daughter's imminent collapse, rushed to Raena's side. As Raena completed the final, intricate steps of her dance, she lost consciousness and crumpled to the ground. Queen Isadora caught her just before she hit the cold, wet stones, her heart heavy with concern.

***

At last the time has arrived, as we gathered in a narrow crevice deep within the mines, Kael detailed the final steps of our plan. We huddled around him, our faces etched with a mixture of hope and trepidation.

"Alright, here's what we need to do," Kael began, his voice barely a whisper.

"I've prepared enough of the concoction for each of us. We'll apply it to our shackles simultaneously, using these crude brushes I've fashioned from discarded materials."

He paused, looking each of us in the eye.

"Once our shackles are weakened, we can break them with a swift strike from a rock or other hard object. But we must be cautious. If we're discovered before we've freed ourselves, it's all over."

We nodded in agreement, and we exchanged determined glances. It was clear that we were all aware of the stakes. There was no turning back now. Gavril stepped forward, his voice calm but firm.

"We'll need to synchronize our actions. When the guards change shifts during the rain summoning, that's our window of opportunity. We must act quickly and efficiently. There can be no hesitation."

We nodded, our hearts pounding in our chests, the gravity of the situation sinking in. Each of us carried the weight of the lives that depended on our success. As the hour approached, we could feel the tension mounting. The very air around us seemed to crackle with electricity, our nerves frayed as we prepared to take the greatest risk of our lives. My mind raced, a torrent of thoughts and emotions threatening to consume me. I could feel the anger that had been smoldering within me for years, fueled by the suffering of my people, finally threatening to burst into an uncontrollable inferno. The determination to see this through, to free myself and my fellow slaves, pushed me forward, even as the voice of doubt whispered in the darkest recesses of my mind.

The rain summoning began, bringing a cacophony of thunder, the torrential downpour outside the mines offering us a measure of cover. The guards and mine overseers were preoccupied, leaving us with the brief window of opportunity we so desperately needed. My hands shook as I dipped the makeshift brush into the vial of Kael's concoction, the viscous liquid clinging to the bristles. I exchanged a resolute nod with Gavril and Kael, our unspoken understanding clear – it was now or never. With a deep breath, I carefully applied the potent substance to the shackles that bound me, my heart pounding in my chest as the acidic mixture began to hiss and bubble, eating away at the metal. I glanced around, noting the same mixture of anticipation and fear reflected in the eyes of my comrades.

As the weakened shackles strained against our wrists, I looked to Gavril and Kael, waiting for the signal to break free. The seconds ticked by, each one feeling like an eternity as the thunder rumbled overhead. Finally, Gavril gave the signal, a swift nod of his head, and we struck our shackles with all the strength we could muster. The sound of metal snapping echoed through the mine, mingling with the cacophony of the storm outside. A fierce sense of triumph surged through me as the broken chains fell away, the weight of years of bondage lifted from my body. But there was no time for celebration, for we were far from safe. Now, we had to make our escape. With hearts pounding and adrenaline coursing through our veins, we crept through the shadows, each step a silent prayer that we would not be discovered. The storm continued to rage above, masking our movements as we inched closer to the surface, and, we hoped, to freedom.

Our escape route had been meticulously planned, winding through the least monitored sections of the mines. We were like shadows, slipping between the flickering light of the torches that sporadically illuminated the rocky tunnels. Every clatter of chains, every echo of a distant voice made our hearts skip a beat, the specter of discovery a constant threat. My mind was a whirlwind of thoughts, the anticipation and fear intertwining in a dance as wild as the storm above us. Images of the overseers, their cruel smiles, the whip in their hands, kept flashing in my mind.

"*Not tonight*," I told myself.

"*Tonight, we break free.*"

The memories of my people's suffering fueled my resolve. The countless days in the mines, the scars, both physical and mental, the echoing cries of torment – they were all engraved in my soul, a constant reminder of why we needed to succeed.

"Stay close," Gavril's voice barely reached me over the deafening rain. His eyes were alight with a fiery determination that reflected my own. We had all lost too much to turn back now. We pressed on, our progress painstakingly slow. With every step, we edged closer to the surface, to the world outside, a world from which we'd been cruelly ripped apart.

Suddenly, a distant clatter echoed through the mines, followed by the muffled voices of the guards. We froze, our breaths hitching in our throats. Had we been discovered? I could feel the icy tendrils of fear snaking its way around my heart, squeezing it in a vise-like grip. The guards' voices grew louder, their words indistinguishable but the tone unmistakably urgent. Gavril signaled for us to press ourselves against the rocky wall, our bodies merging with the shadows. The voices grew louder, and then, much to our relief, gradually faded. We allowed ourselves to breathe again, a collective sigh echoing through the tunnel.

"We need to move. Now," Kael urged, his voice shaking slightly. His eyes met mine, and I saw the same burning determination there, the same desperate need to be free. With renewed urgency, we pushed forward, clawing our way through the oppressive darkness.

My senses heightened, every sound - the patter of rain above, the distant murmur of voices, even the steady rhythm of our own breaths - was amplified, echoing menacingly in the narrow confines of the tunnel. When we neared the surface, a gust of wind laced with the scent of rain and freedom rushed to meet us. My heart pounded in my chest, the rhythm syncopating with the thunder that roared overhead.

"We're close," Gavril breathed, his eyes reflecting the storm raging outside. The tunnel ended abruptly, opening to the tempestuous night. The guards were mere silhouettes against the rain-soaked landscape, their attention focused on the massive containers they were scrambling to fill. Their laughter and casual banter drifted towards us, a grotesque melody that starkly contrasted with the gravity of our situation. Gavril and Kael shared a glance, and then with a nod, we stepped out into the storm. The rain felt like salvation, each drop washing away years of torment, fear, and submission. Yet, it was a fleeting moment of respite. We were still in the heart of danger. We moved with the shadows, the darkness our only shield against the prying eyes of the guards. My heart pounded a relentless drumbeat in my chest, echoing the fear and anticipation coursing through my veins.

Every step was a calculated risk, every breath a silent prayer. Thoughts of the overseers discovering our empty chains, the alarm that would inevitably follow, and the brutal retribution that would be meted out if we were caught fueled my resolve.

"No turning back," I muttered under my breath, the words barely audible over the storm's cacophony.

My inner fire, that indomitable spirit that had seen me through countless beatings and endless days of toil, roared defiantly. A shout cut through the sound of the rain, followed by a pointed finger. My blood ran cold. Had we been spotted?

But the guards' attention was diverted towards a fellow overseer who'd slipped, his precious container of water spilling. Laughter echoed through the storm, the guards oblivious to the drama unfolding in their midst. And then, we were past them, the mine and its horrors disappearing behind a curtain of rain. An expanse of untamed wilderness stretched before us - a world free from chains and whips, a world where we could simply exist.

The storm continued to rage around us, a testament to the chaos within. Yet, amid the thunder and the rain, a sense of hope kindled within me. We were free, against all odds. We had defied our captors, our fate, and had emerged from the depths of despair into the promise of a new dawn.

"Tonight, we are no longer slaves," I vowed, my words devoured by the storm.

But as we vanished into the desert, I felt a pang of unease. Something gnawed at the back of my mind, a sense of foreboding that I couldn't shake off. A strange sensation, like a ripple in the fabric of my being, echoed within me, intensifying with each step we took. It was as though an invisible thread that connected me to something - or someone - was being stretched thin, on the verge of snapping.

Raena. Her name resonated in my mind, a haunting melody in the cacophony of my thoughts. She was the princess, the untouchable, living a world apart from the suffering we endured. There should have been no reason for her to be in danger, but this unsettling feeling kept gnawing at me, a silent scream in the back of my mind.

I tried to dismiss it, attributing it to the stress and fear of our escape. But the feeling wouldn't abate. It clung to me, a spectral shroud that no amount of logic could dispel.

"Something's wrong," I muttered to myself, the words barely a whisper in the howling wind.

"What?" Kael, ever vigilant, had picked up on my murmur.

"It's... It's nothing," I lied, shaking my head.

Now was not the time to discuss inexplicable feelings, not when our lives hung by a thread. But as we pressed on, navigating the treacherous desert under the storm's wrath, I couldn't shake the feeling. A sense of dread, like an icy hand clutching my heart, only grew stronger. It made no sense. She was a princess, swaddled in the safety of her castle, far away from the horrors of the mines. And yet, my gut churned with a foreboding that I couldn't ignore.

Raena was in danger. I didn't know how or why, but I felt it in my very core, a primal instinct that was impossible to ignore.

"Is everything okay, Ash?" Gavril asked, his brows furrowed in concern.

I looked at him, my gaze lingering for a moment too long. There was a question in his eyes, an unspoken query that I wasn't ready to answer.

"I'm fine," I lied again, clenching my fists to hide their trembling. My voice was steady, belying the turmoil raging within me.

But as the storm raged on, so did my unease. It was a phantom pain, a ghostly sensation that refused to leave. Something was terribly wrong. And as much as I wanted to dismiss it as a figment of my overactive imagination, I knew better.

Raena was in danger. And I was powerless to help.

21

—— · ₀° ☆: *.) .* :☆° . ——

The storm raged outside and the streets and squares of the city turned into jubilant scenes of celebration. The people of Varidia rejoiced in the rain, children darting about with arms outstretched, their laughter echoing through the air. Adults followed suit, their joyous cheers punctuating the rhythmic patter of the raindrops. The rainfall was more than just a respite from the heat; it was a symbol of hope, a promise of life and prosperity after long, parched stretches of desert sun. Water collectors were set up across the city, funneling the precious rainfall into large reservoirs. Even as they celebrated, the people worked tirelessly, ensuring that not a single drop of the goddess' gift was wasted. The city was alive with energy and hope, a stark contrast to the quiet concern that gripped the royal palace. Inside the palace, the mood was somber.

Princess Raena lay motionless on her grand bed, her skin pale and her breathing shallow. The royal physician, a man of advanced years and vast experience, looked over her with a furrowed brow. His practiced hands moved with a calm precision as he examined the princess, his face a mask of deep concern. King Lucius, now weighed down by worry, stood by his wife Queen Isadora, their hands entwined. Beside them were their son, Prince Caspian, and Raena's fiancé, Zarek. Aldric, the visiting prince, completed the anxious assembly.

"Her vital signs are stable," the physician reported, his voice hushed in the quiet room.

"But her consciousness... it's as if she's locked away inside her own mind. She shows no reaction to external stimuli. It's unlike anything I've seen."

"Is there nothing you can do?" Queen Isadora asked, her voice barely more than a whisper.

"I have administered several restorative potions, but they've had no effect," he replied.

"Her body is not weakened, it is her spirit that seems to have retreated."

Silence fell over the room as the weight of the physician's words settled in. This was uncharted territory; there were no known cases of a mage entering such a state after a successful Rain Summoning.

"What do you mean her spirit has retreated?" Prince Caspian asked, breaking the silence.

"What could possibly cause such a thing?"

"That, I do not know," the physician admitted, his voice heavy with regret.

"I can only speculate that the enormous power she channeled during the ritual had unforeseen consequences."

Zarek stepped forward, his face lined with concern. His hand reached out to clasp Raena's, his touch gentle. The room was heavy with a silence that was only broken by the distant sound of the rain outside. Zarek's voice, when he finally spoke, was filled with desperation. "There must be something we can do. Some...some spell, some remedy. Anything."

The physician sighed heavily, a sorrowful look in his eyes.

"I wish there was, Lord Zarek. I have used all known methods within my reach. Her life-force is strong, her body healthy. It is her consciousness that has retreated inward, and I do not possess the means to reach it."

King Lucius, who had been silently observing the exchange, finally spoke, his voice deep and authoritative.

"Then we must find someone who does. Seek the scholars, the sages, anyone who may have knowledge about this. We must leave no stone unturned."

Throughout the city, the celebrations continued unabated, the populace oblivious to the royal family's plight. Days turned into nights, and the rain continued to pour, blanketing the city in a cool, soothing mist. The city's reservoirs were filling up, the parched land drinking greedily from the sky. As the seven-day storm approached its end, scholars, mages, and healers from across the kingdom were gathered in the palace, poring over ancient texts, consulting mystical artifacts, and casting divination spells in the hopes of finding a solution. The palace was abuzz with activity, a stark contrast to the serene stillness of the princess's chambers, where Raena lay, her condition unchanged. Throughout the course of the rain-soaked week, Zarek hardly ever left Raena's side. He sat beside her, holding her hand, whispering words of encouragement and love, and offering silent prayers to every deity he knew. Sleep was a stranger to him, chased away by his worry and the constant vigil he kept. The princess's chambers became his world, a space filled with an agonizing mix of love, hope, and despair.

He adamantly refused to leave her side. His heart ached at the sight of her, so vibrant and full of life not long ago, now lying so still and silent. He brushed a lock of her hair away from her face, his touch gentle and filled with longing.

"Raena," he whispered, his voice choked with emotion.

"You must come back to us."

Caspian watched his brother-in-law-to-be from the door of the room. He had always admired Zarek's strength and determination, but now he saw a different side of him, a vulnerability that he had never witnessed before. He approached Zarek, placing a comforting hand on his shoulder.

"Zarek, we will find a way. Raena is a fighter, and we are not going to give up on her."

Zarek turned to Caspian, his eyes filled with a desperate hope.

"I can't lose her, Caspian. She's my world, my everything."

Caspian nodded, understanding the depth of Zarek's feelings. He was his sister's most ardent supporter, her love, her partner.

"We all feel the same, Zarek. Raena means the world to us too. We will do everything in our power to bring her back."

Aldric, who had been quietly observing the conversation, finally spoke.

"We are exploring every avenue of knowledge we can. Scholars from across the kingdom are pouring over texts and ancient lore as we speak. I am confident that we will find a solution."

"I wish I could share your optimism, Aldric," Zarek replied, his voice barely more than a whisper. He turned his gaze back to Raena, his hand never leaving hers.

"But it's hard to hold onto hope when the love of your life is lying here, trapped in a world we cannot reach."

Aldric, although never having experienced such profound love, could understand Zarek's anguish. He offered a small, reassuring smile.

"In my experience, Zarek, it's precisely in these moments, when everything seems lost, that hope becomes our strongest ally. We will not abandon Raena, and we will not lose hope."

***

Within the quiet confines of her own mind, Princess Raena was far from unconscious. She found herself in a world of dreams, a realm that felt as real as the world she had left behind. This realm was not bound by the laws of reality but by the whims and fancies of her subconscious. Raena found herself walking along a mist-shrouded path, her surroundings unfamiliar and strangely beautiful. In this dreamscape, her typically confident and bold demeanor was replaced by a sense of curiosity and wonder. The rain-soaked foliage around her glistened with a surreal brilliance, casting a kaleidoscope of colors that danced and shimmered like the water that had enveloped her during the Rain Summoning. As she ventured deeper into the dream, a mysterious figure appeared in the distance, their form obscured by the swirling mists. Raena felt an inexplicable pull towards this enigmatic presence, her curiosity piqued. She called out to the figure, her voice echoing through the dreamlike landscape.

"Who are you? Show yourself!"

The figure remained silent, their form shifting and coalescing like the mists that surrounded them. Raena's impatience grew, her stubborn nature reasserting itself. She was a princess, after all, and she was not accustomed to being denied answers.

"I command you to reveal yourself!" she demanded, her tone imperious and authoritative.

As if in response to her command, the figure stepped forward, emerging from the mists. Their face remained hidden, their form indistinct and ever-changing. They raised a hand, beckoning Raena to follow them, their movements fluid and hypnotic. Raena hesitated, torn between her natural caution and an overwhelming desire to uncover the truth behind this enigmatic apparition.

Her curiosity won out, and she followed the figure as it led her through the dream, her heart pounding in anticipation. The further she ventured, the more the dreamscape seemed to evolve and change, becoming darker, more mysterious. The taste of rain lingered on her lips.

Raena delved deeper into her dream, a voice whispered in her ear. "Princess Raena, the path you walk is treacherous and unknown. The power you wielded has unlocked doors within your soul, doors that lead to secrets long forgotten."

Raena frowned, her arrogance and confidence rising to the surface. "I am not afraid. I am the Princess of Varidia, and I have conquered far greater challenges than this."

And as if in response, the dream shifted once more. Raena found herself standing in front of a grand and imposing door, its surface etched with intricate symbols that seemed to pulse with a life of their own. The door creaked open, revealing a realm of swirling mists and shadows. In the midst of the fog, two figures materialized. The first figure was that of a woman, her form shimmering like a mirage. She was radiant, an ethereal beauty that was impossible to ignore, yet her face remained obscured, hidden behind a veil of brilliant light. Raena felt a strange connection to this figure, an inexplicable familiarity that stirred something within her. Beside the woman, a second figure emerged. This one was distinctly masculine, his presence equally powerful and enigmatic. Like the woman, his face was obscured, adding to the mystery of his identity. He stood tall and commanding, his silhouette imposing amidst the swirling mists. Raena approached them, her heart pounding in her chest. "Who are you?" she demanded, her voice echoing through the dreamscape.

But the figures remained silent, their identities hidden behind their shimmering forms. The dream morphed once again, the foggy landscape dissolving around Raena to reveal a vast, boundless ocean. She gasped in surprise, her eyes wide as she took in the sight. Varidia was a desert planet; she had never seen so much water in one place. The ocean stretched out to the horizon, its surface reflecting the colors of the dream-sky above. It was beautiful and terrifying all at once. The woman figure appeared again, standing atop the waves, her form shimmering with a radiant light. She spread her arms wide, and as she did, the ocean seemed to respond, the waves rising and falling in a rhythmic dance. She was a part of the ocean, her energy intertwined with the water, a sense of power and tranquility radiating from her.

Raena, drawn by the spectacle, stepped closer. Her feet touched the edge of the water, and she could taste the salt in the air, the cool spray of the ocean mist against her skin. It was a sensation she had never experienced, and it sent a thrill of excitement coursing through her. The woman figure turned to face Raena, her form still shrouded in mystery. Raena felt a profound sense of connection to her, a familiarity that transcended the boundaries of the dream. She reached out towards the figure, her hand trembling slightly.
"Who are you?" she asked again, her voice echoing across the expanse of the ocean.

Before the woman figure could respond, the man figure stepped forward, his form solidifying from the mist. He reached out, placing a hand on the woman's shoulder. His touch seemed to send a ripple through the dream, the landscape shifting once more. Raena found herself standing on the precipice of a great chasm, the ground crumbling beneath her feet. Fear gripped her heart as she teetered on the edge, the abyss yawning before her.

"Who are you?" she demanded, her voice echoing off the unseen walls of the chasm.

But the figures remained silent, their identities still shrouded in mystery. The chasm yawned wider, and Raena stumbled, her heart pounding in her chest. She reached out, her hand groping for something solid, something real. But there was nothing. Just the cold, empty air of the dream. The dream began to fade. The figures, the chasm, the ocean, all dissolving into a swirl of colors and shapes. Raena reached out, trying to hold onto the dream, but it slipped through her fingers like smoke.

22

— · ˚ ☆: *.⊃ .* :☆˚ . —

A sense of disorientation filled Raena's senses as her eyes slowly fluttered open. The rich tapestry of her royal chambers greeted her, the familiar sight bringing a strange sense of comfort. Her body felt heavy, every muscle languid and sore. She moved to sit up, but a wave of dizziness washed over her, forcing her back onto the plush pillows. She remembered fragments of her dream, the taste of rain, the mysterious figures, the boundless ocean, and a sense of profound revelation. She felt a connection to that dream, a part of her that was still anchored in that otherworldly realm. Yet, it was slipping away from her, like wisps of smoke carried by the wind. She frowned, looking around the room, her memory a haze. Her gaze fell on a figure slumped in a chair by her bedside - Zarek.

She found herself reaching out, her hand trembling as she lightly touched his arm. At her touch, Zarek stirred, his eyes blinking open to meet hers. He woke with a start, his eyes, hazed with sleep, meeting hers. The shock registered on his face, followed by disbelief. He blinked, as if he was expecting her image to fade away, a cruel trick of a dream.

"Raena?" he breathed, his voice quivering, as if he dared not believe it. She gave a weak smile, her hand reaching out to touch his. He flinched at the contact, his gaze darting to her hand and then back to her face.

"Zarek..." she whispered, her voice hoarse and fragile.

He was by her side in an instant, his hand reaching out to tenderly touch her face. He studied her intently, his gaze filled with a mix of love and fear, as if trying to memorize every detail of her features.

"You're awake..." he murmured, his voice trembling with emotion. He leaned down, pressing a reverent kiss to her forehead.

"You're really awake."

"I... I think so," she replied, her own emotions bubbling to the surface.

She felt a tear escape her eye, sliding down her cheek. Zarek gently brushed it away, his touch feather light.

"You've been asleep for over a week," Zarek said softly, his voice barely a whisper.

"We didn't know when... if... you would wake."

His eyes, a vibrant emerald green, were haunted as they held hers.

"I feared...I feared I'd lost you, Ren."

Raena felt her heart ache. She had no recollection of what had happened, only the faint echoes of a dream that felt too real, too complex to be just a figment of her imagination. She looked at Zarek, his face pale and drawn, a testament to his unwavering devotion. She tried to speak, but her voice came out as a raspy whisper.

"Zarek... I'm sorry, for worrying you" she managed to croak, her throat aching with the effort.

Zarek shook his head, his expression softening.

"Don't apologize, I'm just glad you're back with me."

Zarek gently extricated his hand from hers, rising to his feet.

"Let me get you some water," he said, his voice soft. His gaze, however, held an intensity that belied his calm demeanor.

Moving across the room, he took a glass and filled it with water from a crystal decanter. The sound of the liquid splashing into the glass was a quiet symphony in the silent room. He returned to her side, Zarek's hand was steady, the glass of water held with a gentleness that was a stark contrast to the turmoil of emotions he'd just expressed. He presented it to her, his eyes meeting hers with a softness that only she was privy to.

"You must drink," he said, his voice firm yet tender.

"Your body needs to regain its strength."

Raena nodded, reaching out to accept the glass. Her hand shook slightly, the weight of it heavier than she remembered.

"Seems I can't even manage a glass of water," she muttered with a trace of her typical arrogance. It was forced, she knew, an attempt to regain a semblance of her usual confident facade.

Zarek's lips quirked in a fond smile. He carefully slid one arm behind her shoulders, lifting her gently, while his other hand held the glass to her lips. She drank deeply, the cool water soothing her parched throat.

"Easy, love," Zarek cautioned her gently, pulling the glass away after a few moments.

She had always been the confident one, the stubborn one who never needed help. Now, in her weakness, she was relying on Zarek. It was a new experience, one that both confused and comforted her. As she finished the water, she noticed Zarek studying her, a soft smile playing on his lips. He seemed to be holding back a comment.

"What?" she asked, the word more of a croak. But she raised an eyebrow in challenge, a silent dare for him to go on.

"I was just thinking," he began, setting the glass aside and helping her settle back against the pillows.

"When we were children, you used to boss me around. You'd command me to fetch you water from the oasis, even though it was just a few steps away."

She snorted at the memory, a faint smile tugging at her lips.

"And you would actually do it."

His chuckle was low and warm.

"I was besotted, even then. Always running around, trying to win the princess's favor."

Raena's lips curved in a more genuine smile now.

"Well, it seems not much has changed. You're still at my beck and call, Lord Zarek."

His laugh was a soft rumble in his chest.

"For you, my princess, always."

With each passing minute Raena regained some of her strength, so she recounted what she could remember of her dream to Zarek.

"It was... strange," she admitted, her gaze distant as she tried to recall the details.

"I was in a place... it was unlike anything I've ever seen. There was rain... and an ocean."

"An ocean?" Zarek's eyes widened in surprise.

Varidia was a desert planet, after all. They were both Water Mages, but they had only ever manipulated the water from the underground reservoirs and the scarce rainfall. An ocean was a foreign concept, a vast expanse of water they'd only read about in the ancient texts.

She nodded.

"And there were these... figures. A man and a woman. I couldn't see their faces, but I felt... drawn to them. Especially the woman. I... I think I know her, Zarek. But I can't remember from where."

Zarek was silent, his gaze thoughtful. His hand gently squeezed hers, his thumb tracing soothing circles on her skin.

"We'll figure it out, Raena. Together."

Zarek stood up and leaned down to press a tender kiss on Raena's forehead.

"I'll be right back. I need to let your family know you're awake, and I'll bring you something light to eat."

The palace was quiet, the usual hustle and bustle muted as if the entire household was holding its breath, waiting for news about their princess. Zarek made his way to the royal quarters, his steps echoing in the hushed silence. Upon reaching the door, he hesitated. His hand rose to knock but paused mid-air. Taking a deep breath, he steeled himself and rapped his knuckles against the polished wood.

The door opened, revealing the worried faces of Raena's parents. The King and Queen's expressions shifted from anxiety to hope as they took in Zarek's face.

"She's awake," he announced. Relief washed over the royal couple, their hands clasping together in silent prayer.

They thanked Zarek for his unwavering loyalty, his dedication to their daughter only solidifying their approval of their engagement. His next destination was the kitchen, where he requested a simple meal to be prepared for Raena. Auguste, set to work immediately, preparing a light soup with fresh bread on the side. With the tray in hand, he made his way back to Raena's chambers. Zarek entered the room, his gaze immediately seeking out Raena. She was sitting up against her pillows, looking stronger than before.

"I hope you're not expecting a feast," he said, setting the tray on the bedside table.

Raena rolled her eyes.

"I wouldn't dream of it, Zarek. I'm not that unreasonable."

He laughed, pulling up a chair beside her.

"I could argue that point, but I won't. Not today."

He picked up a piece of bread, dipping it in the soup before holding it out to her. She rolled her eyes at him again, but opened her mouth anyway, allowing him to feed her. Their quiet reprieve was interrupted by the opening of the chamber door. The royal physician, entered, followed closely by Raena's parents, her brother, Caspian, and visiting Prince Aldric.

"I heard my sister is finally awake," Caspian said, his voice filled with relief. He was a year older than Raena, with warm hazel eyes and messy brown hair. His usually jovial demeanor was tinged with worry. Aldric, the prince from the neighboring kingdom, he was of a similar age but held a sterner countenance. His eyes, however, held a warmth as they landed on Raena.

"It's good to see you awake, Princess Raena," he greeted.

"Hard to get rid of me," Raena quipped, despite the rasp in her voice. She offered them a weak smile.

The physician stepped forward, his experienced gaze assessing Raena. He pressed a cool hand to her forehead, checked her pulse, and asked a series of questions about her condition.

"Good, good," he murmured, mostly to himself.

"You'll need plenty of rest, your Highness, but it seems you're on the mend."

Raena was clearly not in the mood for a lecture.

"I've been resting for over a week, Eamon," she said, a hint of her usual stubbornness peeking through.

"But you also need to regain your strength," Zarek chimed in, offering her another spoonful of soup.

She shot him a look that could have withered a lesser man, but he merely chuckled and held the spoon steady.

With a huff, she accepted the soup, much to everyone's amusement.

"Always a handful, isn't she?" Caspian joked, earning him a glare from Raena.

"And you're always a pest, Caspian," she retorted, causing laughter to fill the room. It was a welcome sound, a sign of returning normality.

Prince Aldric watched the exchange with a soft smile, the love Zarek held for Raena was palpable, and Aldric respected that.

Eamon cleared his throat, drawing everyone's attention back to him. "Your Highness, I will prepare some herbal remedies to help you recover more rapidly. They should help with your strength and overall well-being."

Raena's father, the King, nodded in agreement.

"That sounds like a wise course of action, Eamon. Thank you."

Eamon nodded.

"There's thyme for strengthening the immune system, chamomile for calming, and fenugreek for digestion. A mixture of these, brewed into a tea, should be consumed three times a day."

Raena scoffed lightly.

"Herbal tea? Really Eamon, you make it sound like I'm on my death bed."

Her father, King Lucian, spoke up then. His voice was warm, but firm.

"Raena, it's important that you take this seriously."

She shot her father a defiant look, but then sighed.

"Fine. But I don't see why I can't use magic to speed up the recovery."

Eamon's gaze sharpened at that.

"No, Princess. I strongly advise against that. Your body has been through a great ordeal. Using magic now could further drain your energy and delay your recovery."

Zarek added, his voice calm and supportive.

"Ren, you're one of the most powerful Water Mages I know, but even the mighty oasis needs time to refill after a drought."

Caspian smirked at Zarek's analogy.

"Well put, Zarek."

Raena's sighed knowing she can't argue with all of them.

"Alright, herbal tea and rest it is."

Her mother stepped forward, taking Raena's hand in hers.

"That's my brave girl."

Eamon excused himself to prepare the herbal remedies.

"I shall return shortly with the first dose of tea, Your Highness," he said before making his exit.

The queen, still holding Raena's hand, gave her a reassuring smile.

"You'll be back on your feet in no time, dear. Just be patient with yourself."

Raena scowled, her impatience apparent.

"I don't do 'patient' very well, Mother."

King Lucian chuckled knowing his daughter well, Caspian grinned, "Maybe this is the universe's way of teaching you a lesson in patience."

Raena narrowed her eyes at her brother.

"Don't make me throw this soup at you, Caspian."

Prince Aldric couldn't help but chuckle at the sibling banter. He offered a reassuring smile to Raena.

"Rest assured, Princess, we'll all be here to support you during your recovery."

Raena's parents took their leave, wanting to give their daughter some space and privacy. Caspian and Aldric remained, sitting at the foot of Raena's bed. Zarek, ever attentive, continued to feed Raena small spoonfuls of soup.

"You know," he said softly.

"I never doubted that you'd wake up. You're far too stubborn to let something like this keep you down."

Raena smirked.

"You always know just what to say, don't you, Zarek?"

He grinned.

"It's a gift."

23

——— · ˳˚ ☆: *.) .* :☆˚. ———

The storm had been both a curse and a blessing. The relentless rain turned the desert into a quagmire, each step a laborious chore. But it was also our salvation, providing us with much-needed water and a respite from the scorching desert sun. As demons, we were hardy creatures. Our blood ran hotter than that of humans, warding off the chill of the rain-soaked nights, and our bodies were built for endurance. Yet, despite our inherent resilience, the journey was a brutal test of our fortitude. Our destination was a small settlement, a speck on the vast canvas of the desert. We moved under the cover of the storm, our figures barely discernible against the backdrop of the howling wind and torrential rain. Kael led us. He was our beacon, his resolve unyielding despite the hardships we faced. He'd heard whispers of this place while serving in the decadent halls of the privileged, rumors of a secret organization that aided escaped slaves. The possibility of such an alliance was a ray of hope in our bleak circumstances. Yet, I couldn't shake off my apprehension. I was born a slave, raised in the mines. Deception and betrayal were as familiar to me as the chains that had once bound me. Trust was a luxury I couldn't afford, not when the stakes were as high as they were now.

"Are you sure about this?" I asked Kael, my voice barely audible over the roaring storm.

He turned to look at me, his eyes hard but understanding.

"No," he admitted. "But it's the best chance we have."

I grunted, looking away. The thought of putting our fate in the hands of strangers was disconcerting. Yet, I knew Kael was right. We were outlaws now, fugitives. We needed allies, no matter how dubious. The rain continued to pour as we trudged through the desert, our bodies pushed to their limits. But it was the prospect of freedom, of a life beyond chains and whips, that spurred us on. The rain was relentless, but so were we. Days blurred into nights, the storm a constant companion. Our bodies ached, our spirits wavered, but our resolve held firm. We were demons, born of fire and grit. We would not be broken. The first sight of the settlement was a balm to our weary souls. It was a small cluster of buildings, huddled together like a band of refugees seeking shelter in the unforgiving expanse of the desert.

We approached with caution, wary of the unknown. The storm had eased, the rain now a drizzle. The scent of wet earth was overpowering, a stark contrast to the sterile smell of the mines. Gavril, signaled for us to stop. His sharp gaze swept over the terrain, scrutinizing every nook and cranny for potential threats. He was a seasoned warrior, his instincts honed from years of survival in the harsh mines.

"We're not walking into a trap, not if I can help it," Gavril muttered, his eyes never leaving the settlement. His voice was a low growl, the statement more of a vow than a mere comment.

"Good," I agreed, my own gaze mirroring his wariness.

"We've come too far to be caught now."

"Let's approach from the shadows," I suggested.

"We can gather information without revealing ourselves."

Then, Kael sighed.

"We have to trust someone, Ash," he said, meeting my gaze head-on. His voice was calm, yet laced with a hint of darkness born from his past.

"We can't fight this battle on our own."

His words stung. Trust was a double-edged sword, a weapon that had been wielded against us more times than I cared to count. But as I looked at him, his words sinking in, I knew he was right. We were out of options. We needed allies, a refuge, a hope. The settlement was a gamble, but it was one we had to take. We ventured closer, the settlement unfolding before us. It was more of a village really, a haphazard collection of buildings lined with barrels and containers catching the last drizzles of rain. People, both humans and demons, scurried about their tasks under the grey sky. The sight of other demons, however downtrodden, living outside the mines stirred something within me - a spark of hope or perhaps the bitter taste of envy. But mostly, it was anger - raw and burning - at the injustices that my kind endured. The mages' rain, a resource we were denied, collected freely in their barrels, while we had to scrabble for every drop. Kael guided us into the alleys, away from prying eyes. His demeanor was calm, collected, his every movement exuding an air of nonchalance, a stark contrast to the turmoil I knew simmered beneath the surface.

"Let's find that tavern," Kael suggested, his eyes scanning the area. His voice held a note of authority, a reminder of his days in the privileged halls where he had to learn the art of control and deception.

Gavril grunted in agreement, his eyes never straying far from our surroundings. His muscular form was tense, ready to spring into action at a moment's notice. We slipped into the tavern like shadows, unnoticed and silent. The room was filled with a motley crowd, the air thick with the smell of damp clothing and stale alcohol. We each found a spot, strategically scattered across the room, our eyes and ears open. The hum of conversation filled the air, the words blending into a steady murmur. We kept our heads low, our expressions neutral. The inhabitants, a mix of demons and humans, were as varied as the stories they carried. Gavril had positioned himself by the entrance, a silent sentinel with a watchful eye. His gaze flickered over each newcomer, analyzing and assessing. I knew he would be the first to act if things went south.

Kael, on the other hand, had chosen a seat at the bar. He sat with an easy grace, his posture relaxed yet alert. His eyes held a distant look, as if lost in thought, but I knew better. He was absorbing everything, the conversations, the atmosphere, the subtle dynamics playing out around us. I had found a spot near a group of locals, their loud chatter providing a cover for my eavesdropping. I listened, my mind sifting through the words for any scrap of useful information.

"I heard there's been a breakout from the mines," one of them was saying, his voice slurred with alcohol.

"Yeah, I heard it too," another chimed in.

"They say the slaves used the Rain Summoning to make their escape. Clever bastards."

A shiver ran down my spine. They were talking about us. I glanced at Kael, meeting his gaze across the room. He gave a subtle nod, a silent acknowledgment. I turned my attention back to the conversation, listening as they moved onto other topics. But my mind was whirling. We were the talk of the settlement. We needed to move fast, find allies before our pursuers found us. The night wore on and we gathered pieces of information, snippets of conversations that painted a picture of the settlement. It was a place of desperate hope and silent despair, a refuge for those who had nowhere else to go.

Finally, Kael rose from his seat, a signal that it was time to regroup. We met in a quiet corner, away from prying eyes. Kael's gaze was serious as he shared what he had learned.

"There's a man here, a healer, a demon" he said, his voice low.

"He's been helping demon slaves. I think he's part of the organization we're looking for."

I looked at Gavril, seeing my own trepidation reflected in his eyes. It was a slender thread of hope, but it was something.

"We need to find him," I said, determination steeling my voice.

Kael nodded, his expression resolute.

"I heard he operates in the shadows, under the guise of a simple apothecary. We should start there."

Gavril grunted in agreement, his eyes never straying far from our surroundings. His muscular form was tense, ready to spring into action at a moment's notice. As we left the tavern, the rain had finally come to a halt, leaving the settlement damp and cool. The containers lining the streets were filled with precious rainwater, a resource we could scarcely imagine having access to back in the mines. We navigated the narrow alleys, Kael leading us with confidence. He had a knack for blending in, for picking up information without ever drawing attention to himself. He was a survivor, shaped by his past and honed by necessity. The apothecary was a small, unassuming building, tucked away in a quiet corner of the settlement. A dim light flickered behind the window, casting eerie shadows on the surrounding walls. It looked like any other shop, we entered the apothecary one by one, trying not to draw attention to ourselves.

The interior was cluttered with shelves filled with bottles, jars, and pouches, each labeled with the name of some herb or concoction. The scent of herbs and spices hung heavy in the air, mingling with a faint metallic tang. An older demon, his skin lined with age and his eyes sharp, stood behind the counter. He regarded us with a mix of curiosity and caution. Kael approached him, his demeanor casual yet deliberate.

"We're looking for a healer," Kael said, his voice barely above a whisper.

"A demon who helps his own kind."

The older demon's gaze flicked between us, weighing our intentions.

"I am but a simple apothecary," he replied, his tone guarded.

Kael leaned in closer, his voice tinged with urgency.

"We need your help. We're running out of time."

A tense silence stretched between them, the air thick with unspoken words. Finally, the older demon let out a slow breath, his eyes narrowing.

"Follow me," he said, and disappeared through a concealed door behind the counter.

We exchanged wary glances before following him into a dimly lit back room. The healer, if that's who he truly was, closed the door behind us, sealing us in with our fate.

"Now," he said, his voice low and grave, "tell me your story."

***

The room was heavy with silence, the healer, an older demon named Orlon, studied us, his gaze thoughtful. We waited, each of us holding our breath. His decision would shape our path.

Finally, he spoke, his voice carrying an undercurrent of respect. "You've been through much. Your will to survive is commendable."

"But survival isn't enough," I found myself saying, my voice steady. "We want to fight. To end this slavery, this... injustice."

Orlon's eyes bore into mine, assessing my determination.

"A fight against the mages is no small endeavor. It's a path of blood and pain."

"We're no strangers to either," Gavril grunted, his arms crossed over his chest.

Orlon nodded slowly.

"That's true. But this is a different kind of battle. It's not just physical strength that matters. It's strategy, intelligence, patience."

He paused.

"I'm willing to help. But you must understand that what we do is dangerous. The organization I work with is small, secretive. We help free demon slaves and offer them a chance at a new life. But our existence is precarious. One wrong move, and we'll be discovered."

We nodded in understanding, the weight of his words settling heavily upon us.

"This settlement," Orlon continued, "is a secret haven for both demons and human nulls. The mages have no power here, but we must keep our presence hidden from them."

The thought of a place where we could exist without fear of persecution was both comforting and unbelievable. I glanced at Kael, whose eyes were filled with a mixture of hope and uncertainty.

"Our organization is dedicated to freeing demons, but we do not wish to spill blood unless absolutely necessary. We must be careful, tactical, and above all, patient."

Kael spoke up, his voice soft yet determined.

"We understand the need for caution, but we can't just stand idly by while our people suffer."

Orlon nodded, his eyes filled with a shared sorrow.

"I know, but we must choose our battles wisely. We have to be prepared for the long journey ahead and the sacrifices we will have to make."

Gavril grunted, a hint of skepticism in his eyes.

"And what happens when subtlety isn't enough?"

Orlon met his gaze evenly.

"We adapt, and we fight if we must. But bloodshed is the last resort. It only brings more pain."

"First, you must learn to live among us, to understand our ways and the delicate balance we maintain. Only then can you truly become part of our cause."

In the days that followed, we integrated ourselves into the settlement, learning its customs and traditions. We discovered a community that was a stark contrast to the world outside, a place where demons and human nulls coexisted in harmony. We met the others, demons and human nulls who had also found their way to this haven. Their stories were as varied as ours, a tapestry of pain and resilience. I found myself drawn to their strength, their will to survive. In their company, my own resolve solidified.

24

—— · ₒ ° ☆: *.) .* :☆° . ——

While we grew accustomed to the life in the settlement, we also learned the inner workings of the organization. We attended clandestine meetings, discussing strategies and planning operations to help our enslaved brethren. Gavril, ever the pragmatist, focused on the practical aspects of our new life. He trained harder than any of us, pushing his physical limits and learning the layout of the settlement like the back of his hand. His skepticism lingered, but he dedicated himself fully to the cause. Kael, on the other hand, was like a fish in water in the intellectual environment. He poured over maps and documents, learned the code language, and familiarized himself with the politics of the settlement. His trauma was a constant companion, but he wore it like armor, turning it into a force that drove him. I found myself stepping into a leadership role. My anger towards the mages, my desire for justice for my people, was a burning flame that drew others to me. I organized training sessions, coordinated tasks, and made sure that everyone was taken care of. I was determined to be the leader my people needed.

Our evenings were often spent in the company of Orlon. His wisdom and experience were invaluable. He taught us about the history of the demon race, about our culture and traditions that had been suppressed by the mages. He taught us about the power of unity, of standing together against a common enemy. Through it all, the looming threat of discovery hung over us like a dark cloud. We knew that if the mages discovered the settlement, it would mean the end of everything we were fighting for. One evening, we found ourselves in the local tavern, a lively place buzzing with stories and laughter. Gavril was engaged in a game of darts with a couple of other demons, while Kael was in a quiet corner, lost in conversation with a human null, likely discussing some esoteric topic. I was at the bar, nursing a glass of the local brew, when I overheard a group of demons at a nearby table. They were talking about the water mages, their voices hushed. I caught a few words – "princess", "collapsed", "Rain Summoning". My interest piqued, I moved closer, trying to catch more of their conversation.

When I was close enough, I turned to them, my tone casual. "Couldn't help but overhear," I started, nodding towards the empty seat.

"Mind if I join?"

There was a moment of silence as they assessed me, their eyes scrutinizing. Then, one of them gestured to the empty seat.

"Be our guest."

I thanked him and sat, trying to appear nonchalant.

"Heard you talking about the princess of the water mages," I said, meeting their gaze one by one.

"What happened?"

One of them, a demon with a scar running down his face, leaned back in his chair.

"Heard it from a contact in the city. During the last Rain Summoning, she apparently collapsed. Just fell to her knees, unconscious."

"Any idea why?" I asked, keeping my tone casual.

Scar-face shrugged.

"They say it's exhaustion. That she's been overworking herself. But who knows the truth?"

The conversation shifted then, taking a turn I hadn't expected. The demons, buoyed by their shared hatred of the mages, began to make crude jokes at the princess's expense. Their laughter rang harshly in my ears, their words a jarring contrast to the concern I felt. Each joke was more vulgar than the last, their laughter growing louder. My grip on the glass tightened, the edges digging into my palm. I could feel the heat of anger rising within me, a familiar flame that threatened to consume my self-control.

"Maybe she just needed a good lay," one of them suggested, a smirk on his face, his eyes gleaming with crude amusement.

That was the final straw.

In a flash, I was on my feet, my fist connecting with the smirking demon's face. He fell backwards, crashing into the table and scattering the drinks. The tavern fell into a stunned silence, all eyes on us. Shock and confusion were etched across the faces of the demons at the table. They couldn't understand why I would defend a water mage, someone who represented the very enemy we were fighting against. Before things could escalate further, I felt a hand on my arm. I turned to see Kael, his eyes calm yet firm.

"Ash," he said quietly, his voice steady despite the tension in the air.

Gavril was by his side, his gaze scanning the room for any threats. His hands were empty, but I could see the readiness in his stance, the willingness to fight if needed. The room remained silent, I turned, Kael and Gavril following suit, and walked out of the tavern. The cool desert air hit my face, calming the residual anger. I looked at Kael, then at Gavril, their silent support a comforting presence.

I knew I had made a scene, had reacted impulsively. But I couldn't bring myself to regret it. Once we were a safe distance away from the tavern, Kael broke the silence.

"Ash," he began, his voice calm and measured. He did not reprimand me, nor did he question my actions. Kael understood all too well the emotions that had driven me.

"I know what it feels like. To worry about someone who is supposed to be your enemy."

His words hung heavy in the silent night, the echoes of past hurts evident in his voice. Kael had loved once, and it had cost him dearly. His love had been for a mage, a woman who had betrayed him and left him with scars that ran far deeper than the surface. I glanced at him, a silent understanding passing between us. Despite his harsh experiences, he understood my feelings for Raena. I didn't need to voice them, he just knew. Gavril joined us then, his large frame coming to a halt beside me. He didn't voice his concerns or his confusion. But in his eyes, I saw the question he didn't ask. Why? Why did I care for a mage?

"I know she's a mage," I said, my voice barely above a whisper.

"And I know what they've done to our people. To you, to Kael, to me. But she... she's different."

Gavril remained silent, his gaze moving between Kael and me. He didn't understand, not like Kael did, but he accepted my words. He trusted me, despite his confusion.

"Let's head back," Kael suggested, his voice carrying a hint of finality. There was nothing more to be said, not then.

We made our way back to our shared quarters, the tension of the evening slowly dissipating.

——— · ｡° ☆: *.☽ .* :☆° . ———

25

A month had passed since Raena's awakening. Her recovery was progressing well, and she was once again able to roam the palace freely. Elras, her dedicated demon servant, was with her every step of the way, ensuring she didn't overexert herself. One evening, Elras was helping Raena tidy her chambers when he noticed an unopened pile of scrolls, still bound together by a thin leather strap. They were dust-covered, clearly having been forgotten in the chaos of the past weeks.

"Your Highness," Elras called, his voice coarse but respectful. "Found these old papers. They ain't like nothin' I seen before."

Raena turned to look at him, raising an eyebrow curiously.

"Let me see them, Elras."

She took the scrolls from him, eyes widening as she recognized them.

"Oh, I'd forgotten about these! We bought them in the market before the Rain Summoning. Zarek, Caspian, and Aldric couldn't make head nor tail of them." Elras scratched his head, peering at the writing.

"Ain't entirely sure, but... I reckon I recognize some of it. It's old, old demonic. Real ancient."

Raena looked surprised.

"Old demonic? Can you read it?"

Elras shrugged.

"Not much, but maybe some."

Raena's eyes sparkled with excitement.

"Well, what are you waiting for? Translate what you can!"

Elras squinted at the text, moving his finger slowly over the symbols. "This bit... it says 'water'... 'power'... and 'balance'. And this... 'great cost'."

Raena frowned, intrigued by the cryptic phrases.

"Water, power, balance, and great cost? Sounds ominous."

Without wasting any time, she summoned Zarek, Caspian, and Aldric to her chambers. When they arrived, she showed them the scrolls and relayed what Elras had translated so far. Zarek was the first to speak, his tone thoughtful.

"This could be significant. These scrolls could hold ancient knowledge, or they could be a warning."

Caspian, nodded.

"We should consult someone who can read ancient demonic. It may give us more insight."

Aldric agreed.

"Knowledge is power, after all."

Zarek furrowed his brow in thought.

"My father deals with a lot of the demon affairs. He might know someone who can translate this."

Raena nodded.

"That's a good idea, Zarek. We'll speak to him tomorrow."

The next morning, they found themselves standing in front of an imposing structure in the city. It was a stark structure, austere and unadorned, save for the kingdom's crest etched above the grand entrance. This was the Demon Administrative Center, a place where demon slaves were bred, trained, and managed under the watchful eye of Lord Cadmus, Zarek's father. Making their way through the entrance, they couldn't help but feel a sense of unease. The atmosphere was thick with the sense of dominance and control, making the air itself feel oppressive.

"Keep your wits about you," Zarek cautioned as they entered. The inside was a hive of activity, with administrators bustling about and demons being led in and out of various rooms. They were ushered into a luxurious office, where Lord Cadmus was perched behind an ornate desk. His eyes were sharp and calculating as they entered, a smirk playing at his lips.

"Ah, the young royals," he drawled.

"To what do I owe the pleasure?"

Zarek stepped forward, a single scroll held carefully in his hands.

"Father, we've come across something unusual. We believe this scroll is written in ancient demonic."

Lord Cadmus' interest was piqued. He held out a hand for the scroll. "May I?"

Zarek handed it over and Lord Cadmus unfurled it, examining the text. His brows furrowed in concentration.

"Indeed, this is ancient demonic. Not often seen these days."

Raena wasted no time.

"Can you or someone here translate it?" she asked.

Lord Cadmus leaned back in his chair, regarding them with an aloof smile.

"Indeed, I could translate it. The question is... why should I? What's your interest in this, and where did you obtain such a relic?"

Raena met his gaze evenly.

"We purchased it at a market. As for our interest, it's purely academic".

Zarek added.

"We thought it might provide some insight into the ancient times. Perhaps a history of the demon race or some other forgotten knowledge."

Lord Cadmus studied them for a moment, his eyes flicking between the scroll and their faces.

"Forgotten knowledge is often forgotten for a reason," he said, rolling the scroll.

"And yet, curiosity is the bedrock of all discovery, Father," Zarek interjected, his tone light but his gaze steady.

"Is it not?"

Lord Cadmus huffed, amused despite himself.

"You have your mother's tenacity, I'll give you that." His gaze shifted to the scroll again.

After a pause, he looked back at them, eyes narrowed.

"This scroll... it's an account of when the demons invaded our world."

There was silence as they processed his words. The history they knew had always painted the demons as native to their world, enslaved after an uprising.

"That's impossible," Aldric finally broke the silence, disbelief clear on his face.

"Demons have always been here. That's the history we know."

Lord Cadmus shrugged nonchalantly.

"History is often rewritten by the victors. Nonetheless, the script here paints a different story. A tale of an invasion, not of an uprising."

"But why would someone hide this?" Caspian asked, his brows furrowed in confusion.

Lord Cadmus leaned back in his chair, steepling his fingers.

"That's a question for another time," he said, his gaze drifting to Zarek.

"What I'm more interested in is where you obtained this scroll, and if there are others like it."

"We bought it from a merchant in the city," Raena replied, cautious.

"He had several other scrolls in the same script."

Lord Cadmus' eyes lit up with interest.

"And where might these other scrolls be now?"

Zarek stepped in before Raena could answer.

"Safe and secure. We thought it best not to carry all of them around."

Lord Cadmus gave a dry chuckle.

"Indeed. That's smart. Very well, I will translate this one, but I am interested in seeing the others."

Pausing for a moment, Lord Cadmus appeared thoughtful.

"There is much about demons that even I don't know, despite my position. There are many well-kept secrets surrounding them, and perhaps it is time to share some of that knowledge with you."

He looked at Raena and Zarek pointedly.

"After all, Zarek, you are my heir, and Raena, you are to become my daughter-in-law and future queen."

Lord Cadmus stood up from his chair, gesturing for them to follow.

"I believe it's time for a tour of this facility. It will be enlightening for all of you, I'm sure."

As they followed Lord Cadmus through the winding corridors of the Demon Administrative Center, they saw the various aspects of demon management. They followed Lord Cadmus through a labyrinth of corridors, their echoing footsteps swallowed by the stone walls. Their first stop was a large room filled with rows of desks and harried-looking individuals bent over stacks of parchment.

"This is where we manage the day-to-day affairs of the demons," Cadmus explained, a hint of pride creeping into his voice. "Assignments, sanctions, housing, sustenance - everything is regulated from here."

Raena looked around, a frown marring her features.

"It looks more like an office than a center for demon affairs."

Cadmus merely chuckled, a sound devoid of warmth.

"Indeed, my dear. Managing demons is no different than any other administrative task, once you strip away the mystique."

The group continued on, eventually arriving at a room filled with rows of neatly organized shelves, each containing countless scrolls and tomes.

"This is our extensive library, where we keep records of demon history, their abilities, and any relevant research," Lord Cadmus explained, his voice dripping with pride.

"It is an invaluable resource for those who seek to understand the true nature of these creatures."

Aldric, ever the opportunist, asked.

"May we borrow some of these texts, Lord Cadmus? We would like to learn more about them."

Lord Cadmus raised an eyebrow.

"Perhaps, but only after I have reviewed them myself. There are some secrets that are best left undiscovered by those not prepared for the consequences."

The next stop on the tour was a dimly lit chamber filled with cages, each housing a demon in various stages of development. The air was thick with a mix of fear and despair, and they couldn't help but feel a sense of unease as they observed the creatures.

"These are our breeding chambers," Lord Cadmus stated matter-of-factly.

"We carefully select and breed demons with specific traits, ensuring a steady supply of powerful and obedient servants for the kingdom."

Zarek, unable to hide his distaste.

"Is this truly necessary, Father? These creatures are living beings, after all."

Lord Cadmus' eyes narrowed, his voice cold.

"It is not our place to question the order of things, Zarek. Our world depends on these demons and their powers. It is our duty to ensure that they are controlled and utilized for the benefit of the kingdom."

Lord Cadmus then led them to a smaller room adjacent to the breeding chambers. The room was filled with an assortment of glass vials containing liquids of varying colors. He picked one of the vials, a deep purple liquid shimmering within.

"These," he began, holding the vial up to the light, "are our tools of persuasion." His smirk was almost predatory.

"A particular pheromonic potion, if you will."

Raena arched a brow.

"Pheromonic potion? You mean like some sort of love potion?"

Lord Cadmus gave a dry chuckle.

"Not quite, my dear, it goes beyond that, something much more powerful. It is especially effective on demons, making them particularly attracted to another demon or an individual."

Caspian, the ever-curious one, couldn't help but ask.

"And what purpose does this serve?"

Cadmus, put the vial back to its place.

"Control, young Caspian. Control. With this potion, we can direct a demon's actions, make them more compliant, or even use them as a means to an end."

The cold, calculated way Lord Cadmus spoke sent a shiver down Zarek's spine. It was a blatant reminder of the ruthless and cunning nature of his father.

Lord Cadmus smirked.

"It can be employed to ensure the successful mating of select demons, or even as a means of controlling rogue demons by having them become infatuated with one of our own."

Aldric, unable to hide his fascination, leaned in to examine the potion.

"It must be quite powerful to have such an effect on them."

Lord Cadmus nodded.

"Indeed, it is. But it must be used with the utmost caution. In the wrong hands, it could cause utter chaos."

Zarek, asked.

"What precautions do we take to ensure that this potion doesn't fall into the wrong hands?"

Lord Cadmus looked at his son, a hint of approval in his eyes.

"The recipe and knowledge of its existence are highly classified. Only a select few are allowed access to the potion, and it is always used under strict supervision."

Raena remained quiet, her mind buzzing with this new information. As she glanced at the vial Lord Cadmus had held, she couldn't help but think of Ash, his aggression —it all suddenly made a chilling sort of sense. He must have thought she had used one of these pheromonic potions on him. She hadn't, of course, but now she finally understood his question.

"I trust you understand the significance of what I have shown you," Lord Cadmus said, his gaze sweeping over them all.

"The power we possess over these creatures is not to be taken lightly."

Raena, her voice brimming with defiance, retorted.

"These creatures, as you call them, have feelings, consciousness. They're not just tools to be used."

Lord Cadmus merely smirked.

"You have much to learn, Princess. And hopefully, time will teach you."

Their next stop was a vast, open space that was filled with the sound of clashing metal and guttural roars. A closer look revealed it to be a training room where demons were being put through rigorous drills under the watchful eyes of heavily armed trainers.

"Welcome to the heart of our operations," Lord Cadmus announced, an ominous satisfaction seeping into his voice.

"Here, we train and condition the demons to follow our commands without question."

The sight was harrowing. Demons of varying sizes were chained and directed by handlers using. Some demons were forced to lift heavy weights or run until they collapsed from exhaustion. Others were made to fight each other, the clanging of their chained fists against one another echoing through the chamber. The air was thick with the scent of sweat and blood. Aldric grimaced, clearly uncomfortable, while Caspian's eyes widened in shock. Raena could feel a sickening knot forming in her stomach, and Zarek's jaw clenched tightly at the sight.

"This is monstrous," Raena whispered, her voice tight. Lord Cadmus merely shrugged, seemingly unfazed by the spectacle.

"Discipline, Princess," he replied, his voice as cold as ice.

"Only through rigorous training can we ensure their obedience. Any sign of rebellion is swiftly and effectively dealt with."

As they watched, they saw demons of all shapes and sizes being put through their paces by stern, unyielding trainers. Whips cracked, and magical spells were cast, each strike or incantation meant to reinforce the demons' submission. Raena bit her lip, her heart aching for the tormented creatures. Zarek, remained silent, watching the scene with a mixture of fascination and disgust. Caspian, on the other hand, was struggling to comprehend the purpose behind such harsh methods.

"Surely there must be a better way to handle them," he suggested.

Lord Cadmus, replied coldly.

"There is no room for softness in this world. The demons are dangerous, and we must use every means necessary to ensure their compliance."

Their next destination was a room that sent a chill down their spines.

"This is the punishment room," Lord Cadmus explained, his voice devoid of any emotion.

"When demons defy our authority or prove themselves disobedient, they are brought here to be reminded of their place."

The air was charged with fear and anticipation. An array of cruel devices lined the walls: spiked collars, whips embedded with shards of magical crystals, iron cages barely large enough for a demon to curl up in. The floor was stained with dark splotches, a silent testament to the violence that occurred here. In the center of the room was a large, circular pit. Within it, a demon was chained, its eyes filled with terror. A man stood over it, his hand glowing with a strange, green light. With a swift, heartless motion, he sent a wave of magic towards the demon. It roared in agony as its body contorted.

The group watched in stunned silence. Even Aldric, usually so flippant, had turned pale. Raena, her heart pounding, turned to Lord Cadmus, her eyes blazing with anger.

"This is wrong," she said, her voice steady despite the horror unfolding before her.

"These demons... they're sentient. They feel pain, they have thoughts and emotions. How can you justify this?"

Lord Cadmus merely looked at her, his eyes cold.

"It is a necessary evil, Princess," he said.

"We must do what is needed for the survival and prosperity of our kingdom."

Aldric, despite his usual stoicism, was the first to break the silence that hung heavily in the room.

"And yet," he said, his voice low, "I can't help but wonder if the price we're paying is too high."

Lord Cadmus turned, his eyes narrowed slightly.

"These beasts, as sentient as you believe them to be, would not think twice about tearing us apart if given the chance," he replied, his voice steady.

"Our kingdom's prosperity comes first."

Aldric, despite his initial fascination with the breeding program, could no longer hide his discomfort. He shifted on his feet, a troubled look on his handsome face. He glanced at Caspian, who was still staring wide-eyed at the pit.

"I... I didn't realize it was like this," Caspian muttered, breaking the silence. He glanced at Zarek and Raena.

"Is there nothing we can do?"

Raena remained silent, her gaze fixed on the tormented demon in the pit. She could feel the anger bubbling within her, but she bit her tongue. She knew better than to challenge Lord Cadmus further. Not here, not now.

Zarek, catching Caspian's glance, sighed.

"It's complicated, Caspian. This... it's been the way of things for as long as I can remember."

Lord Cadmus, seemingly satisfied that they had grasped the severity of the situation, finally moved to leave the room.

"Come," he commanded, not bothering to check if they followed. "There is still much to see."

Continuing the tour, the group's mood had significantly darkened, one chamber contained a collection of enchanted collars, designed to cause intense pain to the wearer whenever they resisted their handler's commands. Caspian, usually the jester, was somber and silent, his eyes reflecting the horror of what they were seeing, as they watched a young demon child being painfully bound by its enchanted collar, its cries for mercy falling on deaf ears. Raena couldn't help but think of Ash. She wondered how he'd been treated, if he had endured the same harsh training and punishment. Her heart ached at the thought. Zarek, too, was deep in thought. His father's methods were harsh, yes, but they also kept their kingdom safe. He was torn between his duty and his heart. After hours of touring the facility, they found themselves back in Lord Cadmus' office. The warmth of the office was a stark contrast to the chill they had felt in the punishment room. Lord Cadmus gestured for them to sit down, as he himself took a place behind his desk. His stern face softened slightly as he addressed them again.

"I know what you've seen today might be difficult to process," he started, his voice echoing in the silent room.

"But you must understand, we don't do this out of cruelty. We do it out of necessity."

Raena found herself scoffing at his words, her arms folded over her chest as she glared at him.

"Necessity? Is that what you call it?"

Lord Cadmus sighed, leaning back in his chair.

"Princess, I understand your outrage. Truly, I do. But these demons...they are not like us. Their minds are wild, their instincts savage. If left to their own devices, they would turn this kingdom to ashes."

The room fell silent again. Even though Raena was still seething, she couldn't ignore the underlying truth in Lord Cadmus' words. She had seen Ash's aggression first hand, the animalistic ferocity in his eyes.

Caspian, his voice still shaken, asked.

"But surely there must be a more humane way to control them, to work with them rather than against them."

Lord Cadmus shook his head.

"Humane, you say? These creatures have brought destruction and chaos to countless civilizations before ours. They cannot be reasoned with, only controlled."

Raena, her voice wavering, pressed on. "But have we ever tried? Have we ever tried to understand them, to reach out to them as equals?"

Lord Cadmus scoffed.

"The naivety of youth. You speak as if they are our kin. They are not. They are monsters that we have harnessed for our own benefit. And it is only through our unyielding control that we maintain the delicate balance that keeps our kingdom safe."

Zarek, feeling the weight of his father's words, hesitated before speaking.

"But Father, what if there's a better way? What if there's a chance for us to coexist peacefully, without all this suffering?"

Lord Cadmus fixed his gaze upon his son.

"Do not forget, Zarek, that it is our duty to protect the kingdom, and that sometimes requires difficult decisions. Your heart may be swayed by the plight of these creatures, but remember that our people rely on us to ensure their safety and prosperity."

Aldric, despite his discomfort, voiced the question they all had. "What makes them so dangerous, Lord Cadmus? Is it their strength? Their abilities?"

"Yes, and more," Cadmus replied.

"They possess powers we can scarcely comprehend. Fire that can melt stone, speed that can outmatch the wind, strength that can crush iron. They're a force of nature, untamed and unpredictable."

"But none of the demons we've encountered possess such abilities," Zarek pointed out, his brows furrowed in confusion.

Lord Cadmus' eyes hardened at Zarek's challenge, but instead of snapping back, he exhaled deeply, his demeanor changing. His usual haughty confidence seemed to wane, replaced by a solemn seriousness that was both surprising and somewhat unnerving.

"In ancient times, my son," Cadmus began, his voice grave, "demons were far more powerful than the ones we deal with today. They held powers that could bend the very fabric of reality, control elements, and command forces beyond our comprehension."

Aldric raised an eyebrow, skepticism apparent in his tone.

"And how do you know this, Lord Cadmus? Have you seen such a demon?"

"I have not," Cadmus admitted, "but our ancestors did. It's written in our ancient texts, coded in our architecture, etched into our history. Demons nearly conquered our realm once. They were not of this world and wreaked havoc until they were subdued."

Raena's eyes widened.

"And you're just telling us this now?"

Cadmus' gaze met hers unflinchingly.

"This history is not known to many. The knowledge of the demon's true power is dangerous in the wrong hands. The last thing we want is for the demons to remember what they once were."

Caspian shifted uncomfortably in his seat.

"But if they were so powerful in the past, why have they become... well, weaker?"

Lord Cadmus leaned back in his chair, his eyes staring at some distant point as he spoke.

"The truth is, we do not know exactly how our ancestors achieved this. The ancient texts are frustratingly vague on that point. The ancients somehow found a way to weaken the demons, to trap them in our realm, and diminish their powers. The exact methods, the spells, or whatever it was that they used, are a mystery to us. That's one reason why I'm so interested in the scrolls you found."

His eyes shifted towards Raena.

"They're ancient, filled with secrets that could potentially shed light on how the ancients achieved what they did. It's imperative that they are studied carefully and that they do not fall into the wrong hands."

Aldric was silent for a long moment, processing the magnitude of the information they had just been given. He finally spoke, his voice low, "So, you're saying that if these demons rediscover their true capabilities... they could be a genuine threat to us all?"

Cadmus nodded, his gaze hardening again.

"Exactly. We cannot afford to let that happen. Our methods may seem harsh, but they are necessary."

Zarek's mind raced, the implications of the revelation piling on the anxiety he already felt. He stole a glance at Raena. Her face was pale, her eyes wide. His heart ached at the sight.

"We'll ensure the scrolls are safe, Father," he said quietly, clenching his fists in resolve.

Lord Cadmus nodded, approving his son's determination.

"Good," he said, his voice reverberating through the silence of the room.

"Remember, what you have heard here today must remain a secret. The fewer who know about this, the better."

He then turned his attention to Aldric, his gaze piercing.

"As for you, Prince Aldric, I have no doubt that your own kingdom will educate you further on this matter, given your future responsibilities as king. You are to be trusted with much, and I expect you to handle this information with the seriousness it deserves."

Aldric nodded, accepting his words with a stoicism that belied the whirlwind of thoughts in his head.

"Understood, Lord Cadmus," he said, his voice firm.

Cadmus then turned back to all of them.

"Now, I must insist that you bring me those scrolls as soon as possible. Time is of the essence, and we cannot afford to dawdle."

Raena's eyes flashed defiantly.

"We will bring you the scrolls, Lord Cadmus," she declared, her tone firm. "But this does not mean we are your pawns. We are mages in our own right, and we will also look for answers."

Cadmus's lips curled into a sardonic smile.

"I wouldn't expect anything less of you, Princess Raena," he replied, a hint of begrudging respect in his tone.

"Just remember, in this delicate matter, caution will serve us all better than haste."

With that, he dismissed them, and the group slowly rose from their seats. The revelation still hung heavily in the air, making the silence between them feel stifling. Zarek offered Raena a comforting look, but she merely nodded, her expression unreadable. Caspian, however, couldn't help but break the silence as they exited the facility, his usual cheerfulness dulled.

"Well, that was heavy," he muttered, attempting a joke.

"Anyone up for a swim to lighten the mood?"

Aldric gave him a sideways glance, shaking his head slightly.

"Not now, Caspian," he said, his voice unusually serious.

"Let's just get those scrolls to Lord Cadmus."

—— · ₒ˚ ☆: *.) .* :☆˚ . ——

Life at the settlement fell into a rhythm, a dance of routine and learning, of shared stories and shared dreams. We worked during the day, our tasks varied and challenging. By night, we became students of history, of strategy, of the lore of our race. Amid all this learning, another form of education took place - Kael was teaching us how to read and write. The mages had denied us this basic right, keeping us ignorant to maintain their control over us. But here, under the cover of the desert's night, we were reclaiming that right.

Kael was patient, breaking down the complex scripts into simpler parts, guiding us through each stroke. We practiced late into the night, our fingers stained with ink, our minds filled with new words, new possibilities. Kael was patient and kind, always ready to explain things in a way we could understand. It was strange, sitting with books and scrolls spread out before us, tracing the foreign symbols with our fingers. But with each passing day, the strange symbols started making sense, started forming words and sentences. One day, while we were hunched over a particularly complex text, Gavril broke the silence.

"I never thought I'd be doing this," he said, his voice carrying a note of wonder.

"Learning to read, to write. It's… it's not something slaves do."

Kael paused, setting down his quill.

"It's not something slaves are allowed to do," he corrected gently. "Knowledge is power, Gavril. That's why the mages don't want us to have it."

Gavril was silent for a moment, processing Kael's words. Then, he nodded, picking up his quill again.

"Then let's make sure we use this power well."

With every passing day, our bond grew stronger. The three of us were united in our determination to help our people, to bring about change. Our friendship had become a lifeline, a source of strength in the face of adversity. Our knowledge expanded and with it so did our understanding of the world around us. We began to see the subtle nuances of the mage's rule, the delicate balance of power that kept them in control. And it became clear that if we wanted to make a difference, we needed a plan.

One evening, as we sat around a small table in our humble dwelling, we began to discuss our options. Kael, ever the strategist, had been carefully considering different approaches, weighing the risks and rewards of each.

"We need to be careful," Kael said, his voice low and serious.

"Any move we make will have consequences. We must be prepared to face them."

Gavril nodded in agreement.

"We can't just charge in, we need a plan that minimizes the risk to our people."

I leaned back in my chair, my mind racing with possibilities.

"What if we found a way to weaken the mages from within? To turn their own people against them?"

Kael's eyes narrowed, considering my suggestion.

"It's not impossible. There are factions within the mage society that aren't happy with the current regime."

"But how do we do that?" Gavril asked, his brow furrowed.

"We're slaves, remember? It's not like we can just walk up to them and start a conversation."

A sly grin spread across my face.

"That's where our new language skills come in handy. We infiltrate their society, using the very knowledge they tried to deny us."

At my words, Gavril and Kael exchanged a glance. It was Gavril who broke the silence first.

"And how do you propose we 'infiltrate their society'?" He asked, skeptically, his thick brows furrowing further.

"We're not exactly inconspicuous, Ash."

Gavril had a point. We were demons - our horns and our red eyes were unmistakable signs of our lineage, signs that marked us as 'other', as 'less than'. But I had been thinking about this, about our distinctiveness, and I had an idea.

"We don't need to blend in to infiltrate," I said, leaning forward, my hands flat on the table.

"We just need to be... overlooked."

Kael tilted his head slightly, a sign I had come to recognize as him being intrigued.

"Go on," he encouraged.

I took a deep breath, gathering my thoughts.

"Think about it. The demons and the nulls, we're everywhere in their society. We serve their food, clean their homes, build their cities. They see us every day but they don't really look at us. We're invisible to them."

"Which gives us an advantage," Kael finished for me, his eyes shining with understanding.

"We can be their servants, their laborers. We can listen, observe, gather information."

Gavril nodded slowly, his initial skepticism fading as he saw the potential in my plan.

"We can use their arrogance, their ignorance against them."

"Exactly," I said, a wave of relief washing over me.

"We play the part of the obedient slaves. We listen, we learn. And when the time is right, we strike."

"But," I continued, my voice steady despite the enormity of what I was suggesting, "we need to expand. It can't just be the three of us. We need our people, all of them, in on this."

Kael's brow furrowed, a hint of concern in his eyes.

"You mean a spy network?"

"In a sense," I said, nodding.

"We have demons in every corner of their cities, in every noble household, in pleasure houses, in their beds. If we can get them to pass on what they hear, what they see... it could change everything."

Gavril grumbled, crossing his arms over his chest.

"That's a big 'if', Ash."

"It is," I agreed, "but I believe we can do it. We can teach them, just as Kael taught us. We give them the tools to communicate secretly. We give them a reason to hope."

"I think Orlon might already have something like this in place," Kael mused, tapping his quill against the table.

"He's always had his ear to the ground, so to speak. He might be willing to help us expand it."

"We'd need to speak to him, of course," I said, glancing at them both. "He should know what we're planning."

Gavril snorted, though there was a hint of a smile on his face.

"So, we're becoming spies and educators now?"

"Seems like it," I said, grinning back at him.

"Alright," Kael said, pushing back his chair and standing.

"Let's do this. We have a lot of work ahead of us."

***

Finding Orlon was easy, as usual he was at his apothecary preparing healing remedies.

"Orlon," I greeted him, trying to sound as casual as possible.

"We need to talk."

Orlon wiped his hands on his trousers, turning to face us. His gaze was shrewd, assessing.

"What's this about, Ash?"

I glanced at Kael and Gavril.

"We have a plan," I said.

"To fight back. To change things."

Orlon's gaze sharpened, a hint of curiosity in his eyes.

"Go on."

I laid out our plan in detail, from the infiltration to the creation of a spy network, our goal to expose the cracks in the mage society and drive them apart. As I spoke, I saw a mix of emotions play across Orlon's face – skepticism, concern, and a flicker of hope.

When I finally finished, Orlon was silent for a long moment. Then, he sighed, rubbing a hand over his face.

"You're talking about revolution, Ash," he said.

"War."

"Not war," I argued.

"Liberation. Freedom."

Orlon shook his head.

"I won't condone violence, Ash. I won't condone the eradication of mages."

"I don't understand," Kael interjected, his voice edged with frustration.

"Why are you protecting them, Orlon? After everything they've done to our people?"

Orlon looked at Kael, his eyes filled with sorrow.

"I'm not protecting them, Kael. But there are innocent mages who have nothing to do with the enslavement of our people. We can't punish them for the sins of others."

Gavril scoffed, his impatience apparent.

"You expect us to believe there are 'innocent' mages? They've all benefited from our suffering."

"Not all mages are the same," Orlon countered.

"Some are just as trapped in this system as we are. They're born into a society that tells them they're superior, that it's their birthright to rule over us. Many don't question it because they don't know any better."

I clenched my fists, the fire inside me growing hotter.

"But we can't just let them continue to enslave us, Orlon! We need to take a stand, show them that we won't be subjugated any longer."

Orlon looked at me with a pained expression.

"I understand your anger, Ash. I feel it too. But if we resort to violence and bloodshed, we become no better than those we're fighting against."

Kael stepped forward, his voice soft but resolute.

"We're not asking for a bloodbath, Orlon. We want to dismantle the system, not destroy every mage in existence. Our goal is to bring about change, to create a world where demons and mages can coexist as equals."

I couldn't help but notice something in Orlon's demeanor. He seemed to speak with a certain understanding, almost as if he knew the mages personally. It was something I had noticed before, but it was more pronounced now.

"Orlon," I began, a hint of suspicion in my voice.

"You speak as if you're personally acquainted with the mages. Is there something you're not telling us?"

Orlon hesitated, a guarded expression crossing his face.

"I... I have connections. Not all mages are our enemies, Ash."

"What do you mean?" Gavril asked, suspicion coloring his voice.

Orlon sighed, finally revealing a closely guarded secret.

"The benefactor of our secret organization, the one who helps us maintain our settlement... is a mage noble."

The room fell silent, the weight of his revelation settling over us. I felt a mixture of anger and disbelief, struggling to understand how someone from the very group oppressing us could be our ally.

"How can we trust them?" I demanded, my voice raw with emotion. "How do we know they're not using us for their own gain?"

Orlon met my gaze, his eyes filled with a quiet determination.

"This mage has risked everything to help us. They've shown nothing but compassion and understanding for our cause. I've seen their actions, Ash, and I believe they truly want to help."

"But why?" Kael finally asked, his voice barely a whisper.

"Why would a mage help us?"

Orlon gave a slight shrug.

"He doesn't agree with the enslavement of our people. He wants change as much as we do."

I felt my blood boil at Orlon's words, my hands clenching involuntarily.

"And we're supposed to believe that?" I spat, the bitterness in my voice echoing off the small room's walls. "Believe that a mage, someone from the same class that treats us worse than beasts, wants to help us? You expect us to trust them?"

Orlon's gaze met mine unflinchingly, an unexpected fire in his eyes. "I understand your reservations, Ash. But we have to look at the bigger picture. This is a chance for us to turn the tide, to fight back."

"No, Orlon," Kael interrupted, his voice low and steady.

"You need to understand something. Every mage, every single one of them, is complicit in our suffering. They may not be directly responsible, but they're not innocent. They benefit from our pain, our servitude. They live in luxury while we suffer. They quench their thirst while we choke on sand."

His words hung in the air, a stark reminder of the harsh reality we lived in. I watched as Orlon's face hardened, his eyes flickering with a mix of emotions.

"I have seen their cruelty firsthand, Orlon," Kael continued, his voice barely a whisper now.

"I have experienced their viciousness, their disregard for our lives. I bear the scars, physical and mental, of their so-called superiority. And I am not alone. Every single one of our people suffers, even now."

Orlon was silent, his gaze locked onto Kael's. There was a moment of tense silence before he finally spoke, his voice barely audible.

"I... I understand."

"We appreciate the help this mage provides," I said, breaking the silence that had settled over the room.

"Truly, we do. But we cannot forget, not even for a moment, the suffering our people endure. We must do whatever it takes, Orlon, to free them."

Orlon sighed heavily, rubbing a hand over his face.

"I understand your sentiments, Ash, Kael. I do. And I agree with you. Our people's suffering is paramount. But we must be careful. Any misstep could cost us dearly."

"Yes, we must be careful," Gavril chimed in, his voice calm yet firm. "But we cannot afford to be overly cautious, Orlon. We've been living in fear for too long. It's time we take our fate into our own hands."

Orlon took a deep breath, his gaze moving from me to Kael and finally to Gavril. He gave a slow, solemn nod, the weight of our words seemingly sinking in.

"Alright," he said quietly. "I'm with you. Whatever it takes."

Silence fell over the room once more, but this time it was a silence filled with resolve and determination. Orlon's gaze was heavy when he met mine, a nod of understanding passing between us.

"I have a small network of spies within the mage society," he confessed, his voice barely above a whisper.

"They're not much, but they've been feeding me information. It's how I've managed to keep our settlement hidden and safe."

Kael raised a brow at this, a spark of interest in his eyes.

"Can we use them?" he asked, his tone measured.

"Can they help us expand our network?"

Orlon nodded, looking thoughtful.

"It's risky, but it's possible. They're mostly lower-ranking mages and a few servants who are sympathetic to our cause. We'd have to be careful, ensure they're not discovered."

"A calculated risk," Gavril muttered, crossing his arms.

"But one that could give us the upper hand."

"I agree," I said, my mind racing with possibilities.

"We need to start somewhere. This could be our foundation."

Orlon looked at each of us, a grim determination on his face.

"We'll need to plan carefully, figure out who we can trust. And remember, our benefactor or other mages can't know the full extent of our plan."

"Why not?" Gavril asked, his brow furrowed in confusion.

"He's on our side, isn't he?"

Orlon sighed, shaking his head.

"While he disagrees with the enslavement, I doubt he'd condone outright rebellion. We risk losing his support if he thinks we're planning to betray his own kind."

"So, we move in shadows," Kael concluded, his gaze hard.

"Even within our own ranks."

"Yes," Orlon agreed.

"We can't afford any leaks. Our plans, our lives, and the lives of our people depend on this."

"We'll start with your spies, Orlon," I decided, my vo ice firm.

"We need to figure out who we can trust, who's willing to take the risk. From there, we can expand our network, slowly, carefully and add our own people to it."

"Agreed," Kael said, nodding.

"We also need to work on our communication. Find a way to pass messages without arousing suspicion."

I sighed, rubbing my forehead.

"Alright. So we have a plan. We expand our network of spies, gather information, and start undermining the mages' rule. We stir up dissent, make them question their own system. And all the while, we prepare for the possibility of a direct conflict."

27

—— · ₀° ☆: *.) .* :☆° . ——

The group walked through the palace corridors, their footsteps echoing in the quiet. As they approached Raena's chambers, her heart pounded in her chest, a sense of dread washing over her. She pushed the door open, her eyes scanning the room. Her gaze fell on the table where the scrolls should have been, but it was empty. Raena's heart skipped a beat, her breath hitching in her throat. "They're... they're gone," she stammered, feeling a chill run down her spine.

Zarek quickly moved to her side, his brow furrowing as he looked at the empty table.

"Are you sure this is where you left them?" he asked, though his tone made it clear he didn't doubt her.

"Of course, I'm sure!" Raena retorted, her voice rising in pitch.

"Elras arranged them for me just yesterday!"

At the mention of the demon servant, Caspian perked up, a hopeful glint in his eyes.

"Then maybe Elras knows where they are!" he suggested, trying to inject some optimism into the situation.

"Binda!" Raena called, summoning her loyal maid. Moments later, Binda appeared, a worried look on her face.

"Fetch Elras, immediately."

While Binda hurried off, the group waited in tense silence, their minds racing with possibilities. When Elras finally arrived, he bowed low, eyeing the group curiously.

"You called for me, Princess?" he asked, his voice tinged with confusion. Raena gestured towards the empty table.

"The scrolls, Elras. Where are they?"

A flicker of surprise crossed Elras's face, and he quickly moved to the table, his eyes scanning the surface.

"But... I left them right here," he muttered, sounding genuinely baffled. "I haven't moved them since yesterday."

The room fell into a heavy silence, each person trying to process the fact that the scrolls were missing. Raena felt a knot form in her stomach, the weight of the situation sinking in. Without the scrolls, they had no hope of understanding the demons' true power or preventing a potential disaster.

"I... I don't understand," she finally managed, her voice barely above a whisper.

"Who would take them?"

Zarek squeezed her shoulder reassuringly, though his eyes held the same worry.

"We'll find them, Raena," he said, his voice resolute.

"We have to."

Aldric was the first to break the silence.

"We need a plan," he stated, his tone calm but firm.

"These scrolls won't find themselves."

Zarek nodded in agreement, casting a concerned glance at Raena.

"Aldric's right. We need to be systematic about this."

Elras, still looking guilty and bewildered, spoke up hesitantly.

"I'm real sorry, Princess Raena. I swear I didn't do nothin' with them scrolls."

Raena, though visibly upset, shook her head at Elras.

"I don't believe you took them, Elras," she said, her tone softer. "But we need to figure out who did."

The room was filled with a palpable tension as they all pondered their next move. Suddenly, Caspian, who had been uncharacteristically quiet, clapped his hands together.

"Well, it's clear as a desert spring to me!" he declared.

"We need to conduct an investigation!"

They all turned to look at him, their expressions varying from surprise to skepticism. Aldric raised an eyebrow at his friend.

"And since when are you an expert in investigations, Caspian?" he asked, a hint of amusement in his otherwise serious tone.

Caspian shrugged nonchalantly.

"I'm not. But we're all smart, and we've got a mystery to solve. Plus, how hard can it be? We'll start by retracing our steps and asking around. Someone might have seen something."

Zarek looked at Caspian thoughtfully, then turned to the others. "He's got a point. It's a start, at least."

Raena nodded, her determination returning.

"Alright," she agreed, standing up and dusting off her dress.

"Let's start with everyone who had access to my room. Binda, Elras, we're going to need your help."

Elras bowed deeply, looking somewhat relieved.

"Anything you need, Princess," he replied. "I just want to make things right."

Binda nodded as well, her face showing concern but also readiness.

"Of course, Princess Raena. We'll do everything we can."

Raena looked around at the gathered group, her expression serious. "Don't mention the scrolls to anyone. Simply say that something valuable has gone missing from my room."

The group began their investigation, questioning palace staff and retracing their steps from the previous day. Despite their efforts, however, they found no trace of the missing scrolls or any clue as to who might have taken them. Raena, feeling frustrated and helpless, gathered her friends in her chambers once more.

"We've been at this for hours, and we have nothing to show for it," she huffed, her arms crossed.

Caspian tried to maintain his optimism, but even he couldn't deny the facts.

"Maybe the thief already left the palace," he suggested, hoping to provide some direction.

Aldric nodded, his expression pensive.

"It's a possibility. If that's the case, then the scrolls could be anywhere by now."

Zarek, who had been quietly contemplating, finally spoke up.

"I think it's time we informed my father about this," he said, his face taut with concern.

Aldric shot him a sharp look.

"Lord Cadmus?" he questioned, clearly surprised.

"But Zarek, you know how he is about the demon affairs."

"I do," Zarek replied, nodding.

"But he needs to know. The scrolls are too important."

Despite the gravity of the situation, Raena couldn't help but let out a huff of annoyance.

"I can't believe I'm saying this," she muttered, "but you're right, he needs to know."

Zarek nodded and left the room, leaving the remaining three in a tense silence. Aldric ran a hand through his hair, his face etched with worry.

"This is bad, Raena," he said, looking at her.

"Those scrolls... they might contain dangerous information."

"I know, Aldric," Raena replied, her voice a mere whisper as she looked out the window towards the barren desert.

"The stakes are high, but we have to keep faith. We'll find them."

While Zarek was away informing his father, the remaining group continued their search. They combed through the palace, asked more questions, and even ventured into the city, but the scrolls remained elusive. When Zarek returned, he looked more serious than ever.

"My father is... concerned," he reported, choosing his words carefully.

"He's doubled the guard and has ordered a thorough search of the city."

***

The dawn light was just beginning to bathe the palace in its golden hue as I sat on my balcony, looking out over the lush gardens and sparkling water fountains. It was a sight that always brought me a sense of tranquility. But today, the stark contrast between the vibrant greens of the garden and the arid desert beyond the palace walls only served as a harsh reminder of the world outside. The world I had glimpsed at the Demon Administrative Center. The memory of the demons at the Center flooded back to me, their cries echoing in my ears, the terror in the eyes of the children imprinted in my mind. It was horrifying, enraging. I knew the demons were dangerous, but no one, especially not children, deserved to be treated with such brutality. A dark silhouette stands out in my memory, his golden eyes holding a defiance that sends a shiver down my spine. I can't help but wonder about him. What is he doing? How is he being treated in the mines? Is he holding up? His image burns in my mind, a constant reminder of the reality I've been shielded from for so long.

I shake my head, trying to rid myself of these thoughts, but they persist, persistent as a desert storm. I know they're dangerous. I've heard of the destruction they can cause, the chaos they can sow. But the demons are not just monsters, they're sentient beings. And the fact that they're tortured, even the children... it's unforgivable. "Stop it, Raena," I mutter to myself.

I can't afford to think like this. It's dangerous, it's imprudent, it's... it's not me. I've always been firm, always made the tough decisions. I'm a princess, for god's sake, I'm supposed to uphold the kingdom, not question its ways. But then again, am I not also supposed to stand for justice, for compassion? If not me, then who will question these practices? Who will ensure that justice is served? "Stop it," I admonished again, my grip on the railing tightening. "You can't afford to be conflicted. Not now, not when so much is at stake."

But there it was - conflict. I tried to squash it down, to pretend it wasn't there, but it was like trying to hold back the ocean with a broom. The more I thought about it, the more it gnawed at me. "Since when did I become so sensitive?"

I muttered to myself, my brows furrowing in frustration. I was the princess of this kingdom, a water mage with a duty to my people, and here I was, wrestling with emotions for a demon and his kind.

"Zarek is my future. I am his future. This... infatuation with Ash... It's just sympathy. Yes, that's it, sympathy for his plight."

I stood up, pacing back and forth on the balcony, my heart pounding in my chest like a drum. I had to be strong, I had to do what was right for my kingdom. But what was right? Turning a blind eye to the torture of demons, or standing up against it?

"I can't just sit here and do nothing," I resolved, turning back towards my chambers. I had resources, I had influence, and by the gods, I was going to use them.

Summoning Binda, I instructed her to prepare boxes of food and containers of water. The palace had enough to spare, and it was the least I could do. Though it was a small gesture, it was a start.

Next, I called for Darius, the captain of my guard.

"Darius," I began, "you will accompany Elras to the Zulmar mines. Ensure he delivers the food safely and returns unharmed." His brow furrowed, the only sign of his confusion.

"As you command, Princess," he said, saluting me before leaving. I sighed, turning my attention to the last task at hand.

Finally, I summoned Elras.

"Elras," I began.

"I have a task for you. I want you to go to the mines, with Darius. You're to deliver supplies, food, you are to leave at once."

The surprise on Elras' face was clear, but he quickly composed himself.

"Yes, milady," he responded, his voice rough yet filled with gratitude. "I be honored to do this for you... for them."

"You are to check on them, especially on Ash, deliver the supplies and tell me how the overseer has been treating the slaves since I last was there."

His gaze sharpened at Ash's name, but he simply nodded.

"As you command, princess."

With Elras and Darius on their way to the mines, I knew I had to act quickly. There was another matter I had to address - the missing scrolls. While I trusted Elras, I was no fool. He was a demon, after all, and one of the few people in the castle who knew about the scrolls and their contents. It was imperative to search his living space and his usual workspaces while he was away.

Gathering my resolve, I sought out my fiancé Zarek, my brother Caspian, and our mutual friend Aldric. I found them in the palace courtyard, practicing their water magic. Their expressions changed to curiosity as I approached, sensing the urgency in my stride.

"Zarek, Caspian, Aldric," I began, trying to maintain a calm demeanor.

"I need your help. Elras is on a mission to the mines, and we must use his absence to search his quarter and workspaces for the missing scrolls."

Zarek's intelligent eyes narrowed, and his mouth formed a thin line.

"Elras, you say? Are you sure, Raena? He's been loyal to you."

"I know," I replied, my voice firm.

"But we can't ignore the possibility. He's a demon and had access to the scrolls. We must be thorough."

Zarek simply nodded, understanding my point.

"Alright, we will do it, for the safety of our kingdom."

Aldric, nodded stoically, his handsome features set in determination.

"We'll be discreet, Raena. You can count on us."

I looked at each of them, grateful for their support.

"Thank you. Let's split up to cover more ground. Caspian, you and Aldric check his living quarter. Zarek, you're with me. We'll search his workspaces."

The four of us reconvened later in the day, our search having come up empty. No trace of the scrolls was found. I couldn't help but feel both relief and disappointment. Elras was innocent, but the scrolls were still missing. I sifted through Elras's usual places, my heart pounded with a strange mix of hope and dread. The idea of Elras betraying us was painful, but if he wasn't the culprit, then the mystery of the missing scrolls only deepened. Hours passed, and the sun was setting when we regrouped. Our faces were dust-streaked and weary, but none of us had found anything. Zarek's expression was grim as he shook his head.

"There's nothing in the workspace," he reported.

"No hidden compartments, no loose floorboards... nothing."

Caspian's usually bright eyes were dull with disappointment.

"Same with his quarter," he said, sounding as frustrated as I felt.

"I couldn't find anything either," I admitted, my heart heavy. The relief at Elras's innocence was overshadowed by the frustration and worry that the scrolls were still missing. Who else knew about them? Who else had the means to take them?

Aldric's stoic demeanor held, but I could see the concern in his eyes.

"We need to find another lead. The scrolls are too important to give up on."

"I agree," I said.

"We'll keep searching. We'll find them, no matter what."

Later that evening, Elras returned from his mission to the mines.

"Princess Raena," he began, bowing slightly as he stopped in front of me.

"I've delivered the supplies, just as ye commanded."

"Thank you, Elras," I nodded, appreciating his efforts.

"And what of the slaves? The overseer?"

Elras paused, his gaze shifting uneasily before he spoke again.

"The overseer... he's still as harsh as ever, milady. But there's more. Three slaves, they've escaped. Ash was one of 'em."

My heart skipped a beat at his words.

"Escaped?" I echoed, my mind whirling.

"Do you know where they might have gone?"

Elras shook his head.

"I'm sorry, milady. I don't know. They disappeared into the desert, and... well, you know how vast it is."

I nodded, a flurry of emotions roiling inside me. Relief that Ash had escaped the brutal mines. Worry over his survival in the harsh desert. Frustration over our lack of progress with the scrolls. It was a lot to process.

"I see," I murmured, more to myself than to Elras.

"Thank you for the information, Elras. You've done well."

28

— · ₒ˚ ☆: *.) .* :☆˚ . —

Months had passed since our conversation with Orlon, and our small organization had grown, fueled by determination and the hope of liberation. We'd managed to establish a network of spies, both demons and null humans, who had infiltrated the mage society and were providing us with valuable information. Each day, we learned more about the mages' weaknesses, their secrets, and the cracks in their oppressive regime.

"We've managed to recruit three new sympathizers," Orlon reported one evening, shuffling a pile of parchments on the wooden table we'd commandeered for our meetings.

"One of them is a mage's scribe, another is a kitchen servant, and the third... The third is a guard."

"A guard?" Kael echoed, his eyes narrowing slightly.

"That's a high-risk position."

Orlon nodded, his face drawn.

"Yes, but he has access to places the others don't. It could be beneficial."

Gavril grunted, leaning back in his chair.

"Or it could be a setup."

"We'll need to vet him thoroughly," I said, the weight of our task settling heavily upon me.

"We can't afford a mistake."

"According to our sources," Kael began, his gaze locked onto a parchment.

"There's a public gathering scheduled in two weeks. Most of the high-ranking mages will be in attendance."

Gavril smirked, his eyes gleaming with a dangerous light.

"Sounds like a perfect opportunity to stir some trouble."

"No," I cut in sharply, meeting his gaze head-on.

"We're not ready for open rebellion. Not yet. We need to keep gathering information, keep building our network."

"How many are we now?" I asked Orlon, looking over the expanding settlement.

"We're close to a thousand," he replied, a hint of pride in his voice. "And more arrive each week."

"Word is spreading," Kael observed, his gaze distant.

"Soon, we'll be a force to be reckoned with."

"And what then?" Gavril asked, his voice cutting through the air like a knife.

"When do we act? When do we take the fight to them?"

"Soon," I answered, my gaze steely.

"But not before we're ready."

Despite the intense heat of the desert and the constant threat of discovery, our community thrived. We were a motley crew of misfits and outcasts, but we were united by a single purpose - freedom.

"We need to plan our next move," Orlon said one evening, my gaze focused on the map spread out before us. It was marked with the locations of known mage compounds, each one a potential target.

"We're not yet strong enough for a full-scale assault," Kael mused, his fingers tracing the map.

"But we could start disrupting their operations, sabotage their water supplies."

Gavril snorted, a wry smile on his face.

"A little desert taste for them, eh?"

"The main water supply is heavily guarded," Kael said, pointing at the map.

"But there are several smaller reservoirs that are less secure. They're used to supply individual compounds."

I nodded, tracing the routes to the reservoirs with my fingers.

"If we could introduce something to the water, a contaminant..."

Gavril's eyebrows shot up.

"Poison them?"

"Not poison," I corrected, shaking my head.

"We're not murderers. But if we could make the water undrinkable..."

"Orlon could prepare a concoction," Kael suggested.

"Something that will spoil the water but won't harm those who drink it."

"Exactly" I agreed, yet with a faint edge of uncertainty.

The room went quiet, the only sound the occasional flicker of the oil lamp casting long shadows over the map. My fingers traced the inked lines on the parchment, marking out the main artery of water flowing into the mage compounds.

"Is this the best course of action, though?" I broke the silence, my voice echoing in the room.

Kael and Gavril glanced at each other before turning their attention to me.

"What do you mean?" Kael asked, his brow furrowed.

"We're growing," I began, my gaze wandering to the window where I could just see the faint outlines of the shanty huts that now dotted the landscape.

"Every day, more come to us. We've created a haven here, a home for those who had none. But with growth comes need. We're low on supplies, the demand is increasing."

"Are you suggesting we focus on gathering resources?" Gavril asked, leaning forward in his chair, his elbows resting on the worn-out table. His eyes, reflecting the lamp's glow, were focused on me.

"Partly," I answered.

"We've been so focused on striking out that we might be neglecting our own defenses. Our settlement is expanding, and so too is the risk of being discovered. We must be prepared for that."

Kael nodded, his fingers absently drumming on the table.

"Ash is right. We need to fortify our settlement, make sure we're ready for any kind of threat. We're a beacon in the dark, it's only a matter of time before unwanted eyes turn our way."

"We can do both," Gavril suggested.

"We can work on fortifying the settlement and continue with our plan to sabotage the mages' water supply. We don't have to choose one over the other."

"But what about water for us?" I interjected.

"We're in the middle of a desert. We can't sustain this growth without a reliable water supply. We either need to start stealing it from the mages, or find a way to create our own."

"And in the cities?" I continued, my tone a little more subdued, my gaze locking with each of theirs.

"We need safe houses, places our sympathizers can hide, and our people can rest when they go into the cities. It's too risky to keep everyone here."

"That's a gamble," Gavril retorted, his eyes narrowed.

"If we start building safe houses in the cities, we risk exposure. One wrong move, one slip-up, and the mages will be on us."

"I understand the risk," I replied, my voice steady.

"But it's a risk we'll have to take. We can't keep operating from the shadows. If we want to free our people, we need to establish a presence in the cities. We need to show the mages that we're not afraid."

Kael remained silent, his gaze locked onto the flickering flame of the oil lamp. After a long, contemplative pause, he finally spoke.

"Ash is right. We need safe houses, places we can operate from within the cities. But we need to be smart about it. We can't just choose any place. We need to pick locations that offer easy escape routes and remain inconspicuous."

"And about the water," Kael continued, his fingers tracing over the map.

"We do need our own source. But until we find it, we need to consider stealing. Hitting the smaller reservoirs could work."

"Stealing isn't the only option," I said, an idea taking form in my mind. The room fell silent as I gathered my thoughts.

"What if we kidnapped a mage? A water mage."

The silence deepened, each of us contemplating the weight of that proposition. Finally, Orlon, who had been quiet until now, gave a thoughtful hum.

"Kidnapping a mage?" Kael asked, his voice filled with disbelief. "That's a dangerous game, Ash. If we're caught, they'll come down on us with full force."

"I know," I replied, my voice firm but weary.

"But we're running out of options. We need water, and we need it badly. If we don't do something drastic, we'll never be able to keep up with our growing population."

Orlon finally spoke up, a worried look on his face.

"I agree we're desperate, but kidnapping a mage... that could jeopardize us in more ways than one."

"How so?" Gavril questioned, leaning forward with interest.

Orlon sighed, his hands folded neatly on the table.

"Our benefactor, if word got out that we've kidnapped a mage, we might lose that support."

"If it comes to that," I began, my voice echoing in the quiet room, "it should be a secret. A secret among us, and us alone."

Kael studied me for a moment, then slowly nodded.

"Ash has a point. As long as we're careful, and we make sure the mage we take can't be traced back to us, it could work. It's a risk, yes, but so is everything else we're doing."

Orlon looked at each of us in turn, a somber expression on his face. "Let's not rush into anything. We'll start with the less risky strategies first. Strengthen our settlement, establish safe houses, and steal from the smaller reservoirs. We'll continue searching for a sustainable water source. As for the... other plan, let's keep it as a last resort."

"We'll need to build escape routes, places to hide in case of a surprise attack. And we should train everyone, not just the fighters. Everyone should know how to defend themselves and their home."

"Good point, Orlon," Gavril commented, his gaze hardening.

"I'll start organizing the training tomorrow."

"And I'll work on potential escape routes and hiding places," Kael added, his focus already shifting to the map.

"I'll look into the reservoirs," I declared, my mind racing with possibilities.

"We need to figure out their schedules, their weak points, everything."

"Be careful, Ash," Kael warned, his eyes meeting mine.

"If the mages even suspect we're stealing from them..."

"I know," I cut in, my gaze never leaving his.

"I'll be careful. I won't get caught."

We spent the rest of the night planning, strategizing, and preparing. Orlon shared his knowledge of the city's layout, pointing out potential safe houses and escape routes. Gavril devised a training regimen that would prepare our people for any possible scenario. Kael and I worked on a plan to infiltrate one of the smaller water reservoirs, using the city's sewer system to access it undetected.

"The sewers are filthy, and they're crawling with vermin," I noted, grimacing at the thought.

"But they're also unguarded and mostly forgotten. It's the perfect way to get in and out without being seen."

Kael agreed, his face reflecting the grim determination that matched my own.

"We'll need to map them out, know them better than the back of our hands. It's going to be dangerous, but if we're successful, it could be the key to our survival."

"We'll need a small team," I continued, my mind already assembling a list of potential candidates.

"Fast, stealthy, and able to keep their mouths shut."

"I can think of a few," Gavril chimed in, a glint of mischief in his eyes.

"They're not much for words, but they can move like shadows when they need to."

"Good," I nodded, feeling a sense of hope kindle in my chest.

"We'll start training them immediately."

Over the next few weeks, we put our plans into action. Our settlement began to transform, fortifications rising from the sand, escape tunnels being dug, and our people training tirelessly under Gavril's watchful eye. Meanwhile, Kael and I ventured into the city under the cover of darkness, mapping the sewers and studying the reservoir.

—— · 。° ☆: *.☽ .* :☆° . ——

29

The city was a cacophony of life, the heartbeat of a thriving desert metropolis that pulsed under the scorching sun. Sun-bleached buildings of sandy hues rose up, their surfaces shimmering under the heat. Their domed rooftops and arched windows spoke of the desert's architectural tradition, while the colorful, fluttering banners added a dash of vibrancy to the otherwise monotonous landscape.

Tucked away in the heart of the city was a humble tavern, a haven for those seeking respite from the relentless sun. Its entrance was flanked by wooden barrels, the aroma of ale faintly wafting from them. Above the entrance, a rusted sign creaked in the gentle desert breeze, the words "The Sand Serpent" barely discernible under layers of dust and age. Inside the tavern, the air was cool, a stark contrast to the heat outside. The stone floors were cool to the touch, and the walls held back the desert's relentless heat. The only sources of light were the sunbeams streaming through the small windows and the flickering lanterns hanging from the wooden beams, casting dancing shadows that played along the tavern's interior.

At a corner table sat three figures, their clothes and demeanor making them blend in with the other patrons. The first was a woman of stunning beauty, her dark hair cascading down her back in loose waves, her clear blue eyes scanning the room. She wore a simple dress of earthy tones, a stark contrast to her usual royal attire, yet it failed to diminish her regal bearing. Beside her, a tall, broad figure hunched over a mug of ale. His red eyes flickered with an otherworldly glow under the hood he wore, his skin was a dark crimson hue. He spoke in a gruff, almost coarse voice, his words laced with a peasant's dialect. The third figure was a woman of average height and unassuming appearance. Her hair was bound in a practical bun, her hazel eyes scanning the tavern with an almost maternal concern. She sipped her drink delicately, her every move indicating a sense of familiarity and comfort in her role.

Their table was littered with mugs of ale and plates of food, their banter mixing with the general hum of conversation within the tavern. The murmurs of the tavern's patrons grew louder as the day wore on, the mixture of voices creating a symphony of local gossip and news. A local trader was boasting about his new venture to the east. He claimed there was a hidden oasis filled with rare herbs, and he intended to be the first to exploit this newfound resource. His words were met with excited chatter and a few skeptical snorts. At another table, a woman spoke in hushed tones about a group of slaves who had reportedly escaped the mines. There were whispers that one among them was a powerful mage, and that they were causing havoc for the mine and guards. A grizzled veteran by the bar was regaling younger patrons with tales of his past battles. He spoke of a formidable foe, a tribe of desert dwellers known as the Sand Vipers, who seemed to have resurfaced recently after years of silence. Meanwhile, a group of merchants speculated about a recent increase in taxes, blaming it on the royal family's supposed extravagance. Their words were bitter, reflecting the discontent that was slowly brewing in the city.

In the midst of all this, Raena maintained her casual demeanor, sipping her ale and laughing at the right moments. Inside, however, her mind was working overtime, analyzing every piece of information. Elras shifted uncomfortably in his seat, his red eyes glancing towards Raena.

"My lady," he began in a low tone, his voice carrying a hint of concern, "this ain't a place fit for someone of your... stature."

Binda, sitting on the other side of Raena, nodded in agreement, her hazel eyes filled with worry.

"Elras is right, milady. The city streets can be dangerous, even for a skilled mage like you."

Raena merely smiled, raising her mug in a mock toast.

"Elras, Binda," she said, her clear blue eyes twinkling.

"I've trained with the best water mages in the kingdom. Besides, no one knows who I am here."

Elras grumbled something inaudible under his breath but didn't press the issue further. Binda, however, wasn't as easy to dissuade.

"Your safety is our primary concern, milady. If anything were to happen..."

Raena cut her off gently, placing a reassuring hand on her arm. "Nothing will happen, Binda," she said, her tone firm yet soothing. "I need to know what's happening in the city, what the people are saying. We can't know what is happening around us if we're blind to what's happening outside the palace."

Binda sighed, her worry lines still prominent. Their conversation was briefly interrupted as the tavern door creaked open, allowing a brief gust of hot desert air to sweep across the room before it was replaced by the cooler, dimly lit interior.

Five men, cloaked and dust-covered, walked in, the murmurs and chatter hushing slightly at their arrival. They settled at the far end of the tavern, their presence adding a layer of curiosity to the room's buzzing atmosphere. Their eyes, alert and wary, scanned the room, missing nothing. Elras tensed, his hand instinctively moving to the hilt of his dagger hidden beneath his cloak. Raena's attention, however, was drawn back to the current gossip.

"There's talk among the nulls," a low ranking mage was whispering to his companion.

"Talk of rebellion. They're tired of being treated as less than human, no rights, no dignity."

"Rebellion?" his friend scoffed.

"What can they do? They have no magic, no power."

"Don't underestimate them," the first man warned.

"There's more of them than there are of us. And they're desperate. Desperate people can be dangerous."

The gossip in the tavern continued, a cacophony of murmurs and whispers filling the room as the patrons shared stories and news.

Meanwhile, the cloaked men huddled in their corner, conversing in low tones that were drowned out by the tavern's noise. Every so often, one of them would glance towards Raena, his gaze intense. Elras noticed this and shifted uncomfortably, his hand still gripping the hilt of his hidden dagger. He leaned closer to Raena, whispering, "My lady, one of them fellows is starin' at you."

Raena glanced towards the cloaked men, her gaze meeting the one who had been watching her. He quickly looked away, turning back to his companions. However, Raena could feel his gaze on her, as if he was studying her, trying to see beyond her middle-class disguise. Binda noticed the exchange and her face filled with worry. "Milady, we should leave," she said, her voice barely audible over the tavern's noise.

But Raena waved her off.

"Let him look," she said confidently, taking a sip of her ale.

"He's not the first man to find me fascinating."

Binda looked like she wanted to argue, but she remained silent. She knew better than to question Raena when she was in this mood. Despite her confident words, Raena felt a shiver of unease. The man's gaze was different, more intense than the others. It was as if he saw her, the real her, beneath the middle-class disguise. It was a feeling she hadn't experienced in a long time.

As the night wore on, the tavern's patrons started to leave, their conversations and laughter fading into the night. The cloaked men also stood up to leave. The one who had been watching Raena lingered, his gaze lingering on her before he followed his companions out of the tavern. Once they were gone, Raena let out a sigh of relief. She finished her ale and rose from her seat.

"Time to go," she said, her voice carrying a hint of exhaustion.

Binda and Elras nodded, quickly gathering their belongings and following Raena out of the tavern. As they stepped into the moonlit night, the air was still warm, but a slight breeze provided a welcome respite. Raena, curiosity piqued by the mysterious man's unwavering gaze, decided on a whim to follow the cloaked figures. She motioned to Binda and Elras to stay close and moved silently through the winding alleys, using her water magic, subtly manipulated the moisture in the air to muffle their movements. She walked a safe distance behind them, blending in with the night as her dark attire melded into the shadows.

"Milady, are you sure about this?" Elras grumbled, his large figure cumbersome as he tried to match Raena's stealth.

"These men ain't no common riffraff."

Binda agreed, her hazel eyes filled with worry.

"Elras is right, milady. It's too dangerous."

Raena, however, dismissed their concerns.

For a moment, they trailed the men through the winding streets of the city, the sand beneath their feet muffled. However, as they turned a corner, they found the street ahead empty. The men had disappeared.

"Damn," Raena muttered under her breath, scanning the surroundings for any sign of the men.

Elras sighed, his breath misting in the cool desert night.

"We lost 'em, milady."

Binda looked relieved.

"Thank goodness. Now, can we please go back home?"

Raena gave a resigned nod, her mind still focused on the mystery men. Who were they?

"Alright," Raena finally conceded, her tone slightly dejected.

"Let's go home."

As they turned back, Raena took one last glance at the deserted street. The night was quiet, the earlier bustle of the city a stark contrast to the silence. She couldn't shake the nagging feeling that the man's gaze had stirred within her. She knew that something was wrong, caravan raids, discontent among the nulls, and that mysterious man who had looked at her in a way no one else had in months. The sun rose high and hot over the desert city the next morning, the golden rays lighting up the palace in a warm glow. Raena awoke, the memory of last night's events still fresh in her mind. She pushed herself up from her bed, her dark hair a wild cascade around her shoulders, and stretched, her clear blue eyes squinting against the sunlight streaming in from the window.

She dressed in a comfortable attire, a simple yet elegant dress befitting her status as a princess, and walked to the dining hall for breakfast. The palace servants, brought her a delicious meal of fresh fruits, flatbreads, and some local cheese. Raena ate in silence, her mind preoccupied with the events from the night before. After breakfast, she decided to take a walk around the palace corridors to clear her mind. As she turned a corner, she almost collided with Zarek. His gaze was focused on a parchment in his hands, completely oblivious to his surroundings.

"Zarek!" Raena exclaimed, a bit surprised. She quickly composed herself, a teasing smile pulling at her lips.

"What's got you so lost in thought?"

Zarek looked up from the parchment, his usual charm replaced with a tense grimace. He sighed and ran a hand through his hair.

"One of my family's water reservoirs was hit last night," he said, his voice filled with frustration.

"It was one of our smaller, less guarded ones, but it still held a considerable amount of water."

"Stolen?" Raena frowned, crossing her arms over her chest.

"Who would dare to steal from your family?"

"That's the question, isn't it?" Zarek muttered, his eyes returning to the parchment in his hands.

"We've had our differences with some families, but this is a new low."

Raena's blue eyes flared with indignation.

"Such audacity," she muttered, straightening her back and holding her head high.

"What are you planning to do?"

Zarek sighed, looking almost helpless, a sight so rare that it caught Raena off guard.

"I'm not sure. We've always had disagreements, but nobody has ever resorted to stealing water."

"The guards didn't see anything unusual. No signs of forced entry, no footprints, nothing. It's as if the water just... vanished."

"Vanished," Raena echoed.

"Just like those men last night."

Zarek frowned, looking at her in confusion.

"What men?"

Raena waved off his question, her mind racing.

"Never mind that. Listen, Zarek. There's been talk around the city... talk of discontent among the nulls. People are unhappy, the taxes are too high, and the living conditions... well, you know how it is."

A flicker of understanding passed over Zarek's face.

"You think this has something to do with the stolen water?"

"I'm not sure," Raena admitted.

"But it's possible, isn't it?"

Zarek looked thoughtful, running a hand through his hair.

"It's a possibility, but... the nulls? Really? They've never been this bold before."

Raena shrugged.

"Desperate times call for desperate measures. People will do a lot when they're pushed to the edge. And it's not just the nulls. There's been an increase in caravan raids as well. Something's happening, Zarek."

Zarek sighed, rolling up the parchment.

"I can't argue with you there, something is happening. I'm on my way to a council meeting now to discuss what happened last night. My father is already there."

Raena's eyebrows rose.

"A council meeting? And you didn't think to invite me?"

He shot her an amused look.

"Well, I was under the impression that you found council meetings as appealing as a sandworm."

She huffed, crossing her arms.

"That doesn't mean I don't want to be informed."

"I stand corrected then," he said, bowing slightly with a playful grin. "Would Her Royal Highness, Princess Raena, The Radian Jewell of the Desert grace us lowly council members with her presence at the meeting?"

Raena scoffed at his theatrics, but she couldn't help the smile tugging at her lips. His gaze softened, and he reached out, tucking a loose strand of hair behind her ear.

"Be careful. I don't like the idea of you getting involved in all this. It's dangerous."

Raena rolled her eyes, though she appreciated the sentiment.

"I can handle myself, Zarek."

"I know you can," he said, his eyes filled with a mix of admiration and concern.

"That's what worries me."

Together, they made their way to the council chamber, where the meeting was already in progress. Raena could feel the tension in the air, as influential mages debated the recent events.

"...such audacity, to steal water from the house of Xantheer!"

One council member bellowed.

"Such sacrilege will not stand!"

"Indeed!" another agreed.

"This is a clear violation of our sacred customs. The perpetrator must be found and dealt with accordingly!"

Raena's father, King Lucian, nodded at his daughter with a mixture of surprise and approval.

"Ah, Raena. I'm glad you've decided to join us. We were just discussing the recent events plaguing our city."

Raena took her seat next to her father, Zarek settling into his own spot nearby next to his own father. Lord Cadmus, Zarek's father, was in the midst of a heated argument with another council member. His voice boomed across the room.

"Whoever committed this heinous act must be found and made an example of! Such audacity cannot go unpunished!"

The other council member, a thin, aging mage, raised a shaking hand in protest.

"Now, now, Cadmus, let's not jump to conclusions. We have no evidence to point us in the right direction."

"Evidence?" Lord Cadmus spat, his eyes narrowing.

"We have a city in turmoil, water stolen from my own family's reservoir. What more evidence do we need?"

The room fell silent. Raena glanced at Zarek, who was watching the exchange with a thoughtful frown. She could see the wheels turning in his head, and she knew he was thinking about their earlier conversation.

Finally, one of the council members muttered.

"Could it be the Nulls?"

A gasp echoed through the room, the mere mention of the Nulls - the non-mage population of the city - enough to cause a ripple of surprise and disbelief.

Cadmus sneered.

"The Nulls? Those powerless wretches wouldn't dare."

The thin mage, refusing to back down, retorted.

"Oh, Cadmus, always so quick to underestimate those you deem beneath you. The Nulls have every reason to act against us. We control their water, their lives. Desperation can drive people to do unimaginable things."

Raena saw the opportunity to interject, her voice sharp and commanding.

"The Nulls have no magic, but they have their ways. We cannot dismiss them without investigation."

"Are you suggesting we waste our time investigating those pitiful creatures?" Cadmus scoffed, his face contorting in disgust. "We should focus on our own."

"Father, Raena has a point," Zarek interjected, calmly.

"We cannot afford to ignore any possibility. We must consider all potential threats, regardless of their origin."

King Lucian, who had been observing the exchange, finally spoke up. "I agree with my daughter and Zarek. We must consider every possibility. It would be foolish to disregard any potential leads."

The council members muttered amongst themselves, some in agreement, others dissenting. The atmosphere grew tenser as the debate continued, insults and accusations flying through the air like daggers. At this point, Lord Eran, a young mage with a kind, patient demeanor, spoke up.

"I must agree with Lord Zarek and Princess Raena. We cannot turn a blind eye to any potential suspects. We must be thorough and fair in our investigation."

Cadmus rolled his eyes, exasperated.

"Fair? This is about justice, not fairness! We must maintain order and protect our interests!"

"Evidently, your interests involve turning a blind eye to half the city!" Eran shot back. The room gasped; Eran was known for his gentleness, not his sharp tongue. Cadmus's face turned a shade darker, his lips curled into a snarl.

"You impudent whelp! I've crushed insects more threatening than you!"

Eran merely raised an eyebrow, unfazed.

"And yet, here we are, your family's water reserves depleted, and you, clueless as to who did it. Perhaps those insects weren't as insignificant as you thought."

Zarek's eyes flickered between the two men, his face a mask of neutrality. Raena, on the other hand, was barely suppressing a smirk. She'd always appreciated Eran's unexpected spine. Cadmus was about to retort when King Lucian raised his hand, silencing the room.

"Enough. We are not here to bicker and squabble like petty merchants. We are the ruling council of this kingdom, and we will act as such."

Cadmus reluctantly backed down, shooting Eran a final venomous glare before retreating into sullen silence. Lucian's gaze swept the room, his voice commanding.

"We will conduct an impartial and comprehensive investigation. All possibilities will be considered. That is my final word on the matter."

The council members, even Cadmus, nodded in submission.

The King's word was law, and none dared dispute it.

30

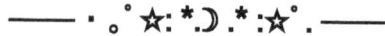

Once the meeting adjourned, Zarek and Raena found themselves standing in the grand corridor, the echoes of the council's argument still ringing in their ears. The once intimidating room, filled with harsh words and louder egos, was now eerily quiet. Zarek released a long-held breath, running a hand through his hair in an absent-minded gesture.

"Well, that was more intense than usual."

Raena let out a laugh.

"And you enjoy these meetings?" she asked, looking at Zarek with a playful smile.

"I find them... enlightening," he replied, matching her grin.

"The council members' true colors show when under pressure. It's... educational."

Raena shook her head, her dark hair catching the light.

"You and your peculiar idea of fun," she quipped.

"Although I must admit, I didn't expect Eran to stand up to Cadmus like that. It was quite a sight."

Before Zarek could respond, two figures appeared at the end of the corridor. Caspian, Raena's younger brother, strode forward with his usual careless swagger, prince Aldric trailing behind him. Both had missed the council meeting, and from the look on Caspian's face, he was eager to find out what he had missed.

"We heard the shouting all the way from the training grounds," Caspian said, his eyebrows furrowing in worry.

"What's all the fuss about?"Raena exchanged a look with Zarek before answering.

"Let's just say it was an... eventful meeting. But then again, when is it not?"

Caspian's grin widened.

"Oh? I missed the old windbags throwing tantrums at each other? What a tragedy!"

"More than tantrums, brother." Raena retorted, her tone serious despite the jesting words.

"Our water reserves are being stolen."

Aldric stepped forward.

"The water is being stolen? From the reserves?" His voice was measured, but there was an undercurrent of concern that did not go unnoticed.

"Indeed," Zarek replied, his casual demeanor belying the seriousness of the situation.

"And it's not just a trickle. Enough water has been taken to cause alarm."

"Stolen? By who?" Caspian asked, concern replacing his initial amusement.

"That," Zarek chimed in, "is what we intend to find out. The council will conduct a thorough investigation. In the meantime, we should be vigilant."

Aldric crossed his arms, his gaze distant.

"I suppose it's also worth looking into the water gathering and storing methods. If someone's stealing, they've found a flaw in the system."

"And we need to plug that flaw before we drain dry," Zarek nodded, appreciating Aldric's insight.

"Cadmus won't be happy about this," Caspian commented.

"It's going to ruffle his feathers."

Zarek rolled his eyes.

"Father's feathers are perpetually ruffled, Caspian. This will just be an added gust of wind. He was less than pleased about the idea of investigating the Nulls."

"And what of the demons?" Aldric's voice was low, serious, causing everyone to turn to him.

"Well…" Zarek began.

"Father was convinced it couldn't have been them. He thinks they're incapable of such actions."

Aldric merely nodded, his gaze distant. Caspian, however, was less reserved.

"I'll bet he didn't like that idea either, did he?"

"Understatement of the year," Raena laughed, her hand waving dismissively.

"He was livid."

Zarek's expression grew more serious, he glanced at Raena, "Speaking of things that may ruffle feathers," he began, his tone thoughtful, "the annual ball is quickly approaching."

Raena sighed, rolling her eyes.

"Of course. How could I forget? A grand celebration amidst rising taxes and whispers of rebellion. Just what we need."

"Actually, that's not the part I was referring to," Zarek added, a wry smile playing on his lips.

"I was thinking about the traditional dance of the betrothed."

Raena shot him a disbelieving look.

"That dance? The one we practiced as children, with you invariably stepping on my toes? You believe now is the time for that public spectacle?"

Zarek chuckled, a touch of mirth in his eyes.

"Yes, my love. We have to dance. Together. In front of everybody. A grand spectacle for all to see, and speculate."

"Could the timing be any worse?" Raena groaned, sinking against a nearby wall.

"The Nulls already think we're wasteful. An extravagant ball is going to validate their beliefs. Not to mention the fact that I'll have to parade around in a gown that costs more than their annual salary. It's just...it's not right."

"You're not wrong, Raena," Aldric chimed in.

"But we must remember that the ball is a tradition, deeply ingrained in our society. Not holding it would also cause uproar, especially among the nobles. It's a double-edged sword, really."

Caspian, attempted to lighten the mood.

"Oh, come now! Think about the feast! The music! The...uh...dancing..." He trailed off, wincing at Raena's glare.

"Jokes aside, Caspian," Zarek said, "Raena has a point. The ball could exacerbate tensions. But Aldric is also correct. It's tradition, and canceling it might be interpreted as a sign of instability or fear. We're stuck between the hammer and the anvil as it were."

"It seems we are," Raena agreed, her blue eyes troubled. She sighed again, this time running her fingers through her dark hair.

"I suppose there's no use whining about it. We must carry on with our duties, as expected."

"And on that note," she added, her gaze flitting to each of the men in turn.

"I have another duty to attend to. The ball gown won't fit itself, you know."

Caspian's grin was infectious.

"The trials and tribulations of a royal," he teased, earning him a quick smack on the arm from Raena.

"It seems we are," Raena agreed, her blue eyes troubled. She sighed again, this time running her fingers through her dark hair.

"I suppose there's no use whining about it. We must carry on with our duties, as expected."

"And on that note," she added, her gaze flitting to each of the men in turn.

"I have another duty to attend to. The ball gown won't fit itself, you know."

Caspian's grin was infectious.

"The trials and tribulations of a royal," he teased, earning him a quick smack on the arm from Raena.

Shaking her head in mock exasperation, Raena started down the hall.

"I must take my leave, gentlemen. Try not to create any more catastrophes while I'm gone, won't you?"

After she disappeared around the corner, the men fell into contemplative silence.

"Well, gents," Caspian finally broke the silence.

"I believe we have a lot to consider."

"And a ball to prepare for," Aldric added, a touch of resignation in his voice.

"Indeed," Zarek replied, watching the corner where Raena had disappeared.

"Indeed we do."

***

Raena swept into the room reserved for her fitting, the lush, intricately woven rugs muffling her footfall. Sunlight filtered through the high, narrow windows, glinting off of the polished brass mirrors that lined the walls. Arrays of precious stones, beads, and threads were laid out on a large mahogany table, shimmering like a cache of pirate's treasure under the gentle sunlight. In the middle of this delicate pandemonium stood the seamstress, a slender, hunched Null woman named Emilia. She was one of the few who managed to distinguish themselves in their craft, catching the eye of the royals. Raena often marveled at the precision of her work, the care with which she manipulated even the most stubborn fabrics into forms of breathtaking beauty. Emilia turned, her eyes, cloudy with age, brightening as she spotted Raena.

"Your Highness," she bowed, her voice trembling with reverence and a hint of nervous anticipation.

"The dress is ready for the first fitting."

Raena gave her a nod, her lips curving up in a small, encouraging smile. She was very aware of the disparities between her world and Emilia's, and she had always tried to treat her with the respect she deserved. The dress, a glorious cascade of deep blue silk embroidered with silver threads, was hung on a wooden mannequin. It was a masterpiece, painstakingly crafted to highlight Raena's slender figure and complement her dark hair and fair skin. The bodice was designed to fit snugly, studded with tiny sapphires that shimmered in an echo of her eyes. The skirt flared out, an ocean of silk that ruffled and flowed with the slightest movement. Raena couldn't help but take a step back, her eyes wide as she took in the magnificent creation.

"Emilia," she breathed, her gaze shifting to the humble seamstress, "it's... it's exquisite."

Emilia beamed at the praise, her weathered face crinkling into a wide smile.

"Thank you, Your Highness. It was a labor of love. Now, if you would please undress, we can begin the fitting."

Raena complied, allowing herself to be swept up in the detailed and well-practiced routine of the fitting. She stood still as Emilia adjusted the bodice, her fingers deft and confident as she pinched, tucked, and smoothed the material. The Null woman's concentration was absolute, her focus narrowed down to the smallest stitch. The outside world, with all its troubles and tribulations, seemed to fade away. The opulence of the dress, the attention to detail, the delicacy of the needlework - it all conspired to create a bubble of tranquility. Eventually, Raena found herself once again fully dressed, the gown fitting her like a second skin. She turned to face the mirror, the sight that greeted her taking her breath away. The dress, with its deep blue hue and sparkling sapphires, made her skin glow, her dark hair seem richer, her blue eyes brighter.

"Emilia," Raena whispered.

"Thank you."

Emilia's eyes softened, her wrinkled hand reaching out to gently pat Raena's.

"It's my honor, Your Highness. Now, let's make sure every stitch is perfect for the ball."

Just as Raena began to respond, the fitting room door creaked open, causing both women to glance up. Standing in the doorway was Zarek, his gaze immediately finding Raena. He stilled, his breath catching at the sight of her in the opulent dress. The setting sun threw golden rays of light around her, making her seem ethereal and otherworldly.

"By the gods, Ren," Zarek breathed, his usual cheeky grin replaced by an expression of awed reverence.

"You look... absolutely radiant."

Raena, though no stranger to Zarek's flattery, felt a blush creep up her cheeks at his words. She knew Zarek - knew his playful nature, his fondness for jest - but the sincerity in his voice and eyes was unmistakable.

"Always one for a dramatic entrance, aren't you, Zarek?" Raena shot back, unable to suppress a smile. She elegantly rotated on her heel, the silky fabric of her dress swirling around her.

"One could say you're early, or that you're woefully late. After all, Emilia and I are nearly done."

Zarek strode into the room, his gaze never leaving Raena. Emilia, sensing an intimate moment brewing, tactfully excused herself.

"If you'd excuse me, Your Highness, Lord Zarek, I'll leave you two alone."

With that, she shuffled out of the room, leaving Raena and Zarek alone amongst the twinkling beads and shimmering silks. Zarek approached Raena, his fingers gently brushing over the sparkling sapphires adorning her bodice.

"Ren," he murmured, his fingers tracing a stray lock of her dark hair, "I can hardly believe the sight before me. You are... stunning. The stars themselves will be envious at the ball."

Raena's blue eyes met his, a playful smirk tugging at her lips.

"Just make sure you remember how to dance, Zarek. Or it'll be the stars laughing, not envying."

Zarek chuckled, the sound echoing around the grand room.

"Oh, my love, have faith. When the time comes, we'll glide around the ballroom as though we were born for it."

Slowly, almost teasingly, he extended his hand towards her, his fingers brushing lightly against the smooth skin of her bare arm. He let his touch travel up her arm, igniting a trail of goosebumps in its wake, before resting it on her waist. His eyes, a mesmerizing emerald green, locked onto hers, sparkling with a mischievous glint. His voice taking on a theatrically serious tone.

"Or are you implying that I, the heir of the House of Xantheer, the finest dancer this side of the Barren Sea, would falter at our ball?"

His outrageous claim caused a burst of laughter to bubble from her lips, the sweet sound echoing through the room. Zarek's heart fluttered at the sound, his grin widening in response. Raena, unable to resist the contagious energy that Zarek seemed to radiate, let her hand slide into his.

"You, the finest dancer?" she said, her eyebrow arching in mock skepticism. "I think that remains to be seen, Lord Zarek."

"Oh? I'm not too sure if should I be more concerned with the dance or with the number of hearts you'll break at the ball, Raena."

His voice dropped low, a whisper that resonated deeply within the quiet of the room. His eyes sparkled mischievously, and a playful smirk pulled at the corners of his mouth.

"Zarek, I do believe you're jealous," Raena chided with a smirk, her fingers moving to fiddle with the topmost button of his tunic.

"You should know better. My heart is already claimed."

His hand moved to cover hers, halting her playful actions. The intensity in his gaze deepened, his voice taking on a seductive timbre.

"Yes, and the man who has your heart, Princess, he's the luckiest bastard in all the realm."

Raena felt a delicious shiver run down her spine at the gravelly earnestness in his voice. There was a tantalizing tension between them, electrifying the air and making her heart race.

"I suppose he is," Raena responded, her smirk softening into a flirtatious smile as she felt Zarek's thumb gently stroke the back of her hand. He was tantalizingly close now, the space between them electrified with an energy that was palpably intense.

"However," she continued, her voice dropping to a sultry whisper as she traced her other hand along the prominent lines of his chest through his tunic, "is he prepared for all the jealous eyes that will be on him, Lord Zarek?"

There was an irresistible spark in her eyes, a devilish allure that made Zarek's heart pound. He leaned into her touch, his hand leaving hers to run up her arm, his fingers ghosting over her delicate collarbone. The spark of desire in his eyes matched hers.

"Let them be jealous, Raena," he murmured, his voice husky. His gaze flickered to her lips before returning to her eyes.

"They can look all they want, but they can never touch... never have what is mine."

With his hand cradling her jaw, he leaned in closer, his lips a breath away from hers. His eyes searched hers, the intensity of his gaze causing her to lose her breath. He was so close now that she could feel the heat radiating off him, could smell the heady scent of him. The fitting room suddenly seemed too small, too confining.

"But tell me, my mischievous princess," Zarek breathed against her lips, his thumb tracing her lower lip with a tender caress that sent sparks of desire coursing through her, "do you think you can keep yourself from breaking my heart?"

Before Raena could respond, Zarek's lips were on hers, a possessive, fiery kiss that left her gasping for breath. The taste of him was intoxicating, alluring. His hands were firm against her, one hand in her hair, the other gripping her waist, pulling her flush against him. It was a dance of tongues and passions, a dance far more seductive than any that could ever be performed in a ballroom. Raena's heart pounded in her chest as she gave herself over to the kiss, her arms sliding up around his neck to draw him closer. As they broke apart, both panting lightly, a wicked glint appeared in Zarek's eyes. His hand drifted lower, tracing the curve of her waist before he gently lifted the edge of her dress. His fingertips ghosted along the bare skin of her thigh, causing her to shiver in anticipation.

"My apologies, princess," he murmured, his voice husky with desire. "I can't help but explore this masterpiece you're clothed in... and what's beneath."

Raena met his gaze boldly, her own desire flaring in her azure eyes. She wanted this, wanted him. The tension in the room was near palpable, their heavy breaths the only sound in the quiet room.

Zarek leaned in closer, his breath hot on her ear as he whispered, "My jewel... may I...?"

The words were left hanging, a silent question in the air, but the intent was clear. His fingers trailed higher up her thigh, igniting a trail of fire along her skin, setting her senses ablaze.

"Yes," Raena found herself whispering in reply, her heart pounding in her chest.

"Yes, Zarek."

With her approval, Zarek knelt before her, his hands skimming up her thighs as he pushed the silk of her dress higher. His eyes never left hers, the desire in them burning brighter than the desert sun. And then his mouth was on her, his tongue moving in ways that drew gasps and shudders from her. She clutched at his shoulders, her knuckles white as wave after wave of pleasure coursed through her. Every flick, every touch, sent her spiraling further into bliss. He was relentless, teasing her until she was a quivering mess, panting his name. Once he'd brought her to the edge, he pulled away, pressing a chaste kiss to her inner thigh before standing. He smoothed down her dress with a satisfied smirk on his face, his gaze holding a devilish gleam.

"You are so beautiful," he whispered.

"I want to see you naked tonight, may I visit your quarters?" Raena, still breathless from Zarek's intoxicating ministrations, could only manage a nod, her azure eyes wide and full of desire.

"Lord Zarek," she murmured, her fingers sliding up to trace the line of his jaw, "if you don't visit, I'd consider it a grave insult."

Her playful tone was a stark contrast to the flush on her cheeks and the rapid beat of her heart. Zarek's eyes shone with delight at her response, a soft chuckle escaping his lips. He covered her hand with his own, pressing a warm kiss to the back of her fingers. His gaze was full of unspoken promises, his intent clear.

"My love," he whispered, the rough timbre of his voice sending shivers down her spine.

"I would never dream of causing such an offense."

The promise in his voice sent a thrill of anticipation coursing through her. The image of his hands on her bare skin, the feel of his mouth on her, was still fresh in her mind, a tantalizing promise of what was to come. There was a wicked glint in his eye as he straightened up, letting her hand fall back to her side. With one last lingering look, Zarek exited the fitting room, his touch lingering on her skin and his promise echoing in her mind. The room felt emptier without him, his presence having filled it with an electric tension that was now noticeably absent. But the promise of the night to come was a heady thought, and Raena found herself eagerly looking forward to it.

—— · ˳° ☆: *.) .*·☆° . ——

31

Weeks turned into a busy blur, each passing day a symphony of hard work and quiet victories. We stole water from the smaller, less-guarded reservoirs of a local noble family. It was a dangerous operation, but we executed it flawlessly. Our men would slip into the sewers under the cloak of darkness, navigating the labyrinthine tunnels with a precision honed by relentless practice, and siphoning off just enough water to go unnoticed. Meanwhile, the fortifications around our settlement took form, the raw, parched sand giving way to stone walls and hidden tunnels. Gavril was a taskmaster, driving our people hard, but always with a glint of pride in his eyes as he watched them grow stronger and more capable each day. Our network of safe houses across the cities expanded, built within the modest establishments operated by nulls. We communicated using coded language and hidden signs, a language that was ours, belonging to the rebellion and to no one else. One evening, as we gathered around the map once again, I looked at Kael and Gavril, my comrades, my brothers in arms. The lantern light carved shadows into their determined faces, highlighting the strain of our relentless fight but also the strength that radiated from them.

"We've done well," I started, breaking the silence that had fallen over us as we pored over the map.

"We've managed to secure a steady supply of water, our defenses are coming along well, and we've established footholds in the cities."

Gavril grunted in agreement, running a hand over his stubbled chin. "The training's paid off. Everyone's holding their own. It's a start."

Kael, however, looked up at me, his eyes thoughtful.

"Yes, it's a start," he echoed Gavril's sentiment.

"But there's still a long way to go. The mages are not fools. They'll notice the missing water eventually."

"I know," I nodded, my gaze locked onto the sprawling city represented on the map.

"Which is why we need to stay one step ahead. We can't afford complacency. The moment we start thinking we're safe, that's when we'll lose."

Orlon shuffled into the room then, his face drawn.

"News from the city," he announced, his voice trembling slightly. "Our benefactor sends word that the mages are growing restless. They've noticed the diminished water supplies."

Silence fell over the room like a shroud, the weight of the news sinking in. The mages were suspicious, which meant we were in danger. But we were far from defeated. We were the desert wind, silent, invisible, relentless. And we wouldn't be stopped, not until our people were free.

"There's more," Orlon began, unfolding a scrap of parchment, his fingers shaking slightly.

"The mages are hosting a grand ball in a fortnight. A celebration of their rule, and they're bringing the Water Heart to the palace as a symbol of their power."

The Water Heart, the source of the mages' command over water. It was believed to be an ancient artifact, a relic of a time long lost. My mind raced. If we had the Water Heart, we could have a powerful bargaining chip, free ourselves from the suffocating grip of the mages. And there was something else. The demon slaves working in the mines. The Water Heart could be our bargaining chip to free them.

"I want to steal it," I declared, my voice echoing in the silence that followed Orlon's revelation. Gavril choked on his drink.

"Steal the Water Heart? Ash, have you lost your mind?"

"Lost it?" I asked, a dry smile curving my lips.

"Or just found it?"

"Think, Gavril," I continued, my tone leveling.

"If we get our hands on the Water Heart, we dictate terms. We wouldn't be in the shadows anymore. We could bring our people out of those mines."

His eyes were wide, unblinking, but there was an unmistakable hint of understanding there. Orlon watched us quietly, the lines on his face deepening with concern.

"Ash," he started, "stealing the Water Heart... it's not just rebellion. It's war."

"And what have we been preparing for, if not war?" I countered.

Kael, his eyes flicking between us, finally broke his silence.

"Ash... it's risky. More than anything we've attempted before."

"But it could change everything," I insisted, turning to him.

"You know what those mines are like. You know what it could mean to free those trapped in there."

He closed his eyes, a single nod indicating his agreement. Gavril grunted, his gaze falling onto the map again.

"We're not just going up against the mages at the palace. We're walking into a den full of vipers wearing the finest silks and the sharpest smiles."

"I know," I said, my voice dropping to a whisper.

"And we'll walk among them, disguised as one of their own."

I saw Orlon's eyebrows lift at my words.

"The glamour necklaces," he murmured, realization dawning on him.

"We used them when stealing water. We could use them again to hide our demon heritage."

I nodded, a slow smile creeping onto my face.

"Exactly."

"I'll get them ready," Orlon said, pushing himself to his feet.

Gavril turned towards me, a hint of the old fire sparking in his eyes.

"Alright, Ash," he grumbled.

"Let's do it. Let's steal the bloody Water Heart."

I clapped him on the shoulder, feeling a swell of hope rushing through me.

**

The night swallowed the landscape outside, with only a few scattered fires of the settlement piercing the darkness. The desert was a silent, eternal witness of our struggle, of our hopes. I stepped out, seeking solace in its quiet embrace. The tense dialogue and planning left my mind spinning and the stark midnight air brought the much-needed respite. My thoughts wandered. As much as our collective focus was on the Water Heart, my mind inevitably fell upon her. I felt the echo of her presence in the harsh desert wind, her image etched into my mind, the light of the lantern reflecting off her ebony hair and her blue eyes holding a depth that reminded me of the endless sea that we used to hear tales of. Footsteps shuffled behind me and I knew without turning who it was. Kael, his presence as familiar as the rhythm of my own heart.

"You should be resting," he said, his voice low and calming as he fell into step beside me.

"I could say the same about you," I replied, my gaze still fixed on the desert. There was a silence then, but it was a comfortable one. Kael and I had weathered enough storms together that words weren't always necessary. A ghost of a smile touched my lips.

"I saw her, Kael," I confessed, my voice mingling with the midnight wind.

"In the city, at the tavern. I saw Raena."

He remained silent for a moment, his eyes fixed on the vast expanse of darkness before us.

"The princess?" he finally asked, his voice subdued.

"Are you certain?"

"I would know her anywhere," I answered simply.

"She didn't see me, or at least she didn't recognized me" I continued, my voice growing distant as the memory of her played in my mind. A long silence ensued, Kael's gaze still on me. I could see the warning in his eyes, the fear, the painful memories of his own past.

"Ash," he finally said, his voice carrying the weight of unspoken warnings.

238

"You know this... attraction... it's dangerous, she's a mage. A princess. You're a demon. This... it's not just dangerous, it's suicide."

I chuckled lightly, the sound hollow in the silent night.

"And yet, here we are, planning to steal the Water Heart from under their noses. Isn't that suicide, too?"

He fell silent at that, his gaze returning to the infinite expanse of the desert.

"Perhaps," he finally murmured, his voice barely audible over the wind.

"But one is a fight for our people. The other... the other is a battle you're fighting alone, Ash."

"Love and war, Ash," Kael continued, his tone taking on a somber note.

"They don't mix well."

"Who said anything about love?" I replied hastily, too hastily, but the sudden intensity in Kael's gaze told me he didn't buy it. He knew me too well.

"Ash, you're walking a tightrope with a blindfold. You can't see the end, and you can't see the fall. We can't afford to lose you to a mage's charm. Right now, we need to survive first. We need to free our people. And that..." He gestured vaguely towards the direction of the city, where I knew the palace - and Raena - resided.

"That could be a distraction."

There it was, the unvarnished truth. Kael, despite his traumas and his struggles, had an ability to see things for what they were. No illusions, no fantasies. And right now, he was right. But acknowledging that didn't make the reality any easier. I watched as Kael retreated back into the shadows, leaving me alone with the desert, my thoughts, and the haunting image of Raena. As the night stretched on, I realized I wasn't just contemplating theft, rebellion, or even war. I was contemplating a dance with fire, a dance that could consume us all. And yet, I couldn't shake off the feeling, the hope, that this dance might also be the spark we needed to ignite our revolution. But for now, the desert remained our silent witness, the stars our only guide in the impending storm.

—— · ˛ ˚ ☆: *.).* :☆˚ . ——

32

The day of the ball arrived with a flourish, bringing with it a current of feverish excitement that swept through the palace. Servants rushed to and fro, their faces flushed with exertion as they laid out the final touches - lavish platters of exotic fruits and meats, sparkling crystal goblets filled with the finest wines, sumptuous decorations of gold and silver that added to the grandeur of the palace. As evening fell, the palace grounds became a hive of activity. The nobility of the realm, resplendent in their finery, began to arrive in droves. Whispers and giggles filled the air, mingling with the strains of a melody being played by a group of skilled musicians. The atmosphere was electrifying, charged with anticipation and the promise of a night filled with merriment and intrigue. Each guest wore a mask, hiding their identities and adding an air of mystery and intrigue to the night. Gilded, feathered, and bedazzled, the masks were a parade of creativity and artistry, a symbol of high society's extravagance.

Raena stood at the top of the grand staircase, the sapphire-studded mask she wore mirroring the shimmering brilliance of her eyes. It concealed her identity, yet highlighted her alluring beauty, a tantalizing enigma to the crowd below. She descended the stairs slowly, her blue silk dress flowing like a waterfall, catching the ambient light in a mesmerizing dance of shadow and radiance. Her heart pounded in rhythm with the ethereal music wafting through the grand hall, the expectant gazes of the nobility below fueling her anticipation. When she reached the bottom of the stairs, a masked figure detached himself from the crowd. Dressed in a tailored black tunic that accentuated his muscular form, Zarek wore a mask of shimmering emerald, the deep green echoing the hue of his eyes. He stood with the air of a man utterly besotted, his gaze soft yet blazing as he watched his beloved descend the stairs.

"Lady of mystery," he greeted, his voice low and warm, "you have outdone the stars themselves tonight."

His hand extended in invitation, the playfulness of his persona undercut by the depth of feeling in his eyes. Raena's lips curled in amusement, the mystery of the mask not hiding her distinctive smirk. "And you, my lord, are a vision of the night sky, dark and endlessly captivating," she replied, slipping her gloved hand into his.

While the banter between Raena and Zarek simmered, the large double doors of the grand hall were thrown open and the crowd instantly hushed. King Lucian and Queen Isadora, the monarchs of the realm, made their grand entry. They were figures of majesty and grace, their regal presence commanding the attention of every individual present. The King's deep baritone echoed through the ballroom as he raised a glass, commanding silence with his poised presence.

"Noble lords and ladies, we welcome you to our palace. We gather under the vast desert sky, bound by the shared allure of water and magic, bearing witness to an alliance of love and power."

His words carried weight and stirred a ripple of excitement through the ballroom. The Queen then, her voice melodic yet firm, continued, "Tonight, our beloved daughter Raena, and Zarek, heir to the prestigious House of Xantheer, will perform the betrothal dance. Their unity shall be the first drop of rain in our desert, heralding a prosperous future."

A thunderous applause filled the ballroom, the clapping hands akin to the roaring of a river in the quiet of the desert night. Zarek took Raena's hand, guiding her to the center of the dance floor, as the crowd parted to create a circular space for the betrothed couple. The music started, slow and enchanting, the rhythm mimicking the natural flow of water, the lifeblood of their realm.

Their dance was a beautiful tableau of flowing movements and controlled passion, a visible manifestation of their burgeoning affection. Raena moved with the grace of a desert bloom swaying in the night wind, her every movement a testament to her confident beauty. Zarek matched her step for step, his movements displaying the understated strength that lay beneath his persona.

Watching them from the sidelines were two figures, both masked, but their identities known to all. Caspian, Raena's brother, wore a mask of pure white, his hazel eyes shining with mirth. He was a sight to behold, his strong physique adorned in an elegant white suit, making him a perfect foil to his sister's sapphire brilliance. Aldric, the visiting prince, was a vision in crimson and gold. His mask, a blend of the two colors, added an aura of mystery to his handsome features. The casual ease with which he carried himself belied the cunning mind beneath his charming exterior.

"I've half a mind to swoop in and steal Raena away," Aldric joked, his gaze fixed on the dancing couple. His tone was light, the words spoken more in jest than any serious intention.

"And you'd be turned into a human popsicle before you could blink," retorted Caspian, his laughter echoing in the hall. He was all too aware of Zarek's fierce protectiveness over Raena.

Their conversation was interrupted by the arrival of Lord Cadmus, Zarek's father, his authority and power making him a formidable presence.

"Princes," he greeted, his voice a gravelly hum that commanded respect.

"You seem to be enjoying the spectacle. Is it not a sight to behold?"

"It is, indeed, Lord Cadmus," replied Aldric, matching the older man's tone with his own air of respect.

"Your son certainly knows how to command a room."

A satisfied smirk crossed Cadmus' face, visible even behind his mask.

"That he does. He'll make a fine leader."

Aldric turned to Caspian, raising an eyebrow in silent question. Caspian shrugged in response, his eyes darting to where Raena and Zarek were finishing their dance, their movements ending in a beautifully choreographed pose. The room erupted in applause once more, the spectators enthralled by the spectacle they had just witnessed.

"The dance is beautiful indeed," Caspian chimed in, his voice light. "Yet, I wonder if Zarek truly commands the room or if it is Raena who bewitches us all."

Lord Cadmus turned to the young prince, his eyes glinting dangerously behind his mask.

"Bewitched or not, Prince Caspian, remember it is my son who leads the dance. That is the nature of power."

Aldric's lips curved upward in a smile.

"Power is an enticing game, Lord Cadmus. However, the dance... ah, the dance is all about balance, wouldn't you agree?"

"Balance is a luxury only those at the top can afford, Prince Aldric," Cadmus replied tersely.

"In the desert, it is survival that matters."

"The desert can be harsh," Caspian acknowledged, his gaze straying back to his sister.

"Yet, it nurtures its own, yields to those who know how to bend water to their will. That's the beauty of survival, Lord Cadmus. It adapts."

"Adaptation is only part of the story," Cadmus retorted.

"Control is what makes a ruler."

Aldric chuckled, a light and airy sound.

"Control, adaptation, survival... all pieces of the same puzzle, my lord. A dance, if you will."

"Indeed," Lord Cadmus conceded, his gaze returning to the dancing couple.

"A dance it is."

As the final notes of the music fell into silence, the couple paused, their bodies still close. Their breaths were in sync, a testament to their shared dance. Raena's eyes, bright beneath her mask, were locked with Zarek's, their depths reflecting the shared intimacy of the moment. The crowd erupted into applause, their delight echoing throughout the grand ballroom. Stepping apart, Zarek brought

Raena's hand to his lips, placing a kiss on her knuckles before releasing her.

"My lady is parched," he noted, his eyes scanning her flushed face.

Raena laughed lightly, a sound that made Zarek's heart leap.

"The desert heat seems to have followed us inside, hasn't it?"

"Yes," Zarek replied, his smile hidden behind his mask.

"Shall I fetch you something to drink?"

"That would be wonderful, Zarek," she answered, her blue eyes twinkling behind her mask.

Zarek offered a nod of agreement, his gaze lingering on Raena a moment longer before he disappeared into the sea of faces. Alone in the midst of the bustling ballroom, Raena's gaze drifted across the masked figures, their shapes twirling and swirling to the orchestral melody that filled the air. It was then that a figure separated itself from the crowd, moving towards her with an effortless grace that turned heads. His attire was simple but tastefully done, standing in stark contrast to the gaudy opulence around them. His mask, a minimalist piece, shadowed his eyes but did nothing to hide the intensity in them.

"My lady," he greeted, his voice as smooth as the river's flow. He bowed slightly, a perfectly executed move of respect.

"May I have the honor of this dance?"

Raena's eyebrows raised in surprise, her interest piqued by the audacity of the stranger. Despite the grandeur of the ball, few dared to approach the princess so openly, especially with her betrothed present. Yet, here he was, an enigma in the midst of a spectacle.

"And who might you be?" she asked, her voice ringing clear above the soft melody of the orchestra.

"A mere admirer," he replied.

"One captivated by the beauty of the desert's moon."

"Flattery will get you many places," she said, her voice teasing.

"But will it get you this dance?"

"That," he replied, his tone confident, "is entirely up to you, my lady."

Raena found herself intrigued. His allure was more than just his handsome features, it was in his words, his boldness, the way he held himself. It was a stark contrast to the pretentiousness she often encountered, and she found it refreshing.

"Very well," she replied, a smile playing on her lips.

"One dance."

His hand enveloped hers, a firm but gentle grip. As he led her to the dance floor, a hush fell over the crowd, all eyes on them. As they moved in rhythm with the music, there was a wild elegance to their dance, a clear departure from the controlled poise of her dance with Zarek. The stranger led with a quiet confidence, and Raena found herself caught in the charm of the moment, the mystery of her partner adding to the thrill of the dance. Caspian, watching from the sidelines, frowned slightly.

"So, stranger," she said, drawing herself a fraction closer.

"What brings you to our humble palace tonight?"

He smiled, an enigmatic curl of lips.

"The promise of an enchanting evening under the desert stars," he responded, his tone low, intimate.

"And the chance to dance with the most captivating woman in the room."

His audacity had her chuckling.

"And has the evening lived up to your expectations?" she inquired, meeting his gaze with an equally challenging one.

"In some ways," he answered, his voice laced with a hint of amusement.

"It has exceeded them."

Raena smirked, her eyes sparkling with a mix of curiosity and amusement.

"Really? How so?"

He leaned in, his voice dropping even lower.

"Well, I never expected to share such a delightful dance with the radian jewel of the desert herself."

Raena laughed, the sound like the chiming of bells.

"You certainly know how to weave words, stranger."

"Perhaps," he conceded, his smile mirroring her own.

"But tell me, Princess, are you truly as free as the desert wind, or are you bound by chains unseen?"

Raena's laughter faded, replaced by a moment of thoughtful silence.

"A little of both, I would imagine," she admitted.

"One does not become the future queen without a few chains."

His gaze held hers, seemingly captivated by her candid response.

"And do these chains... Does your betrothed... bring you joy?"

The question hung in the air between them, as heavy as the desert heat. Raena, taken aback, held his gaze, her own eyes narrowed in suspicion and interest. This was not mere idle conversation, not mere flattery. This was a probe, an inquiry she was not accustomed to. It intrigued her and put her on edge, all at once.

"Why, stranger," she drawled, a coy smile pulling at her lips.

"That's a rather personal question, don't you think?"

He chuckled, a deep, rumbling sound.

"A fair response. Yet, a dance is more than just steps. It's a conversation, is it not?"

"Indeed, it is," she conceded, her smirk returning.

"And to answer your question, I find joy in many things. My betrothed is but one of them."

He hummed, nodding his head in acknowledgment.

"As the moon finds joy in the stars, yet chooses to dance alone in the sky."

Raena laughed, her heart oddly light.

"Perhaps," she said, a teasing glint in her eyes.

"Or perhaps, the moon enjoys the mystery of the dance more than the constancy of the stars."

Meanwhile, Zarek had procured two glasses filled with a refreshingly cold nectar, water mingled with the sweet fruits of their world. The glasses chilled in his hand, condensation forming on the outside, a testament to the magic imbued within. He turned back to find Raena, his eyes scanning the crowd until they landed on her, dancing with a stranger. A flicker of surprise crossed his eyes, followed quickly by a frown that settled into a hardened expression. He remained in place, his gaze fixed on the pair. Raena, lost in the rhythm of the dance, was only vaguely aware of the reactions of the crowd around her. Their dance continued, the room watching in enthralled silence. Zarek's grip on the glasses tightened, his gaze never wavering from the scene. The sight of Raena, so radiant and carefree with another man, stirred within him a whirlpool of emotions he had yet to fully comprehend. His love for her was a relentless tide, but jealousy was a new beast, its claws sinking deep within him. He watched in silence, waiting for the dance to end, for Raena to return to him. His betrothed, his love, his future Queen.

When the orchestra hit the final crescendo, Raena and the stranger slowed their movements. With a final spin, he brought her to a halt, his hand gently releasing hers. The crowd burst into applause, clearly delighted by the spectacle of the dance. Raena dipped her head in acknowledgment, her eyes never leaving the stranger.

"Thank you for the dance, my lady," he murmured, bowing gracefully.

"It was an honor."

"And a mystery," she replied, mirroring his bow with a slight curtsy of her own.

"Thank you, stranger."

As the crowd erupted into applause, a new figure approached them. He was clad similarly to the first, his mask equally plain and intriguing.

"Begging your pardon, princess," the newcomer said, his voice smooth, holding a hint of an apology.

"I seem to have misplaced my brother. It appears, however, that he's found himself in delightful company."

The first stranger chuckled, his demeanor unapologetic.

"Guilty as charged," he admitted.

"The company was too enticing to resist."

Zarek, his gaze still on Raena, finally made his way through the crowd. The tight grip on the glasses had left his fingers numb, but he ignored the sensation. With an unreadable expression, he approached the trio, his eyes taking in the two strangers.

"Enjoying the party, gentlemen?" Zarek asked, his tone light, but the look in his eyes was anything but.

"I see you've met my betrothed."

"The pleasure was all mine," the first stranger said, turning to Zarek and extending a hand in greeting.

"Your betrothed is a captivating dancer."

Zarek took the stranger's hand, his own grip firm.

"Yes," he agreed, his gaze fixed on the masked man.

"She has that effect."

"I'm afraid we haven't been introduced," the second stranger interjected, attempting to dissolve the growing tension.

"I'm Kael, and this is my brother, Soren."

"Zarek," he replied tersely, then gestured to Raena.

"And I believe you've already met Princess Raena."

"Indeed, we have," Soren said, his gaze sliding back to Raena.

"It's a night we won't easily forget."

— · ₒ˚ ☆: *.⟩ .* :☆˚ . ——

The evening of the ball dawned, its iridescent twilight falling over the opulent mage palace like a veil. As the sun descended, the palace walls, adorned with intricate patterns of diamonds, gleamed and glowed, reflecting the dying rays in a thousand brilliant colors.

Kael and I stood in a distant alley, adorned in clothes that were unfamiliar and uncomfortable, our hands clutching the glamour necklaces. The very air buzzed with the sheer power of the enchantment they held, their golden chains cool against our heated skin. We were about to step into a den of serpents. Serpents draped in silk, armed with deceptively sweet smiles and lethal magic.

I felt Kael's gaze on me, his voice cutting through the thick anticipation.

"Ready?"

I grinned, the exhilaration of our plan washing over me.

"As I'll ever be."

Together, we clasped the necklaces, the world blurring as the magic took effect. I blinked, a strange sensation of lightness sweeping over me. My reflection in a nearby puddle showed a man unfamiliar to me. Human. Unremarkable. Not a trace of my horns or my demon eyes. The necklace had done its work. Kael, too, was unrecognizable. His normally fierce, demon eyes were now a calming shade of blue. His horns, like mine, had vanished. We were, for all intents and purposes, human.

"Let's go," Kael muttered, adjusting his mask as we stepped into the growing throng of mages and nulls making their way to the palace. When we neared the entrance, a heavy, nervous energy settled over me. It wasn't fear, but an intoxicating blend of excitement and dread. Kael must have sensed it, his grip on my shoulder reassuring.

"Remember the plan, Ash," he said, his voice a low murmur that only I could hear.

"Get in, get the Water Heart, get out."

"And if I see her?" I found myself asking.

Kael didn't respond immediately.

"Then you'd best remember who and what you are."

His words were harsh, but necessary. The risks of this dance were high. I needed to remember that. For the sake of our people. With a deep breath, I followed Kael into the fray. The air was thick with the intoxicating scent of magic and exotic perfumes, the undercurrent of whispers and laughter creating an ethereal symphony. Each step I took felt like a dance with danger, every smiling face a potential enemy. Underneath the extravagance and the laughter, there was a war about to unfold, a rebellion simmering. And we, demons dressed as humans, were at its very heart. The thrum of music and chatter grew louder as we navigated through the grand corridors towards the main ballroom. Every corner we turned, every open archway we passed, revealed more of the sprawling grandeur. Ivory columns towered high, cloaked in the shimmer of water magic; moving frescoes narrated tales of mage victories, none of them mentioning the blood of our kin spilt to their glory. I felt a bitter rage well up within me. A quiet, insidious flame stoked by every dismissive glance, by every condescending smile they shot towards nulls in their servitude. I swallowed the acrid taste, schooling my features into an indifferent mask. Now was not the time for recklessness.

Kael's touch on my arm pulled me from my thoughts. His eyes, too, held a storm under their calm surface, echoing the turbulent tempest within me. He gave a slight nod, reminding me of our goal. Remember the plan. Remember our people.

We finally stepped into the grand ballroom, and the sight took my breath away. Thousands of lights floated overhead, casting a soft, shimmering glow on the sea of masked revelers. Beautiful gowns swirled in mesmerizing patterns, the air thrummed with the rhythm of music, laughter, and whispered secrets. As much as the ostentatious display repulsed me, there was no denying the captivating allure of it all. I glanced at Kael. He looked as out of place as I felt, but his face held a grim determination that mirrored my own. Suddenly, the crowd parted, and my breath hitched. There, descending the grand staircase, was the princess. A vision in a dress that shimmered like the night sky. Her mask failed to hide the brilliance of her eyes, as deep and mysterious as the mythical oceans. My heart pounded in my chest, conflicting emotions threatening to drown me. I found myself unable to look away from the woman who unknowingly held my interest, held a piece of my fiery, relentless heart. My heart throbbed with a strange mix of fascination and dread. Kael's warning echoed in my head, pulling me back from the edge. I tore my gaze from her and glanced at him. He was watching me closely, his blue eyes sharp and knowing.

"You'd best remember who and what you are," he murmured again, a grim echo of his earlier words.

I clenched my jaw, the image of Raena's entrancing beauty seared into my mind.

"I haven't forgotten."

The grandeur of the ball continued unabated around us, the intoxicating rhythm of music and laughter creating an illusion of joyous celebration. But beneath it all was the bitter tang of reality, of oppression and disparity. Kael and I were islands amidst this sea of revelry, knowing too well the price paid for every glittering spectacle. Suddenly, a fanfare of trumpets silenced the room. From the far end of the ballroom, atop a dais resplendent in jewels and silk, the King and Queen stood. A hush of reverence fell over the gathering, every eye turning towards the rulers. I studied them with barely veiled contempt, their opulence a stark reminder of our people's suffering.

"Noble lords and ladies, we welcome you to our palace. We gather under the vast desert sky, bound by the shared allure of water and magic, bearing witness to an alliance of love and power," the King's voice boomed, carrying effortlessly across the vast room. There was a smug smile on his face, a show of power to his subjects.

"Tonight, our beloved daughter Raena, and Zarek, heir to the prestigious House of Xantheer, will perform the betrothal dance. Their unity shall be the first drop of rain in our desert, heralding a prosperous future."

A deafening applause echoed through the ballroom as the king concluded his proclamation. All around me, faces gleamed with excitement and anticipation. The buzz of hushed whispers blended with the soft strains of music wafting from a hidden orchestra.

The name Zarek rang unfamiliar and harsh in my ears, a discordant note in the evening's symphony. The king's words twisted in my gut, a sharp, unexpected pang of jealousy flaring up in response to Raena's impending betrothal. A futile emotion, I knew, and yet it seethed within me like a tempestuous flame, threatening to consume my calm façade. The room erupted in cheers and whistles, the crowd parting as this Zarek, led Raena to the center of the dance floor. He held himself with a certain arrogance, an air of entitlement that most mages seemed to wear like a second skin. But it was the way he held Raena's hand that stoked the inferno of my jealousy. The music resumed, a soulful melody with the subtle rhythm of water running over pebbles, and the betrothed couple began to sway.

Despite the glamour necklace, I could feel my demon eyes burn. My gaze was fixed on them, the way Zarek held her, the way his hand rested on her waist, the way they moved in synchrony. Every single detail fueled my silent rage, my heart pounding a fierce drumbeat against my ribs. Kael nudged me, his gaze heavy with understanding. He didn't need to ask to know what was going through my head.

"We're here for a reason, Ash," he murmured, a stark reminder of our mission.

"I know," I replied through gritted teeth, pulling my gaze from the couple to the grandeur of the palace around us.

"But who is this Zarek, and why have I never heard of him?"

"He's the heir to House Xantheer," Kael replied, his voice barely audible over the music and laughter.

"One of the most powerful mage houses. This alliance is a consolidation of power. It's a calculated move."

I watched Zarek whirl Raena around the dance floor. The crowd watched in rapt attention, their applause like the sharp sting of a whip. Suddenly, the music changed tempo, and I watched Zarek lift Raena in a flamboyant spin. My grip on the champagne flute tightened. An irrational part of me wished to tear them apart. But reason prevailed. It had to. We were there with a purpose. Kael's grip on my arm tightened, a silent warning.

"Keep your focus, Ash."

"She is not his," I growled, my voice a low whisper.

Kael's gaze flickered to me, concern etched into the lines of his face. "And she's not yours either," he responded quietly, a harsh truth couched in a calm voice.

"Remember, we're here for the cause."

With a growl I dragged my gaze away from Raena and scanned the room, my eyes landing on a stern figure, watching the dance with a keen eye.

"Who is that?" I asked, nodding towards him.

"That's Lord Cadmus," Kael murmured.

"Zarek's father and the one in charge of demon affairs."

So, that was the man who viewed us as dangerous creatures, pests to be controlled and used. Lord Cadmus, Zarek's father, was a name every demon knew and feared. He was the iron fist of the kingdom, overseeing demon affairs with brutal efficiency. He was as cunning as he was ruthless, his hatred for our kind well-known. My hands itched to wrap around his pompous throat, to show him just how dangerous we could be. But again, reason prevailed. I nodded, filing away the information for later use. Turning my attention back to the spectacle before us, I studied Zarek with a newfound interest, taking in his every detail with a cold analytical detachment. His smug expression, the way he reveled in the attention, the proprietary hold on Raena – it was all infuriatingly familiar. He was his father's son, a reflection of Lord Cadmus, ruthless and arrogant in his power. Just then, as if part of some divine cosmic jest, Zarek detached himself from Raena, mumbling something in her ear that made her laugh, before striding away.

His departure left Raena momentarily unattended, and without thinking, I found myself moving toward her.

"Ash!" Kael's warning hiss was barely audible over the sound of the orchestra. He was quick, but my resolution was quicker.

"My lady," I greeted, bowing slightly.

"May I have the honor of this dance?"

Raena turned to me, her eyes widening in surprise at my abrupt approach. The masks we wore hid our identities, and the glamour necklace concealed my demonic nature, rendering me as anonymous as any other attendee. As I took her into my arms, guiding her across the dance floor, I could feel the ripple of shock coursing through the crowd. I didn't care. For once, the mages' scrutiny meant nothing to me. I was not a slave tonight; I was a man, a man dancing with a woman who ignited a fierce blaze in his heart. Raena moved with grace and ease, following my lead as we swayed to the rhythm of the music. It was a dance Kael had painstakingly taught me, his years as a pleasure slave providing him with a thorough understanding of the mages' customs. I had protested then, balking at the thought of learning anything from the people who enslaved us. But now, I was grateful. Grateful because it meant I could hold her, if only for a moment.

Though she didn't recognize me, there was a familiarity in her eyes, an unspoken connection that sent a shiver down my spine. We were two souls, drawn together in the most unlikely of circumstances, dancing under the watchful eyes of a society that had chosen to subjugate one while elevating the other. Through the corner of my eye, I saw Kael's disapproving gaze. I could almost hear his warning, the caution that underscored his every move. But tonight, under the moonlit sky, amidst the splendor and grandeur of the mage's palace, I chose to listen to my heart. While we swayed to the rhythm of the music, my eyes found Zarek in the crowd. His smirk had faltered, his eyes narrowed at the sight of me dancing with Raena. His possessiveness was as clear as day, and I met it with a defiant smile of my own. I may be a demon slave, bound by chains and laws not my own. But in this moment, with Raena in my arms and the music coursing through my veins, I as free. I was the storm that refused to be contained, the flame that refused to be extinguished. And tonight, I was going to dance.

—— · ˳° ☆: *.) .* :☆° . ——

34

The last note of the orchestra reverberated through the grand hall, an audible punctuation to the dance. As the applause of the crowd washed over us, I released Raena from our shared space, our shared moment.

"Thank you for the dance, my lady," I said, bowing to Raena, the words tasted foreign on my tongue, as though they were ripped from a book of etiquette.

"And a mystery," she responded, the corners of her lips twitching upwards as she offered a graceful curtsy.

She seemed intrigued, and I found myself longing to remain in this moment, to shed the layers of deceit and bare myself to her. But such wishes were dangerous, for they bore nothing but a bitter fruit of despair. The crowd's applause brought me back to the present. I raised my eyes to find Kael making his way towards us, his every movement a testament to his years spent in the treacherous company of the mages.

"My apologies, princess," Kael started, his voice carrying an apology as smooth as silk.

"I seem to have lost track of my brother."

I smirked at his attempt to lighten the situation, to smooth over any suspicions that might have arisen from my audacious act.

"Guilty as charged," I admitted, meeting Raena's gaze.

"The company was simply too enticing to resist."

As we engaged in the elaborate charade, Zarek reappeared, a pair of drinks in his hands. His gaze was cold, penetrating, as it swept over Kael and me.

"Enjoying the party, gentlemen?" His voice was light, a stark contrast to the storm brewing in his eyes.

"I see you've met my betrothed."

"The pleasure was all mine," I replied, extending a hand towards him. The words tasted bitter in my mouth, but I swallowed the disdain. It was not the time for confrontation. Not yet.

"Yes," Zarek replied tersely, taking my hand with a grip meant to intimidate. But I was no stranger to intimidation.

"She has that effect."

Before the tension could mount, Kael interjected.

"I'm afraid we haven't been introduced. I'm Kael, and this is my brother, Soren."

"Zarek," he introduced himself, his tone stiff.

"And I believe you've already met Princess Raena."

Raena. A name that held more power over me than any spell. I met her gaze, holding it for a moment longer than necessary.

"Indeed, we have," I said, my voice holding a depth of emotion I hadn't intended.

"It's a night we won't easily forget."

A burst of laughter interrupted the increasingly strained tableau. My gaze was drawn towards the source of the interruption.

"Pray, dear sister, save a dance for me," a voice boomed, its jovial undertone cutting through the thrumming atmosphere like a silvered knife.

A man I did not recognize approached, his mirth-filled eyes dancing behind his mask. His bow was so grandiose it would have been comical if not for the seriousness of our predicament. Raena's laughter rippled through the crowd, serving to lighten the dense air that seemed to have enveloped us.

"I would not dream of denying you such, dear brother," Raena replied, the playful smirk on her face incongruous with the edge in her voice. I found it strangely captivating.

"But only if you promise not to step on my toes as you did last time." A blush spread across the stranger's face, the shade of crimson stark against his fair complexion. Despite his embarrassment, he let out a deep, hearty chuckle.

"Raena, you wound me! I swear it was an honest mistake."

I observed their interaction with interest, this glimpse into the dynamics of their family revealing more about them than I anticipated. It was a stark contrast to the world Kael and I had been born into, a stark reminder of the reality we were up against.

Kael subtly elbowed me, reminding me of our purpose, of the mask we had to don amidst this sea of facades.

"His name is Caspian," he murmured under his breath.

"He's a skilled mage and not one to be trifled with, despite his easygoing demeanor."

His warning was unnecessary. I had no intentions of underestimating any of the mages here. Just as I was locking that information away, another man approached our small congregation. His attire was just as grand as the rest of the nobility, and his confident stride suggested he was no stranger to these grand halls. A cascade of laughter echoed behind him, the crowd parting for him as though drawn back by an unseen hand.

"Raenas, Zarek, a splendid dance, truly," he enthused with a twinkle in his eye, offering me his hand, not for a shake, but in the traditional mage greeting – a palm against palm, an acknowledgement of equals. An arrogant assumption from the man. I bristled inwardly, but kept the mask of the affable nobleman 'Soren' intact. I placed my hand against his. His touch was cool, suggesting a potential water mage. I suppressed the urge to pull away, the feel of his skin against mine a stark reminder of the power he wielded. Power that had been used to subjugate my people, to shackle us in chains of servitude and prejudice.

"The dance, it's all anyone can talk about," he continued, pulling away and turning his attention to Kael, offering the same greeting.

Kael accepted the greeting with an elegant nod, his fingers pressing against Aldric's in a mirrored performance. The subtleties of high society were a second language to him, each gesture an intricate dance of hidden meanings and unspoken alliances.

"Kael," he introduced himself, his voice smooth as velvet, his demeanor radiating an amicable curiosity that belied the turmoil I knew him to be experiencing.

This world was familiar to him, but not in the way it was for the water mages around us. His familiarity was born of a need for survival, an unwelcome necessity from a past life he was forced to embrace once again. The man, Prince Aldric as he revealed, nodded his head in acknowledgement.

"A pleasure, Kael and Soren," he said, turning back to me. He had a politician's charm, a magnetism that drew in people but always kept them at arm's length.

"I haven't seen you at court before. You are...?"

"Visiting," Kael jumped in smoothly, playing the part of the protective older brother with an ease that made me grit my teeth. "We hail from one of the minor cities. This is our first venture to the capital."

Aldric's eyes flickered between us, his intrigue clearly piqued. "Welcome, then. The palace can be quite overwhelming for first-timers. But fear not, you'll find we are quite hospitable."

While he said those words, my mind swam with images of the inhumane treatment of my people. Hospitable, indeed. I ground my teeth, feeling a bitter taste in my mouth.

"I'm sure we will," I replied, forcing a smile onto my face.

"Thank you for the welcome, Prince Aldric."

"Aldric," Caspian said, slightly hesitant.

"Lady Lysandra looks radiant tonight, does she not?"

Aldric glanced over in the direction of Caspian's gaze, his eyes scanning the woman in question. A coy smile curled upon his lips, as he turned back to him.

"Indeed, she does. She does..." Aldric's voice trailed off, his grin widening as he studied Caspian.

"You know, Caspian, you have been casting admiring glances in Lady Lysandra's direction the entire evening," Aldric teased, his eyes gleaming with mischief.

"If I didn't know better, I'd think you were smitten."

Caspian's face flushed, the tips of his ears turning a rosy hue. He stuttered, trying to formulate a suitable response, his usual eloquence abandoned in his discomfiture.

"I... I mean, she's... you know..."

"A lady of considerable charm, yes?" Aldric supplied, his voice laced with humor. He clapped a hand on Caspian's shoulder, a sympathetic gesture that held a twinge of triumphant amusement.

"Caspian, my friend, you are as readable as an open grimoire."

Raena, standing on Caspian's other side, laughed, a sound that tinkled like chimes in the breeze.

"Caspian, so tongue-tied? That's a rarity. Do you need me to introduce you to Lady Lysandra?"

Her eyes gleamed with devilish amusement, clearly enjoying Caspian's discomfort.

"No, I can—" Caspian began, his cheeks aflame.

"But it's no trouble at all," Raena continued, her voice sweet and her smile teasing.

"After all, what are sisters for?"

From the corner of my eye, I saw Kael stiffen slightly, his gaze locked on Lady Lysandra. The humor drained from his face, replaced by an icy calm that set my teeth on edge. But he recovered quickly, a polite smile masking his temporary lapse.

"Lady Lysandra is indeed a woman of... singular character," he said, his voice impeccably neutral.

Aldric raised an eyebrow, looking between Kael and I.

"You seem well-informed about court ladies for newcomers. Have you met Lady Lysandra before?"

The question hung in the air. For a moment, Kael's eyes flickered with something dark, something haunted. But it was gone so quickly, I might have imagined it.

"No," he answered smoothly, a perfect picture of serene denial.

"But her reputation precedes her. She's quite the talk of the court, isn't she?"

Aldric nodded, chuckling.

"Indeed, she is. Perhaps, we can arrange a meeting for you and Caspian. Two birds with one stone, as they say."

Kael nodded, his smile not quite reaching his eyes.

"That would be most gracious, Prince Aldric. However, we wouldn't want to impose."

Aldric laughed heartily, dismissing the sentiment with a wave of his hand.

"Nonsense! It's hardly an imposition. Besides, it would be remiss of us to not introduce our new guests to the highlights of the court."

"I suppose there's no harm," Kael conceded, though there was a certain tension to his shoulders, a barely noticeable stiffness that betrayed his apprehension. It seemed that Lady Lysandra was a ghost from his past he'd rather not confront.

"But back to the more pressing matter," Aldric smirked, his attention swiveling back to a mortified Caspian.

"How exactly do you intend to win over the fair Lady Lysandra, Caspian? A bold declaration of love, perhaps?"

Caspian shot him a withering look, though it lacked any real venom. "It's not like that, Aldric," he muttered, his face a deep shade of crimson.

"Not like that?" Raena echoed, a mischievous twinkle in her eyes. "Then how is it, dear brother?"

Before he could respond, a stray strand of her hair fell into her face, obscuring one of her eyes. Without thinking, I reached out, tucking it behind her ear. Raena froze, her eyes widening as she looked at me, and I quickly pulled my hand back, chiding myself for the impulsive action.

"I—" I started, but the words stuck in my throat. Raena watched me, her expression unreadable. I expected a lash of her sharp tongue, a biting retort for my audacity, but it never came. Instead, there was a silence, a long, stretching moment that was shattered when Zarek let out a chuckle.

"Soren, my dear man," Zarek began, a wry smile dancing on his lips as he looked at me, "you seem to be a natural with the ladies. Perhaps you should be advising Caspian here instead of the other way around."

Caspian's cheeks flushed again, though whether from embarrassment or indignation, I couldn't tell. Raena was still silent, her gaze on me unreadable. It was disconcerting, to say the least.

"My lord Zarek, you jest, but perhaps there's truth to your words," Kael interjected smoothly, drawing attention away from me. I shot him a grateful look, which he returned with a small nod.

"Yes, I suppose we could all learn from Soren's... natural charm," Aldric chimed in, a smirk curving his lips.

He seemed to enjoy the entire spectacle. Just as the words slipped from Aldric's mouth, a shimmering figure weaved its way through the throng of attendees. Lady Lysandra, a vision of coquettish allure, moved towards us with the grace of a serpent on the prowl. She smiled, a perfectly practiced curl of her lips, her eyes gleaming with curiosity.

"Princess Raena, Lord Zarek," she greeted, her voice as silky as her silver gown, which shimmered under the ballroom's lights.

"I could not help but marvel at your performance earlier. It was as if you two were born to dance."

Zarek offered her a courteous smile, "My lady, your words honor us".

As Lady Lysandra's gaze drifted over us, a curious flicker entered her eyes as they met mine.

"And who, might I ask, is this?" she inquired, her voice all sugar and spice, seemingly innocent but the sharpness behind her eyes betrayed her cunning.

Kael, stepped forward.

"May I introduce my brother, Soren," he said, his voice level, his expression hard to read. There was a certain chill to his demeanor, a hint of frost that hadn't been there before.

"Soren," she repeated, the corners of her mouth curling into a coy smile as she extended a gloved hand in my direction.

"An enchanting dance with the princess, I must say. Few men are bold enough to make such an impression."

I took her hand, bowing over it.

"I am honored, Lady Lysandra," I replied, my voice steady. Kael's teachings had prepared me well, but interacting with the woman brought a rush of apprehension.

There was something deeply unsettling about her, a feeling I couldn't quite place. I shot Kael a subtle look, and he nodded, barely perceptible, offering a silent reassurance. Raena, who had been silent, chimed in.

"Lady Lysandra, you remember my brother Caspian of course."

Her voice was light, a hint of mischief hidden beneath her words. As she introduced the bashful Caspian, the Lady's gaze shifted towards him, an arched brow betraying her curiosity.

"Your highness" she said, her voice a melodic purr as she looked at him, "how could I forget? It has been quite a while, hasn't it?"

There was a playful note in her tone, but I saw Caspian tense up, his face draining of color under the golden lights.

Zarek, observing the spectacle, tried to diffuse the situation, chuckling, "Caspian's become quite the mage while he was gone, you know. He's just a bit... shy."

Lysandra's smile widened, a predatory glint in her eyes as she turned back to Caspian.

"Is that so? Well, we must catch up then," she said, extending her hand towards him.

Caspian seemed to freeze for a moment before he finally moved, reaching out to take her hand. Yet, in his nervousness, his foot caught on the edge of Raena's dress, and he stumbled forward. A gasp swept through the nearby crowd as Caspian went crashing into a nearby table, causing an ornate vase to teeter precariously on the edge. In a desperate scramble to prevent further disaster, Caspian thrust out his hands, intending to use his magic to steady the vase. Yet, in his panic, he misjudged the strength of his magic. A burst of water erupted from his palms, not only stabilizing the vase but also sending a cascade of water splashing over Lady Lysandra. The room fell into stunned silence as Lysandra stood there, drenched from head to toe, the look on her face a perfect blend of shock and fury. Caspian, meanwhile, looked mortified, his eyes wide with terror. A few snickers broke the silence, swiftly followed by the muffled sounds of laughter echoing throughout the hall. Aldric, meanwhile, was trying his best to contain his laughter, though his eyes were filled with mirth.

"Caspian, my dear man," he chortled.

"I meant for you to sweep her off her feet, not soak her to the bone." Feeling a sudden surge of sympathy for the hapless Caspian, Kael stepped forward.

"Perhaps we should help Lady Lysandra," he suggested, though his voice was tinged with a cool detachment.

However, with all eyes on the spectacle unfolding, I subtly signaled to him. It was the perfect opportunity for us to slip away unnoticed. Understanding my intention, he nodded and we discreetly distanced ourselves from the amused crowd.

—— · ₒ˚ ☆: *.) .* :☆˚ . ——

We navigated our way through the grand, marble corridors, dimly lit by an array of jeweled lanterns. The whispers of revelry growing distant, the silence was both eerie and welcome, a sharp contrast to the rambunctious celebration we had left behind. Our masks hid our identities but we were acutely aware that we were trespassing in forbidden territory. The glimmering necklaces around our throats weighed heavy with the burden of our pretense and the lies that they masked. I could feel my heart thrumming in my chest, the adrenaline churning an odd mix of fear and anticipation within me. Kael moved with a practiced ease, a graceful shadow darting amongst the regal opulence of the palace. His knowledge of mage society was a precious asset, one that had served us well thus far. His every action was deliberate and measured, calculated to blend into the aristocratic air of our surroundings.

Our destination wasn't as easily reachable as we'd hoped. The palace was a labyrinth of corridors, winding staircases, and grand halls, each more opulent than the last. We had a map, memorized from countless hours of scrutiny, but the palace in reality was a complex riddle wrapped in grandeur and secrecy. There were guards too, their hawk-like gaze and imposing stance a stark reminder of the risks we were taking. We had to tread carefully, each step meticulously planned, and every word we spoke was carefully weighed. In this world, we were playing a game where one wrong move could lead to our utter ruin. I, Soren to them but Ash to myself, was playing a role that felt alien to me. A servant passed us, her eyes downcast, focused solely on the silver tray she was balancing. Kael intercepted her path with an easy smile.

"We seem to have lost our way, my dear. Could you guide us to the viewing gallery?"

From the viewing gallery there were some straight corridors that lead directly to the vault room, from there it would be easy for us to navigate. The servant hesitated before she finally nodded, giving us a quick, somewhat apprehensive smile. She led us through an array of corridors until we arrived at the threshold of a grand chamber, its opulence a mirror of the grandeur that was the ballroom. She bowed before disappearing back into the labyrinthine palace. The chamber was largely deserted, save for a few lingering nobles engaged in hushed conversations. But it was the figure by the expansive windows near the balcony that seized our attention. A familiar silhouette, framed against the sprawling cityscape bathed in the pale moonlight. It was Elras. Recognizing him despite the palace livery he now wore, I felt a sharp pang of recognition and worry.

Kael gestured towards Elras with a slight tilt of his head, his gaze sharp and calculating. Nodding in agreement, we smoothly navigated our way through the chamber towards him, our demeanor composed, our steps unhurried. Elras was standing alone, staring out at the city as if lost in thought. His hands were folded neatly behind his back, the picture of obedient servitude. As we approached, he straightened, turning to face us. His eyes, hardened by years of servitude and hardship, swept over us without recognition.

"Good evening," Kael greeted, his voice steady, masking the turmoil that must be churning within him.

"You seem to be the only one here who is not lost in revelry."

"Aye, m'lords. My duties leave little time for merriment," Elras responded, his accent, rough and unmistakably lower-class, a stark contrast to the refined lilt of Kael's words.

"Perhaps you could assist us then," I interjected, drawing his attention.

"We were hoping to gain a better understanding of this magnificent palace. We seem to be quite lost," I confessed, a touch of chagrin coloring my words.

Elras's brow furrowed, his gaze drifting between Kael and myself. His eyes, like smoky quartz, held a sharpness – a vestige of his former life, no doubt. But within the harsh lines of his face, I saw no flicker of recognition, no inkling that he knew us for who we truly were.

"Aye, m'lords, the palace can be a confusing place to those not used to it," he conceded, his voice rough like gravel but not unkind. "Would you like me to guide you?"

"That would be most appreciated... brother," I replied, laying my hand on his shoulder in a casual yet familiar manner.

It was a risky move, but a necessary one. Elras stiffened under my touch, his gaze sharpening. I saw him search my face, his eyes flickering with confusion before recognition dawned, his expression turning from shock to disbelief.

"Kael... Ash...?" he whispered, his voice barely audible, his eyes darting between us.

"But how...?"

"Quiet, Elras," Kael hissed, his eyes darting around the balcony, ensuring no curious ears were close by.

"We can't afford to be overheard."

Elras blinked, still seemingly shocked, but nodded, pulling away to maintain the guise of the dutiful servant. His hands trembled slightly, the only sign of his inner turmoil.

"We are not what we seem," I began, keeping my voice low.

"These are glamour necklaces," I gestured towards the glimmering pendants hanging around our necks.

"They mask our demonic heritage."

"And you're here because...?" Elras asked, his gaze darting between Kael and I, fear and hope warring in his eyes.

"We are here for our people, Elras," Kael replied, his tone resolute. "For all of us. We need to bring about a change."

Our old friend nodded, swallowing hard. His gaze traveled over us once more, taking in our disguised forms.

"You... You've changed," he murmured, a note of awe in his voice.

"Not by choice, Elras," Kael said softly, a bitter undercurrent to his words.

"But by necessity."

"We're here to steal the Water Heart," I announced, my voice barely more than a whisper, yet the words resonated with the weight of our intentions. Kael's gaze flickered to me, a silent reprimand for my directness, but it was necessary. Elras needed to understand the gravity of our mission. Elras stood there, silent as a tomb, eyes wide with disbelief. Then he shook his head.

"This is madness," he muttered, his voice little more than a low growl. "The Water Heart is the foundation of the mages' power. They won't just let it go. You'll start a war. They'll hunt you down."

"We're already at war, Elras," I countered, my tone firm, leaving no room for argument.

"They just don't know it yet. And we've been hunted all our lives. This won't change much."

Elras echoed, his voice hollow.

"You're going to get yourselves killed."

"Perhaps," I admitted.

"But it's a risk we're willing to take. For our freedom. For our people."

Elras' expression twisted, torn between loyalty to us, his friends, and the overwhelming dread that was slowly creeping onto his face.

"And if you get the Heart... what then?"

"We will use it as a bargaining chip," Kael replied, his voice steady, his gaze unwavering.

"To negotiate for the freedom of our people."

Elras remained silent for a moment, weighing our words. He looked from Kael to me, his gaze lingering on the glamoured necklaces we wore.

"You're really going to do this, aren't you?" he asked, the resignation in his voice was palpable.

"Yes," I confirmed, meeting his gaze squarely.

"We are."

He exhaled deeply, running a hand over his face.

"And what do you want from me?"

"We need your help, Elras," I stated plainly.

"Your knowledge of the palace. Everything can help."

"But--"

"We won't force you," Kael cut in, softening his tone.

"This is your choice."

Elras nodded slowly, the weight of our words settling around him. "I'll… I'll help you," he finally conceded. His gaze flickered between us once more, a mix of resignation and resolve in his smoky eyes. "If you manage to steal the Water Heart, I can lead you out of the palace."

We exchanged a glance, Kael and I, relief washing over us. This was the first real break we had since this reckless plan had been formed. Elras was a lifeline, an unexpected but welcome ally. Yet, it was hard to ignore the fear lurking in his eyes.

"Wait here," Elras instructed us abruptly, a renewed sense of urgency to his words.

"There's something I need to give you."

Before we could question him, he had disappeared into the shadows of the palace, leaving us alone. While we waited, our gazes returned to the balcony overlooking the city, the revelry of the masquerade ball echoing distantly. I could see the tension in Kael's posture, the way his hands clenched and unclenched at his sides. A servant came to clear away some empty goblets left on a nearby table. She spared us a quick, nervous glance before scurrying away. This close to the action, it was harder to forget what we were doing. With every passing minute, the risk of discovery loomed larger, but I could no more abandon our mission than I could cease to breathe. The fate of our people rested on our shoulders, and that was a burden I was willing to bear, no matter the cost.

"I saw the way you looked at Lysandra."

Kael nodded, his gaze darkening.

"She was... a part of my past. A part I'd hoped to forget. I was... assigned to her for a time," he confessed.

His tone was hollow, devoid of any emotion, but I could see the tumult behind his eyes.

"What was she like?" I asked, curious despite the gravity of our current situation.

Kael's lips curled into a cold smile.

"Vain," he said, the word dripping with scorn.

"A woman of perverse tastes who revels in the power she holds over others."

I shivered slightly, imagining the horrors he must have endured at her hands. The mages were cruel, and their pleasure slaves bore the brunt of it.

"We'll need to be careful around her," I stated.

"She may recognize you."

Kael shook his head, the cold smile morphing into a bitter smirk. "She won't. The mages never really see us, Ash. We are mere objects to them, tools for their amusement. She would no more recognize me than she would a goblet she drank from a year ago."

His words were chilling, but they bore the weight of truth. We were nothing to the mages, expendable and easily replaceable. But that also worked to our advantage; our insignificance was our greatest disguise.

"We're going to destroy them," I vowed.

"For us, for Elras, for every demon slave out there."

Kael's eyes met mine, the intensity of his gaze matching the conviction in my voice.

"We have no other choice, Ash. We must succeed."

As he said that, Elras returned, a nondescript pouch in his hand.

"Here," Elras said, his voice more gruff than usual. He handed over the pouch to us, his gaze hard.

"Pinched 'em from them high an' mighties," he said, referring to the mages.

"They be inked in ancient demonic."

Kael and I exchanged a glance, surprise flickering between us.

"You can decipher it?" I asked, taking in Elras' rugged, calloused hands - the same hands that could, it seemed, trace the elegant strokes of a forgotten language.

"Aye, bits an' bobs," he replied, a self-deprecating chuckle in his voice.

I turned to Kael, silently prompting him to examine the scrolls. As he unfurled the parchment, the ancient markings danced ominously in the soft light. His gaze scanned the symbols — strange, intricate, and somehow hauntingly familiar. "Anything you can make out?" he asked. A nod from Elras, his eyes taking on a faraway look as they traced the foreign symbols.

"Words here and there. 'Power... Binding... River...' Not nearly enough. This needs a proper readin'."

Preserving the delicate parchment, Kael stowed it back into the pouch with a thoughtful hum.

"This could be invaluable," he agreed, "But discretion will be our best friend here."

"Got that right," Elras said, nodding fervently.

"This... if it's got a power to use 'gainst the mages, we need to keep it under wraps."

"They keep the Water Heart in the west wing," he murmured, "Secluded chamber, guarded by just a pair."

"Two guards," I mused aloud, my mind racing with a dozen plans and contingencies.

"We can handle that."

Kael cast a sidelong glance my way, one corner of his mouth lifted in a skeptical smirk.

"I can't help but wonder if it's a trap. Guarding their most valuable asset with a mere duo... It seems suspiciously convenient."

Elras's chest rumbled with a mirthless chuckle, and he shrugged his broad shoulders.

"Ain't no riddle, mates. They simply don't anticipate no one daft enough to make a move on the stone here, within the belly of their power. The Palace, it's like a sacred shield to 'em."

The straightforward logic of his argument settled over us. The audacity of our mission was our advantage. It was a cover in itself. Who, indeed, would attempt to steal the heart of the Water Mages' power from under their very noses, from the stronghold of their opulence and authority?

"The sheer arrogance of it," Kael muttered, his lips curling into a wry smile.

"Believing themselves so untouchable."

"That same arrogance," I added, looking from Elras to Kael, "will be their downfall."

36

—— · ₀˚ ☆:*.⟩.*:☆˚. ——

Guided by the taciturn Elras, we slipped through the labyrinthine palace corridors, avoiding prying eyes and busy servants. The oppressive silence of the palace's secluded wing was punctuated by our soft footfalls, the tense whispers of our clothes, and the muffled music that seemed an echo from another world. Our destination soon loomed before us, grand double doors standing sentinel at the end of an ornate hallway. Two guards, regal in their lustrous blue uniforms, stood watch. Their sharp eyes scanned the corridor, missing nothing. We paused at the edge of an oversized tapestry, hiding in its formidable shadow. Elras melted into the background. I glanced at Kael. His face was a study in composure, a perfect mask of nobility. He gave me a small nod. The charade was about to begin. He straightened, swaying gently, a parody of a drunken noble. I mirrored him, a grin plastered on my face. It was time to play our roles. We stumbled forward, a cacophony of obnoxious laughter bouncing off the walls.

"More wine, dear friend!" Kael slurred, arm draped over my shoulders.

"Only if ye promise not to trip over yer own feet again!" I retorted, my words equally slurred.

We approached the guards, our drunken act in full swing. The pair looked at us disdainfully, hands instinctively moving toward their sides, prepared for any indiscretion. Kael hiccupped loudly, followed by another peel of exaggerated laughter, and we steadied ourselves against the corridor wall. I couldn't help but feel a rush of adrenaline, of danger and exhilaration. It was a deadly dance we danced, and one wrong step could lead to our doom. But Kael was a master of this dance. He grew up in the squalid pit of mage pleasure dens, molded by its cruel rules, and honed by the rigors of survival. He had survived by learning to be more than a slave. To be a performer, a confidant, a mirror that reflected the mages' own vanity back at them. He was the perfectly obedient pleasure slave, and it was that obedience, that ability to hide his true self behind a façade of subservience, that made him the perfect conman. He met the guard's gaze, his eyes glazed and unfocused, the picture of inebriated disorientation.

"Good evenin', gentlemen," Kael slurred, leaning heavily against the door.

"Could ya show us the way to...to..."

"The wine cellar!" I chimed in, stumbling forward, nearly toppling into one of the guards. The man steadied me with a gruff sigh of annoyance.

The guards exchanged a look of pure disdain before one of them pointed down the hall from whence we'd come.

"Take the second right and follow the staircase down," he said. "Now, off with you before we have to remove you."

Kael gave a nod that was more like a head bob, muttered a word of thanks, and turned to leave, pulling me along with him.

"Wait," I mumbled, lurching back towards the guards, my balance seemingly failing me.

"Easy, friend," one of the guards reached out, attempting to steer me away. It was the opportunity we needed.

I twisted, quick as a desert viper, my hidden dagger plunging into the guard's chest. His eyes widened in surprise and his hands went instinctively to the hilt, his strength already fading. At the same time, Kael had spun towards the second guard, the glint of his dagger barely visible as he drove it home with lethal precision. Despite our speed, the first guard, in his final throes, managed to grab at my necklace. With a strength born of desperation and shock, he yanked it from my neck, the magical glamour dissipating in an instant.

His eyes met mine, filled with disbelief and terror as he looked upon my true demonic form.

"Demon..." he gasped out, blood bubbling on his lips. He fell back, dead before he hit the floor, his final expression one of horrified realization.

For a heart-stopping moment, Kael and I locked eyes, understanding passing between us. It was a close call, too close.

I hastily tucked the necklace back under my clothes, the glamour reengaging. To anyone looking, I was just another human, a nobleman, not a demon slave on a deadly mission. Elras appeared then, stepping from the shadows with a grim nod.

"Let's get this done, lads," he muttered, keeping his voice low. His roughened features were set in determination, eyes flickering towards the still forms of the guards.

The chamber doors groaned open, revealing a space that could only be described as a sanctuary. Even in my loathing for the mages, I couldn't deny the stunning beauty of the room. It was a serene tableau of bubbling fountains and gleaming pools, cascades of crystal clear water creating a tranquil melody that echoed through the vaulted ceiling. Greenery spilled from every corner, a lush oasis that starkly contrasted the arid harshness of the outside world. Centered in the room was a magnificent statue of the Water Goddess, Melusine. Crafted from marble, she seemed to emerge from the floor, a cascade of water flowing from her hands into a shimmering pool below. Her serene expression and graceful pose exuded an ethereal calm, a tangible manifestation of the sacred reverence the mages held for their deity. My gaze then fell on the centerpiece of the room, the object of our daring mission—the Water Heart. It was a delicate structure, formed from a unique crystalline material that caught the light and refracted it into a million gleaming hues. The crystal was exquisitely carved into the shape of a blooming lotus, the blossom's petals gently cradling a pool of water so clear it was as if the very essence of life was contained within it. This wasn't just water. It was a symbol of the mages' dominance, a tool of their manipulation, an embodiment of their divine connection to Melusine. I could almost feel the power pulsating from it, a tangible force that prickled my skin with its intensity. A realization struck me. This was the power that had allowed a race of magic-wielding oppressors to enslave my people. A flame of resentment flickered within me, but I pushed it down, focusing on the task at hand. Our purpose was to steal it away from them, to reclaim control of our own fate, not to stand in awe of it. Elras was the first to break the trance.

He moved forward with a purpose, his eyes hardened with determination and years of pent-up anger. His former status as a slave may have been erased by Raena, but the mark it left was as clear as day. Kael and I followed suit, closing the distance between us and the object of our daring mission. The pool housing the Water Heart was encircled by a delicate barrier of runes, designed to keep the sacred water contained and protected. Kael reached out, tracing the glyphs with his finger. As his finger danced across the intricate patterns, Kael's brow furrowed, a mutter of frustration seeping through his teeth. His hand recoiled as if the runes had physically burned him, his usual elegance replaced with a raw display of surprise and anger. "Damn the mages and their protective spells," he spat, flexing his fingers as though shaking off the phantom pain.

Elras stepped up to him, the gruff former miner surveying the runes with suspicion. He extended a calloused hand, trying to mimic Kael's previous action. The barrier of glyphs shimmered at his touch before sparking brightly, sending Elras staggering backward with a pained grunt. He scowled, nursing his singed hand.
"Blasted mages and their bloody sorcery," he growled, his rough voice seething with pent-up frustration.
For a moment, the two of them stood there, nursing their pride more than any physical pain. I stepped forward, my determination refueling at the sight of my comrades' struggle. I felt a sudden urge to shatter this magical barrier myself, to break the cycle of helplessness, to reclaim some semblance of power.
"Stand aside," I told them, my voice a quiet rumble. The fiery passion that often led me was now simmering, controlled but potent.

Kael and Elras exchanged a glance before stepping away, skepticism and curiosity mingling in their expressions. They knew as well as I did that I possessed no magical aptitude. I was a warrior, a leader, a demon - but not a mage. Yet, as I reached out towards the glowing runes, I clung to the glimmer of hope, the reckless optimism that had guided me through our mission so far. My fingers made contact with the barrier, the magical energy crackling against my skin. A searing pain lanced through me, more intense than any physical wound. But instead of recoiling, I held my ground, teeth gritted against the onslaught. I felt an inner fire, a potent force that had nothing to do with magic and everything to do with stubborn resolve, determination, and a relentless spirit. The glyphs flared violently, casting harsh shadows on my determined face. A deafening hum filled the air, and for a moment, I felt the oppressive weight of failure bearing down on me. But just as quickly as it came, it dissipated. The hum faded, the runes dimmed, and the barrier evaporated like morning mist under the harsh desert sun. A stunned silence hung in the air, Kael and Elras gazing at the now accessible Water Heart with wide eyes. I pulled my hand back, flexing it to relieve the lingering sting.

"Quite a touch you got there, Ash," Elras commented, his voice heavy with awe.

Without a word, I reached for the Water Heart. It pulsed with an almost living energy, cool and soothing against my rough hand.

"Let's move," I said, tucking the Water Heart carefully away.

With one last glance at the sacred chamber, we left, leaving the sanctuary in stunned silence.

———　·　.°　☆:　*.⁾　.*　:☆°　.　———

37

We navigated the hallways of the palace with Elras in the lead, his familiarity with the palace layout leading us through the labyrinth of hallways and chambers. His expression was taut, the fiery torchlight reflecting off his grim countenance, and his posture rigid. "Blasted, confounding maze," he muttered under his breath.

His expression was that of a man both loathsome and intimately familiar with his surroundings. Yet for all his grumbling, he moved with a practiced ease. Kael and I followed in his shadow, our nobleman disguises affording us a measure of security. I could feel the gazes of passing servants slide off me, their minds registering our presence but disregarding us as just another group of mages.

Suddenly, a figure emerged from a side corridor, nearly colliding with us. Prince Caspian stood there, a look of surprised recognition on his face as he took us in. His normally immaculate attire was rumpled and his face held an expression of mingled embarrassment and relief.

"Soren, Kael," he greeted, referring to the aliases we had introduced ourselves with earlier. His gaze shifted to Elras, a flicker of confusion crossing his features before he shrugged it off.

"I wasn't expecting to see you here."

A smooth lie slid off Kael's tongue as he stepped forward, a friendly smile on his face.

"Prince Caspian, we were just taking a break from the crowd ourselves."

Caspian seemed to relax at Kael's easy demeanor, a small smile tugging at his lips.

"Ah, the crowd... I suppose we all need an escape from time to time."

I could practically see the wheels turning in Kael's head as he navigated the conversation, steering it away from our clandestine activities. We had to keep Caspian in the dark, both for our safety and his. Meanwhile, Elras, seemed to be biting his tongue, his eyes were darting anxiously down the hallway we had come from, his usual gruff demeanor replaced with tense silence. The conversation took a turn as Caspian mentioned the incident with Lady Lysandra. His face reddened, a mix of embarrassment and resentment brewing beneath his courteous facade. He ran a hand through his hair, a nervous habit I'd noticed earlier in the evening.

"I'm just trying to avoid further mishaps," he confessed, sounding more like a frustrated boy than the powerful mage he was.

While Kael and Caspian chatted, my gaze lingered on the prince. Despite our shared animosity towards mages, there was an air of innocence about him, a far cry from the ruthless, cold-hearted mages I was familiar with. He was a victim of his circumstance, much like us. Kael, sensing the shift in conversation, tactfully guided Caspian's thoughts away from his earlier embarrassment.

"It's not every day we get to attend a ball," he said, bringing a smile back to the prince's face.

With the conversation veering towards safer ground, Elras relaxed, though his gaze still roved the surrounding hallways. We needed to get away, to escape the confines of the palace with the Water Heart safely in our possession. Finally, after what felt like an eternity, we managed to bid Caspian farewell, promising to see him later in the ballroom. As he retreated down the hallway, a sense of relief washed over us. We had navigated the encounter without raising suspicion.

"Damn that was close," Elras finally said, his voice gruff with tension. "Too close."

I nodded, my heart still racing.

"Let's get out of here before we run into anyone else."

Elras led us through the last winding corridor and out into the open. As we emerged, the cool desert night hit us, carrying with it the heady scent of exotic blossoms and the distant sound of music from the ballroom. Kael sighed, a note of relief in his voice.

"We made it," he said softly, looking back at the opulent palace with a strange mixture of awe and distaste.

Yet, our relief was short-lived. No sooner had we stepped away from the palace walls, that the sound of alarm bells echoed through the night air. A pulsating, anxious noise that sent a shiver of fear down my spine.

"By the Great Flames," Elras cursed under his breath.

"They've found out."

Our noble disguises wouldn't do us much good now. If the palace guards were alerted, it wouldn't take them long to notice two nobles strolling away from the palace grounds.

"Elras," I called, catching his attention.

"Come with us."

"What?" he stammered, taken aback.

"I can't, Ash. It would look too suspicious if I disappeared now."

"Elras, we've got the Water Heart. We can start making real changes for our people. We need you with us," I pleaded, hoping the prospect of freeing our people from the water mages would convince him.

Elras was silent for a moment, his face a complex dance of emotions - hope, fear, resignation. Then he shook his head.

"No, Ash," he said firmly.

"I can do more good here. Princess Raena...she's different. She treats me well, go, Ash. Before they catch up."

With a heavy heart, I clapped him on the shoulder.

"Take care, old friend," I said, then turned to Kael.

"Let's go."

——— · ˳° ☆: *.) .* :☆° . ———

38

A murmur of anxious voices filled the king's chamber as trusted advisors, high-ranking officials, and royal family members huddled close. Their expressions were a mix of disbelief and dread as the captain of the guards, a grizzled veteran with a scar bisecting his face, finished his report.

"We found the runes disintegrated. As if someone managed to disrupt the magic entirely. We've never seen anything like this before."

"Could it be an inside job?" one of the advisors suggested, a hint of panic creeping into his voice.

"Preposterous," Lord Cadmus dismissed with a wave of his hand. "Everyone in this palace knows the importance of the Water Heart. To suggest treason is..."

"Logical, father," Zarek interrupted, earning him a stern look from the Lord.

"Given the circumstances, we must consider all possibilities."

"Indeed," King Lucian rumbled, his gaze fixed on Captain Loras. "What about our null servants? Could any of them have done this?"

Captain Loras shifted uncomfortably.

"With all due respect, my King, nulls lack the necessary knowledge or skill to break the barrier. Besides, the magic surrounding the Water Heart would've reduced them to ashes."

"Then it must be the work of a mage," Queen Isadora concluded, wringing her hands anxiously.

"The runes were not merely broken," Zarek chimed in.

"They were undone. Erased."

Lord Cadmus scoffed.

"Are you suggesting that the thief was not just any mage, but one equal in power to our most skilled rune masters?"

Zarek met his father's gaze steadily.

"I'm suggesting we don't know who or what we're dealing with."

Raena's gaze flickered between the arguing men, her mind whirling with thoughts. There was truth in Zarek's words. Whoever had stolen the Water Heart was not only dangerous, they were an enigma.

"Then we must assume the worst," Raena spoke up, commanding the room's attention.

"We are dealing with an enemy who knows our magic and defenses. This isn't an act of petty theft; it's a declaration of war."

"War?" Lord Cadmus echoed, finally, the disdain evident in his voice.

"Really, my dear Raena. Such dramatic declarations."

Zarek flashed his father a disapproving look, though it went ignored. Raena, unperturbed, held Cadmus' gaze evenly.

"What else would you call it, Lord Cadmus?" she countered.

"This is no common thief's act. The Water Heart was our most closely guarded secret treasure, it's the key to our strength, it gives life to our people. Its theft is a blatant attack. If we don't return it, water will be even scarcer than it is now."

"Indeed," Queen Isadora murmured.

"Raena may be right. We cannot afford to be complacent."

King Lucian's brow furrowed deeply in thought.

"And yet, it is unsettling to conceive that we have an enemy capable of such a thing. All our allies... none harbor ill-will strong enough to commit such an act. Why would they? Their lives are also tide to it."

Zarek pushed himself off from the wall.

"Perhaps it's not a question of ill-will. But of desire. The Water Heart holds immense power."

"An enemy who wants power and is willing to incite war to obtain it..." Raena's voice trailed off, her mind running through possible suspects.

"An audacious idea," Lord Cadmus mused.

"Yet, it doesn't answer the question of who."

"I suggest we start questioning the people around us," Zarek said, his gaze scanning the room.

"Our servants, our guests, our allies. Everyone."

"And cause a mass panic?" Lord Cadmus shot back.

"You're not thinking straight, son."

Zarek bristled at the dismissal, his eyes flaring with icy determination. "Panic is preferable to the drought that will befall us if the Water Heart is not recovered. But I suggest we keep this discreet. Only those who need to know should."

Lord Cadmus grunted his approval.

"Discretion is indeed our ally in this matter. Any rumor could invite unsavory opportunists or cause unnecessary havoc. We will handle this matter within the walls of this palace."

Captain Loras, who had remained silent through the discourse, suddenly cleared his throat.

"Your Majesties," he began.

"We could utilize the palace guard. They are loyal and discreet. We could begin investigations immediately."

King Lucian nodded.

"Very well. Captain, you will oversee this task. Keep your men vigilant and discreet."

"As you wish, Your Majesty," Loras bowed his head, face grave.

"And you, Cadmus," the King continued, shifting his gaze onto the Lord, "will ensure the court continues as normal. We need to avoid suspicion."

The Lord bowed curtly.

"What about Caspian and Aldric?" Raena interjected suddenly, "Shouldn't they know about this?"

Cadmus was quick to retort.

"Absolutely not. Aldric is a prince of a neighboring kingdom. This knowledge must not cross our borders."

"Lord Cadmus is right, Raena. This is a matter we should keep within our kingdom until we know more. Alerting others could paint a target on our backs, a sign of perceived weakness. Do you believe another kingdom could be behind this Cadmus?" King Lucian asked.

"Would they risk the water scarcity to gain power?"

Lord Cadmus took a moment to answer, his sharp gaze darting to the high arches of the chamber ceiling.

"It is certainly within the realm of possibility, Your Majesty," he began.

"But a gamble of such magnitude seems... reckless. And yet, we cannot ignore any possibility."

"Even the most desperate kingdom would think twice about inciting the ire of our combined powers," Zarek chimed in.

"Unless they've been blinded by their ambitions or have found a way to harness the Water Heart's magic."

His comment drew several thoughtful looks from around the room. It was a chilling prospect. If an enemy could indeed use the Water Heart, they would hold a devastating advantage.

"Indeed," Queen Isadora added, her voice steady and comforting, like a beacon in the storm.

"The motivations of our potential adversary remain unclear. It could be a power play, a desperate act, or perhaps... a symbol."

"A symbol?" Raena asked.

"A symbol of defiance, perhaps. A statement to challenge our rule."

A pregnant pause filled the room, each individual digesting the implications. To view the theft as an act of symbolic defiance added a new, troubling dimension to the crisis. But it also painted a potential profile of their enemy - brazen, bold, and unafraid.

"Whoever they are," Raena broke the silence, "symbol or no symbol, power-hungry or desperate... We will find them. And they will pay for their audacity."

"No stone shall remain unturned," Zarek pledged.

"The first stone to turn," Zarek continued, "is to analyze the manner in which the glyph was broken. The runes were not simply shattered. They were erased, undone....Such a feat requires a profound understanding of magic, an intimate knowledge of the Water Heart's defenses."

"Only a select few possess such knowledge," Raena broke in.

"Only a handful of our own could have done this."

There was a collective intake of breath at her words. Treason was a word that echoed ominously within the palace walls, a sin incomparable.

"We've taught our mages to honor and protect the Water Heart," King Lucian observed.

"To find one among them capable of such treachery..."

"Before we jump to such dire conclusions," Lord Cadmus said, a note of caution in his voice, "let us not forget the existence of old texts, scrolls, and books that lay in the ruins of our predecessors. There is a possibility that our adversary might have dug out such knowledge."

Zarek nodded, conceding his father's point.

"Indeed, such a source cannot be overlooked. But it strengthens the theory that it is a mage behind this, someone who can decipher and utilize such ancient wisdom."

Queen Isadora looked visibly distressed, her hands clasped tightly in her lap.

"So, we are searching for a needle in a haystack."

"Perhaps," Zarek agreed.

"But this needle has left a unique mark, a signature per se. We must hunt down whoever possesses this particular skill, this understanding of our magic."

"Then we must seek knowledge," Raena declared.

"Dig into our archives, seek out our scholars, consult with our elder mages. We need to understand the method of this... magic dissolution. And, we need to do this covertly."

"A wise plan," King Lucian nodded.

"Let's set this in motion. Captain Loras, quietly arrange for the necessary investigations. Cadmus, oversee the court as usual. We must not let our guard down, nor should we let the realm sense our unease."

———— · ₒ˚ ☆: *.) .* :☆˚ . ————

It was deep into the night next day by the time Kael and I stood before Gavril and Orlon, the last echoes of our tale fading into the confines of our makeshift command center. A sense of satisfaction welled up within me. We were back at our settlement, our base; back amongst our people. Yet, the satisfaction was tinged with concern for Elras who remained behind at the palace. Gavril, with his broad shoulders and stern gaze, listened to our report with a practical silence, occasionally interrupting us with pointed questions. Orlon, on the other hand, watched us with his observant eyes.

"And the Water Heart..." Gavril finally broke the silence, his tone holding a note of awe.

"You've really brought it."

I exchanged a look with Kael before gently pulling the crystalline artifact from the folds of my clothing. As it came into view, a collective gasp filled the room.

The Water Heart was a sight to behold. The artifact caught the sparse light of the room, casting an otherworldly glow across the faces of Gavril and Orlon. Despite my resentment towards the mages, I couldn't deny the mesmerizing beauty of it. I hated the power it represented, yet was enthralled by its magnificence. Orlon was the first to break the silence.

"By the Flames..." he whispered, his usually stoic demeanor slipping. He reached out to touch it, then hesitated, pulling his hand back. "It's... it's beautiful."

"It's power," I said.

"And it's our ticket to freedom."

Gavril nodded, seeming to pull himself from the hypnotic gaze of the Water Heart.

"You've done well," he said, looking at us both with a newfound respect.

"We need to plan our next move carefully. This... this changes everything."

"Indeed it does," Kael agreed, his voice barely above a whisper, as if he feared the weight of our undertaking might shatter the moment. "This is the key to our liberation, but how do we use it to unlock the door?"

Gavril, rubbed his chin thoughtfully.

"We should consider our options," he began.

"Using the Heart, we have leverage over the mages. They will want it back and we can use that to our advantage."

"That sounds easy enough," Orlon interjected, his gaze skeptical. "But how do we even approach them without risking our own lives?"

"We cannot risk revealing ourselves, not now," I said, feeling the responsibility of leadership weighing heavy on me.

"And we certainly can't risk Elras. We need to be smart."

Kael nodded in agreement.

"We need to bring the mages to us, on our terms. We can send them a message. Anonymously."

Gavril frowned.

"An anonymous message, from demon slaves, demanding negotiations for freedom? And you think they'll take it seriously?"

"They will," I said, "if we threaten to destroy the Water Heart."

The room fell into silence as the boldness of Kael's plan washed over us. It was dangerous, reckless even, but it held the potential to work. The mages would move heaven and earth to reclaim the Heart.

"A daring plan," Orlon finally said, breaking the silence.

"But it just might work."

"But we need to be prepared," I warned, meeting each of their eyes. "If this fails, we need to be ready for war."

"Or....Dissension," Kael said simply.

"We don't reveal ourselves as the thieves. Instead, we make it seem as though the theft was an internal job. A faction of the mages, dissatisfied with the current regime. We know there are factions within the mage society that are unhappy with the current status quo. What if one of them stole the Heart to force change? It's plausible, isn't it?"

"It's more than plausible," Gavril admitted, the spark of strategy flickering in his eyes.

"It's a stroke of genius. The mages would turn against each other, their focus shifted from us, and we... we get a seat at the negotiation table."

Orlon frowned, concern furrowing his brow.

"But how do we manage this? It's one thing to suggest it, Kael, but to actually sow the seeds of discord among the mages... It's a dangerous game."

"Indeed," Kael acknowledged.

"But it's a game we're forced to play, Orlon. We've stolen the Water Heart. We're already in peril. The question is: how do we maneuver our pieces on the board to our best advantage?"

"The message," I mused aloud, "the anonymous message threatening to destroy the Heart. It must seem to come from a faction within the mage society, one with the motive and means to pull off such a theft."

"Exactly," Kael affirmed, a shadow of his former self returning to his eyes.

"We'll need to be careful, craft the message in a way that it points to them, but subtly. We don't want the mages to realize they're being manipulated."

Gavril nodded slowly, absorbing the intricacy of our plan.

"It's a delicate operation. But if it works, we'll have the upper hand, and the chaos among the mages will provide us the opening we need."

Orlon's brows furrowed, a hint of concern etching lines onto his otherwise stoic face.

"I worry about the factions dissatisfied with the current leadership. They've been of help to us, either directly or indirectly. It seems...unfair to point the finger at them."

His words hung heavily in the dimly lit room, a stark reminder of the moral quagmire we waded through. It was easy to lose sight of right and wrong in a world where survival often demanded unpalatable choices.

"It's true," I conceded, looking at Orlon, then at the others.

"We're playing a dangerous game here. But remember, we're not just playing for our own lives, but for the future of our entire race. We can't afford to play safe. Not now."

"Remember," I murmured, looking at each of my comrades.

"We are not throwing our friends to the wolves. This is a bluff, a gamble that could change the tides in our favor."

Gavril nodded, his gaze steeling over.

"Then let's play our cards. For freedom."

40

—— · ˚ ☆: *. ☽ .* :☆˚. ——

"   To all those who bear the thirst for change within the fractured halls of the Mage Order. Listen, and let our words reverberate through the deepest corridors of your conscience. The Heart of Water, your sanctified symbol of dominion, the keystone of your power, no longer lies within the protective circles of your palaces. It has been wrenched from its pedestal and now pulses with life in the hands of those who dare to challenge your supremacy. We stand prepared, on the precipice of destruction. A mere thought away from extinguishing its luminescent pulse, severing your sacred link to the realm of Melusine. But we, the shadows that you've shunned and oppressed, offer an alternative path, a path that leads not to the annihilation of your lifeline but towards the possibility of a shared destiny. It's a path that demands reparation, that calls for courage, and above all, mandates justice.

    Renounce the shackles you've placed on demon kin. Release them from the cruel grasp of servitude, recognize their rights to live, to exist, to prosper, as more than just indentured spirits. Acknowledge the nulls, who may not possess your magical lineage but share in your humanity. They've been overlooked, disregarded, shunned to the margins of society despite their contributions, their loyalty, their dreams.

    Restore the balance that has been lost in your greedy pursuit of power. Only then, under the renewed covenant of respect and shared prosperity, will the Heart be returned to your care. It is then, and only then, that we entrust you with its power, its responsibility. It is then that you prove worthy of its possession.

Let these words not be lost in the sands, let them be the winds of change sweeping across this barren landscape.

This is not a plea, it's a call to action. A chance for redemption, for change, for a future where every race, every being, enjoys the privilege of freedom.

Heed this call, for the sake of all that exists under the scorching sun of our shared world."

The king finished reading the anonymous letter they received.

Lord Cadmus was the first to break the silence.

"Outrageous," he spat, his elegant diction splintered by pure disgust. "They call this a 'call to action'? I call it blackmail."

"Is it?" Queen Isadora mused, her calm demeanor a stark contrast to Cadmus's indignation.

"Or is it a call to introspection?"

"Irrelevant," Cadmus retorted.

"This is not about introspection, your highness. It's about our power, our birthright being threatened by faceless insurgents."

King Lucian turned the parchment over in his hand, as if hoping for answers to magically appear on its back.

"A 'shared destiny,' they say," he mused aloud.

"But at what price? The freedom of the demon kin, the elevation of nulls to equal status... These are seismic shifts, changes that would alter the very fabric of our society."

The chamber lapsed into silence again, everyone weighed down by the gravity of the situation. Finally, it was Queen Isadora who broke the silence.

"Perhaps... perhaps we need a shift in perspective," she began slowly. "A change in the way we view our world, our power, our responsibilities. If we treat this as a negotiation rather than a threat..."

"Negotiation? With terrorists?" Cadmus interjected, disbelief etched on his face.

Isadora raised a hand to quiet him.

"Negotiation, Cadmus. With our subjects, our people. Perhaps it is time we listened. For the sake of our kingdom, our reign, and, most importantly, for the sake of the Water Heart."

"No," Cadmus retorted, each syllable sharp as a dagger.

"We must not pander to the rabble. Their demands are outrageous, preposterous, even. Free the demons? They are volatile, unpredictable creatures. Unleashing them onto the society we've painstakingly built could lead to nothing short of disaster. I do not need to remind all of you in this room how dangerous they are."

"Cadmus, we know the history," King Lucian responded firmly, holding up his hand for silence.

"Your objections have been noted. But we are not discussing letting the demons run rampant. We are discussing... reevaluating our system."

Cadmus grumbled.

"And what about the nulls? Are we to raise them to our level? They lack our gifts, our training, our wisdom. That is not an act of fairness, it's a mockery of nature."

"I agree on the matter of the demon kin," Zarek interjected, his tone measured.

"Their potential for chaos is too great. However, we might consider a different stance on the nulls. The nulls are a part of our society, yet we keep them on the periphery. They may not possess our magical capabilities, but they are our people. They work our lands, build our homes. They deserve a voice."

"Yet," Raena's spoke,"Even if we cannot entertain the notion of freeing the demons, can we not make some concessions for them? Must their fate be so dismal?"

Cadmus, taken aback, shot Raena a disapproving look.

"We provide for them, princess. They have shelter, food, and work. What more could they possibly need?"

"But at what cost?" Raena retorted.

"Their servitude is nothing short of inhumane, Cadmus. We chain them, brand them, break them. Is that the cost of their 'provision'? Is it necessary to strip them of their dignity just to keep them under control?"

King Lucian intervened.

"Raena speaks true. The demons may be volatile, they may be dangerous, but they are sentient beings, not mere animals to be broken and enslaved. It is not about what they need. It's about what they deserve - the basic respect that should be accorded to any living creature. Perhaps...we can find some middle ground. They remain our slaves but are treated...better. Not equal to us or the nulls, but better than now."

***

Underneath a sky of blistering cerulean, the royal gardens shimmered like a verdant mirage, a sanctuary of lush green in an otherwise barren world. Vines intertwined with exquisite mosaics, waterfalls cascaded into clear ponds filled with rare, vibrant fish, and blossoms of all hues provided a stark contrast to the endless and majestic peacocks strutted arrogantly, their plumage aglow under the soft twilight. Raena found herself wandering down the central path. She ambled along, tracing her fingers over the blooms, her mind brimming with the echoes of the contentious meeting. The roses prickled her skin, similar to the thorny issues that lay ahead. Freedom, equality, justice – weighty words that seemed to flutter and flit in her mind. Lost in thought, she hardly registered the subtle shift in the air, a whispering rustle that wasn't the wind teasing the leaves. A presence nearby; not quite lurking, but not fully revealing itself either.

"Princess Raena, a gift for your thoughts?"

She turned, her startled gaze falling upon a stranger standing in the dappled sunlight that filtered through the arching branches overhead. He was tall, a handsome figure of man garbed in a cloak that shrouded him in mystery. In his outstretched hand, he held a solitary bloom, its petals the vibrant hue of the setting sun. She studied the man, her gaze unwavering, even as a familiar flutter danced in her stomach, accepting the flower, her hand reaching out for the bloom.

"Is there a reason you're interrupting my stroll?" she asked.

As the stranger bowed slightly, a charming smile played on his lips, "A simple wish to brighten your day, my lady," he replied, his tone low, but not without a hint of playfulness.

Raena studied him, twirling the flower absentmindedly.

"Your face eludes me, but your voice...it rings familiar. Who might you be?"

294

"Soren, my lady," he bowed his head slightly, his lips twisting into an alluring smile.

"We shared a dance at the royal ball not too long ago, remember? I must say, the experience was unforgettable."

"I do recall a dance... it was rather enjoyable, wasn't it?"

"Indeed it was, Princess," Soren responded.

"In fact, the memory of our dance has been a most delightful torment, ensnaring my thoughts since then."

Raena raised an eyebrow at that, a soft laugh escaping her lips.

"A delightful torment, you say?

"Indeed, seeing you now... it reminds me of the rhythm of that dance, the way you moved so gracefully, as if commanding the very elements around you. It was... captivating."

Soren offered his arm, bowing slightly.

"May I walk with you, Princess? I'd love to know what thoughts occupy your mind. You seemed lost in them earlier."

Raena looked at his extended arm, an amused glint in her eye.

"And if I refuse?"

"Then I will respect your decision, as any gentleman should," Soren replied.

"But it would be a shame not to enjoy the beauty of the gardens in good company."

The princess considered him for a moment longer before extending her arm, allowing him to link it with his.

"Very well, Soren. You may accompany me. And in return, perhaps you'll share a few more of your 'torments' with me."

Soren's grin widened.

"Only if you promise not to hold them against me, Princess."

Raena chuckled lightly.

"I make no such promises."

Their footsteps harmonized upon the stone path, leading them deeper into the sprawling gardens. Soren marveled at the lush surroundings, his gaze sweeping over the verdant array of flora which, in its abundance, felt like a mirage set against the harsh desert terrain that dominated their world.

"This garden... it's a marvel," he confessed, his tone imbued with genuine admiration. "A breathtaking oasis amidst a sea of relentless dunes."

"I take it you have a fondness for greenery?"

He bent down, lightly brushing his fingers over a delicate fern, its leaves trembling under the gentle contact.

"I suppose I do," his fingers traced the intricate patterns of the fern leaf, a soft sigh escaping his lips.

"Greenery represents hope, Princess, something the desert lacks."

"I would've thought someone of your stature would be accustomed to such... extravagances."

"I'm afraid that's a misconception, Princess," he corrected with a slight tilt of his head.

"While my family carries a noble title, we lack the wealth that usually accompanies it. Our estate resides near the outskirts of the desert, where water is scarce, and the landscape is as harsh as the life it supports."

"I see," she mused aloud.

"It's not often one hears of nobles living in conditions any less grand than these. Most wouldn't dare acknowledge the disparity of wealth within the nobility. They'd rather keep up appearances, especially when talking to me."

"I imagine that to be true," Soren agreed, his gaze shifting back to her.

"People often put on masks to impress others, especially when it comes to the nobility. I've never been much for pretending. Perhaps it's a fault, but I prefer to see things as they truly are, rather than how we might wish them to be."

"Interesting," she murmured.

"Most nobles in your position would seize the opportunity to ingratiate themselves, tell me whatever they think I want to hear. You're a peculiar one, Soren"

"Is that a bad thing?" He asked, unable to keep the playful note out of his voice.

She raised a single, well-groomed eyebrow in his direction, a slight smirk playing on her lips.

"That remains to be seen."

"Speaking of seeing, I can't help but notice you've been rather contemplative. Care to share what's been on your mind, Princess?"

She paused, seemingly considering her response.

"You're quite forward, aren't you?"

He shrugged, a mischievous grin spreading across his face.

"Only when the occasion calls for it. But in all seriousness, princess," he said.

"You don't have to share if you don't want to. I just hope that during my stay in the capital, however long that may be, we could become... friends. In times of trouble, it can help to confide in someone. Even a peculiar noble from the outskirts."

She was silent for a while, her clear blue eyes studying him intently.

"Friends, then," she agreed, a hint of bemusement on her lips.

"There are few genuine ones. Nobility tends to foster more competitors than confidants."

"An unfortunate truth," Soren nodded in agreement, his tone light but sincere.

"But know this, Princess Raena. While I'm here, you have one less competitor, and one more... friend."

The light in her eyes flickered, something complex and unreadable swirling in their sapphire depths. A hint of a smile ghosted her lips, and she extended her hand towards him. Soren took it, a spark of something electric passing between them at the contact, making him aware of her soft skin against his, and of how perfectly their hands fit together.

"I suppose we shall see, Lord Soren," she murmured, her gaze meeting his once more.

"I do have to warn you, though. I can be a... demanding friend."

He laughed lightly at her warning, the sound echoing through the air around them, soft and warm.

"I expect nothing less, Princess. And for the record, I've been known to be quite relentless myself when it comes to friendships. Though I must admit, I'm looking forward to discovering just how 'demanding' a friend you can be."

"Relentless, are you? I'll be sure to keep that in mind, Lord Soren."

"Please, just Soren. I'm not much for titles, and considering our newfound friendship, we should do away with the formality."

"Very well, Soren," she nodded, "and you should call me Raena then. No need for titles between friends, right?"

"Right," he echoed, his gaze lingering on her just a moment longer than necessary. The corners of his mouth twitched upward in a smile that reached his eyes - a smile that made Raena's breath hitch ever so slightly. He really was quite charming.

The sun was now casting long shadows, painting the garden with a palette of golds and purples. An atmosphere of quiet tranquility settled over them, like the stillness before a storm, charged with a sense of something just out of reach. Soren turned to face her more fully, the sunset illuminating his face, throwing into sharp relief the striking lines of his features. Studying his features, her mind unwillingly traced back to another face – that of Ash. Her heart seized at the thought, and a faint frown graced her delicate features. No, she thought, the similarity was merely a trick of the mind. The dusty, dirt-streaked face of the demon could hardly be compared to the striking visage of the noble before her. Yet, some gut feeling was nagging at her, like a tune she couldn't place but recognized nonetheless.

"You look as though you're trying to solve a particularly challenging riddle, Raena," Soren commented, his voice breaking her train of thoughts.

"I assure you, I'm not as complex as I may seem."

"Perhaps," she replied, pulling her thoughts back to the present. "You remind me of someone, that's all."

His brows furrowed in confusion, the corners of his mouth curling into a small, questioning smile.

"Oh? Anyone I should be jealous of?" His tone was light, an obvious tease, yet she noticed the curiosity in his eyes."

She let out a soft laugh, an involuntary blush creeping onto her cheeks.

"No, not at all," she replied, waving off his question, "just a coincidence, I'm sure."

"I'm glad to hear that," he said, his smile growing wider, a hint of relief in his voice. The atmosphere relaxed a bit, and he shifted the topic back to lighter banter.

"So, you're engaged to that lord Zarek, right? Tell me, what's the story there?"

"Ah, so now it's 'that lord Zarek,' is it? You certainly seem curious about my personal affairs, Soren," she teased, a smirk curving her lips.

Soren raised an eyebrow, a lighthearted chuckle escaping him. "Merely trying to understand my... friend better," he responded, emphasizing the last word.

Raena's smirk deepened.

"Very well then. To satiate your curiosity, Zarek and I grew up together. Our families, being of two of the most influential mage houses in the kingdom, thought it prudent to unite. And thus, an engagement was arranged when we were children."

The idea of Raena being forced into an arrangement without her heart being in it didn't sit well with him.

"And how do you feel about it?" he found himself asking, despite the personal nature of the question.

Raena sighed, looking into the distance, lost in thought for a moment. "At first, I resented the idea," she admitted.

"Being bound to someone because of a decision made by others... it didn't sit right with me. But Zarek... he made it bearable."

Soren tilted his head slightly, intrigued by her candid confession. "How so?"

She looked back at him, her eyes softening.

"He's patient, considerate... He's always been there for me, listened to me when no one else would. He's a remarkable mage, intelligent, clever and... he's got a cheeky side that keeps me on my toes."

Raena laughed softly, a certain warmth spreading across her face as she spoke of Zarek.

"Over time, we grew close, very close. I can't deny that I developed genuine feelings for him."

Soren's smile faltered ever so slightly. Hearing her speak so fondly of Zarek stirred a strange discomfort within him, yet he forced himself to maintain a neutral expression.

"It seems that lord Zarek is indeed a fortunate man," he replied, his voice steady despite the tight knot forming in his chest.

"Oh, don't sound so glum, Soren," she teased, her sapphire eyes sparkling with mirth.

"You asked for the story, and I delivered."

Soren let out a soft chuckle, masking his unease behind a light-hearted facade.

"True, but I must admit, I'm a little jealous of him," he said, his voice playful yet sincere.

"Is that so? Jealous of a betrothal, or jealous of Zarek?" she challenged, her tone teasing.

He chuckled, taking a moment to response.

"I wouldn't say jealous of Zarek. More... envious of his position."

"And what position would that be, Soren? The one of being betrothed to a demanding friend or being the constant target of her mischievous pranks?" Raena asked, leaning in closer to him with a playful gleam in her eyes.

He met her gaze, the intensity in his eyes not quite matching the lightness of their conversation.

"The position of having your regard, Raena," he answered, his voice low and sincere.

"The privilege of knowing you as he does."

A silence settled between them, Raena looked away, her heart pounding against her ribcage. She had been attracted to Ash - a fact that had stirred enough confusion in her already complicated life. And now, Soren, with his charisma and relentless nature, seemed to be provoking similar feelings within her. Soren, noticing her silence, took a step back, his features softening.

"I apologize if I've overstepped, Raena," he said, his tone replaced with a genuine sense of concern.

Raena blinked, pulling her thoughts back into focus. She found herself surprised by the sincerity in his apology.

"No, it's... it's not that, Soren," she reassured him, offering a small, appreciative smile.

"You just caught me off guard."

He studied her for a moment, his eyes flickering with a silent question. With a brief nod, he decided to push just a little further.

"Raena... you speak of your feelings for Zarek," he started, his voice soft yet firm.

"Does that mean you're in love with him?"

It was a question she had asked herself countless times, a question that she still struggled to find an answer to. She hesitated, her gaze falling onto the grass beneath her feet.

"I... I don't know. I care for him deeply, there's no doubt about that. But love? I'm not certain."

She paused, her thoughts drifting back to Zarek. The safety and familiarity he offered were comforting.

"In my heart, I feel a strong connection with Zarek, something forged over years of companionship," she confessed.

"But is it the all-consuming passion that poets speak of, that bards sing about? I'm not sure. I sometimes wonder if I even know what love truly is."

Soren, sensing her discomfort, quickly tried to lighten the mood.

"I see," he said, a playful smile pulling at his lips.

"Then I suppose it's Zarek's long-standing friendship I'm jealous of. He's had years of a head start on me."

After a moment, he leaned closer and continued in a quieter tone, "Actually if I think about it, I'm not jealous of anyone."

His voice was gentle, and there was a sparkle in his dark eyes. Raena felt her heart fluttering as he gazed at her intently. She wondered if he could read her mind or see straight into her heart. She had to admit that his sudden closeness made her feel a bit uneasy, but it was also strangely intoxicating.

"What do you mean?" Raena asked.

"What I meant," Soren continued, his voice still gentle and his tone serious.

"Zarek has had many years to make you feel safe and comfortable with him, to win your friendship and trust. I can't deny or disregard that," he admitted, his voice soft yet determined.

His gaze didn't waver, the usually playful demeanor overshadowed by a newfound resolve.

"But that doesn't mean I can't catch up," he added. His hand slightly brushed against hers, a subtle yet deliberate action that sent a jolt through her system.

Raena's eyes widened in surprise, not only at his unexpected touch but also at the implications of his words. Her mind raced with questions, her heart pounded with excitement, and a hint of fear. What was Soren saying? Was he genuinely interested in her? Despite her engagement to Zarek?

"I intend to win you over, Raena," he said, his voice barely a whisper.

There was no jest in his tone now, only a raw honesty that took her breath away. Raena swallowed, her throat dry. She was attracted to him, there was no denying that. But this... this was something else entirely. He wasn't merely flirting; he was stating his intentions in the most forthright manner possible.

"And how do you propose to do that, Soren?" she asked

Soren's dark eyes sparkled with a mixture of determination and playfulness as he stepped back, breaking their close proximity. He raised an eyebrow, the ghost of a smirk on his lips.

"By showing you that there is more to love than comfort and safety."

"And what else is there?" Raena asked, her voice soft and her heart fluttering.

Not a lot of people apart from those closes to her had been so honest or straightforward with her before. Soren didn't seem to be afraid of expressing himself, and she found that admirable and alluring. Soren moved closer to Raena, his dark eyes glinting in the sunlight as he gazed at her intently.

"More than comfort and safety... There is passion, excitement, and a feeling of connection that runs so deep, it makes you feel like the whole world is yours for the taking. It makes your heart race and your soul feel alive," he whispered.

"It makes everything seem possible and worth fighting for."

His voice was tender and thoughtful, and he seemed to be lost in his own thoughts. Raena felt her heart beating faster as she listened to him speak so passionately. It was beautiful.

"You make it sound so wonderful," Raena said, her voice soft.

"And it is, but it's also terrifying. It can consume you, make you reckless..."

Raena's heart skipped a beat as Soren came closer and caressed her cheek. It was a soft and gentle touch, but it sent a shiver down her spine. She felt a mixture of emotions surging through her, ranging from shock to anticipation to a sense of comfort and safety. She could feel her cheeks blushing, and she found herself holding her breath, unsure of what would happen next. There seemed to be a spark between them, and she felt herself drawn to him more and more with every passing moment. But that would surely be a mistake. She wasn't sure how to respond to his gesture of intimacy, and she could feel herself getting overwhelmed by the intensity of the moment. Soren held her gaze, his eyes studying her gently. She could feel her lips part slightly, wanting to say something, but she couldn't seem to find the words. His thumb traced a line from her cheek to her jawline, his touch light as a feather. There was a question in his eyes, one she found herself unable to answer.

Without uttering a word, Soren leaned in, his eyes never leaving hers. The world seemed to slow as the distance between them lessened. He paused for a moment, as if asking for permission, then pressed his lips gently against hers. Raena felt her mind go blank, her heartbeat drowning out any other sound. Her eyes fluttered shut as she gave in to the unexpected but not entirely unwelcome sensation. Soren's lips were warm and soft against hers, his kiss gentle and hesitant, as if testing the waters. A sudden surge of emotions swelled within her. Confusion, surprise, a hint of fear, and amidst it all, an undeniable spark of thrill. She wasn't sure what she should be feeling, but the one thing she couldn't deny was the intensity of the connection she felt with Soren. The moment lasted for what seemed like an eternity, a strange interlude where the world around them seemed to fade away. Raena, her heart thundering in her chest, barely breathed as she kissed him back. Her hand found its way to his chest, feeling the steady rhythm of his heartbeat beneath her fingers. She wasn't sure how she should be reacting, but her body seemed to have a mind of its own.

The taste of him, the feel of his lips against hers was intoxicating, causing her mind to spin and her senses to become heightened. Soren pulled away gently, leaving just a breath of space between them. His eyes held hers, a mix of intensity and curiosity shimmering in their depths. Raena couldn't quite decipher the look he gave her, it was as if he were trying to see past her exterior and into her very soul.

"I..." she started, her voice barely a whisper.

The words caught in her throat, her mind a whirlwind of thoughts and feelings. How was she supposed to respond to that? She'd never experienced anything so profound, even with Zarek, her feelings had been born out of familiarity and comfort rather than this feeling that seemed to ignite every nerve in her body. Soren didn't interrupt her, his gaze remained fixed on hers, patient, as if he had all the time in the world to wait for her response.

"Soren," she finally breathed, her voice a mix of confusion and curiosity.

"Why did you…".

His face softened, and he lifted his hand, gently tucking a loose strand of hair behind her ear. The small gesture, so tender and considerate, caught her off guard. It was such a contrast to the passionate man she had seen moments ago.

"Because I wanted to," he replied simply, his voice low and sincere. "Because, for a moment there, I thought I might never get the chance again. And because," he paused, his gaze piercing.

"I couldn't stand the thought of not knowing what it felt like to kiss you."

Raena stared at him, speechless. His honesty was disarming, and his words sent a shiver down her spine. She was engaged, on the brink of marrying a man she'd known for years, and yet, here she was, captivated by a man she'd only known for a few days.

Soren watched her in silence for a moment, his expression unreadable. Then he sighed, his hand falling to his side.

"I don't know for how long I'll be in the city, Raena," he confessed, his voice soft.

"But I needed you to know... from the moment I saw you, you were in my heart, my Lunae Lumen."

"Lunae Lumen?" Raena repeated, her voice a soft whisper, a hint of curiosity dancing in her eyes. The term was unfamiliar to her, but it was clear from Soren's tone that it held a significant meaning.

Soren gave her a small, fond smile. His eyes seemed to soften as he explained.

"Lunae Lumen is a term of endearment. It means... moonlight'. For you've unknowingly lit up a part of me that I thought was long lost."

—— · ｡˚ ☆: *.☽ .* :☆˚. ——

41

Raena took a moment to process his words, his confession. Her heart pounded like a drum in her chest. She could feel the warmth of his breath against her face, but something else tugged at her mind, a gnawing thought.

"You must think me a fool," she spat, her blue eyes flashing dangerously.

With a flick of her wrist, she summoned her water magic and a surge of water surged from her palm, pushing Soren backwards. He staggered but managed to remain upright, surprise etched onto his face.

"I don't know what game you're playing, Soren, but if you dare touch me again, I swear I'll have your head!"

Soren stood there, drenched, yet his gaze remained unwavering. His soaked attire clung to his form, highlighting his muscular physique, but he made no move to dry himself. His eyes flickered with a myriad of emotions - surprise, hurt, concern - but not a hint of fear.

"Game?" he chuckled lightly.

"Believe me, this would be easier if it would really be a game, my intentions... my feelings... they are genuine."

Soren's gaze softened as he looked at her, the anger radiating from her stunning in its intensity. He had not expected such a vehement reaction. He should've known better, should've realized that Raena, with her fiercely independent nature, would not accept his confession easily.

"Your title, Raena, means nothing to me," he replied honestly, his voice firm.

"If you were someone else, it wouldn't change the fact that I am drawn to you."

"But it would make things easier," he continued, the intensity in his gaze never faltering.

"If you were anyone else, I wouldn't have to share you with anyone. I wouldn't have to steal moments with you like a thief in the night. I could have you by my side, openly and without any hesitations."

"You're a fool!" Raena spat, rounding on him.

Her eyes flashed with both anger and confusion.

"And you're mistaken if you believe I'd simply fall into your arms because of your sweet words. I'm engaged, Soren. To Zarek!"

The atmosphere seemed to crackle with electricity as she stepped back, her water magic swirling around her in a whirlpool of anger and frustration. Soren watched as she fought against the surge of emotions his confession had stirred. His words were a catalyst, unraveling the tenuous thread of propriety and decorum that she clung to. Without another word, Raena turned and left, leaving Soren standing alone in the garden, rain-drenched and with a sinking feeling in his chest. He watched her retreat until she disappeared, leaving him alone with his thoughts and his torment.

Jealousy, a feeling he was unaccustomed to, gripped him. The image of Zarek, with his smug smiles and easy charm, filled his mind. That Zarek had the privilege of being by Raena's side, of being her confidant, her friend...it infuriated him.

"Damn him," he muttered, running a hand through his wet hair. "And damn me."

He was a demon, a rebel leader masquerading as a nobleman in a kingdom that enslaves his people. And he had fallen in love with a princess who was engaged to another.

What an utter mess he had gotten himself into.

***

Raena marched through the castle corridors, her chest tight with fury. Her fists clenched at her sides, her icy eyes reflecting the churning storm within her.

"The nerve of him," she muttered, glaring at the elegantly woven tapestries as though they were to blame.

Every syllable of Soren's confession replayed in her mind like a broken record, their sincerity sparking a storm of conflicting emotions.

"Thinks he can charm me with pretty words and a heartfelt confession," she scoffed, shaking her head.

"Engaged or not, I am not some tavern wench to be swept off her feet."

The fact that she felt a tug at her heart, a pulse of warmth spreading across her chest at the memory of his words only fueled her anger. She was engaged to Zarek, her childhood companion, the man who had always been by her side. She shouldn't be affected by Soren's words, let alone feel a pang of regret for rejecting him so harshly. In her seething state, she didn't notice the group of men stepping out of a room ahead of her. She collided into a sturdy figure, nearly toppling him over. The familiar scent of aged parchment and mint tea tipped her off, and she glanced up to find herself staring into the disapproving eyes of Lord Cadmus.

"My, my, Princess Raena," Cadmus drawled, regaining his balance. "One might think you're in a hurry. Perhaps if you took the time to observe your surroundings, such collisions might be avoided."

Standing behind Cadmus were Zarek and Lord Eran, their faces etched with lines of stress, a stark contrast to the usually calm and composed demeanor they held. Eran, in particular, looked paler than usual, his kind eyes filled with a quiet worry.

"Apologies, Lord Cadmus," she replied.

"It was not my intention to nearly topple you over. Perhaps if you had more... dexterity, we wouldn't be in this situation."

The older man's eyes narrowed at her brazenness, but before he could reply, Zarek stepped in.

"Raena," he said, the corners of his lips twitching upwards in an attempt to diffuse the situation.

"We were just discussing some... matters. You seem flustered. Is everything alright?""

"I am fine," she replied, attempting a smile that didn't quite reach her eyes.

"Are you sure?" Zarek pressed, looking at her skeptically.

"Because you look like someone just sold the royal horse."

Raena frowned at him, but couldn't help the chuckle that bubbled from her lips.

"Very funny," she replied, the corners of her mouth twitching into a smile.

"Father, Lord Eran, if you don't mind, I'd like to take Raena for a walk," Zarek said, turning to the two men.

"By all means," Cadmus replied with a dismissive wave of his hand, "we have pressing matters to attend to."

With a curt nod, Zarek offered his arm to Raena, who accepted it. They began their walk through the castle's corridors, the tension ebbing away with every step.

Raena glanced at Zarek, her curiosity piqued.

"Zarek," she began, "why did you all look so...stressed?"

Zarek's face turned serious, his playful demeanor melting away like ice in the desert sun. He paused in their walk, leading Raena into an alcove hidden by an ornate tapestry. It was a place they'd frequented as children, a private corner away from prying eyes.

Zarek paused, his lips forming a tight line.

"It's Lord Eran," he finally admitted, glancing at her from the corner of his eye.

"There's suspicion that he might be involved in our current crisis."

Raena blinked at him, taken aback. Lord Eran? Kind, patient Lord Eran? Involved?

"That's... hard to believe," she said slowly, trying to wrap her head around the information.

"I understand your disbelief, my love. I felt the same," Zarek replied, his expression somber.

"But the facts we've uncovered so far... they are... alarming."

"But, let's not discuss it here," looking around cautiously.

"We need to talk somewhere private."

──── · ˚☆: *.☽.* :☆˚ · ────

42

Safe within the confines of Raena's private quarters, a hushed silence blanketed the room. Zarek had a weight to his presence that suggested impending bad news, his usual jovial demeanor dampened. "Zarek, you're beginning to worry me," Raena said, her heart thrumming in her chest.

Her gaze flicked over his face, picking up the deep furrows in his brow and the drawn tightness around his eyes. This was more serious than she'd initially suspected. He took a deep breath, then stepped forward, closing the distance between them.

"Raena," he began, his voice thick with tension.

"We found out something... complicated, about Lord Eran."

Raena frowned, and for a fleeting moment, she wondered if this was some bizarre jest. But the stern look on Zarek's face told her otherwise.

"What could be so serious?" she queried, her voice barely above a whisper.

"He's involved in a clandestine operation," Zarek confessed, his voice barely audible.

"He's been aiding the escape of demon slaves and has been encouraging nulls to advocate for more rights."

Raena's heart skipped a beat, the words echoing in her ears. Lord Eran, the gentle soul who'd treated everyone with kindness, involved in something so radical? It was almost surreal.

"But... why would he do that?"

Raena stammered, her mind racing as she tried to process the revelation. She knew Lord Eran was kind, but this was an entirely different level of compassion, especially considering the dangers he was facing. Zarek ran a hand through his hair, a sigh escaping his lips.

"I think, despite the societal norms, Eran views the treatment of demon slaves and nulls as unjust. He probably felt he couldn't stand by idly anymore. My father thinks he might be involved in the Water Heart theft, at least the organization he created."

Raena closed her eyes, her mind a whirlwind. The repercussions of this were far-reaching, and the political landscape was about to become a battleground. This was a precarious situation, and they were in the eye of the storm.

"I fear what will happen if the truth comes out," Zarek continued, his voice barely a whisper.

"If Lord Eran is indeed involved, he will face severe punishment, probably even death. The councilors won't stand for such a betrayal, especially not from one of their own."

Raena took a moment to let the words sink in, her mind wrestling with the implications of this discovery.

"Do you think Lord Eran knows where the Water Heart is?" she asked, her voice barely a whisper, her eyes searching Zarek's face for any hint of confirmation.

Zarek's expression was hard to read, a myriad of emotions passing over his face. After a tense moment, he sighed and ran a hand through his hair, his gaze downcast.

"When we confronted him about the theft, he seemed genuinely surprised," he confessed.

"He was stunned... and even seemed disoriented. Like he himself didn't know it was missing."

"So, he denies knowing about the theft?"

Raena asked, her heart pounding in her chest.

"But the organization he allegedly formed..."

Zarek cut her off.

"Yes, my father has indisputable evidence of that. But he seemed unaware of the Water Heart's disappearance."

Raena felt a twinge of hope. If Lord Eran hadn't been aware of the theft, there was a chance he might be innocent. But if that was the case, then who had stolen the Water Heart? And why?

"We've always known that Lord Eran advocated for more humane treatment of demons and nulls," Zarek continued, his voice steady. "But... this? It's a significant escalation, and we need to tread carefully."

They fell into silence again, the weight of the situation settling over them like a heavy shroud. Their world was shifting rapidly beneath their feet, and they had no idea what the dawn would bring.

***

In the dim, shabby interior of the "The Sand Serpent", two figures hunched over a rickety table. Their forms were hushed by the night's obscurity, faces illuminated only by the sallow glow of the single, flickering candle on their table. Ash and Kael, under the guise of Soren and Kael, respectively, were deep in a hushed conversation, glasses of amber liquid in their hands. They were in the heart of the town, their anonymity secured by the clamor of raucous laughter and drunken chatter around them and the glamour necklaces they wore around their neck.

"No word of the Heart," Kael said, his voice just above a whisper. His eyes, accustomed to the dim light, flicked about the room, taking note of every patron, every hushed conversation.

Ash grunted, twirling the glass in his hand.

"They'd rather save face than admit they've lost control," he muttered.

Kael shrugged, a wry smile playing on his lips.

"They would not want the common folk to know their prized jewel is gone. Panic would ensue, and questions would be asked."

"Precisely," Ash agreed, his mind wandered to Raena, his mate, and his heart gave a painful throb. Even in their plotting, he couldn't keep her out of his thoughts.

"I see her in your eyes, Ash," Kael murmured, his voice barely audible over the tavern's murmur.

Ash's grip tightened around his glass, his jaw clenched.

"Don't," he said flatly, his fiery gaze met Kael's calm one.

A moment of silence passed between them. Kael's lips parted as if to speak, but he thought better of it. He sighed, his gaze shifting to the worn wooden table.

"Fine. So, what's the next move?" he asked, attempting to steer the conversation back to their primary mission.

"The mages are blinded by their arrogance," Ash began, a spark of determination lighting his eyes.

"They underestimate us, and that's their downfall. We stir up the dissatisfied factions within their society, pit them against each other. We need to spread the word in the undercurrents of society, whispers that the royal family lost the Heart."

"Ah," Kael said, the hint of a smile tugging at the corners of his mouth.

"I see where you're going. Cast doubt and fear in the hearts of the public. Question the invincibility of the mages' rule. We'd be weakening their image from within."

"Exactly," Ash replied, a determined spark in his eyes.

"A king is only as strong as his subjects believe him to be."

Kael allowed a moment of silence to pass before he spoke again. He set his empty glass on the table, focusing his gaze on Ash.

"Are you okay with this, Ash?" he asked, his voice barely a whisper. "This will affect Raena too."

At her name, Ash's gaze hardened, and he looked away. He knew that, of course he did. But what choice did he have? He was leading a rebellion for the freedom of his people. Personal feelings had to be set aside. Yet, the thought of causing Raena any distress filled him with a deep, gnawing pain. He looked back at Kael, his expression steely.

"I am aware," he said, his voice barely above a whisper.

"But this is about our people, Kael. It's about a future where we're not living in constant fear. What other choice do we have?"

Kael didn't reply immediately, his gaze deep and contemplative. He studied Ash, his friend, the torment in his eyes

314

visible even in the dim tavern light. The battle between the man and the cause he was fighting for was raw and poignant.

"I understand," Kael said softly. He reached over to clasp Ash's shoulder, offering a supportive squeeze.

"But you can't ignore your feelings, Ash. They are as much a part of you as our mission."

Ash scoffed at that, pulling away from Kael.

"Feelings are a luxury we can't afford," he grumbled, downing the rest of his drink in one gulp.

Kael sighed, knowing better than to argue when Ash was in such a mood. He had seen his friend like this before, the fiery determination, the stubborn refusal to accept anything less than victory. It was one of the things that made Ash a born leader, but it was also his Achilles heel. A new wave of patrons were flooding in, their cheerful chatter adding to the cacophony of noise. Among the faces, Ash noticed a few disgruntled mages, their expressions grim as they talked in hushed tones. The game had begun. Ash turned back to Kael, his expression resolute.

"Let's get to work," he said, standing up.

It was time to fan the flames of rebellion. A revolution was brewing, and they were at its heart.

43

—— · ₒ˚ ☆: *.) .* :☆˚ . ——

Servants moved silently around the table, serving steaming platters of exotic fruits, fresh bread, and savory meats. Kael sat next to Caspian, conversing in soft tones and sharing the occasional laugh, while Soren held a more reserved air, his gaze flicking across the faces around him, analyzing and assessing.

"It's been quite a week," Aldric said, his voice echoed in the grandeur of the room.

"I don't believe I've seen you two since the ball. How are you finding the court?"

"Interesting," Kael replied, his silver tongue effortlessly maneuvering through the conversation.

"Never a dull moment."

Caspian chuckled, his demeanor radiating an easy charm.

"Indeed. Intrigue is our daily bread here."

A servant refilled their glasses with a rare vintage, the ruby liquid catching the light, and Kael saw his opportunity. Leaning back in his chair, he casually brought up the topic he was interested in.

"Speaking of intrigue," he began, swirling the liquid in his glass.

"I've been hearing strange rumors, disturbing ones. I assume they are nothing more than whispers among the gentry."

Caspian paused, eyeing Kael, while Aldric looked on with apparent interest.

"Oh?" the prince inquired.

"And what might these whispers say?"

"Something about the Water Heart," Kael answered casually.

"Stolen, they say."

For a moment, the room was filled with silence. Caspian's expression wavered for a moment, his easy charm replaced with a hint of concern.

"Stolen?" he echoed, laughing, but there was a lack of warmth to it. "That would be quite a feat. The Water Heart is well protected."

"Indeed," Kael agreed, eyes twinkling with secret amusement.

"But you know how rumors are, they tend to exaggerate the truth. I assumed you would find it as amusing as I did."

Ash, his demeanor a stark contrast to Kael's nonchalance, added, "Some say it was an inside job. A faction within the mage society, discontent with the current state of things. They're demanding changes."

"Changes?" Aldric cut in, his eyes narrowed in suspicion.

"What sort of changes?"

"Well," Ash continued, his gaze steady, "they believe that the demon kind have been treated unjustly, that they deserve freedom. They also think that the nulls should be granted more rights."

Aldric scoffed at that, Caspian spoke.

"The nulls and demons... wanting more rights... that is quite a tale. But I find it hard to believe that anyone among us, the mage society, would be capable of such actions."

"Or maybe it's simply that we find it hard to believe that someone among us would have the audacity to demand change," Ash countered.

Just as Ash's words hung in the air, a soft rustle of silk announced the arrival of Lady Lysandra. The dining hall seemed to freeze for a moment as she entered, resplendent in her morning attire, sparkling in jewels and wrapped in the most exquisite fabrics. As she swept into the room, the men rose from their seats in a customary show of respect.

"Lady Lysandra," Caspian greeted, bowing low, his face flushed. "What a pleasure to see you again. Please, join us."

Lysandra graced the table with a dazzling smile, her eyes flicking briefly over Kael and Ash before focusing on the prince.

"Caspian," she purred, gliding into the chair he held out for her. "How charming. A breakfast invitation. It's quite a change from the... events at the ball."

Kael's stomach clenched at her mention of the ball. The memory of the last time he saw Lysandra was still vivid, a dark stain on his past that he had no desire to revisit. But he had been trained well. He pasted a polite smile on his face and inclined his head in her direction.

"Lady Lysandra," he said, his voice even.

"You look as radiant as ever."

She gave a soft laugh, her gaze sweeping over him with an interest that made his skin crawl.

"Why, thank you. Lord Kael was it...?"

"Bane," he replied smoothly, the false name rolling off his tongue. "Kael Bane."

"A pleasure," she said, her interest in him fleeting.

"And your brother Soren?"

Ash's gaze was cool as he nodded toward her.

"Soren Bane," he replied curtly.

His dislike of Lysandra was barely veiled. But he held his anger in check, mindful of his role and Kael's warnings. As a server filled Lysandra's cup with tea and a plate with the morning fare, she turned her attention back to the table.

"And what fascinating conversation has entwined you gentlemen this morning?"

"We were discussing the outrageous rumors floating around lately," Caspian volunteered.

"Rumors?" Lysandra turned her gaze on him, her perfectly arched brows rising in intrigue.

"The rumored theft of the Water Heart, my lady," Kael explained, his voice smooth and measured.

"Ah, the fabled Water Heart," she chuckled.

"Stolen, you say? What an amusing fancy."

"It seems there are some in the court who find the concept less than amusing," Ash interjected.

"There's talk of an inside job. Of a faction within the mage society demanding... changes."

Lysandra's amusement faded at that.

"Changes?"

"Demon kind and nulls to be granted more rights," Ash said plainly.

Lysandra paused, her lips parting slightly in surprise. Then she laughed.

"What a preposterous notion. The mages fighting for the rights of nulls and demons? I cannot think of a more entertaining folly."

"Yet, the rumors persist," Kael reminded her gently, his gaze not leaving hers.

"One might wonder if there is a kernel of truth to them."

"Well," she shrugged, her lips curving in a dismissive smirk.

"One can only wonder. After all, rumors are a dime a dozen in this court."

The conversation was again interrupted as Raena glided in with Zarek trailing slightly behind. With practiced grace, the men rose from their seats. Caspian was the first to greet his sister, his face splitting into a wide grin.

"Little sister," he greeted, the familial affection evident in his voice.

"You're looking bright-eyed this morning."

Raena returned his warm greeting, her gaze meeting each face in the room before finally resting on Ash. Her eyes narrowed slightly, before she composed herself.

"Lady Lysandra," she acknowledged, her voice cool, her eyes not leaving Ash.

"And the Bane brothers, I see. A pleasure, as always."

Ash met her gaze steadily, his heart pounding in his chest. Raena's presence always had that effect on him.

"Princess Raena," he returned her greeting, dipping his head in a respectful nod.

"Quite the gathering this morning," Zarek commented.

"I trust breakfast has been pleasant?"

"Indeed," Kael replied.

"The conversation, too, has been quite... enlightening."

Raena's gaze was still locked with Ash's.

"And what has been the subject of such fascinating discourse?"

"Rumors, Princess," Ash said.

His voice was low, almost a whisper, but each word reverberated through the room.

"Rumors of an alleged theft of the Water Heart."

"Oh, how ridiculous," Lysandra chimed in again, the condescending smile on her lips failing to reach her eyes.

"Lord Zarek, surely you can put these wild speculations to rest? As a member of the council, you would be privy to such things."

Zarek's eyes, moved across the faces in the room before landing on Raena. A silent communication passed between them, their years together allowing an understanding only they shared.

"Indeed, rumors have a way of taking a life of their own," Zarek finally said, his gaze steady.

"While it is true that a faction within our society seeks change, the Water Heart is far from the reach of such... trivial disturbances. The Heart remains under the council's watchful guard."

Lysandra's eyes darted from Zarek to Raena, her lips curling into a smug smile.

"Such absurdities. Surely not a soul among us water mages could harbor such drastic thoughts?"

"Every society has its dissidents, Lady Lysandra," Kael said, his voice mild, his face impassive.

"Even ours."

"And what does the council plan to do about such dissent?" Lysandra questioned, her brow arched high.

"Surely such foolishness cannot be tolerated."

Zarek inclined his head, acknowledging her concern.

"The council is indeed discussing a course of action, Lady Lysandra. There may be some concessions considered."

Lysandra looked momentarily taken aback, her lips parting in surprise.

"Concessions?" she echoed, aghast. "Surely, you jest!"

"Jest?" Zarek echoed, his eyes betraying a gleam of amusement. "Hardly, Lady Lysandra, these are delicate matters of policy. Necessary, you might say."

Aldric voice his thoughts.

"Concessions could imply negotiation. It might be wiser to demonstrate our might instead. We hold the water. We hold the power."

As his words resonated around the table, Kael studied Aldric with keen interest. Here was a man who, like many, believed power was the key to control. It was a mindset Kael understood well, a mindset he used to navigate his way through the labyrinth of the mage society.

"And yet," Kael mused aloud, his tone careful, "overbearing might has been known to incite rebellion. Moderation, my dear Aldric, is often a wiser course."

It was Ash who picked up the thread next, his voice steady.

"You speak of concessions, Lord Zarek, but how far are you willing to bend? What would these concessions entail?"

His gaze drifted to Raena, finding her watching him with a curiosity that sent shivers down his spine. Zarek's gaze narrowed, ever so slightly, at Ash's question.

"We are considering a reformation of the treatment of the demon class."

Lysandra's laughter, harsh and abrupt, cut through the air like a knife.

"Reformation? What a preposterous notion!"

She downed a gulp of her crimson wine, eyeing Zarek with an incredulous stare.

"Not quite as preposterous as you may think, Lady Lysandra," Zarek countered, his gaze unwavering.

"We do not seek to grant them freedom, only to better their conditions."

Raena, with her gaze on her orange juice, added.

"It's not an act of charity, but a means to prevent revolt."

"Revolt," Lysandra scoffed, shaking his head.

"Those demons and nulls, revolting? It would be like watching sheep take on a pack of wolves."

The imagery was indeed absurd, and yet, Ash, hidden beneath his glamour, felt a surge of indignation. These humans saw his kind as cattle, as mindless creatures devoid of will, of spirit.

"I would caution against underestimating any being, Lady Lysandra," Ash stated, his voice firm. His own mockery of her sentiment was carefully veiled.

"One may find surprise in the most unlikely of places."

Lysandra raised a brow at that, giving him a considering look.

"An intriguing point of view, Lord Soren. One almost might think you have a soft spot for these creatures."

The insinuation hung in the air like a veil of smoke, and for a moment, Ash felt the pang of danger. He took a sip of his wine, his calm exterior belying the tumult beneath.

"On the contrary, Lady Lysandra," he responded, leaning back in his chair.

"I simply value a healthy respect for all forms of life. It is a wise mage who sees the potential in all creatures, wouldn't you agree?"

Lysandra studied Ash for a moment longer, then, with a wave of her hand, dismissed the notion.

"Romantic notions," she murmured, refilling her glass.

"But this is no place for sentimentality. It is a question of control."

Aldric, who had been quietly listening, finally voiced his thoughts.

"Isn't control achieved through fear? Demonstrate our power, and they will think twice before stepping out of line."

Raena frowned, looking at Aldric.

"Fear breeds hate, Aldric, not loyalty. We need a balance between authority and respect."

"Pretty words, Raena," Lysandra sneered.

"But pretty words do not rule a world."

"Intriguing," Kael murmured, his gaze pensive.

"These concessions, should they materialize, what would they encompass, Lord Zarek?" He lightly stirred his tea, a picture of relaxed curiosity. His past dealings with Lysandra had taught him to tread lightly around such a volatile creature.

Zarek considered Kael, his eyes calculating.

"Several possibilities are on the table," he began, slowly.

"Including improvement of living conditions, restriction of the harsher disciplinary actions, and perhaps..." he paused, choosing his next words with care.

"... educational opportunities, to name a few."

"Education?" Lysandra snorted, disdain clear in her voice.

"What need does a demon have for education? They are tools, nothing more."

Ash's blood boiled at her words. He swallowed his fury, reminding himself of the charade he was to maintain. The room grew perceptibly warmer, the air stifling and heavy, as if a fire roared unseen within its confines. Beads of perspiration trickled down foreheads and the fragrant aroma of blossoms in the nearby gardens grew heady. Lysandra, loosened the collar of her elaborate dress, fanning herself with a hand.

"It seems the weather conspires against us this morning," she commented, wiping her forehead with a delicate handkerchief.

"It is unseasonably warm."

Suddenly, Lysandra's handkerchief ignited, going up in flames in an instant. She shrieked, dropping the flaming cloth onto the fine marble floor, where it fizzled out as if doused by unseen water. Panic reflected in her wide eyes. A gasp echoed around the room, followed by a brief stunned silence. The temperature within the room seemed to return to normal as quickly as it had changed, leaving everyone to question whether they had imagined the whole event.

"To unpredictable weather and even more unpredictable discussions," Caspian proposed, raising his glass high.

His words had the intended effect, coaxing a smattering of hesitant chuckles from the room's occupants. Still, a layer of unease hovered in the air, as palpable as the lingering smoke from Lysandra's handkerchief.

—— · ˳˚ ☆: *.) .* :☆˚ . ——

44

With breakfast ended, the group got smaller, lady Lysandra saying her goodbyes and Zarek departing to deal with council business. Caspian slumped back in his chair, a wry smile on his lips. "Well, that went smoothly," he commented, running a hand through his hair.

Aldric chuckled, clapping his friend on the shoulder.

"Smooth as a desert sandstorm, my friend. At least this time lady Lysandra managed to keep her clothes dry."

He rose from his seat, stretching and groaning theatrically as he did so.

"Well, enough of this indoor drollery, I say! What say we move this gathering outdoors? I propose a friendly game of archery. After all, it's a fine day, and I do believe we could all do with a change of scenery."

Raena perked up at the suggestion.

"That sounds wonderful, Aldric! I could use the practice, after all." She pushed away her half-empty plate, already excited at the prospect of displaying her skills with the bow. Ash and Kael exchanged a glance. Their training at the rebel settlement had included weaponry, but neither of them favored a bow.

Caspian perked up, "I'm in," he said, rising from his seat.

"What about you, Soren?"

Ash looked at Kael.

"We'd be delighted," he said, answering for both of them.

The air was cooler in the gardens, the greenery offering relief from the scorching sun. The mage's palace boasted an elaborate archery range, with targets at varying distances and heights. Aldric and Caspian selected their bows, well-versed in the sport. Kael and

Ash, on the other hand, were novices. Kael took the bow that was handed to him, his fingers tracing the taut string and smooth curve of the wood. His fingers ached at the unfamiliar sensation. Years of servitude had not included this type of recreation.

Raena went first, her shot swift and accurate, embedding itself neatly into the center of the target. There was a smattering of applause, as the next arrow pierced the air. Her raven hair catching the sunlight, the princess exuded an aura of confidence that commanded attention, her form flawless in the execution of the shot. The arrow struck true, once again embedding itself in the heart of the target. Ash could not deny the swell of admiration that rose within him, alongside an emotion he was still coming to terms with — a fierce, undeniable affection. He found himself stepping forward before he was aware of his own intention.

"Princess, if I may?" He asked, gesturing to the bow in her hand.

Raena looked at him, surprise evident on her face. But she passed him the bow with a smirk.

"Are you planning to show me up, Soren?"

"Nothing so presumptuous," he replied, accepting the weapon. His fingers grazed hers in the process, an electric current passing between them.

"Just looking to learn from the best."

Her eyes flicked to their hands and then back to his face, a strange look passing over her features before she quickly masked it. But he had seen it, and it gave him a glimmer of hope. With a sigh, he nocked an arrow, his grip unfamiliar with the bow's delicate balance. His first shot went wild, eliciting a chuckle from the princess. His cheeks heated in response but he shrugged, affecting an air of nonchalance.

"May I?"

Raena moved closer, her hands lightly adjusting his grip and stance. Her touch was fleeting, almost like a water ripple. Yet, it left an undeniable imprint, a memory etched into his skin. The world seemed to fall away, leaving just the two of them in that moment.

The whispers of the wind, the rustle of the leaves, the warmth of the sun, all melded into a timeless snapshot. The stakes of his true identity, the looming revolution, the stolen Water Heart - they all blurred at the edges of his mind, losing focus. His second shot was better, the arrow landing closer to the center of the target. The small victory felt hollow compared to the warmth spreading through him from her praise.

Kael's eyes were worrisome as he watched them, their camaraderie blossoming before his eyes. His brother was treading a dangerous line, and he could only hope they wouldn't all pay the price. When it was his turn, Kael held the bow with the reverence of a novice. With a deep breath, he let the arrow fly. It shot through the air, carving a golden path in the dying sunlight before it thudded onto the edge of the target. It was not the center, but considering it was his first time, it was an accomplishment. Caspian clapped him on the back, a genuine grin on his face.

"Not bad, Kael." His words, though meant in jest, brought a small smile to Kael's face.

As the day wore on, the archery range was filled with friendly competition and shared laughter. Every so often, Ash would catch Kael's eye, an unspoken understanding passing between them. Despite the laughter and the lightness, they were far from forgetting their purpose. They found a moment of respite and stood apart.

Once out of earshot, they moved into the shadow of a tall column, their expressions turning grave. Kael's blue eyes reflected a concern that mirrored Ash's own. Their charade was starting to wear thin, the edges fraying with every passing minute.

"They won't grant freedom to our kind," Kael voiced out what had been haunting Ash's mind.

Ash's jaw clenched in response, his gaze darkening with an anger that he struggled to keep at bay.

"No, their entire civilization is built upon the oppression of our people. They would not throw it away that easily. We need to push them harder," he muttered, his fingers unconsciously curling into fists.

He involuntarily relaxed as Raena's laugh, light and melodic, reached their ears. Ash's gaze drifted back to her, his heart tugging at the sight. The beautiful princess, was proving to be more than just a spoiled noble; she was becoming the anchor to his stormy emotions. Her smile, her fiery spirit, they were the light piercing through the darkness of his discontent.

"What do you suggest?" Kael inquired, his eyes darting towards the crowd to ensure their conversation remained undetected.

Ash was silent for a moment, his gaze unfocused as he pondered their course of action. A reckless idea had been sprouting in his mind, one he knew Kael wouldn't approve of. But he also knew it was the push they needed.

"We need to give them a taste of their own medicine," he finally said, his voice low but firm.

"They've been comfortable in their power for far too long. They need a jolt... a reminder that power is a double-edged sword."

Kael frowned, clearly anticipating the direction Ash was headed. "And how do you propose we do that, Ash? We are here under a guise. Any overt act could expose us."

"Tomorrow," Ash began, his gaze unwavering.

" We attack where it hurts them the most: their lyrium supply. We have allies on the inside who can arrange it to look like an accident."

"Lyrium is their main source of power, and with the Heart gone..." Kael pointed out, his voice lined with worry.

"Such a move would put the city in chaos."

"Exactly," Ash confirmed, a dangerous glint in his eyes.

"Chaos creates opportunities, opportunities we can exploit to free our brothers from the mines. It's time we take our fate into our own hands, no more soft maneuvers."

Ash was about to elaborate further when a familiar, light laugh echoed in the background. He looked up to find Raena making her way towards them, her beautiful face etched with curiosity and a hint of concern. His heart thudded in his chest as she approached, her sky blue eyes holding a question that he wasn't sure he was ready to answer.

"Soren, Kael," her gaze flitting between the two.

"You've been away for a while. Is something the matter?"

Their masks of deceptive joviality fell back into place, Ash conjuring a grin onto his face.

"Nothing of concern, Princess," he responded, his tone light.

"Just a bit tired after all the competition, I reckon."

Kael nodded in agreement, his charming smile hiding the turmoil within.

"Yes, your brother was a tough opponent. He has quite the skill with the bow."

Raena laughed, the sound like a balm to Ash's troubled heart. "Caspian has always been good with it. Perhaps you can challenge him to a rematch tomorrow?"

"We would be honored, Princess," Ash replied.

Tomorrow, they would make their move.

45

——— · ｡° ☆: *.) .* :☆° . ———

As the day waned, the group retired to the grand veranda that overlooked the palace's sprawling gardens.

"A day well spent, wouldn't you say?" Aldric said.

"It was indeed, your highness," Kael conceded.

Caspian, flush with his victory, came to stand next to his sister, his pride evident in his wide smile.

"But, I think the day is far from over. We must celebrate!"

Raena, following her brother's cue, ordered a servant standing at the edge of the veranda.

"Fetch us the best vintage from the cellar. And some of those spiced canapés from the kitchen, oh and some of Auguste's deserts" she commanded, her tone accustomed to obedience.

"My dear sister, always trying to spoil us!"

Raena shrugged, a teasing smirk playing on her lips.

"Well, someone needs to appreciate my refined taste," she retorted, eliciting a round of laughter from the group.

Ash watched her, an inexplicable warmth spreading through him. She was an enigma, a maze of contradictions that he had come to adore. Her arrogance was paired with a stubborn intelligence, her mischief with an unexpected kindness. In another world, in another time, he could see himself falling hopelessly in love with her. Kael, standing by Ash's side, noticed his lingering gaze. He nudged Ash gently, Ash rolled his eyes but couldn't stop the ghost of a smile that had formed. Soon, the servants returned with trays laden with bottles of glistening liquors and plates of exquisite appetizers. The aroma that wafted through the air was intoxicating, a mélange of spices and sweetness that promised a delicious treat.

Raena picked up a bottle.

"To Caspian's victory," she declared, her tone full of jest and warmth. The cheer that erupted was deafening, glasses clinking together in a symphony of celebration. Aldric, with a self-satisfied smile, leaned over the tray of desserts that had just arrived.

"You simply must try these," he urged, lifting a small pastry delicately between his fingers.

"They are simply to die for."

Ash's eyes flicked to the small pastry in Aldric's hand, a hint of recognition lighting his gaze. He recalled the sweet taste of those desserts when he had first tasted them at the mines. The thought of Raena offering him that sweet morsel was a memory that had stayed with him. Picking one up, he chuckled softly.

"Mm, I remember these," Ash murmured, more to himself than anyone else. But in the quiet that had fallen, his voice carried, and heads turned to him. Their heads turned towards him, their expressions curious.

Caspian asked, a smile on his face, "Oh, and where might you have tasted these, Soren?"

Caught off-guard, Ash stumbled over his words.

"I...uh...".

But before he could think of a plausible explanation, Kael stepped in smoothly.

"At the Royal Ball, of course," he said, flashing Ash a quick glance. "They were served at the dessert table. It was quite the spectacle, wasn't it, brother?"

"Ah, yes," Ash said, seizing the lifeline Kael had thrown him.

"It was indeed. Such a spread of desserts, I've never seen anything like it."

There was a general murmur of agreement, Raena adding with a laugh "Oh, Auguste can indeed be quite... extravagant," she said, taking a small bite of the pastry and savoring its sweet taste.

"He has a flair for the dramatic, that's for sure."

Aldric joined her laughter, his own chuckle rich and warm. "Extravagant is an understatement, Raena. Auguste's creations are a spectacle in and of themselves."

Caspian, chuckling, added.

"And the drama doesn't stop at his desserts. You should see him when he's in the kitchen. It's like watching a play unfold."

The group erupted into laughter, the image of their pompous chef orchestrating his culinary dramas proving too amusing to ignore. Kael, however, watched the scene unfold with a thoughtful gaze, his mind turning over their words. This shared laughter, this camaraderie, this was what they were fighting for. A world where such moments were not just the privilege of a few but the birthright of all. As more rounds of drinks made their way around the table, the banter grew louder and the laughter more boisterous.

"It's quite simple, really," Aldric slurred, struggling to keep his balance on his chair.

"Every time a person utters the word 'water,' they take a shot."

"Wait, like the water we drink or water as in...?" Caspian started, looking a bit confused, only to be cut off by his sister.

"Caspian, you're already behind," Raena chastised, pointing at his glass.

"That's one shot for you."

A chorus of laughter ensued, Caspian, looking a bit flushed, rolled his eyes but obediently took his shot. The alcohol was beginning to do its work, causing the group to forget their inhibitions and delve deeper into silliness and laughter. Raena turned to Ash with a teasing glint in her eyes.

"Soren, what do you prefer, wine or... the alternative?" she asked, a barely suppressed smirk playing on her lips. Ash caught on to her game, and the corner of his mouth curled up in a smirk.

"Well, Princess, I'm rather fond of the grape's juice," he said, raising his glass and taking a sip to emphasize his point, effectively avoiding the forbidden word.

This prompted another round of laughter, Raena shaking her head at Ash's smooth reply. Caspian, despite his inebriated state, tried to participate in the fun.

"Did you know," he began, trying to balance himself on his chair, "Did you know that our kingdom's most prized wine is made with the purest...uh, H_2O?"

A second of silence followed, and then the room erupted in laughter, Raena playfully smacking her brother on the shoulder.

"That's cheating, Caspian!" she said through her laughter.

Caspian blushed and conceded, sheepishly picking up a shot glass and drinking it down. The warmth was infectious, and Ash found himself chuckling along with them, momentarily forgetting the world beyond this night. With the alcohol working its magic, Aldric tried to share a tale. But his attempt to dodge the word 'water' was futile, and he ended up taking a few more shots, his face flushed with the warmth of the liquor and his failed attempt to stay within the rules of the game. Kael watched the scene unfold, a small, uncharacteristic smile playing on his lips. This moment, filled with laughter, felt strangely comforting. He was aware of the masks they were wearing and the stakes of their mission, but he allowed himself this one night, this singular moment to revel in the joy of being part of something so human. Caspian and Aldric, both thoroughly drunk, were engaged in a heated debate over which type of alcohol was better. The others' argument escalated to the point that they were shouting at each other, with Caspian claiming that wine was the best while Aldric disagreed and said that liqueur was the superior choice. Ash took another sip of his wine and calmly suggested that they settle their argument through a drinking contest.

"Let's do it," Caspian said, his eyes bright with anticipation.

Aldric was quick to agree, saying, "It's settled, then. First one to pass out loses."

Raena, already quite inebriated, chimed in, her speech slurred and uneven.

"Wait, wait, wait. I... I want to... join in too. Why should... why should boys have all the... the fun?"

She swayed a little in her seat, looking at Ash and Kael with sparkling eyes.

"Caspian... Aldric... Soren... Kael..." she pushed glasses filled to the brim in front of each one of them.

Her hand faltered a bit, causing some of the amber liquid to spill onto the table. The rich smell of the alcohol wafted up, mixing with the earlier lingering aromas of the desserts. Ash frowned at the sight, his eyes holding a note of caution as he regarded the princess.

"Princess, you might want to take it easy," he said, a hint of concern in his voice.

"Don't even think 'bout saying no, Soren. 'Twas your idea after all."

He blinked, the veranda slightly spinning as he looked at her, his concern for Raena overriding his amusement.

"Raena, maybe you should—"

"No, no... no," she protested, wagging a finger at him, her words tumbling out haphazardly.

"You... you are... part of this. No escaping, Soren."

Begrudgingly, Ash picked up his glass, glancing at Kael.

"This is a terrible idea," he muttered, though the edges of his mouth curled up, his resolve crumbling in the face of Raena's infectious laughter.

As demons, they could metabolize the alcohol far more efficiently than humans, but even they had their limits. Caspian, having lost his equilibrium entirely, leaned on Aldric for support. The words coming out of his mouth were barely coherent, but his enthusiasm was undeterred.

"Soren... Kael... welcome... to the cha-cha-allenge!"

Aldric, though equally inebriated, managed to keep a somewhat straight face.

"Prepare...to be humbled, my friends."

Raena interjected, "Enough chatter. Drink up."

All glasses in hand, they toasted with a hearty, albeit slurred, cheer, "To...to a night of...cheer?" Caspian suggested, the spinning enough to make him fumble his words.

"Cheer it is!" Aldric echoed with a laugh, the lot of them clinking their glasses together in the center of the table before tipping the contents down their throats.

Aldric was the first to slam his empty glass back onto the table, followed by Raena who giggled, nearly missing the table with her own. Ash, with a tight grip on his self-control, set his glass down with measured precision while Kael's was a smooth motion. Aldric, his face flushed, squinted at Ash and Kael.

"You two... you two... You're keeping up... so well," he said, pointing at them with a wide grin, his words drawled out.

Ash, replied with a twinkle in his eyes.

"Comes with... years of... practice."

He smirked, his speech noticeably clearer than the others, even though the veranda was spinning for him too.

"And a... hardy constitution," Kael added, causing a round of laughter to ripple through the group.

"Perhaps... perhaps, we should... involve you two... more often...", Caspian managed to comment, his words half-lost in his laughter.

Raena, caught up in the laughter, tried to rise from her seat, her attempt foiled as she swayed dangerously. Caspian, with a brotherly instinct, reached out to steady her. Just then, a stern presence swept over the group, capturing their bleary attention. Binda, Raena's longtime maid, stepped forward with a concerned frown etched into her otherwise kindly face. Behind her stood Elras, his expression pinched as he too took in the sight of the drunk mages, his gaze fell immediately on Ash and Kael. His eyes widened, worry flickering in his depths for a moment before he schooled his features into neutrality.

"Princess Raena," Binda started, her voice a soft yet firm reprimand. "It is quite late. Perhaps it would be best if we were to retire for the evening?"

Raena, still leaning heavily on Caspian, looked up and tried to focus her eyes on Binda. She hiccuped, an infectious giggle slipping out before she could catch it.

"Binda... Elras, is that you?" she slurred, her hand gesturing grandly toward her two companions.

"Meet... meet my friends... Soren and... Kael."

Binda offered Ash and Kael a nod, the proper etiquette of a royal maid evident in her demeanor.

"Sirs," she greeted, her voice not without a note of concern.

Kael, despite his tipsiness, managed a gracious bow of his head in response, a habit ingrained from his years of servitude.

"We are honored," he said, his words remarkably clear considering the circumstances.

Ash glanced at him before nodding to Binda and Elras.

"It's good to meet you," he said, though his words, too, were more slurred than earlier in the night.

"Binda, Elras, come... come join us!"

Raena beckoned them over, sweeping her arm wide with a grand flourish, her glass nearly tipping in her loose grip.

Binda hesitated, her eyes flickering with worry as she exchanged a glance with Elras.

"Princess, it's unbecoming to--"

"No, no...no," Raena protested, silencing Binda with a dismissive wave of her hand.

"You... you are... family. You should join, too. No more... objections."

Ash watched the exchange in silence, a bit dazed from the alcohol but still lucid enough to feel a surge of surprise at Raena's behavior. He was so used to the casual cruelty of the mages that this... this was unexpected, and it warmed something in him.

"Princess, I must insist..." Binda began, her eyes flicking towards Elras. He stood there, silent and conflicted, his gaze lingering on Ash and Kael. 'If only you knew,' he thought, his worry for his demon friends well-concealed behind his neutral expression.

With a subtle elbow, Binda nudged Elras, her eyes imploring him to back her up. But the tall demon just shuffled awkwardly in response, glancing warily between the princess and his disguised friends. Binda straightened herself, giving Raena a stern look. "Princess, as your maid and confidante, I must advise that we retire. The hour is late and the wine has... clearly taken its toll," she said, the edge of reproach in her tone evident.

Raena merely giggled again, leaning her head back against the plush chair, her eyes swimming with merriment.

"Binda, don't worry... I'm not going anywhere... just yet." She slurred, her finger wagging in the air.

"Not until we finish our... our game."

Ash, watching the exchange, felt a pang of empathy towards Binda. The maid cared deeply for Raena, it was clear. Raena pointed at Ash.

"Look here, Soren... You'll keep an eye on me, won't you?" she slurred, her eyelids heavy with drink.

Ash, now significantly under the influence of the potent drink, found himself nodding, the promise slipping easily from his lips, despite the strange circumstances.

"I...I swear it, Princess," he declared, managing a surprisingly sobering level of sincerity.

"I'll...I'll protect ya with my life."

He then tried to straighten up in his chair, an attempt at displaying a sober demeanor that failed hilariously as he almost toppled over, only to be caught by Kael's quick reflexes. Kael chuckled, shaking his head in a mixture of amusement and disbelief.

"We both will," he added, addressing Binda, "you have my word." There was a lightness to his voice, a playful undertone that suggested he was enjoying the night's unexpected turn.

"You see, Binda?" Caspian exclaimed, gesturing wildly at Ash and Kael.

"Our new friends are gonna...gonna look after her... So, you don't...you don't have to worry."

Aldric, joined the chorus of reassurances.

"Truly, Binda, it will be fine. We'll...uh...make sure she gets to bed soon. We just...uh...need to finish our game first." His words were slow and punctuated by lazy gestures, his usual sharp wit dulled by the drink.

Their assurances seemed to do little to alleviate Binda's concerns, her brow furrowing even more as she considered the group. With a sigh, Binda bowed slightly.

"Very well, Princess. However, I urge you to not stay up too late." She glanced at Elras.

"Elras, we should retire for the evening. The princess has made her decision."

The undercurrent of worry in her voice was unmistakable. Raena waved her hand dismissively, her eyes struggling to focus.

"Yes, yes... Go rest, Binda, Elras. I'll be fine, truly... We all will." Raena sighed contently as she looked around at her friends.

"Now, where were we in the game?"

"Uh...we were...we were drinking," Aldric stated, almost matter-of-factly, raising his glass in demonstration, his slurred speech punctuated by a hiccup.

Raena chuckled, the sound loud and carefree in the quiet room. "That... that we were," she agreed, the wine making her usually sharp words sloppy and unrestrained. She grabbed her own glass, its contents sloshing dangerously as she raised it in a sloppy toast. "To... to the game, then."

"To the game, princess," Ash said, his words holding a hint of affection.

"And may the best mage win."

—— · ｡˚ ☆: *.☽ .* :☆˚. ——

46

Caspian was the first to succumb to the wine's potent spell, his head drooping lower with each passing moment until he was sound asleep. Aldric soon followed, slipping into a comfortable sleep against the armrest of his chair, a peaceful smile gracing his face. Raena was stubbornly trying to stay awake, but the alcohol was winning. Her eyes were barely open, and her words came out more incoherently as time passed. She was drifting between sleep and wakefulness when Ash gently intervened, removing the now empty glass from her hand.

"Enough, princess. Time to sleep," he said, his voice softer than before.

She made a small noise of protest, but didn't resist as he carefully rearranged her on the plush chair, making her comfortable. With Caspian, Aldric, and now Raena asleep, Ash turned to Kael, finding his friend also swaying a bit, but still conscious. They shared a look Elras appeared, bearing a tray laden with bottles of cool water. "Thought you might need these," he whispered, his voice hoarse from the hour.

Ash gratefully accepted one of the bottles. He took a long drink, the cold water soothing his burning throat, before splashing some of it on his face. The cool sensation seemed to bring a little clarity back to his clouded mind. Kael, following Ash's example, did the same. He took a deep drink, water dribbling down his chin, then splashed the remainder over his face. His golden hair, once perfectly styled, now clung wetly to his forehead, but he didn't seem to care. He gave a long sigh, shaking off the effects of the alcohol with every droplet that fell from his face. After a moment, Ash turned his attention back to Raena. She was dozing now, her breathing shallow and her head lolling against the plush back of the chair. Despite her intoxicated state, there was a serene beauty about her that touched Ash deeply. He felt an urge to protect her, stronger than anything he had ever felt.

"Elras," Ash said, his voice slightly slurred but firm.

"I'll take her to her room."

Elras blinked in surprise but nodded.

With as much grace as his current state allowed, he bent down and carefully scooped her up in his arms. She was light, her body fitting comfortably against his chest. A small sigh escaped her lips as she nestled into him, her face nuzzling against his neck, her breath warm against his skin. It was a small gesture, unconscious and innocent, but it sent through Ash, a strange mixture of pleasure and fear. Ash's gaze drifted back to Kael, his eyes narrowing slightly in concern. Kael stood still, seemingly sturdy, yet the light sway of his tall form betrayed the toll the alcohol had taken.

"Kael," Ash began, his voice just above a whisper, not wanting to disturb the peaceful slumber of Raena in his arms. He motioned towards Caspian and Aldric, both still dozing peacefully in their seats. "See if you can find a servant to help them to their quarters. We'll meet at the palace gates after I've taken Raena to her room."

Kael nodded and stumbled lightly towards the door, his graceful demeanor making even his unsteady steps seem somewhat elegant. With Kael preoccupied, Elras took the lead, guiding Ash through the grand corridors of the palace towards Raena's chambers, their footfalls echoed off the cold marble, the only sound breaking the deep silence of the night. Raena nestled further into Ash's arms, her breath falling in sync with his steady heartbeats. The sight of her, so vulnerable yet trusting, reignited a fierce protective urge within him. It was a strange yet comforting sensation, one he hadn't expected but readily accepted. He couldn't help but shake his head at the absurdity of it all. Here he was, a demon slave disguised as a mage noble, walking through the grand corridors of a palace ruled by mages, carrying a princess who was as oblivious to his true identity as she was to the fact that she was his soulmate.

Finally, Elras stopped before an intricately carved door.

"Her room," he murmured, his gaze a strange mixture of concern and relief as he pulled out a key and unlocked it.

Ash nodded in gratitude, a silent acknowledgment passing between the two. With Raena cradled in his arms, he gently pushed open the door, stepping into a room that smelled of spring and Raena's sweet scent. He moved cautiously into Raena's chambers, the soft glow of moonlight filtering through the sheer curtains casting a gentle light across the room. It was a room befitting a princess, lavishly furnished, yet with an inviting warmth. There were traces of Raena in every corner - from the open book on the bedside table to the mint tea nearby. He carefully lowered Raena onto the bed, her relaxed form sinking into the plush mattress. Her breaths remained steady, a soft sigh of contentment escaping her as Ash gingerly removed her shoes, setting them aside.

His hands hesitated for a moment before pulling the soft silk coverlet over her. She looked peaceful, her dark lashes resting against her high cheekbones, lips slightly parted. He brushed a strand of hair from her face, his eyes tracing her peaceful features. Despite the circumstances, one thing was clear to Ash - his feelings for Raena were real, as raw and visceral as his desire for freedom. With one final lingering look, Ash rose, preparing to make his exit.

"Soren..." Raena murmured, her voice clouded with sleep.

Her hand reached out, catching Ash's wrist in a surprisingly firm grip. He froze, heart pounding as he turned back to her.

"Stay... stay with me."

The words were a slurred mumble, her half-lidded eyes not fully conscious, but the intent behind them was clear. Ash looked at her, his mind a whirlwind of thoughts. This wasn't a part of the plan.

But looking down at her, at Raena in her vulnerable state, reaching out for him, Ash felt his resolve waver. He sighed, the sound filled with a mixture of surrender and affection.

"Alright, my moonlight, I'll stay for a bit" he replied softly, trying to keep his voice steady despite the wave of emotions crashing over him.

He settled himself onto the edge of the bed, keeping a respectable distance but staying close enough to comfort her. His hand found its way to hers, fingers intertwining in a soft embrace.

He watched her, his eyes tracing the contours of her face, the faint flicker of her half-lidded eyes fluttering under the weight of her intoxication.

"Soren," she murmured again, her voice laced with the syrupy sweetness of her intoxication.

Her fingers drifted across his cheek, tracing the outline of his jaw. "You know, you're pretty good-looking for a mage from the border." A laugh, warm and unguarded, escaped his lips. He closed his eyes momentarily, savoring the warmth of her touch and the intimacy of the moment. When he opened them, he found her watching him, a mischievous glint in her eyes despite her inebriation.

"I...I like you, Soren," she confessed, the words tumbling out of her mouth in a slurred whisper.

For a moment, Ash was speechless, stunned by the unexpected confession. This wasn't how he had pictured this moment, yet he couldn't help but chuckle at the absurdity of it. He wondered how much of it she would remember in the morning, and how much he would have to pretend to forget.

"Raena...", he started, unsure of what to say, what to feel.

He was torn between the joy of hearing those words and the dread of the consequences of what he had to do. Before he could say anything else, Raena's fingers found his lips, silencing him.

"Shhh," she whispered, her eyes half-closed, her fingers tracing a slow, distracted path upward.

His breath hitched as she unknowingly brushed against his invisible horns, her touch light and exploratory. His skin tingled where she touched, the sensation travelling down his spine, amplifying his awareness of her. His heart clenched in his chest, the fear of discovery battling against the warmth spreading through him.

With a perplexed furrow of her brow her fingers traced the outline of his invisible horns.

"Is... is there something there?" she asked, her voice barely a whisper, her eyes still mostly closed.

Her fingers continued to explore, tracing the curved outlines of his horns as her brow furrowed in confusion.

"Hmm? Soren," she murmured.

"Your cheek... it feels... it feels different."

She giggled, a drunken sound that bubbled up from her throat.

"I must be... must be so drunk... It's like... like my hand is floating", her hand danced in the air, seemingly clutching at nothing

"Yes, my moonlight, you must be very drunk," he took her hand in his, gently prying it from his horns, and placed a soft kiss on her knuckles.

Her skin was warm under his lips, and for a brief moment, he let himself savor the touch, the intimacy. As he released her hand, he watched as she softly snored, her eyelashes fluttering against her cheeks as she sank further into sleep. His heart felt heavy in his chest. With great reluctance, Ash pushed himself to his feet. The room seemed to spin slightly as the aftereffects of the alcohol caught up with him. He steadied himself, taking a moment to regain his composure. He traced the edges of his invisible horns, a bitter chuckle escaping his lips at the thought of her reaction if she knew the truth.

He bent down, pressing a gentle kiss to Raena's cheek, her skin cool and soft against his lips. The scent of her, sweet and intoxicating, filled his senses, leaving a profound ache within him. She murmured something in her sleep, a soft sound that tugged at his heartstrings.

"Goodnight, my lunah," he whispered into the silence of the room, the words heavy with unspoken longing and regret.

He stole one last look at her peaceful form before stepping out of the room, the door closing silently behind him. He navigated through the winding corridors of the palace, his pace steady yet unhurried. As he neared the palace gates, the silhouette of Kael came into view, his friend's form hunched over, clearly struggling to maintain his balance. It was a humorous sight, but one that was also strangely comforting. Here was a fellow demon, trying to navigate this strange world just as he was.

"Kael," Ash greeted his friend, his voice a tad slurred despite his best efforts. Kael merely grunted in response, his gaze never leaving the intricately carved gates before him.

"Did you have fun?" Ash asked, a teasing smile tugging at his lips.

He watched as Kael straightened up, the motion slow and clearly laborious. The silver-tongued demon turned to him, his usually sharp eyes now hazy with drink.

"The mages are...interesting," he said, his words slow and deliberate as he fought off the effects of the alcohol.

His lips twisted into a wry smile.

"Never handled a bow before, yet they insisted I take a shot."

Kael rubbed his temple, his fingers tracing the contour of the glamour necklace hidden beneath his collar.

"Oh, ball of joy! Can't remember the last time I was this inebriated."

The sight of the usually composed Kael swaying on his feet brought a genuine smile to Ash's face.

"Next time," Ash said, taking a step to steady his friend, "we might need to pace ourselves."

He received a grunt in response, but the corner of Kael's mouth twitched upwards, revealing his amusement.

The two demons stumbled away from the palace, their steps echoing through the empty streets. As they disappeared into the night, the palace seemed to sigh, a sense of anticipation hanging heavy in the air. The revolution was near, the wheel of destiny had started turning, and nothing would ever be the same again.

***

Milton Keynes UK
Ingram Content Group UK Ltd.
UKHW032320221024
449917UK00001B/118

9 798227 735928